Alan Savage ̶ ̶ ̶ ̶ ̶ ̶ ̶ ̶ ̶
established aut̶ ̶ ̶ ̶ ̶ ̶ ̶ ̶ ̶
with a deep pe̶ ̶ ̶ ̶ ̶ ̶ ̶ ̶
tary affairs. ̶ ̶ ̶ ̶ ̶ ̶ ̶
Savage are *Otto̶ ̶ ̶ ̶ ̶,*̶ ̶ ̶ ̶
Queen of Night and *Queen of Lions.*

THE LAST BANNERMAN

ALAN SAVAGE

WARNER BOOKS

A *Warner* Book

First published in Great Britain in 1993
by Little, Brown and Company

This edition published by Warner Books in 1994

A CIP catalogue record for this book
is available from the British Library.

ISBN 0 7515 0848 9

Printed in England by Clays Ltd, St Ives plc

Warner Books
A Division of
Little, Brown and Company (UK) Limited
Brettenham House
Lancaster Place
London WC2E 7EN

'There is a remedy in human nature against tyranny, that will keep us safe under any form of government.'

Samuel Johnson

CONTENTS

China at the Time of the Manchus

THE BARRINGTON FAMILY

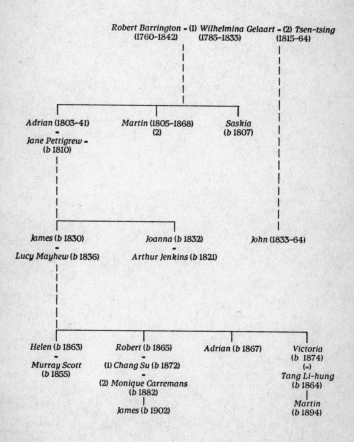

Robert Barrington = (1) Wilhelmina Gelaart = (2) Tsen-tsing
(1760–1842)   (1785–1833)   (1815–64)

Adrian (1803–41)   Martin (1805–1868)   Saskia
-    (2)   (b 1807)
Jane Pettigrew -
(b 1810)

James (b 1830)   Joanna (b 1832)   John (1833–64)
-    -
Lucy Mayhew (b 1836)   Arthur Jenkins (b 1821)

Helen (b 1863)   Robert (b 1865)   Adrian (b 1867)   Victoria
-    -   (b 1874)
Murray Scott   (1) Chang Su (b 1872)   (=)
(b 1855)   Tang Li-hung
(2) Monique Carremans   (b 1864)
(b 1882)
James (b 1902)   Martin
(b 1894)

BOOK THE FIRST
The Dowager Empress

'O conspiracy!
Sham'st thou to show thy dangerous brow by night,
When evils are most free?'

William Shakespeare, *Julius Caesar*

I

THE MASSACRE

A single bell tolled from the campanile of the French Roman Catholic cathedral situated on the west bank of the Grand Canal, opposite the city of Tientsin. This summer of 1870 was hot and humid and the mournful dirge had been heard from time to time for several days now, its reverberations spreading across this greatest of man-made waterways. The sound caused the coolies working the sweeps of the passing sampans to look up in alarm as they made their passage from Nanking and Shanghai on the Yangtse-Kiang to the Pei-ho. The smaller river gave access to Peking, the capital of the mighty Ch'ing Dynasty, rulers of all China.

The constant tolling irritated the guards at the viceregal palace, also on the canal bank and only a short distance from the cathedral; they stamped their feet in anger and discomfort and reflected that it was just as well the Viceroy was absent.

But the noise also shattered the peace of the narrow streets of Tientsin itself. The city sprawled on the east bank of the canal, protected by an outer wall of baked mud, with an inner curtain of high, crenellated stone surrounding the Tatar City. People listened to the tolling and muttered at each other; they knew what it meant – an interment was taking place at the Roman Catholic cemetery behind the cathedral.

The cathedral, only consecrated the previous June, was an eyesore to most Chinese. It was a huge, clearly expensive building, covered in grotesque architectural features, far too large for the size of the Catholic Christian population in Tientsin. But that was a French matter. What concerned the Chinese was that the French had arrogantly determined to build their church on the site of a temple burned by themselves and their British allies during the war of 1861; just as these unspeakable Barbarians had built their consulate on the site of an imperial villa, also destroyed in that brief, and for the Chinese and their Manchu overlords, disastrous conflict.

Such excrescences were the visible signs of the defeat suffered by the House of Ch'ing. Many Chinese hated the Manchus, who two centuries before had swept out of the north behind their eight banners to destroy the Empire of the Ming. But they hated the foreign devils more. They longed for the Emperor to give the signal for them to rise up and drive the Barbarians into the sea. But the Emperor was only a boy, ruled by his mother and his stepmother, the two Dowager Empresses. And they did nothing but remain locked away in the Forbidden City, within the high purple walls that guarded Peking from the outside world.

In the meantime, the Barbarians lorded it over their victims, and even, it was being muttered, sacrificed Chinese infants to their demon god. Was that bell not tolling for the burial of a small child? It had tolled more than a dozen times this last month. There was cholera in the city, but no one knew for sure that each bell had been for a natural death. There were those who wished to find out.

*

In the Convent of St Vincent de Paul, situated just outside the walls of the city, the tolling of the bell seemed louder still. However inadvertently, the nuns were the centre of much suspicion. Sister Françoise wiped her forehead with the back of her hand in a mixture of exhaustion and despair as she gazed at the tiny body in the cot, its features contorted as it reached for air, its mouth hanging open because of the dehydration induced by the cholera which was killing it.

On the far side of the room Sister Aimée gave a little sob. At twenty-two, she was the youngest of the ten nuns in the convent. She had volunteered to work in China the moment she had completed her novitiate, three years before. She was a pretty girl, not very tall but slender and elegant even in her white robe and cowl. She came from a good family, and had travelled to the East with wildly romantic notions. Now those notions were being dissipated in an atmosphere of stench and sorrow.

Sister Françoise went across the room to stand beside the girl. Sister Françoise was herself only thirty, but she had spent eight years in China, and she was tall and strongly built. Monsieur Fontanier, the French Consul, who often visited the convent, was fond of saying that it was a crime Sister Françoise should be locked away in eternal virginity – her heavy-breasted body had surely been designed by God for motherhood.

The nuns enjoyed Monsieur Fontanier's visits; he was an earthy reminder of the world they had renounced. But nothing had made them smile these past few weeks.

The door opened and Sister Adèle hurried in. Small and dark and swarthy, the oldest of the nuns, she always hurried, exuding energy. 'Well?' she demanded. 'Moping?'

'They are both dying, Sister,' Françoise said.

'What can we do, but save their souls?' Sister Adèle demanded. 'Hurry now, Mother Superior wishes to speak with you both.'

Françoise and Aimée washed their hands, went downstairs to Mother Stanislaus's office, and waited at the door. Mother Superior was endeavouring to teach the wife of a newly arrived French official something about the Chinese language. 'You understand, madame,' she said. 'When the CH carries the apostrophe, it is pronounced like a Q. When it does not, it is pronounced like a soft J, or perhaps an X would be more accurate. Thus CH'ING is pronounced Qing, and CHING is pronounced Xing.'

'I will never understand it,' complained Madame Denain. 'What of the Dowager Empresses? How are they pronounced?'

'Their titles are, respectively, Tz'u-an, pronounced Tzoo-an, who is the Senior Empress, and Tz'u-hsi, pronounced Tzoo-she, who is the Junior.'

'And their real names?'

'They can no longer be known by their real names, madame. Only by their titles.'

Madame Denain looked ready to scratch her head. 'I have never heard of two dowager empresses at the same time.'

'This is China, madame. Tz'u-an was the principal wife of the late Hsien-feng Emperor, but Tz'u-hsi, a junior wife, is the mother of the present Emperor.'

'Whose name is T'ung-chih, pronounced Tung-xih,' Madame Denain said triumphantly.

'No, no, madame. That is not his name. He is the T'ung-chih Emperor.'

'Then what is his name?'

'His name was Tsai Shun before his accession. But that too may never be used again.'

'And he is the son of the late Emperor, Wen Tsung Hsien Huang-ti. But you said his father was named Hsien-feng.'

Mother Stanislaus sighed. 'His father was the Hsien-feng Emperor, and was so known when he was alive. When he died, he was given a reign name, which, as you say, is Wen Tsung Hsien Huang-ti. That is the only name he may be known by, now. The Chinese do not practise an absolute system of dates, like us, you see, madame. Each emperor is given a reign name after his death, and all events during his reign are related to the year of his accession.'

'I'll never understand it,' Madame Denain said again.

'Well . . . let me try to give you an example. Our Emperor is Napoleon III, am I correct?'

'Yes.'

'Before he was Emperor, he was Napoleon Bonaparte, but now he is Emperor, no one would call him Monsieur Bonaparte, would they?'

'I suppose not.'

'There you have it. But the Chinese system would go one step further. When the Emperor dies, he would be given a posthumous title, such as, shall we say, Restorer of the Empire. That would be his name for history. Is that easier to understand?'

'I suppose so,' Madame Denain said. 'But there is something else I do not understand. Why do Chinese have two names, and the Manchus only one?'

'Simply because Manchus do not have surnames, madame.' Mother Superior saw the two nuns waiting at the door. 'Ah, Sisters. I have work for you. There are baptisms waiting; Ling has brought in two waifs.'

She turned back to her pupil, while Françoise and Aimée exchanged glances. None of the sisters approved of Mother Superior's behaviour in the business of Chinese children, however much they recognised that she was a good woman who sought only salvation for as many of these heathens as possible. But to offer money for child orphans, who might already be suffering from the disease, simply that they could be baptised before death, seemed somehow ... *un*Christian.

Obedience was the rule; the two young women hurried down the stairs to the central courtyard, where Ling Su-chan, the doorman, waited with two small girls, aged about three. 'Where did you get them?' Françoise asked.

'From my friend, Sung,' Ling explained.

'You are sure they are orphans?'

'Of course, Sister. How else could they come here?'

Françoise stooped and picked up the first of the girls. 'You will be safe here,' she said; she spoke fluent Mandarin.

'I want to go home,' the girl said.

'You will be safe here,' Françoise repeated; she wished

she could feel she was telling the truth.

*

When Ling Su-chan left the convent that afternoon, he went straight to the house of Sung Wan-li. The two were very good friends; from time to time they were lovers – Sung's wife did not object and Ling was unmarried.

'The Mother Superior is very pleased,' Ling told his friend. 'She wishes to know when you will have more orphans for us.'

'Where is my money?' Sung asked.

Ling gave him the bag of silver coins.

'It is becoming more difficult,' Sung said. 'The next will be more expensive.'

'I will tell the Mother,' Ling agreed.

When he was gone, Sung's wife Ting Shan came to sit beside him. 'What you do is very wicked,' she told him.

'Do you feel wicked when you are spending these coins?' he demanded.

'No good will come of it,' she said.

*

The next day, as he went about his business, Sung was seized by several men who held a knife to his throat to prevent him crying out as they pushed him into a darkened alley, where they bound and gagged him, put a sack over his head, and dumped him in the back of a cart and covered him with rags before wheeling him to a house just within the Tatar City. Here he was taken from the cart, the gag was removed, and he was marched into the presence of the Manchu merchant, Chiang-hung. 'Where are my daughters?' Chiang-hung asked.

'Daughters? I know nothing of your daughters,' Sung protested.

'You were seen yesterday, close by where they were playing,' Chiang-hung said. 'And when their sister went to fetch them they were not to be found. We have searched all night. Now I am told you were the last person to see them. Tell me where they are.'

Sung licked his lips. 'I know nothing of your daughters,' he repeated.

Chiang-hung made a gesture, and his men stretched Sung on the floor, holding him there while his pantaloons were removed.

'I know nothing of your daughters,' Sung shouted.

Chiang-hung's people fondled Sung to make him come erect, then they squeezed the glans open, and thrust long wooden splinters between the lips. Sung screamed, again and again, and went soft. But the men kept forcing the wooden slivers into the flesh. 'You will never know pleasure again,' Chiang-hung told him.

'I will tell you,' Sung shouted. 'I will tell you.'

Chiang-hung moved his hand, and the splinters were withdrawn; they were covered in blood.

'I was given money,' Sung panted, his body writhing; he was unable to keep still with the pain. 'By Ling Su-chan, from the convent. He was paid by the Frenchwoman there.'

'For my children?'

'For any children. I did not know they were your children. I saw them playing and thought they were orphans.'

'Why do they wish our children?'

Sung licked his lips again. He had no idea why the Mother Superior should wish Chinese children to be brought to her. But it had to be for a sinister reason: she was a foreign devil. On the other hand, if Chiang-hung were to be told his children were in danger ... but his children could still be saved.

'Put the wood back,' Chiang-hung said.

'No,' Sung shrieked. 'I will tell you. They seek orphans for their priests to sodomise. They force the anal passage open and have their way with them. Orphans. I thought your daughters were orphans.'

'They are sodomised?' Chiang-hung's brows gathered

into a frown. 'You stole my children for sodomy?'

'I did not know,' Sung begged. 'I did not know.'

'Enough,' Chiang-hung said. 'Dispose of this carrion, and let us discover the truth.'

One of the men wrapped a length of thick cord round Sung's neck and drew it tight.

*

'It is an outrage,' declared Father Maurice. His always red face was more puce than ever, the high colour having spread even to his bald head. 'I have never heard of such a thing. You must do something, Monsieur Fontanier.'

'Oh, I shall do something.' Tall and thin with a bristling moustache, the ex-soldier, who had taken part in the conquest of this land with the forces of General Montauban nine years previously, was just as irascible as the priest, and he held the Chinese and Manchus in utter contempt. 'I shall wring somebody's neck.' He got up from behind the desk. 'Denain, fetch my sword and pistols, and arm yourself as well. These devils only understand force. Now, tell me again, Father, exactly what has been done.'

Denain, the Consulate Chancellor, had only recently arrived in China, with his wife. He hurried to obey his superior, whom he held in considerable awe.

Father Maurice gave a noisy sigh. 'A group of men, led by that rascal Chiang-hung, desecrated our cemetery the night before last. They dug up the recent burials, exposed the corpses of those poor children, and began claiming they had been sacrificed to some heathen god after having been raped by our priests. They inflamed the mob, and then went to the magistrates and demanded a search be carried out of the convent; Chiang-hung had the effrontery to claim that his own daughters are in there.'

'And they are not?'

'Of course not. Mother Stanislaus deals only in orphans and the children of converts. She is desperate, with so many people dying of cholera, to save as many of these infant souls as she can.'

'A truly pious woman,' Fontanier said devoutly.

'Well, when the magistrate issued his order that the convent be searched, I refused to accept it. What, allow a bunch of Chinese villains into our sacred ground, to insult our nuns?'

'You acted entirely correctly,' Fontanier declared, strapping on his sword belt and thrusting two revolvers into it. 'And now you say he has brought an order from Ch'ung-hou himself?'

Ch'ung-hou was the Superintendent of Trade in the northern ports, and, in the absence of the Viceroy, the senior Manchu official in the city.

Father Maurice held out the scroll. 'The search party will arrive at three this afternoon, and if not admitted freely, will force an entry. There. That is what it says.'

Fontanier snatched the order, tucked it into his pocket. 'We shall see about that, Father. Go back to the convent, close the doors, and leave this business with me. I shall stuff this paper down Ch'ung-hou's throat, by God. Denain, follow me.'

He marched out of the consulate, mounted his horse, and walked it down the street, Denain, also armed and mounted, at his heels. Chinese pedestrians scurried to and fro before the hooves of his horse; the aggressive ill-temper of the French Consul was well known.

Fontanier dismounted before the offices of the Trade Superintendent, and stamped inside, still followed by Denain, who was endeavouring to look somewhat placatory, as the Chinese clerks started to their feet in dismay. 'His Excellency is busy, your excellency,' one of them protested as Fontanier marched towards the inner door.

'Out of my way, you lout,' Fontanier shouted, seizing the man by the shoulders and hurling him to one side. Then he threw open the doors to the inner office.

There were three men in the room. Ch'ung-hou was a

typical Manchu, not very tall but heavily built, with drooping moustaches and a thrusting lower lip; like the Chinese, he wore a long blue tunic over matching pantaloons, and a round blue hat. He had been seated at his desk, but now he rose in anger. 'What is the meaning of this?'

The other two men, Chinese merchants to whom he had been speaking, hastily moved to the sides of the room.

'There is your meaning,' Fontanier snapped, throwing the order on to the desk. 'How dare you order my people to open their doors to your filthy minions?'

Ch'ung-hou picked up the rather crumpled parchment, glanced at it, and then looked up at the Consul. 'It is for the best.'

'Best?' Fontanier shouted. 'Best?'

'The people are angry. They are convinced that your nuns are mistreating small children and even sacrificing them in an attempt to halt the cholera epidemic. This anger will not go away unless the reason for it is disproved. And the only way it can be disproved is for a magistrate to examine the convent and determine that there is no truth in the rumours.'

'I'll not have it. And what of the desecration of our graves?'

'That was regrettable, Monsieur Fontanier. But when people are concerned for their children—'

'I demand that this order be rescinded. If necessary, I will bring in French troops from their cantonments to protect the convent.'

Ch'ung-hou's eyes flashed with rage. 'No Barbarian soldiers will enter this city. The treaty says so.'

'You think I care for treaties when my nuns are in danger of being raped?'

'No one is going to harm your nuns, Monsieur Fontanier.'

Fontanier picked up the parchment and thrust it at Ch'ung-hou. 'Rescind that order, immediately. I command you.'

Ch'ung-hou snorted. 'You, command me? Your effrontery

amazes me. Leave my office before I have you thrown out.'

'By God, you impudent yellow devil!' Fontanier shouted, drawing his sword. Ch'ung-hou leapt backwards, falling over his chair, and Fontanier made a sweep with the sword, scattering various articles from the desk.

'Help!' Ch'ung-hou screamed. 'Help me!'

The door behind them burst open to admit several Chinese clerks, who encountered the two merchants, attempting to leave.

'We are attacked, monsieur!' Denain shouted.

'Yellow devils!' Fontanier snarled. He drew one of his revolvers with his left hand and fired at Ch'ung-hou; the bullet missed and smacked into the wall beside the Superintendent's head. Fontanier then turned round and fired again, twice, at the men in the doorway. One fell, and the others ran. Denain had now also drawn a revolver, and the two Frenchmen charged through the outer office, firing at anyone who moved; another Chinese gave a howl of pain and collapsed on the floor.

Fontanier threw open the outer doors and glared at the crowd which had gathered outside. It was, at the moment, an entirely peaceful crowd, merely bewildered by the rumours of what was happening inside the offices. 'Out of my way!' Fontanier shouted, brandishing his sword.

One of the Chinese stepped forward. 'With respect, your excellency—'

'Attacked!' Fontanier yelled, and fired. The bullet missed the man but struck someone behind him. The crowd surged backwards, and then forward again. Denain also fired, and the two men ran for their horses. But the crowd reached them as they mounted. Fontanier struck right and left with his sword, threw away his empty revolver and drew the second, but was dragged from the saddle before he could use it. His sword was wrenched from his hand, as was his revolver, but the mob were not interested in using the weapons; they wanted to get their hands on the man himself. He gasped and shouted as the clawing fingers tore at his clothes, gouged at his eyes, were even thrust into his mouth to tear it apart. Within seconds his shrieks had faded, and like Denain he was just a bloody mess.

But still the fingers tore at his flesh.

*

No Chinese city was ever less than noisy. Apart from the constant hum of overcrowded humanity and the barking of dogs, there was the continual eruption of fireworks, singly or in batches as someone either celebrated or drowned his sorrows.

Yet today the noise level was higher than usual. The sisters were in any event on edge, because of the order which had been served, and the likelihood that they would have to open their doors and submit their cells to prying heathen humanity at three o'clock that afternoon. Father Maurice had hurried back from his meeting with the Consul to assure them that it would not be necessary, but Mother Stanislaus was a woman who believed in always preparing for the worst. She had had everyone in the convent – the nine sisters, the twenty-odd Chinese converts who worked there, and several other Europeans who happened to appear during the morning – hard at cleaning and mopping.

The healthy children had all been bathed and dressed as well as the convent could afford; the sick had been at least washed and their linen changed.

Now they were ready. Which was probably just as well, Sister Françoise thought, as they had had no word from Monsieur Fontanier. The Consul was an amusing fellow when he was in a good mood, but in Françoise's opinion he was largely a bag of hot air and his pronunciamentos about what he intended to do seldom amounted to much; she expected to see the magistrate and his people appear at any moment.

Meanwhile the noise in the city grew. It was Sister Aimée, excitable as ever, who went up on to the roof of the convent and came screaming back down the stairs to tell them that the cathedral was on fire.

'Aimée, you are impossible,' Mother Stanislaus declared. 'You will attend me in my office after vespers and I will cane you for causing such an alarm.'

'It is burning, Mother,' Aimée insisted. 'Why do you not go and see for yourself?'

The other sisters were already hurrying up the stairs to stand on the roof and gaze in horror at the smoke billowing skywards to the west. 'That is undoubtedly the cathedral,' declared Father Paul, Father Maurice's junior.

'What are we to do?' Mother Stanislaus demanded.

'Perhaps we should pray,' suggested Sister Adèle.

They all turned towards Father Maurice, who had just joined them, and was also staring at the cathedral in consternation.

'I must fetch the Consul,' Father Maurice declared. 'He will have to turn out the troops.'

He went down the stairs, but Ling Su-chan, standing by the doors, advised against going out. 'There are a lot of people out there, monsieur,' he explained. 'I do not think you would be able to get through.' Ling was very agitated, because he had heard nothing from Sung.

Father Maurice chewed his lip in indecision, then started as there came several bangs on the door. 'It will be Monsieur Fontanier,' he said optimistically.

'Those are Chinese,' Ling told him, listening to the imprecations being shouted beyond the wood. 'They wish to enter.'

'It is not three o'clock yet,' Father Maurice protested.

'I do not think it is the magistrate, monsieur.'

Father Maurice turned to look at the stairs, and at Mother Stanislaus and Father Paul, who were standing there. Beneath them, the converts, men and women, were gathered, and above them, in the doorway to the nuns' quarters, the sisters waited.

'What are we to do?' Father Maurice asked.

'Refuse to admit them,' Father Paul said.

'Yes,' Aimée cried from above them. 'Tell them to go away.'

'Do be quiet, Aimée,' Mother Stanislaus said. 'What are they shouting, Ling?'

'That if you do not admit them they will knock the door down.'

'Can they do that?' Father Maurice asked in alarm.

'I think so, monsieur. There are very many of them.'

'Then we must open the doors,' Mother Stanislaus decided. 'They wish to search the place. Very well. Sisters, you will attend your duties. Stand beside the cots of your patients. And remember, be calm and unafraid at all times.'

Françoise looked at Aimée, who was biting her lip. But Mother Stanislaus had to be obeyed. The sisters returned up the stairs and dispersed themselves; Françoise and Aimée went to the sickroom, where one child was hardly conscious, while the other was very agitated and had attempted to get out of bed, but being so weak had merely fallen to her hands and knees and been unable to move.

'That was very naughty of you,' Françoise said severely, and scooped her from the floor. Aimée had pulled back the sheets and the child was inserted beneath them, and covered again.

'I do not wish strangers to come in here and see them like this,' Aimée grumbled.

'If it will stop all this stupid talk, then it is for the best.'

'We should be in our cells. They will go into our cells. They will steal things.'

Françoise gave her a hard look. Any self-respecting sister should not possess anything worth stealing. But everyone knew Aimée kept little personal treasures, brought with her from France, and allowed her by Mother Stanislaus because her uncle was a count.

'If there is a magistrate in charge,' Françoise said as reassuringly as she could, 'he will not permit anything to be stolen.'

They listened to a sudden upsurge of noise: Ling had opened the doors. The convent echoed to yells and shouts and cackles of laughter, and the immense rustle of humanity.

Then there was another sound, a sharp, shrieked exclamation.

'That was Mother Superior!' Aimée gasped.

The noise grew, and came closer.

'We must get away,' Aimée panted.

'We cannot leave,' Françoise said.

There was nowhere for them to go.

Aimée dropped to her knees and began to pray. Françoise remained standing, left hand clutching her crucifix, gazing at the open door. The sounds had become bestial, and were very close. She heard Sister Adèle's voice, high-pitched, begging for mercy. Was *she* going to beg?

Several men ran past the door, stopped, looked in, and then came in. Françoise found herself inhaling, drawing air into her lungs with such intensity she thought they might burst.

'Please . . .' Aimée began.

The men whooped their joy. Perhaps they had been disappointed in the others; Françoise knew that she and Aimée were the two most handsome of the sisters. The men ran at them and began tearing at their clothes. Françoise felt an enormous urge to hit them with her crucifix, but she made herself stand still.

'The children!' Aimée was shouting. 'The children!'

The men were not interested in the children. They stripped the two nuns naked, pausing only to gaze in amused amazement at the shaven heads, then threw them to the floor and raped them. Françoise did not resist; Aimée fought with the shrieking desperation of someone who could not believe such a thing could ever happen to her, slender white legs flailing to and fro before they were seized and pinned to the floor. Françoise's legs were still; she accepted the futility of resisting. She was aware only of revulsion and pain, of the certainty that they were going to die.

But not until their tormentors were ready. When the men were sated, the two nuns were dragged to their feet and driven along the corridors and down the stairs, before shouting, laughing men and women, many with blood on their hands and clothes, who pulled at the white bodies, pushed them to and fro, grasped their breasts and buttocks and put their hands between their legs. Gasping and weeping, even Françoise now, they were hurled to the floor in the courtyard and raped again. They were only dimly aware of the naked, mutilated bodies – Mother Superior, Father Paul and Father Maurice, Ling and several of the converts – lying to either side of them.

But now it was to happen to them as well, as she and Aimée were pulled to their knees, and they watched the knives coming closer. Their torment was still only beginning.

*

'Have you heard the news from Tientsin?' asked Tz'u-an.

Thirty-four years old, the Senior Dowager Empress had lost to fat much of the beauty which had distinguished her when, as the Lady Niuhuru, she had been presented to the Hsien-feng Emperor as a concubine; her elevation to empress had followed very shortly. But Tz'u-an had never truly come to terms with her choice as wife by the Emperor, and even less with his early death which had left her principal regent for her infant stepson, the T'ung-chih Emperor. That had been nine years ago, nine years of turmoil and strife, both inside the Empire and against the Barbarians who battered at the coasts and rivers, seeking trading privileges, when all she had wanted was to mind her garden and read her books. Now this . . . she had broken with etiquette by calling, unannounced, on her colleague.

It took a great deal to excite Tz'u-an from her normal placidity, but for all the apparently calm certainty with which she moved through life, she was underneath a bundle of anxieties. If she was content to leave the day-by-day ruling of the Empire to Tz'u-hsi, she could never forget that she *was* the Senior Dowager Empress, as named in the last words of the late Hsien-feng Emperor, and as indicated by her title. Therefore hers was the ultimate responsibility for the preservation of the Manchu Empire and the Ch'ing Dynasty which ruled it.

Yet she also knew that it was the mental strength of her co-Empress and Regent which maintained that Empire.

Tz'u-hsi was a year older, although, as the Lady Lan Kuei, she had been presented to the Court on the same day as Niuhuru, eighteen years before. But it was not simply a matter of age that left Tz'u-an always seeking the direction of Tz'u-hsi. Nor was it simply because she was barren, and Tz'u-hsi was the mother of the T'ung-chih Emperor. It was a matter of personality. Tz'u-an had always sought only the quiet joys of life; Tz'u-hsi had always sought power – it had been Tz'u-hsi's angry energy and determination that had saved them both during the palace intrigues which had swirled around the head of the Hsien-feng Emperor as he lay dying, and which had propelled them to their present position of omnipotence.

She stood now, at her window, looking down at the garden deep within the palace complex of the Forbidden City in Peking, watching her son at play. The T'ung-chih Emperor was fourteen, a happy boy who delighted at leading mock armies, even as he neglected his studies. But his nose never lacked a dribble, and he coughed incessantly. He had inherited his father's weak constitution, and no one could doubt that the Empire again tottered on the brink of a succession crisis.

Tz'u-hsi turned at the interruption. At thirty-five, her once slender figure had also filled out, as was visible even beneath the flowing robes of an empress, and her cheeks were fuller than they had once been. The determinedly pointed chin remained, however, as did the glorious raven hair, lying loose on her shoulders and down her back – in the privacy of her own apartment she was bareheaded. More important than these, her black eyes were unchangingly deep, looking at the world with purposeful intensity.

She was not alone. Tz'u-hsi was never alone. Her favourite

eunuch, Chang Tsin, was at her side; they had been friends since childhood. Also present was the Manchu soldier, now a general, Jung-lu, tall and powerfully built. He was the same age as Tz'u-hsi, and also had been her friend since her family's flight from the Yangste city of Wuhu before the advance of the T'ai-P'ing in 1851. It was widely accepted that he had been her lover since the death of the Emperor – or perhaps even before, some said darkly. That he, a whole man, should be permitted the sort of access to the Forbidden City normally reserved only for princes of the House of Ch'ing, was evidence of Tz'u-hsi's disregard for either law or tradition where her own requirements needed to be met.

For both reasons Jung-lu was loathed by Tz'u-an; she considered that for a dowager empress to take a lover was an insult to the imperial family. But she had never been able to stand up to Tz'u-hsi.

'The French are Barbarians,' Tz'u-hsi declared. 'Did their soldiers not burn the Summer Palace, nine years ago? It is just retribution that the mob should burn their cathedral.'

'Many of their people were killed,' Tz'u-an said. 'Will they not make war upon us again?'

'This time we will be more prepared for them,' Tz'u-hsi said, with a glance at Jung-lu, whose face shone with martial ardour.

Tz'u-an sighed. She knew that nothing had changed regarding the relative strengths of the Manchu Banner Army and the Barbarians. If the war was renewed, the men from across the sea would still possess the better generals, the better weapons, and above all, that indefinable elan which seemed to carry them from victory to victory without the possibility of a check. 'You mean you will pay them an indemnity,' she said bitterly.

'We will do whatever has to be done,' Tz'u-hsi told her. 'This massacre was carried out by the Chinese, not the Manchus. The Barbarians will have to understand this. It may be necessary to execute one or two people. But there will be no war.'

'How can you say that?' Tz'u-an cried. 'Do not the Barbarians prefer to make war than anything else?'

Tz'u-hsi smiled, a slight relaxation of the tight lips. 'That is true, Tz'u-an, but I have heard that they are now making war upon themselves, in Europe. They have no time to war with us. If they wish an indemnity, as you say, we will pay it . . . until we are ready to throw them into the sea.'

This was her dream, to atone for all the insults and humiliations the Barbarians had heaped upon the Dynasty during the previous thirty years.

*

Wong Li stammered as he bowed before the ladies seated on the verandah overlooking the garden of the Barrington Shanghai residence. 'The Marshal,' he gasped. 'The Marshal comes.'

'Here?' Jane Barrington gave one of her imperious frowns, while her daughter-in-law gasped, and spilt tea into her saucer.

The two ladies made a considerable contrast, for if they both wore the starched white gowns and broad-brimmed white hats, the white boots and lace gloves regarded as de riguer for daytime apparel by European ladies in the Chinese tropics, they were in every other way as different as could be imagined.

Jane Barrington was sixty years old, her once magnificent head of auburn hair now perfectly white, but her bone structure as defiantly perfect as ever in her youth. She had married into this family in her late teens, and when her husband Adrian, the elder of the two Barrington brothers who had taken over the huge trading concern created by their pirate father, had been killed, she had married again – his younger brother.

That scandal might have rocked the British community in the Far East – as with Tz'u-hsi and Jung-lu, many people had concluded that Jane and Martin Barrington had been

adulterous lovers while Adrian had still been alive – but
Martin Barrington had gone from strength to strength,
whatever the domestic calamities which had seen his
stepdaughter captured and maltreated by the T'ai-P'ing and
his half-brother executed.

Martin himself had died two years previously, in 1868, but
the House was more secure than ever, thanks to the
friendship of his stepson James – Jane's child by Adrian –
with the Junior Dowager Empress: they had been friends as
teenagers before the menace of the T'ai-P'ing had fallen
across the valley of the Yangtse-Kiang.

James's wife Lucy had none of Jane's arrogance. The
daughter of an unimportant factor, when she had arrived in
Shanghai the Barrington star had already been high in the
heavens. She had never aspired to rise to that eminence.
James Barrington had married her when his personal
fortunes had been at their lowest ebb, not in a financial
sense, but in the rape of his sister and his own inglorious
conduct when faced with the T'ai-P'ing. She had been
grateful for his attention, had sought only to make herself
into a good and dutiful wife, and continued to live entirely
in the shadow of her formidable mother-in-law.

She had mothered four children, but the death in infancy
of her firstborn, a boy, had left her even more humble in her
relationship with the rest of the family. She had stood back
and watched as James had regained both his courage and his
sister, and taken the family fortunes to a new high. She felt
out of her depth much of the time.

Thirty-four years old, Lucy Barrington was a pretty rather
than handsome woman, with soft features, and a soft body
as well. She still provided her husband with much solid
comfort in the privacy of their own bedroom. But for the
rest, the plane on which this family lived left her bemused,
and actually to have a viceroy come to call, unannounced . . .
She was on her feet, bodice heaving, pink spots in her
cheeks, as the Chinese magnate came through the drawing
room before an anxious Wong.

One of the great strengths of the Ch'ing had always been their ability to discover and appoint able subordinates, and for all the laws which dictated that the conquered Men of Han, the native Chinese, should wear the humiliating pigtail, and that their women were forever barred from entering the royal family, even as concubines, they had always been prepared to give talented Chinese authority. Never had they sought the aid of the Chinese more than in combatting the T'ai-P'ing, and, amongst others, that bitter and bloody struggle had thrown up Li Hung-chang.

Li himself, told to raise an army to defeat the so-called Heavenly King, had not been above learning from others. He had watched the way men like the American Frederick Ward and the Englishman Charles Gordon had recruited and trained that magnificent body of men which had come to be known as The Ever-Victorious Army, and had applied their methods to his own troops. His 'Hunan braves' had become justly renowned, and with the death of Ward and the return of Gordon to England, it had been Li Hung-chang who had finished off the T'ai-P'ing and gained a deserved reputation.

Since then he had gone from viceroyalty to viceroyalty, ever more trusted by the Dowager Empresses. Now aged forty-seven, he was at the height of his powers. Unusually tall for a Chinese, powerfully built, with long moustaches and a thoughtful expression, he presented few indications, either in dress or manner, that he was one of the wealthiest and most powerful men in the land. Nor had he ever forgotten the loyal and consistent support given to him by the House of Barrington over the years, or the fact that James Barrington had commanded his artillery during the closing stages of the war.

He paused as he came on to the verandah, hands thrust deep into the loose sleeves of his blue tunic, and gave a brief bow. 'Madame Barrington.' And again, 'Madame Barrington.'

Both ladies had risen, but where Jane acknowledged the greeting with a nod of her head, Lucy almost curtsied.

'This is a privilege, your excellency,' Jane said. 'I am

afraid my son is at the godown.' Both ladies spoke Mandarin fluently.

Li nodded. 'This I know. I will see him shortly. I have come to say goodbye.'

'You are leaving Chekiang?' Lucy was concerned, and only just remembered to add, 'Your excellency'. Li Hungchang was one of the few rocks in a changing world.

'I am afraid so, Madame Barrington. I have been summoned to Peking. I am to be Viceroy of Chih-li Province.'

Jane clapped her hands. 'But that is a splendid post.'

'The best. I wish it were in more fortunate circumstances. Have you not heard the news from Tientsin?'

'No. Is there news?'

'There has been a riot, against the French. The cathedral has been burned, and also the convent. Many people have died, including nine nuns, three priests, and some other Europeans, as well as many Chinese converts.'

Lucy clasped both hands to her throat in horror.

'My God,' Jane commented. 'But why?'

'There has always been much resentment against the French and British for their invasion in 1861,' Li said. He could speak frankly to these people because the Barringtons, however British their ancestry, had been Chinese citizens like himself ever since Robert Barrington, the pirate, had done a deal with the Ch'ing and founded the House. 'Recently there has been an outbreak of cholera in the city, and the people came to believe that the nuns were kidnapping children to sacrifice to the Christian god as a means of ending the plague.'

'That is surely ridiculous,' Jane protested.

'I am sure it is untrue,' Li said carefully. 'But it is equally certain that the mob believed it to be true, and what a mob believes can become true in itself. The situation was exacerbated by the irrational behaviour of the French Consul. Now he too is dead.'

'How terrible for those poor women,' Lucy said. 'Were they . . .' She bit her lip, and glanced at her mother-in-law.

Li Hung-chang waited while Wong brought in a tray of tea and Jane poured. Then he said, 'Yes, I am sorry, Madame Barrington, but they were mutilated. It is the way of mobs.'

Chinese mobs, Lucy thought angrily.

'Will there be war because of it?' Jane was more interested in practicalities. After the devastation of the T'ai-P'ing, which had cost an estimated twenty million lives and left the enormously fertile valley of the Yangtse-Kiang a wasteland which was only just starting to recover, the last thing anyone wanted was another war.

Li Hung-chang gave a wry smile; all his life he had been a soldier. 'It will be my responsibility to attempt to ensure that there is not. The French are very angry, but they are preoccupied in Europe with Germany, so we are told. We hope that the matter will be settled by an indemnity. It grieves my heart, as I am sure it does yours, Madame Barrington, that China, so immense, so strong, should be at this time so weak, militarily. This is one of the matters that must be remedied. Until then ... we shall deal in indemnities.' He finished his tea, and stood up. The ladies hastily stood as well. 'You know that if it is ever in my power to assist the House of Barrington, it shall be done. Ladies.'

He bowed, and followed Wong through the house.

*

'Have you heard the news? Viceroy Li was here,' Lucy said anxiously as her husband came up the steps from the street.

James Barrington stopped to hug and kiss his three children. Helen was seven, Robert five, and Adrian three. They were lively, happy children, only endeavouring to be serious in the presence of their father, whom they feared rather than loved.

James Barrington was a man to be feared. He possessed the Barrington height and breadth, the powerful shoulders and long, no less powerful legs, the jutting chin and big nose of his famous forebears. The uncertainties of his youth were long behind him; in playing a full part in the defeat of the T'ai-P'ing he had grown into a hard, ruthless man, who nonetheless prized his family, and cared for them.

Now he placed little Adrian on the floor and stood up, to embrace his wife in turn. 'Yes. He came to see me, too.'

'Isn't it terrible?'

'We knew he was not going to remain in Shanghai forever.'

'I was speaking of the massacre in Tientsin.'

James held her hand as they entered the house, the children trailing behind, Helen in turn holding each of her brothers by the hand. 'I'm afraid the French rather brought it on themselves, by their habit of treating the Chinese as inferiors, and ignorant inferiors, as well.'

'But those poor women . . .'

'It would not have happened had they not inflicted their religious views on the Chinese, questioned their age-old belief in Buddhism and Confucianism.' He paused to squeeze her fingers. 'I'm sorry for them. They suffered a dreadful fate. But there is nothing we can do for them now. Mother!'

He embraced Jane.

'Li was here.'

He nodded. 'Lucy told me.'

Jane clung to his arm. 'Will there be war?'

'Not if we can help it. We can't afford a war.' He gave a grim smile. 'Not yet. Do not worry about it. Here's a letter from Joanna.'

Jane sat down to read it. To hear from her daughter Joanna, always so sane and sensible, was a relief. Because Joanna, more than any other member of the family, had gone through the hell that had been China ten years before. Taken prisoner by the T'ai-P'ing, raped repeatedly and subjected to every conceivable form of humiliation and mistreatment, she had nonetheless eventually managed to escape, and with her sanity intact.

Moreover, she had even, eventually, been able to face the

prospect of marriage. No member of the family, not even her brother James, with whom she had always been very close, had been able to discover the truth of her relationship with the remarkable American adventurer Frederick Ward. Certainly she had grieved long and deeply when Ward had been killed leading the assault on Tzeki in 1862. But when she had recovered from that tragedy, she had allowed herself to receive suitors, and from them, to the enormous relief of her mother and brother, had accepted the proposal of the Reverend Arthur Jenkins.

Jenkins was several years older than she, but he was a solid, sensible man. What their private relationship might be no one could determine; there has been no children of the marriage. But they appeared to be happy, and Joanna had been delighted when Arthur had been appointed to the Methodist Mission in Port Arthur, the great seaport at the southern end of the Liao-tung Peninsular, which thrust its way down from the north-eastern corner of the Gulf of Chih-li. Port Arthur, because it was ice-free all the year round, had grown into a major seaport, almost able to challenge Shanghai and Canton.

Jane turned the pages slowly as she read the words. 'She makes Port Arthur seem like a dream,' she said. 'I should like to visit there, James.'

'And so you shall,' James said enthusiastically. 'You shall leave as soon as you are ready. Joanna will be delighted.'

Jane raised her head from perusing the letter. 'Are you certain there will be no war?'

'Certain,' James assured her.

*

'In addition to an indemnity and the punishment of the guilty, the French require our recognition of the rights they claim in Cochin-China, your excellency,' Li Hung-chang explained.

In the two years that had passed since the Tientsin

Massacre, as it was called, Li Hung-chang had done everything in his power to appease the French. He had executed
eighteen men, imprisoned twenty-five more. he had paid a vast
indemnity, and sent Ch'ung-hou himself to apologise in Paris.
He had been aided, as Tz'u-hsi had foreseen, by the French
war with Germany, and even more by the French defeat. But
the war was now over, and France was anxious to regain
prestige – the time-honoured European way to do that was to
acquire additional colonies, or at least, trading privileges.

'Then let them have it,' Prince Kung said, speaking as
Chairman of the Tsung-li-yamen, the newly created Department of Foreign Affairs.

Li regarded the Prince with surprise. Kung was a small
man, who slouched in his chair, lower lip thrust forward
petulantly. He had a reputation for arrogance and a quick
temper. But Li also knew that the Prince no longer had the
entire confidence of Tz'u-hsi. They had been allies for many
years, since Tz'u-hsi had been the simple concubine of
Kung's elder brother, the Hsien-feng Emperor, and Kung
had sought all possible help to combat the influence of his
uncles over the throne. Yet their relationship had not always
been smooth. When Tz'u-hsi had seized power in 1862,
Kung had loyally supported her, but soon after they had
quarrelled.

One of Tz'u-hsi's dreams had always been the restoration
of the Yuan Ming Yuan, the fabulous summer retreat built by
the Ch'ien-lung Emperor some miles west of Peking, a place
of delicately fashioned palaces, curving bridges over quiet
waters, and the most luxuriant gardens anywhere in the
world. The Yuan Ming Yuan had been destroyed by the
British in 1861 in revenge for the mistreatment of their
envoys; on seizing power Tz'u-hsi's first act had been to
seek the money for its rebuilding. Prince Kung had led the
Grand Council in refusing the appropriations, on the
grounds that the money was more urgently needed elsewhere. Tz'u-hsi had had to accept defeat, but she had herself
turned elsewhere in the House of Ch'ing for support, and

found it in Kung's somewhat sleepy younger brother, Prince Ch'un. She had even found a wife for Ch'un, her own younger sister, thus bringing the Imperial family closer into her own orbit. She and Kung had quarrelled, violently, by report, and on one occasion she had had her erstwhile aide forcibly expelled from her apartment.

Since then they had appeared to become reconciled, but Li refused to accept that Kung could take such a decision as to grant the French a free hand in that vast area of South-East Asia which comprised the ancient kingdoms of Vietnam, Laos and Cambodia, without higher reference.

'With respect, your excellency,' he ventured, 'it will be necessary to have such a decision authorised by the Dowager Empresses.'

Prince Kung gave a grim smile. 'By Tz'u-hsi, you mean, Marshal Li; Tz'u-an seldom attends to business. You shall have the Empresses' signatures as your warrant; they are preoccupied at the moment – His Majesty is to marry.'

*

The two Dowager Empresses sat together to interview the girls who would be brought before them. There were not very many, for only the daughters of the highest and most powerful Manchu mandarins had been allowed to compete for the ultimate prize open to any Manchu woman, that of becoming an imperial concubine, with the prospect of possibly being chosen as Empress.

The reception had been planned and organised by Tz'u-hsi. She was well aware that had such rigorous rules been applied twenty years ago, she would not be here now; her father had not only been a nonentity, but had also been disgraced for having fled his post as Intendent of South Anhwei Province before the march of the T'ai-P'ing. But however many rebellions had been distracting the Empire in 1852, the Hsien-feng Emperor and his mother had sat securely on the Dragon Throne. Today Tz'u-hsi had too many enemies, had created

them by her arrogant determination to rule in the name of her
son. She needed the continued support of the grandees who
had first placed her in power. Quite apart from her humiliation
over the rebuilding of the Yuan Ming Yuan, only a couple of
years previously she had had to acquiesce in the decapitation
of one of her favourite eunuchs, who, sent on a mission to the
south, had attempted to lord it over the local viceroy. Now her
only hope of perpetuating her position was through the
support of her son, soon to be of age.

One by one the twelve girls were brought before the
Empresses and Chang Tsin, in a private room off the
audience chamber. There they were asked questions about
Chinese history and art, and required to quote from the
classics. They were then stripped naked and examined for
blemishes by Chang Tsin while the Empresses watched.

Tz'u-hsi could remember her own examination, the ordeal
it had been. There had been some sixty girls presented for
the bed of the Hsien-feng Emperor, and twenty-seven had
been chosen. She had been the very last, Niuhuru the very
first. Well, she reflected, Niuhuru might still be the very first
lady in the land, but she was now the second.

The ordeal of the examination was not purely to discover
blemishes of either education or physical perfection; it also
sought to establish character by the way in which the girls
reacted. Most of them were quite overcome. Tz'u-hsi
recalled that her own elder sister, Te Shou, had been
distraught – and thus had lost her chance; while *she* had not
only answered all the questions boldly and confidently, but
had submitted to the pawing fingers of the then chief eunuch
with nothing more than a becoming blush.

These girls were a poor lot, a mass of trembling limbs and
shaking hair. With one exception. Her name was Alute, and
she was exceptionally beautiful, slender rather than sturdy as
was the case with too many Manchu girls, with small,
delightful features, straight legs, and splendidly full breasts
– but then at eighteen she was older than was usual with girls
presented for imperial concubinage.

She took everything that was said to her, asked of her, or done to her, with a slight frown, but revealed no other emotion, and when she had dressed again and left the room, Tz'u-an clapped her hands with delight. 'She will make a perfect mate for the Emperor.'

She is *too* beautiful, Tz'u-hsi thought. She is more beautiful than I was at her age, or am now; she could even replace me in the T'ung-chih's affections, especially if she has a character as strong as she has revealed.

She said aloud, 'Do you really think so, Tz'u-an? I have been looking at her pedigree.'

'So have I,' Tz'u-an said. 'She is the daughter of Ch'ung-ch'i. He is a most faithful supporter of the Dynasty.'

'She is also the great-granddaughter of Prince Cheng,' Tz'u-hsi snapped. Prince Cheng had been one of those imperial princes who had tried to seize power when the Hsien-feng Emperor died, and had been forced to commit suicide when the Empresses had triumphed.

'That was a long time ago,' Tz'u-an said. She was setting up, in her usual placid way, to be stubborn, Tz'u-hsi knew.

'I still do not think she is suitable,' Tz'u-hsi argued. 'If you wish to have a member of Ch'ung-ch'i's family, let us take the girl Wan-li. She is the aunt of this girl Alute, although she is actually younger. She will in every way be suitable.'

'By all means let us have Wan-li as well,' Tz'u-an conceded.

'We cannot have both an aunt and her niece,' Tz'u-hsi protested.

'Why not? It has happened before. It is the girl Alute who matters.' Tz'u-an raised her head to gaze at Tz'u-hsi, and Tz'u-hsi gazed back. In public, the two Empresses were careful always to present a totally united front; in private they differed quite often. The disagreements were always about domestic matters; Tz'u-an had no interest in or knowledge of affairs of state. As the Senior Dowager Empress, she was required to affix her signature to any imperial decree above that of Tz'u-hsi, but she was content that Tz'u-hsi and Prince

Kung should tell her that it was for the good of the Empire. She was only interested in the good of the imperial clan, and in this regard she was prepared to assert herself.

And she was the senior. Her decision would always carry the day, as long as she lived – which was no reassurance to Tz'u-hsi, as she was actually the elder of the pair.

But Tz'u-an, as always, was prepared to be both practical and placatory. 'I have the perfect solution,' she declared. 'Why do we not let the Emperor see the girls, and decide for himself?'

Tz'u-hsi's jaws clamped together.

*

The T'ung-chih Emperor stood at a window of his apartment and looked down on the garden where the girls were walking, as instructed: no choice had been made as yet.

His mother waited at one shoulder, Tz'u-an at the other. Chang Tsin hovered discreetly in the background.

'We wish you to decide who is the most beautiful,' Tz'u-an said.

'Who you would most like to make your empress,' Tz'u-hsi corrected softly.

The T'ung-chih's nostrils flared. He might be only fifteen years old, but he looked far older with his constant sniffle and his thin body. Most observers regretfully concluded that he had inherited his father's frail physique; he had been a sickly child as well. This was in fact true, but nature had been assisted in its destructive process by the boy's own vices and the determination of those around him to pander to those vices.

Chang Tsin, the head Eunuch, was the boy's mentor. The T'ung-chih had hardly reached puberty when the eunuch had brought prostitutes, both male and female, to his bed. A few years later the Emperor and his favourite were stealing out of the Forbidden City at dead of night to visit the transvestite brothels in their search for pleasure.

Chang Tsin undertook these adventures with the full

knowledge and consent, indeed the encouragement, of his mistress. Tz'u-hsi knew that her domination over her son was tenuous; the T'ung-chih Emperor was possessed of an imperious awareness of his prerogatives – with every year he asserted himself more and more. But he was a slave to his lusts, and she intended to make sure that he remained so, as long as she was the one who provided the outlets he sought. She refused to accept that his health might suffer through his sexual precocity. All emperors had always been pandered to by some member of their families, usually a mother or stepmother, and many of them had lived to become strong men. That the T'ung-chih was showing no signs of accomplishing this was undoubtedly, in her opinion, due to the physical weakness he had inherited from his father. He would either survive or he would not. That lay in the lap of the gods. Tz'u-hsi had never possessed a strong maternal instinct: she had always reflected that by Confucian law it was her son's duty to love her, not necessarily hers to reciprocate.

It was *her* future that concerned Tz'u-hsi. This had always been her sole concern, ever since she could remember. When that handsome Barbarian James Barrington had proposed marriage, she had thought only of the wealth such a husband could bring her. She had been furious when her father had forbidden the match.

Now she understood that that had been the first manifestation of that good fortune which had never deserted her, even when her affairs had seemed most desperate. She had risen from the depths again and again, been banished by her husband, been condemned by his uncles, been left an outcast ... but she had been there when it mattered, and now she was Dowager Empress.

She had not travelled so rocky a road, and come this far, to yield any of her prerogatives ... especially to a chit of a girl who was also the great-granddaughter of one of her bitterest enemies. The problem was knowing whom to trust. Indeed, the only *man* in the entire empire she could trust absolutely was Jung-lu.

Perhaps there was another. Almost she smiled as she gazed at the parading girls. She had no doubt that James Barrington still loved her. He had virtually said as much when he had been summoned to Peking to receive his reward for his part in defeating the T'ai-P'ing. But James Barrington remained a Barbarian; he would not be able to help her in the Forbidden City.

'Well, Your Majesty?' Tz'u-an said. 'Have you made a choice?'

'There can be only one choice, Mother,' the T'ung-chih said; he called both the Empresses mother – Tz'u-hsi sometimes wondered if he was sure which one of them had actually carried him. 'The girl Alute.'

Tz'u-hsi snapped one of her nails.

2

THE TEA PARTY

Chang Tsin opened the door of Tz'u-hsi's bedchamber, inhaling the somewhat stale air in the room. Normally he slept in here himself, on the floor at the foot of the bed. But that was not required when the Empress entertained Jung-lu.

That the Junior Dowager Empress maintained a lover was well known in Peking; in a society dominated by tattle-telling eunuchs it was impossible to keep any secrets. Most people condemned her, less for immorality than for lese-majesty, that a woman who had shared the bed of an emperor should stoop so low as to seek solace in the arms of an ordinary human being – even if he was a famous general who had once saved her life. Chang Tsin knew better. Tz'u-hsi, with her strong passions, could have had a hundred lovers and perhaps still not be satisfied. Instead, she remained faithful to this one man, a man she had known, and, Chang Tsin suspected, loved, long before she had been sucked into the imperial orbit. Jung-lu was the man she should have married – but he could never have given her the power she so craved and now needed to survive.

Chang Tsin stood just inside the door and gave a gentle cough. He was rewarded with a heave of the covers, as Tz'u-hsi sat up, and Jung-lu, who was always embarrassed to be discovered in bed with his mistress, even by a eunuch, sank lower.

But as far as Chang Tsin was concerned, Jung-lu was a nonentity. Tz'u-hsi was really his, and he loved her with total commitment. He had loved her when they had been children together, she the daughter of a mandarin and he just a slave boy required to amuse her. His love for her had caused him to be cropped and sold away from the family, but she had not forgotten him, and as soon as she had been able, had brought him back to her side and made him the most powerful eunuch in the land.

As such, he also had more enemies than any other eunuch. His star was tied to hers, and should she fall, he would crash with it. But this certainty, which had to happen one day, concerned him less than the possession of her. Because while Jung-lu might share her bed as required, and even push his great member into that so desirable slit, he had as much importance as a dildo. It was Chang Tsin who bathed his mistress each day, who dressed her and waited on her, who, with his soft fingers, satisfied her desires in a way Jung-lu could never hope to achieve. It was Chang Tsin who possessed her.

He loved her best first thing in the morning. As the day wore on, as she donned her lacquered make-up and her heavy gowns and encased her immensely long nails in their silver-sheathed finger-stalls inlaid with kingfisher feathers, as she thrust her cornelian and gold hairpins into that upswept raven hair, and most of all as she issued decrees and sat in judgement on matters of state importance, she became increasingly remote.

She returned to him in the afternoons, when it was her great pleasure to take part in amateur theatricals, a pastime which also amused her son the Emperor, and in which eunuchs were required to play most of the roles. But then she had to be shared with so many others, especially the T'ung-chih.

First thing in the morning, sitting up in bed, naked; her

magnificent hair loose and clouding over her face and past her shoulders; her breasts, large for a Manchu, and still high and firm, trembling slightly; her body warm as toast; she was the most desirable woman in the world. For could not eunuchs also know desire, even if it must be forever unsatisfied?

'What is it, Tsin?' Tz'u-hsi's voice was low.

'The Marshal is here . . .'

'At this hour?'

'He has much to report, Majesty.'

'How is the Emperor this morning?'

'I have not heard, Majesty. There has been no report from the imperial apartment.'

Tz'u-hsi listened to the wind whistling outside the palace. It was January, 1875 by Barbarian reckoning. The Emperor was entering his nineteenth year and for the past two years had been at least the de jure ruler of China, but his recurring ill-health, and his preoccupation with his beautiful bride, as well as the continuing crisis with the French over the Tientsin Massacre, had caused him to leave most of the power in the hands of his mother – an arrangement which well suited Tz'u-hsi, even if he had from time to time asserted himself, as when he had discovered she was again appropriating funds to rebuild the Yuan Ming Yuan, and had commanded the work to stop.

Tz'u-hsi had been very angry about that. She had been equally angry when he had gone against precedent, and received the Barbarian ambassadors in audience without requiring them to perform the kowtow, kneeling before him to bang their heads nine times upon the floor. He had even allowed them to set themselves up in Peking – in the Tatar City – although their buildings were called legations instead of embassies. But she had had to accept such affronts. Her son was the sole fount of her power. Not that she had any doubt that Alute was working on her young husband – he was three years her junior – to assume his proper prerogatives and consign both Dowager Empresses to an honourable retirement.

Tz'u-hsi thought her detestable daughter-in-law was a
true scion of the traitor Cheng! And, as she was far healthier
than her husband, one day she would rule this land, as
Dowager Empress herself.

Thus now Tz'u-hsi was anxious. The Emperor had been
'visited by the celestial flowers' the previous December, and
although in his youth he had undergone the Chinese method
of innoculation against smallpox – in which a diseased scab
was placed in the nostril – the illness had left him even
weaker than usual.

Tz'u-hsi got out of bed, and Chang Tsin held up her robe
for her to wear. Then she sat down while he placed her feet
in her slippers, and remained sitting as he gathered her hair
away from her face and tied it with a bow of yellow silk. The
Dowager Empress could never appear in public in such
déshabillé, but if it was a matter of national importance . . .

The bedclothes heaved again. 'Stay,' Tz'u-hsi said, and
went to the door, which Chang Tsin hastily opened for her.

Li Hung-chang waited in the centre of the antechamber.
He was alone. Only he of all the men in China would have
dared drag the Dowager Empress from her bed, would have
dared expect that she would come to him without having
spent two hours at her toilette.

At the sight of her he dropped to his knees and lowered
his forehead to the floor. 'Up,' Tz'u-hsi said. 'What has
happened now?'

Before the Tientsin Massacre she had known this man
only casually, and by repute. In the immediate aftermath of
that crisis, as French and British and American gunboats had
hurried up and down the rivers and threats had been issued,
she had come to appreciate Li's value both as a patriot and
a negotiator; since the death of Tseng Kuo-fan the previous
year, he had become the most important of her Chinese
ministers. Perhaps he had been too willing to make amends;
her own instincts had always been towards defiance. But his
methods had been remarkably successful. If the French were
now penetrating Cochin-China on a vast scale, they were

receiving a succession of bloody setbacks from the Vietnamese people, whom Tz'u-hsi well knew to be about the most
recalcitrant in her empire. And to her pleasure and amusement there was no way they could relate the resistance they
were encountering to her government – even if she was
secretly encouraging the 'rebels' to destroy the Barbarians
wherever possible. The French, in their new desire to be
friends with the Ch'ing so that their progress in Vietnam
would not be officially impeded, had even sent officers to
train the new Chinese Army, and had built a huge arsenal at
Foochow for the use of that army.

If she could now create a navy . . .

'Today the gods are with us, Majesty,' Li said, rising to his
knees. 'A ship arrived in Tientsin a week ago, and the mails
have this day reached us. Majesty, the British have agreed to
send a mission to aid us in creating an imperial navy.'

'Can we trust them this time?'

She could never forget that when she had first tried to get
the British to help her create a navy, ten years before, their
agent had merely made off with a quarter of a million taels
of Chinese silver.

'I believe so, Majesty. The man Lay was a scoundrel. This
agreement has been made with the British Government.'

Tz'u-hsi sat down. 'The French will give us an army, the
British a navy. When last we were at war, the British and the
French were allied against us.'

'That is true, Majesty. But I have it on the best authority
that the British and the French really hate each other, and
would do anything to harm each other.'

'We must remember that. We shall welcome this British
mission. We must determine how best to deal with them.
Send word to Shanghai, to James Barrington, that we wish
him to attend us here in Peking.'

Li frowned. He liked James Barrington personally, and he
had the highest respect for him as a man, as a soldier and as
a businessman. But he disliked the concept of involving a
Barbarian in essentially Chinese affairs . . . and he disliked

even more the thought that the Empress had a weakness for a Barbarian.

'He will tell us how to deal with the Englishmen,' Tz'u-hsi asserted. 'Was there anything else?'

'There will be certain concessions demanded by the British, Majesty. I believe they will require permission to build a railroad.'

Tz'u-hsi had seen photographs of railroads, as they existed in England and the United States; she was still a little hazy as to their purpose. 'Why?'

'To connect our major cities, Majesty. This is to increase the facility with which goods, and peoples, can be moved from one place to another.'

'Is there danger to us in this?'

'The British will say not, Majesty. However, they will claim the right to operate these railways, and they will use them, I suspect, to penetrate the interior of China.'

'We will have to study the matter,' Tz'u-hsi said. 'For the moment, we will give neither a nay nor a yea.' Her head moved as there came a knock on the outer door. This was urgent.

Chang Tsin opened the door to admit one of the Emperor's eunuchs, who stumbled into the room and fell to his knees.

Tz'u-hsi rose, her body trembling. 'Speak!'

'Majesty! The Emperor . . .'

Tz'u-hsi ran from the room, Chang Tsin at her heels. The eunuch followed them.

Li Hung-chang watched them go, then looked at Jung-lu, who was standing in the inner doorway, fully dressed.

'The Emperor?' Jung-lu asked.

'It is the crisis,' Li said.

Like Chang Tsin, both Li and Jung-lu depended for their future upon the continuance in power of the Dowager Empress.

*

'He cannot breathe,' Alute moaned. 'He cannot breathe.'

The T'ung-chih Emperor gasped and moaned, his emaciated body twisting to and fro. Tz'u-hsi stood above him, Chang Tsin as ever at her shoulder. There were three other eunuchs in the room.

Tz'u-hsi frowned as she took in the situation. The bedclothes were tousled, and both the Emperor and Alute were naked. 'What have you done?' she demanded, her voice harsh.

'He sent for me, Majesty,' Alute wailed. 'He wished me. We . . . we made love. And then he started to cough . . .'

'You have killed my son!' Tz'u-hsi declared. 'With your insatiable lust!'

'I am his wife. He sent for me!'

Tz'u-hsi snorted. 'Have you informed Tz'u-an?' she asked.

'I sent for you first,' Alute said. 'You are his mother.' Alute glared at her through her tears. 'Do you not love him at all? You are unnatural!'

Tz'u-hsi did not take offence; her brain was already ranging into the future. Alute, and the other three concubines, had shared the Emperor's bed for two years, and there was no word of children. Tz'u-hsi's thoughts were drifting towards what would happen when the Emperor died. There would be a difficult time ahead. But she had surmounted difficult times often enough in the past. All that was necessary was prompt action.

'Yes,' she said. 'He is my son. But he is also the Emperor, and Tz'u-an is the Senior Dowager Empress. Send for her immediately.'

Tz'u-an, who had supported her so loyally at the last succession crisis, would be more important than ever at this one. Whatever their recent differences.

By the time Tz'u-an arrived the T'ung-chih Emperor was dead. Predictably, Tz'u-an threw herself into a paroxysm of grief, elaborately shared by Alute and the Emperor's other three concubines. Tz'u-hsi felt that of them all, Alute alone was genuine in her behaviour.

And herself. The Emperor had been the fruit of her loins, the only male child sired by the Hsien-feng Emperor, for all of his sixty concubines. The Hsien-feng had already been a sick man when she had gone to his bed. She had had to use all of her arts, the arts of the whore no less than the arts of the woman, to make him enter her at all. But he had been her destiny, and her efforts had produced this pitiful thing lying before her.

It had been a painful birth, and the boy had lived a mostly painful life. For someone so essentially strong and healthy as herself, it had been difficult to accept that this really was her son. *Was* she unnatural? Had she never loved him? But then, she wondered, had he ever loved her? They had been partners, thrown together by fate, more than mother and son. Besides, she had known this day was coming, for years.

*

Tz'u-hsi immediately summoned a meeting of the Great Council, which included the imperial princes as well as the most important mandarins in Peking. It was still hardly dawn, and a bitter winter's day. An icy wind flowed south from the mountains of Jehol, and hailstones thudded on the pagoda roofs of the imperial palace as the great men struggled out of their wet cloaks and took their places.

Prince Kung was there, together with his younger brother, Prince Ch'un. Where Kung looked watchful, Ch'un merely looked as sleepy as ever. As he was married to Tz'u-hsi's sister, and was therefore twice her brother-in-law, a relationship that carried more weight than that of uncle to the dead Emperor, he had got into the habit of leaving most decisions to her.

Li Hung-chang was also there; Tz'u-hsi knew that in him she would find total loyalty. Jung-lu was not present, but he was in the antechamber, where he could be summoned if necessary; waiting with him was a squad of his Peking Field

Force, the elite Imperial Guard.

The other mandarins – there were a total of twenty-five present – looked collectively anxious. This was the first time in the history of the Ch'ing Dynasty that an Emperor had died without leaving at least one heir; usually in the past there had been too many. 'May we offer Your Majesty our deepest and most sincere condolences,' said the scholar Wan Li-chung.

Tz'u-hsi graciously inclined her head. 'I thank you. I thank you all. But now is the time to think of the future.'

'With respect, Your Majesty,' Prince Kung said, 'Tz'u-an is not present.'

Tz'u-hsi gave him a quick look. 'Her Majesty is too deeply grieved by the death of the Emperor. She will agree to whatever we decide here today.'

The mandarins exchanged glances. That Tz'u-hsi and Tz'u-an did not always see eye to eye, especially in matters concerning the Dynasty, was well known. 'We have given much thought to the title to be bestowed upon the Emperor,' Prince Kung began.

'That is for later consideration,' Tz'u-hsi said. 'As of this moment, the Empire is without an emperor. This must be our first resolve.'

Another exchange of glances. 'With respect, Your Majesty, should we not wait?' asked Ch'ung-ch'i, Alute's father. 'For at least a few weeks. It is possible, even now, that the new Dowager Empress may be with child.'

Tz'u-hsi shot him a glance. 'There is no new Dowager Empress,' she snapped. 'A Dowager Empress can only be established by the will of the deceased Emperor. The T'ung-chih has made no such will. There must be an emperor. Now.'

Ch'ung-ch'i looked around the table, but found little support – or at least, little will to oppose Tz'u-hsi. He therefore decided to abandon that idea, however tempting. 'Then the senior living prince of this generation is Prince P'u-lun.'

'How can you say that?' Prince Kung demanded. 'Prince P'u-lun is no more than two months old. My own eldest son, Tsai-cheng, is eighteen. He is the oldest prince of this generation.' It was his turn to look around the table; no one could doubt that Prince Tsai-cheng had inherited much of his father's talent and force of personality.

'But, with respect, your highness, Prince P'u-lun is still the correct choice,' Ch'ung-ch'i insisted. 'Prince Tsai-cheng is first cousin to the T'ung-chih. There is no precedent for a first cousin succeeding; rather has this always been avoided in the past. Prince P'u-lun is the grandson of the eldest son of Hsuan Tsung Ch'eng Huang-ti, the great Tao-kuang Emperor.'

'He is not suitable,' Tz'u-hsi announced.

Ch'ung-ch'i looked at her in consternation. He had assumed he was forwarding her own choice.

'His father was not a true grandson of the Tao-kuang Emperor,' Tz'u-hsi said. 'He was adopted.'

'Adopted children have the same legal rights as blood children, Your Majesty,' Wan Li-chung said mildly, taking up Ch'ung-ch'i's idea. 'As for the succession, there was a case during the time of the Ming, where the son of an adopted son became emperor.'

'And his reign was a disaster,' Tz'u-hsi retorted, and then almost smiled. 'Was he not taken prisoner by our own Manchus?'

Several of the mandarins nodded their agreement.

'Then what is to be done?' Ch'ung-ch'i asked. 'If the Prince Tsai-cheng is not eligible.'

'The accession of the first cousin,' Li Hung-chang said quietly, 'is, as you say, Ch'ung-ch'i, not customary. But it is not forbidden by law.'

All heads turned towards Prince Kung.

'That I cannot permit,' Tz'u-hsi said. The heads turned back again. 'Prince Kung is my most trusted and valued councillor,' she told them.

The Prince cleared his throat, remembering their violent

disagreement of ten years previously.

'The Empire cannot possibly afford to lose his services,' Tz'u-hsi went on. They all understood the force of this argument: by Confucian law, no father might kowtow to his own son. If Prince Tsai-cheng were to be made emperor, Prince Kung would have to retire from public life. But few of the mandarins could doubt that Tz'u-hsi had a much more important reason for declining to accept Tsai-cheng; as the Prince was eighteen years old, were he to become emperor, Tz'u-hsi's 'behind the curtain' rule would immediately end.

'In these circumstances,' Tz'u-hsi said, 'I have decided that the most appropriate successor to my son shall be Prince Tsai-t'ien.'

The room was absolutely quiet, as heads turned to look at Prince Ch'un. For Prince Tsai-t'ien was Ch'un's son ... by Tz'u-hsi's own sister Kai Tu. More important yet, he was only four years old.

Ch'un seemed to realise what had been suggested. 'Your Majesty!' he cried. 'My son cannot be emperor.'

'Why not?'

'Well ... why ...' He gazed at the mandarins. 'He too is first cousin to the T'ung-chih.'

'Prince Ch'un is right, Your Majesty,' Wan Li-chung said. 'To choose a first cousin at all would be a great break with tradition, and would distress the people. But if there is no other choice, then surely it must be the eldest of the Emperor's cousins.'

'I have already stated my reasons for being unable to accept Prince Tsai-cheng,' Tz'u-hsi said. 'As for tradition, as Li Hung-chang has said, tradition is not the same as the law.'

'I should not know what to do,' Ch'un muttered.

'You have nothing to do,' Tz'u-hsi told him. 'Save know the pride of having fathered an emperor of the House of Ch'ing. You will retire from public life, as you have always wished to do. Nothing will change. Tz'u-an and myself will continue as regents for the Emperor. Nothing will change.'

Once again, silence. Everyone present knew that was the desired end, from Tz'u-hsi's point of view. Nothing would change, for at least a dozen years. 'Such a proposal will have to be put before the scholars,' Wan Li-chung said.

'It is our decision to take,' Tz'u-hsi insisted.

'Where there is such irregularity, Your Majesty . . .'

Tz'u-hsi glanced at Li Hung-chang. He did not fail her. During the argument back and forth he had been sizing up the situation, and making a judgement. 'Tz'u-hsi is right,' he said. 'It is our decision to take. Why are you so afraid to make such a decision? It is clear to us all that there is a considerable difference of opinion, and have we not all the right to our own opinions? Let us put the matter to the vote, here and now, that we may know each other's opinions, and respect them. And that we may reach a decision.'

Tz-u-hsi frowned at him, but he smiled benignly.

'You mean to vote, now, in front of each other?' Wan Li-chung asked, uneasily. Like everyone else, he knew that Jung-lu was waiting in the antechamber . . . and that Tz'u-hsi had a very long memory.

'Yes,' Li said. 'Let us have done with wrangling. It is a simple matter of choice. There have been three names put forward as possible candidates for emperor. The first was Prince P'u-lun. Let all who favour the choice of Prince P'u-lun as emperor hold up their hands.'

There was a moment's hesitation, while Tz'u-hsi held her breath. She trusted Li absolutely, and knew that he was aware she was the fount of his power, but this seemed an inordinate risk to take. Seven hands were raised, amongst them Wan Li-chung's. But not Ch'ung-ch'i's.

'Then we may assume,' Li Hung-chang said smoothly, 'that it is not the wish of the majority that Prince P'u-lun be our next emperor. The second name put forward was that of Prince Tsai-cheng. Everyone present who wishes this, please raise their hands.'

Three hands moved upwards immediately. The remainder

looked at Prince Kung. But Kung's hand remained resting on the table. His eyes were half shut. He was clearly realising that it was necessary for him to remain at the centre of government if anyone was to provide a counterweight to Tz'u-hsi.

The three who had instinctively voted for the obvious choice looked left and right guiltily, then slowly lowered their hands.

Tz'u-hsi smiled.

'There remains the third candidate, Prince Tsai-t'ien,' Li Hung-chang said. 'All those in favour?' He raised his hand.

The remaining fourteen hands went up, including those of Prince Kung and, after a brief hesitation, Prince Ch'un.

'Then it is decided,' Li Hung-chang said, 'by the Great Council of State, that Prince Tsai-t'ien shall be the new Son of Heaven. It but remains for us to choose his reign name.'

'May I propose,' Ch'ung-ch'i said, 'that the new Emperor be named the Kuang-hsu. Of Glorious Succession. Is that not fitting?'

The other mandarins and the princes stared at him. But Ch'ung-ch'i was not given to sarcasm; clearly he genuinely considered it a suitable name.

'The Kuang-hsu,' Tz'u-hsi said. 'It is a fitting name.'

*

'You are a great scholar, Li,' Tz'u-hsi observed when they regained the privacy of her apartment. 'Tell me, has any emperor ever been selected in so egalitarian a fashion?'

'I doubt it, Your Majesty. But the word to use is democratic. That is the word used by the Western Barbarians.'

'You and your Western Barbarians! It was unseemly. And how did you know we would win the vote?'

'Is it not my business to know, Your Majesty? As for being unseemly, it is the end that matters, not the means. I would hope that you have achieved what you wished.'

'Yes,' Tz'u-hsi said. 'I have achieved what I wished.'

'But there yet remains a task, Your Majesty. A task in which I am helpless.'

'Yes?'

'By the Will of the late Hsien-feng Emperor, whatever is decided by the Great Council to become law must bear the signature of Tz'u-hsi at the bottom ... and Tz'u-an at the top. Will Tz'u-an sign this decree, Your Majesty?'

Tz'u-hsi nodded. 'That must be my first task,' she agreed.

*

Tz'u-an listened to what Tz'u-hsi had to say in silence. Since the death of the Emperor she had neither bathed nor changed her clothing; she wore no make-up and her eyes were swollen with tears. She presented a stark contrast to Tz'u-hsi, who wore the imperial yellow robe decorated with vermilion dragons, whose hair was piled on top of her head and concealed by an enormous winged head-dress, and whose cheeks and lips were obscured by the heavy rouge as her eyes were masked behind the kohl outlines.

'That is not right,' Tz'u-an said. 'It is against tradition.'

'Tradition is an accident,' Tz'u-hsi said patiently. 'Something happens, often through force of circumstances, and because it has happened, once, it is thenceforth called a tradition. Our only tradition should be what is best for the Dynasty and the Empire.'

Tz'u-an sniffed. 'And this is best for the Dynasty and the Empire?'

'Yes. It is essential that we maintain the continuity of our policies, which are to make the Empire strong enough to resist the encroachments of the Barbarians. This can only be achieved if you and I remain in control of affairs.'

Tz'u-an sighed. 'I no longer wish to remain in control of affairs. I wish to retire.'

Tz'u-hsi was tempted to remind her co-Empress that she was already virtually retired. 'You may do what you wish, as long as you will affix your seal to imperial decrees when required.'

'Decrees of which you approve.'

'Decrees of which we both approve, Tz'u-an. Like this one.' She thrust the paper at Tz'u-an. 'Will you not affix your seal?'

Tz'u-an took the paper, read it, then sighed again and carried it to her desk.

Tz'u-hsi smiled.

*

'I think it has all been most satisfactory,' Tz'u-hsi said, as Chang Tsin undressed her for bed. 'Now that Tz'u-an has signed the imperial decree, we shall wait a suitable length of time, and then announce the accession of the Kuang-hsu Emperor. I think a month will be sufficient.'

'With respect, Your Majesty, a month may be too long.'

'It can hardly be sooner, Tsin, or people will accuse me of unseemly haste. They accuse me of so much, already.' She sighed, and stretched out in the middle of her huge four-poster bed, pillowed on her hair. 'Come to me. I need soothing tonight.'

Chang Tsin knelt beside her, but did not immediately touch her. 'It will need to be sooner than that, Your Majesty. There is talk that the Lady Alute is pregnant.'

Tz'u-hsi's head turned sharply. 'Talk? Eunuch talk?'

'The lady's eunuchs, Your Majesty. In a month, the rumour may be confirmed.'

Tz'u-hsi sat up. 'It is her doing. She seeks to delay the announcement.'

'You have already said you mean to delay the announcement, Your Majesty. But . . . suppose the lady *is* with child?'

'Is it possible?'

'All things are possible.'

Tz'u-hsi bounced off the bed. 'Give me a robe, and send for Ch'ung-ch'i.'

'Ch'ung-ch'i, Majesty?'

'She is his daughter.'

'But . . . he would be very pleased at such news.'

'He will not remain pleased for very long,' Tz'u-hsi said. 'Haste.'

Chang Tsin hesitated, but it was difficult to argue with Tz'u-hsi when she was in this mood; it always had been, even when they had been children together.

'You will also summon Prince Ch'un.'

'And Prince Kung, Majesty?'

'No, Tsin. I wish Prince Ch'un, the father of the new Emperor. And send for Jung-lu as well,' Tz'u-hsi added, as Chang Tsin turned towards the door.

*

Jung-lu was first to arrive, looking very hot and bothered. 'I had assumed you would sleep alone this night, Your Majesty.'

'And thus you have been with another woman!'

'Your Majesty . . .' But his obvious embarrassment betrayed him.

Tz'u-hsi smiled, and laid her hand on his arm. 'Do you not know by now that I will forgive you anything, so long as you serve me, Jung-lu? Wait in the outer chamber, but listen to everything that is said, and be prepared to act.'

'There is to be trouble?'

'I do not think so. I am about to frighten an old man who is already frightened. To death.'

*

Prince Ch'un was next to arrive, as usual trembling with apprehension.

'There is a crisis,' Tz'u-hsi informed him. 'I had hoped to manage matters with proper decorum, but this is impossible. The death of my son must be announced without delay, and also the name of the new emperor. Prince Ch'un, you will go to my sister's house immediately, with an escort of Jung-lu's Peking Field Force, and you will wrap up your son so that no man may recognise him and bring him to me, here in the Forbidden City.'

'But, Your Majesty . . . the mourning?'

'There will be a proper mourning period. The important thing is that when the death of the T'ung-chih is announced, his successor is already installed.'

'But, Your Majesty, the Empress Alute . . .'

'Is a matter I propose to deal with now. Go and fetch the Kuang-hsu Emperor.'

Prince Ch'un hurried from her presence.

*

Tz'u-hsi seated herself in the high-backed chair in her antechamber. It took nearly an hour for Chang Tsin to leave the Forbidden City, go to Ch'ung-ch'i's house, wake the old man, and bring him to the palace, but Tz'u-hsi was content to wait. Waiting hardened her resolve.

In her girlhood, she had been an innocent, who wished simply to give pleasure and obtain wealth in return. The greatness, the responsibility of belonging to the Dynasty had but slowly grown on her. It had been brought to fruition when the British and the French had marched on Peking in 1861. She and Prince Kung had been the only two members of the Imperial Household who had wished to stay and face the Barbarians in battle; the rest had wished to flee to the mountains of Jehol.

That incident had earned her the respect of Kung. Equally had it earned her the hatred of most of the Hsien-feng Emperor's other advisors, mainly his uncles. She had then for the first time realised that her life was in danger, as a disturbing influence on the Son of Heaven.

For more than a year she had sought to do nothing more than keep alive. But when the crisis had arrived, with the death of the Hsien-feng and the attempt on her life, she had reacted violently and with steely determination. It had been the first time she had condemned anyone to death, but she had not flinched: it had been them or her – and her son.

She had accepted then that such a situation might arise again. Now it had, and she knew she must act with as much ruthlessness as in the past. Even if she had been fond of Alute, she could not doubt that were the girl to give birth, her son would be named Emperor, and herself Dowager Empress, displacing the two older women, and her first actions, as she would be under the control of those relatives who could not forget that Tz'u-hsi had executed her great-grandfather, would be to seek revenge.

A revenge which would not merely encompass herself, Tz'u-hsi knew. It would necessarily include the Kuang-hsu Emperor, and his family. There could be no weakening now.

Ch'ung-ch'i was a mixture of exhilaration and abject fear. He wished only to please Tz'u-hsi, and to be summoned to her private apartment in the dead of night, presumably to discuss affairs of state, promised advancement beyond his wildest expectations. But if she was displeased . . .

A glance at her face told him she was displeased. He fell to his knees before her chair.

'Your daughter, my late son's wife,' Tz'u-hsi said, each word dripping from her lips like vitriol, 'is spreading a rumour that she is pregnant.'

Ch'ung-ch'i raised his head, gave Chang Tsin a nervous glance. 'I will inquire, Your Majesty.'

'There is no need,' Tz'u-hsi told him. 'I know the rumour is false. My son was impotent.'

Ch'ung-ch'i opened his mouth and then closed it again, like a fish out of water. He had never heard that before: there had been no suggestion of it when Alute had been summoned to the Emperor's bed.

'Only I knew this,' Tz'u-hsi said. 'I, and a few faithful servants.' She too glanced at Chang Tsin. 'Your daughter's behaviour is most reprehensible.'

'I will speak to her severely, Your Majesty.'

'I doubt that will assist matters now, Ch'ung-ch'i. As you are aware, a new emperor has been chosen and is already in the Forbidden City.' Which was stretching the truth. 'The Emperor's death will be announced today, and also the accession of the Kuang-hsu.'

'Today, Majesty?' Ch'ung-ch'i was aghast at such unseemly haste.

'These are troubled times,' Tz'u-hsi told him. 'Thus you will understand that your daughter's claim may well inflame passions and cause much distress to our people.'

'I will forbid her to speak of it, Your Majesty.'

'Can you forbid what she may speak of in secrecy? She will be like a canker, eating away at the heart of the Dynasty and the Empire.'

'Your Majesty,' Ch'ung-ch'i begged. 'Tell me what I must do.'

Tz'u-hsi gazed at him for several seconds, then spoke softly. 'I am sure that Alute grieves for my son, perhaps more than she is truly aware. I am sure that as the years go by, her grief will become insurmountable, and she will become a burden to her entire family, but most of all to herself.'

Ch'ung-ch'i swallowed. 'Your Majesty . . .'

'Thus I am also sure that it would be a kindness to the Empress were this undoubted fact pointed out to her,' Tz'u-hsi continued, still speaking softly.

'Your Majesty, you cannot ask me to do such a thing to my own daughter.'

'Not even when it is a kindness? You have other daughters, have you not, Ch'ung-ch'i?'

'Yes, Your Majesty.' Ch'ung-ch'i was trembling.

'And sons as well.'

Ch'ung-ch'i was shaking so much he could not speak.

'A father must always remember that his duty is to *all* of his children, never just one,' Tz'u-hsi admonished. 'Just as a child must always understand that his, or her, duty is to the whole family. In this case, you, as a father, should remember that if the Empress *were* found to be pregnant, it could only be by a man other than the late Emperor, and that would be treason. Such a crime would involve her entire family in her guilt.'

Ch'ung-ch'i looked ready to burst into tears.

'Go now, and consider what I have said,' Tz'u-hsi told him. 'Remember your duty to your family. And remind your daughter of hers.'

Chang Tsin opened the outer door, and Ch'ung-ch'i saw Jung-lu standing there, arms folded, sword hanging at his side. He stumbled from the room, head bowed.

*

'Barrington!' Tz'u-hsi smiled at her favourite Barbarian. 'It has been too long.'

'And for me, Your Majesty.'

James straightened from his deep bow to look at the woman he had once kissed and asked to marry him. Her only reply had been to ask, in turn, if he would make her very rich. He had promised to do so, but although she had then said yes, he suspected she had never meant it, even had her father not interfered. Very rich is a relative term.

Lan Kuei, the Little Orchid, had been sixteen years old when he had proposed. In this spring of 1875 she was approaching forty. Concealed as she was by the heavy make-up of a Dowager Empress, there was little memory of the girl he had loved and wooed, but he supposed that even were she to remove the make-up, there would be little left for him to recognise. She had undoubtedly put on weight; that was to be expected. But there was also a hardness about her eyes he had first glimpsed the last time they had met, when, following the death of her husband and Hsien-feng Emperor, she had pulled off that astonishing coup d'état which had elevated her to become the most powerful woman in the Empire, perhaps the world. Queen Victoria might rule the greatest empire in the world, but she ruled with the consent of her ministers; Tz'u-hsi had executed those of *her* ministers who had opposed her seizure of power.

Now she indicated a chair close to her own. 'Is your family well?'

'Indeed, Your Majesty.'

'You must keep me informed of their health. I have recently learned that you have been blessed with another daughter.'

'She was born only four months ago, Majesty.'

'And she is well?'

'She appears so, Majesty.'

'As I have said, you are blessed. What have you named her?'

James was well aware that Tz'u-hsi was not above laying traps, even for him. 'The Empire is in mourning, Majesty. No child can be named until the twenty-seven months have elapsed.' Just as no marriages could be performed, and even the dead could not be buried with due ceremony.

Tz'u-hsi almost smiled. 'But you have chosen a name, Barrington. To be given the child when the time is right.'

'Yes, Majesty. We will call her Victoria.'

'After your Empress.' Her lip curled. 'No doubt she will be very beautiful. You must keep me informed of her progress. Write to Chang Tsin.'

The eunuch beamed; he and James Barrington were also old friends.

'I will do so, Your Majesty. May I offer you my deepest condolences upon the death of the T'ung-chih Emperor.'

Tz'u-hsi inclined her head.

'And upon that of the Empress Alute, Your Majesty.'

'It is very sad,' Tz'u-hsi said. 'The poor girl grieved so deeply. Very sad. I know that in the West suicide is regarded as a crime against your religion, but it is not so here in the East. We have a more practical view of things. I am sorry that Alute is dead, but is was her decision, and I must respect her for it.'

'Of course, Your Majesty. Is it permissible to ask after the health of the Emperor?'

'He is a fine, sturdy boy,' Tz'u-hsi said proudly. 'You know I have adopted him as my own son?'

'Indeed, Your Majesty.'

'And why should I not?' she demanded. 'He is of my blood.'

'Of course, Your Majesty,' James again diplomatically agreed.

'But I have summoned you here because you can be of assistance to me.' Her face softened into a half-smile. 'Again, James. There is a mission coming from Britain, to advise us on the creation of a modern navy.' Her mouth twisted. The memory of Lay's machinations was still a bitter one.

'That is good news, Your Majesty.'

'You will be my minister to deal with them. They are your people, but you are mine. You will not fail me.'

James bowed his head.

*

James could not help but be aware of the tensions in Peking, the obvious suspicion amongst most of the mandarins and great Manchu chieftains that Tz'u-hsi would bend, or break, any rule that stood in her way, regardless of traditions which stretched back thousands of years into antiquity. This was confirmed when he visited Robert Hart, the Irishman who had been appointed Controller of Customs by the Tsung-li-yamen, the new department created by Li Hung-chang to deal with Barbarian matters. The various indemnities imposed upon China over the past thirty years were being paid out of customs revenues, and Li had decided that a Barbarian was most capable of handling this vital part of imperial business, both honestly and efficiently.

Hart, tall and thin, confident and pragmatic, was the type of Barbarian respected by the Chinese, even if his unshakeable honesty continually frustrated them. He in turn respected James Barrington as another rock of integrity in a corrupt world.

'You may depend upon it, Barrington,' he observed. 'Your friend, the Dowager Empress, is intent upon ruling this land for the good of the Ch'ing, nobody else.'

James was forced to agree with him. He was also aware, however, that as long as Tz'u-hsi had Jung-lu and his Peking Field Force at one shoulder, and Li Hung-chang with his reputation and his very real support amongst the native Chinese – the Men of Han as they called themselves – at the other, and as long as she never attempted to rule in her own right instead of in the name of an adopted son, her position was unassailable, if only because of the comforting thought that in a dozen years the Kuang-hsu Emperor would be of an age to rule himself, and Tz'u-hsi would then *have* to retire, gracefully or not. To start a civil war for the want of waiting twelve years seemed pointless to the essentially pragmatic Chinese mentality.

Equally was James aware that, like Jung-lu and Li, his own future depended firstly upon supporting the Empress, and then, if possible, being able to make the transition to serving the Kuang-hsu when the time came. This involved, for the time being, experiencing some of the hostility felt towards Tz'u-hsi's desire to create a modern army and navy. For the Chinese were very ambivalent about military matters. Their own Confucian ideals rated soldiers the lowest form of society, while elevating the poet and painter and philosopher on pedestals to be worshipped. Side by side with this admirably Christian point of view, however, was a desire to be left in peace and a deep-rooted hatred for the Barbarians who had brought fire and sword to their seaports and now sought to lord over them even in the interior. Thus they wanted the Manchus, who had so vigorously conquered them two hundred years before, to protect them and defeat the Barbarians, even while they were proud that they had so absorbed the conquerors that – apart from the hated sumptuary laws which dictated that the Chinese should wear the pigtail as an indication of their inferiority – it was difficult to tell one people from the other.

James had to explain this to Captain Lang, head of the advisory mission from Britain, when he arrived. He also had to explain that far from there being inexhaustible wealth in China, as all Barbarians supposed, he would have to operate within a very limited budget; there *was* enormous wealth in China, but a large percentage of the taxes collected remained in the hands of the provincial viceroys, and the money which did reach Peking was also likely to be hived off by ambitious eunuchs, or by the Junior Dowager Empress herself. 'Will you make me very rich?' she had once asked him. Since then she had taken care of that ambition herself.

He knew she had not lost her dream of rebuilding the Yuan Ming Yuan. He could only hope that she would have the sense to put the army and navy first.

*

Hardly had Lang arrived than the Empire was plunged into a new crisis. Ch'ung-hou, still regarded by many as responsible for the Tientsin Massacre, had been sent to Moscow to negotiate the settlement of the Russo–Chinese boundaries following the suppression of a long-running revolt amongst the Muslim tribesmen of the north-west. To the consternation of the Manchu hierarchy, the somewhat innocent mandarin was duped by the Russians into conceding a vast area of territory always hitherto considered inalienably Chinese.

Tz'u-hsi was furious, and Ch'ung-hou's head was saved only by the intervention of the Western Powers on his behalf – even Queen Victoria wrote a personal letter to the Dowager Empress, much to Tz'u-hsi's gratification – but it seemed extremely likely that there would be a war with Russia. Tz'u-hsi was all for this; Li Hung-chang wanted to negotiate, but on learning that Charles 'Chinese' Gordon of hallowed memory was in India, he invited the hero of the T'ai-P'ing revolt to Peking, to advise on defensive measures.

Gordon duly came, and used the opportunity to visit his old friend and comrade-in-arms James Barrington at Shanghai. 'The situation is militarily hopeless, of course,' he said. 'China is a huge, inert, helpless dragon. On the other hand, she can never be conquered, simply because she is so huge.'

He gave the same judgement to the Great Council. 'If you truly wish to fight,' he told them, 'declare war, allow the Russians to invade, abandon Peking, take to the mountains and the rivers, and let your enemies simply run out of steam. Then massacre them.'

The Great Council was horrified, and Hart, as Sinophile as James himself, denounced Gordon as having gone mad. Gordon went home, and thence to Khartoum and death; Li Hung-chang negotiated the usual indemnity and regained the disputed territory, and everyone breathed a great sigh of relief.

Even, secretly, Tz'u-hsi.

*

War with Russia might have been avoided, but war with the elements was ever-present. The next winter was one of the worst ever recorded. The Yellow River burst its banks and millions of acres of north China were flooded. Thousands of people died and thousands more lost their livelihoods, while the river itself, when it finally subsided, was found to have changed its course, not for the first time in its history.

Yet China, that massive, inert dragon, as Gordon had described it, shrugged itself dry and staggered on with the business of surviving.

*

During these years, his new duties required that James spend a great deal of time away from home, but he could do this with some ease, as the House of Barrington was well managed by the various Chinese clerks he had trained, and he could look forward to his two sons succeeding him in the business. At least, he hoped he could do so. Robert, as he entered his teens, showed a great deal of talent, but his tastes lay towards the military rather than the mercantile, and he clearly saw himself as a reincarnation of his famous great-grandfather, the founder of the House, whose name he bore.

Still, he was a good-humoured and enthusiastic young man. The same could not be said of his younger brother. As he emerged from childhood, Adrian Barrington was disturbingly introverted and sullen, a solitary boy who seemed to have no friends, even amongst his own brothers and sisters, much less amongst the sons of the other English merchants who attended the school in the International Concession outside Shanghai. Only his grandmother seemed able to bring any animation to his features.

James took more pleasure in his daughters. Victoria, so long delayed – she was seven years younger than Adrian – gave every evidence of developing into a great beauty, with her flawlessly carved features and deep blue eyes, so strangely contrasted to her wealth of dark hair. Helen, who was seventeen in 1880, was altogether softer, with her mother's golden hair and sparkling green eyes. She attracted men as honey attracts bees, and when James returned home from one of his visits to Peking he never knew which aspiring beau would be occupying his front porch.

Helen seemed able to deal with all her admirers with equanimity, but at the beginning of this year of 1880 James discovered that she was seeing a young American missionary more often than any of the others. 'Murray Scott, sir,' the young man said, vigorously shaking James's hand. 'Baltimore.'

'Where is your mission?'

'Well, sir, we haven't started one yet. Mr Barrington, I'm here with Jonas Appleby ... you'll have heard of Jonas Appleby, sir?'

James frowned. He had indeed heard of Jonas Appleby, a very aggressive man who considered that China should be penetrated even further and at the point of a bayonet, if necessary, so that the 'heathen savages' could learn the word of God.

'Mr Appleby plans to open a mission up the Huang-ho, that which they call the Yellow River,' Scott said enthusiastically. 'It will be my privilege to assist him.'

James's frown deepened. 'The Huang-ho has never been opened for Westerners.'

'Can the word of God be restricted because of the obstinacy of a few yellow men?'

'A few hundred million yellow men, Mr Scott. Who happen to own this land.'

'It is our duty, sir, to bring the benefits of civilisation to the heathen.'

'Mr Scott,' James said. 'You are well on the way to making me angry.'

'Papa!' Helen protested.

'He'll hear me out,' James insisted. 'The Chinese people may be heathen in the eyes of a few misguided Westerners, Mr Scott. But their civilisation is ten times older than ours, and so are their religious beliefs, which in any event are far more acceptable than many tenets of Christianity.'

'Sir!' Scott was on his feet. 'You blaspheme.'

'As do you, every time you mock a Buddhist priest.'

'As for speaking of them as civilised, have you forgotten that dreadful massacre in Tientsin, just ten years ago?'

'By no means. I wonder if you would tell me how many massacres of blacks there have been in the southern United States since the end of your civil war? The nuns in Tientsin were at least suspected of witchcraft.'

Scott's face was flushed and angry.

'Oh, sit down, man,' James invited. 'And have a drink.'

'I do not drink alcohol, sir.'

'Maybe you should. It broadens the mind.'

'I must take my leave. Good day to you, sir. Mrs

Barrington. Mrs Barrington.' This last to Jane.

'I'll walk with you to the door,' Helen said.

'Surely that was uncalled for, James,' Lucy said as the young people left the room.

'I think it was very called for,' Jane commented. 'Some of these missionaries seem determined to cause trouble.'

'And then holler for help when they get it,' James growled.

'Well, I can tell you that Helen will be very upset,' Lucy said. 'She has confessed to me that she likes Mr Scott more than any other caller.'

'Him?' James cried. 'You're not suggesting . . .'

'He may have changed his mind. But I do believe he was considering asking for Helen's hand.'

'Considering? That whippersnapper? And would you seriously consider allowing your daughter to marry a missionary? And then to disappear up into the interior?'

'If that is what she wishes to do, yes,' Lucy said, with unusual determination.

*

It appeared that this was indeed what Helen wanted to do. James was tempted to play the heavy father and forbid her, but he knew that would cause a family crisis, which was the last thing he desired.

'I would just like to be sure,' he told her, 'that you are genuinely in love with this fellow, and not merely trying to spite me, or to atone in some way for any murkiness in our past.'

'I would not dream of trying to spite you, Father. I love Murray, and he loves me. As for our past, well . . . it *has* been pretty heathen, hasn't it? And Aunt Joanna married a missionary.'

'I would have thought one in the family was sufficient,' James grumbled. 'Very well, Helen. If that's what you want to do, I'll give it my blessing. You'll remember we're here if the going gets rough.'

'Of course I will.' But she remained angry; she did not kiss him good-night.

*

No sooner had the engagement been announced than most disturbing news arrived from Chang Tsin: Tz'u-hsi had been taken ill. Chang was not very explicit about the cause or the symptoms – he was more concerned with her sudden loss of power, as Tz'u-an and *her* eunuchs were forced to take control of the government, and with his fears that the situation could become permanent.

James was well aware that Tz'u-hsi's death or permanent incapacity would have a profound effect upon his own affairs. There was no point in going to Peking himself, as only Tz'u-hsi herself could give him permission to enter the Forbidden City, and she was in no position to do that, but he tried to find out what he could through his agents. He learned that immediately before the onset of her illness, Tz'u-hsi had dismissed Jung-lu after a quarrel. Over what? Had Jung-lu strayed once too often? Or had he dared to criticise once too often? Either way, as no one could offer any definite symptoms, it seemed most likely that the Junior Dowager Empress was suffering some kind of menopausal breakdown.

It was with a profound sense of relief that in October he received a letter from Chang Tsin, to say that his mistress had recovered and was again transacting business.

*

The wedding of Helen Barrington and Murray Scott was celebrated in great style, although to James's disgust Helen insisted upon being married by Jonas Appleby himself.

'She's gonna be a real credit to our little community up the river,' Appleby told him. 'Your little girl has it all, Mr Barrington, looks, talent, enthusiasm ... and she speaks Chinese like a native.'

'She is a native, Mr Appleby,' James reminded him.

Lucy was at least content, and Jane, from her own experience, was of the opinion that where people loved it was best to let them get on with it. James felt that perhaps he had, after all, over-reacted. And in the new year concern over Helen was forgotten as there came another disturbing letter from Chang Tsin, now James's regular correspondent.

'I would but beg you, Barrington,' the eunuch wrote, 'always to remember that greatness is constantly surrounded by rumour, and that by its very nature, greatness can never repudiate such calumnies. Keep this thought constantly before you: the Dowager Empress is guilty of only one crime, if it can be called a crime, and that is to seek the greatness of the Dynasty, for that way lies the true greatness of the Empire.'

It was a mystifying missive, but the rumour arrived soon behind it: that all had not been as it seemed with the death of the Empress Alute.

*

'He is a cur,' Tz'u-hsi declared. 'He was always a cur.'

'And now he is dead, Majesty,' Li Hung-chang said.

'To say such things,' Tz'u-hsi grumbled.

'People believe what a man says on his deathbed, Majesty.'

'It is a pack of lies, slanders.'

'Nonetheless, Majesty . . .'

Tz'u-hsi exploded into rage. 'And you believe such calumnies!' she shouted. 'You, of all people, Li! Who can I trust if not you? I am surrounded by wretches.'

Li Hung-chang, for all his size and habitual calm, looked ready to flee. He had never seen his mistress in such a mood. The veins stood out on Tz'u-hsi's forehead, and her lips were drawn back to expose her teeth, gleaming white. 'You will make it known!' she shouted. 'I will have the heads of my calumniators. Even the highest! Make it known! And remember it yourself!'

Li Hung-chang rose from his knees and backed from the audience chamber. Chang Tsin waited at the door, and stepped outside with him. 'She is very angry,' Li gasped. 'She will have a fit. All I did was report what is being whispered in the bazaars, what Wan Li-chung is supposed to have said on his deathbed. Now I have angered Her Majesty.'

He was plainly terrified. 'It is but a mood,' Chang Tsin reassured him. 'Believe me, Marshal Li, Tz'u-hsi has too great a regard for your talents and loyalty ever to be truly angry with you. I promise you, the next time you are received by Her Majesty, she will be as gracious as ever in the past.'

Li departed, shaking his head, and Chang Tsin hurried in to the audience chamber. Tz'u-hsi had left her chair and was standing at the window, idly fanning herself. She had lost weight during her illness but now looked better, and stronger, than for some time.

'His excellency is very upset, Majesty,' Chang said.

'And so he should be, bringing such rumours to me,' Tz'u-hsi said. She was again completely in control of herself, but then, Chang Tsin knew that she had always been in complete control of herself. Tz'u-hsi's rages were very carefully calculated.

'Nevertheless, Majesty, Wan Li-chung does seem to have repeated the substance of your conversation with Ch'ung-ch'i shortly before the Empress's death.'

'And how did he learn of it? What has Ch'ung-ch'i to say for himself?'

'He swears he repeated that conversation to no one, Majesty.'

'Am I expected to believe him?'

'It is true, I understand, that the event has lain heavy on his conscience these past four years. It is a sad thing for a man to introduce his own daughter to opium, and then to ensure that she takes enough of it to kill herself. But he swears his undying loyalty to you and to the Dynasty, Majesty. That Wan Li-chung should make such an accusation and then commit suicide is merely unfortunate. But such an accusation can never be anything more than calumny.'

'Rumours, calumnies,' Tz'u-hsi muttered. 'People believe what a man says before killing himself. It can be no coincidence that these rumours began while I was ill, while my enemies supposed I would not recover. Well, I shall prove them mistaken. All of them. You have taken steps to counteract these calumnies?'

'I have written to all who matter, Majesty.'

'You have written to Barrington?'

'Of course, Your Majesty.'

'And what is his reply?'

'I have not yet received one, Your Majesty. But Barrington, like Li, like all the great mandarins, will rally behind you. Of this I am sure.'

'Because they have no choice. But you are right. No one can prove my involvement. We will just ride it out, Tsin. As we have ridden out so many crises in the past, you and I. And now we will seek out the guilty, and punish them.'

'Yes, Your Majesty. There is just one problem.'

Tz'u-hsi turned to face him.

'The rumours have reached Tz'u-an. I have been told this by Chung Kuo-fan.' Chung Kuo-fan was Tz'u-an's chief eunuch.

'Go on.'

'Chung Kuo-fan has told me that Tz'u-an is very upset. That . . .' He hesitated.

'Go on,' Tz'u-hsi repeated.

'She has said some harsh things, Majesty. She remembers how you had your own nephew made Emperor, and this angered her. She remembers how you have broken other traditions. Now she says that you are guilty of causing the Empress Alute's death. She has called you a murderess to her eunuchs.'

Chang Tsin bowed his head in anticipation of an outburst of anger, but for several minutes Tz'u-hsi was silent. When she did speak, her voice was soft. 'How can she say such things against me? Has she proof?'

'She has told her eunuchs that her proof lies in her knowledge of you, of your character, Majesty. Chung Kuo-fan has told me this.'

'Ha! She can make what she likes of that kind of proof. With her eunuchs!' Tz'u-hsi's tone was contemptuous.

'She also says that you have bullied her into agreeing to breaches of the law and of tradition, ever since the death of the Hsien-feng, Majesty.'

'Bullied her? How else am I to obtain her signature on our decrees? She shows no interest in government. Everyone knows she has done virtually nothing these past months while I was incapacitated.'

'Chung Kuo-fan says she is thinking especially of the selection of the Kuang-hsu Emperor. She says that was a crime.'

Tz'u-hsi glared at him. 'Why are you saying these things to me, Tsin? Am I truly interested in what Tz'u-an confides to her eunuchs?'

'Tz'u-an says she will sign no more decrees simply because you present them to her, Majesty. She says she will sign none at all, unless Prince Ch'un is dismissed.'

Tz'u-hsi frowned. 'She said that? Does she wish to bring all government business to a halt?'

'I think perhaps, after her taste of power last year, she wishes to take more of an interest in government business, Majesty. Perhaps to rule. As she has the right. And more than that, Majesty. Chung Kuo-fan has told me that Tz'u-an possesses a document, signed by the Hsien-feng Emperor before his death, authorising Tz'u-an, as Senior Dowager Empress, to order your execution if you ever attempted to rule arbitrarily. Chung Kuo-fan says his mistress have given much thought as to whether such a document should ever be used.'

Once again Chang Tsin expected an outburst of rage, but

Tz'u-hsi merely returned to her seat. 'Your friend is imagining things,' she said quietly. 'Were there such a document, I would know of it.'

'The very rumour of the existence of such a document, Majesty, could assist your enemies.'

Tz'u-hsi considered for some minutes. 'Tz'u-an has no need for such rumours,' she said at last, still speaking quietly. 'As you say, she has the right to rule. She is the Senior Dowager Empress, as long as she lives.' She looked at the eunuch, and gave a bright smile. 'We must mend our bridges to Tz'u-an. Together, we are everything; divided we are nothing, and so is China. Chang Tsin, you will deliver a message to Tz'u-an, from me. You will invite Her Majesty to take tea with me, that we may discuss these calumnies that are being spread about me. You will tell her that I wish her advice on how best to prove my innocence. Go now.'

*

Tz'u-hsi hummed as she sat in her garden with her ladies. She had taken up painting in her leisure moments, and now she sat before her easel and daubed at her canvas while her little dogs, called Pekingese because they were bred in the city, gambolled about her feet. The painting purported to represent the Ornamental Water, the great artificial lake within the Forbidden City, with its many curved bridges, its pagoda-roofed summer houses, and its massed flowers along the banks. It was certainly a blaze of colour.

The ladies whispered to each other that never had they seen Tz'u-hsi so contented, indeed so domesticated as she had been the last couple of days. Why, for her tea party with Tz'u-an she had even entered the kitchens herself and with her own hands baked a set of cakes.

'These are for Her Majesty alone,' she told them. 'They are her favourite, milk cakes.'

The ladies were of course aware of the rumours which were sweeping the Forbidden City, and indeed Peking, if not all of

China, that Ch'ung-ch'i had fed his own daughter opium, and made her smoke it until she died. And that the great scholar Wan Li-chung, an old friend of Ch'ung-ch'i, had sworn on his deathbed that Ch'ung-ch'i had been driven to it by Tz'u-hsi. As they were *her* ladies, they were in no position to condemn her, even if they considered her guilty; were Tz'u-hsi to fall they would fall with her. But they marvelled at her equanimity when it was also known that during her illness a considerable party had grown in opposition to her rule, and that this opposition party was seeking the leadership of the only person in the Empire who could legally oppose her: Tz'u-an.

Tz'u-hsi listened to their whispers, and if she could not catch the words, she had no doubt what they were saying. As they were her creatures, what they said, or thought, was of no importance. Only the Dynasty, only the Empire mattered. Given that simple philosophy, anything she might have done, anything she might have to do, was ordained by the gods.

Chang Tsin entered the garden. 'The Empress comes, Majesty.'

Tz'u-hsi rose from her seat, and laid down her brush. The dogs barked as their mistress slowly walked across the grass to the arbour from beneath which Tz'u-an was at that moment emerging, accompanied by two eunuchs and several ladies.

'Tz'u-an,' Tz'u-hsi said. 'It is so very good to see you. For too long you have not come to visit me.'

'Well, it is some time since you have visited me,' Tz'u-an riposted.

'I know. I am kept so busy with affairs of state. But now I understand that you wish to take your proper place beside me in ruling this great empire.'

Tz'u-an glanced at her, but was too innately polite to remind her fellow Dowager Empress that her proper place would be *before* her. 'We have much to discuss,' she remarked.

'This I know. But let us sit down and have some tea, and we will find the discussion much easier.' Tz'u-hsi sat beside Tz'u-an. 'I have managed to procure some milk cakes for you.'

'That was very good of you.' Tz'u-an took one of the cakes and bit into it, then saw that Tz'u-hsi was not eating. 'Will you not have one?'

'I do not like milk cakes,' Tz'u-hsi said. 'They are all for you. Now, I know what it is you wish to discuss: these rumours that have been spread by Wan Li-chung's eunuchs. Eunuchs! They are a menace to our society.'

Tz'u-an ate another milk cake; always inclined to plumpness, since her widowhood she had abandoned all attempt to control her figure, and was now very stout indeed. 'All rumours have a foundation in fact, Tz'u-hsi,' she pointed out.

'I know. And it is true that perhaps Ch'ung-ch'i did encourage his daughter to take an overdose; no doubt he saw how much she was grieving for her husband, and it moved his heart.'

'And you had no part in it?'

'I too saw her grief, and was concerned by it. I may have mentioned how sad she was to her father.'

'You admit this?' Tz'u-an was so surprised by Tz'u-hsi's demeanour that she ate a third cake.

'I admit it to you, Tz'u-an, as we have been friends for so very many years, and have survived so many crises together. I would admit it to no one else.'

'But you have admitted it to me,' Tz'u-an said.

'Because I am very sorry about it. Left as I am to exercise power on behalf of both of us and our adopted son, the Kuang-hsu, perhaps I forget how men wait upon my every word, and from time to time misinterpret it. When I think of poor Alute . . . But there it is. If you would share my burdens, as you once did, I should be greatly relieved.'

'Then I shall. I am relieved, too, to hear you express your regret for what has happened. But what of Ch'ung-ch'i? He must be punished. The wretch reveals no remorse.'

'In public, Tz'u-an. I assure you that in private he suffers agonies of conscience. But he is a most faithful supporter of the Dynasty. I cannot find it in my heart to punish him.'

'Sometimes you are too soft, Tz'u-hsi,' Tz'u-an said. 'We will have to consider the matter. Equally, we must make sure nothing so sad ever happens again.'

'Then we are friends,' Tz'u-hsi said.

'We have always been friends, Tz'u-hsi. We became friends when we waited to be interviewed by the Hsien-feng's mother, and you discovered that I was related to your mother.'

'Happy days,' Tz'u-hsi said. 'And the Hsien-feng. How I mourn him.'

'As do I,' Tz'u-an agreed.

'You were his favourite. His Empress.'

'I was his Empress,' Tz'u-an conceded. 'I think you were ever his favourite, Tz'u-hsi.'

'From time to time,' Tz'u-hsi said. 'I do not believe he trusted me.'

'How can you say that?'

'Well, is it not true that he gave you a document authorising my execution should I ever try to seize power?'

Tz'u-an laughed. 'Yes, he did give me such a document.'

'He never gave me one about you,' Tz'u-hsi grumbled.

'Well, he knew such a thought would never cross my mind. It was only your ambition he feared, Tz'u-hsi.'

'Nevertheless, it is hurtful to me, to think that our husband so distrusted me,' Tz'u-hsi said. 'I should like to see this document, if I may.'

Tz'u-an laughed again. 'It no longer exists. I destroyed it, many years ago. How could I ever wish your execution, Tz'u-hsi?'

'Ah,' Tz'u-hsi said. 'That was kind of you, Tz'u-an. Are you sure it is destroyed?'

'Yes, I am sure. I burned it myself.'

'You have no idea how that knowledge relieves my mind,' Tz'u-hsi said. 'Will you not have another milk cake?'

3

THE SUMMONS

James Barrington bowed as he entered the audience chamber. 'Your Majesty. I am happy to see you looking so well after your illness.'

Tz'u-hsi sat in her high-backed chair, her face placid; in place of her usual yellow gown embroidered in green and red, she wore plain white. 'Barrington! It is good to see you. It is always good to see you.'

'May I offer my sincere condolences, Majesty.'

'It is a sad time. There have been many of these, recently, Barrington. My country has been going through a difficult period, no less than I. Do you know, I grieved for my son, even as I grieved for his widow. But I knew he was not long for this world; his health was never sound. And Alute ... I could see her grief was dragging her down, and try as I might, she would not be comforted. But Tz'u-an, to be taken ill so suddenly, quite without warning! One minute she was alive and laughing, her usual self, and the next, she was dead. Things like that shake one's belief in the logic of life.'

'But how did she die, Majesty?'

'Who can tell, Barrington? Some kind of explosion within her body. It happened very quickly. That at least is a blessing.'

'In Europe, Majesty, there would have been a post

mortem, to determine the cause of death.'

Tz'u-hsi's eyes flashed. 'Europe!'she snapped. 'Truly are they Barbarians. What, would you have a common surgeon mutilate the body of an empress?' Her tone softened. 'We do not do such things in China, Barrington. As you well know. There is a certain order of conduct, and this must be maintained. We mourn the Dowager Empress. But we must always remember that our principal care is for the living, and the Empire. Tell me of this Captain Lang.'

'Captain Lang is a most efficient officer, Majesty. He is already training sailors, and more important, officers.'

'And what of ships? Has he found us ships?'

'The Captain knows where ships are to be found, Your Majesty. But ships cost money.'

'The money also will be found. Do not worry about the money. I am more concerned with the men. With the officers, as you say. You come from a seafaring family, Barrington. You have commanded ships yourself, for your father.'

'That is true, Majesty. Alas, I am a little old now . . .'

'Old? Bah! You are fifty-one. Do I not know these things? As I am forty-six. Have you forgotten?'

'No, Majesty. I have never forgotten anything about you.'

Tz'u-hsi's smile was roguish. 'Do you regret never having bedded me, Barrington?'

'Majesty!'

Tz'u-hsi laughed. 'Cannot old friends discuss intimate matters? But I understand. You wish to spend the rest of your life enjoying the fruits of your success. Next thing you will be telling me that you wish to go to England.'

'No, no, Your Majesty,' James insisted.

'You must tell me about England,' Tz'u-hsi said. 'I read little of it. I read about France, and Germany, about Russia, hovering on our borders. I read about Spain and Portugal. But about England, no. England never fights any wars, yet the English are everywhere, like ants.'

'Great Britain has fought sufficient wars in her time, and

now controls a mighty empire, Majesty.'

'Like China? There is no empire as mighty as China.'

'Probably not, Your Majesty,' James said, choosing his words with care.

'I read nothing of the British Army. The French say the British have no army.'

'They do not have an army like the French or the Germans, Majesty.'

'Then how can they call themselves great? How can they have an empire?'

'The British Empire is scattered all over the globe, and is kept in being by the Royal Navy, Your Majesty. It is the greatest navy in the world.'

'The navy,' Tz'u-hsi said. 'Yes, I have heard this. Tell me this, Barrington: do you not find it remarkable that this empire, like China, is also ruled by a woman?'

'It is remarkable, Majesty.'

'Two women, ruling the two greatest empires in the world.' Tz'u-hsi observed, with quiet satisfaction. 'Is that not the proper order of things?'

She was in a very good humour, James thought; the best humour he had seen her in for years.

'I have heard that this Empress is also a widow,' Tz'u-hsi went on.

'That is true, Majesty.'

'Two women, with so much in common. Queen Victoria wrote to me, you know, in the matter of Ch'ung-hou. I was pleased to grant her supplication, and spare the wretch's life. Would it not be a fine thing,' Tz'u-hsi suggested, 'for us two women to meet?'

'Ah . . . I am sure it would,' James agreed, his imagination trying to cope with the vision of Queen Victoria and Tz'u-hsi taking tea together.

'Can this not be arranged?'

'I doubt it, Majesty. Queen Victoria would never leave Britain.'

'And I can never leave China. It is a pity.' Suddenly her

tone was brisk. 'But I will have a navy to equal even that of Britain. And I will have a Barrington to command it, as did my forefathers.'

As if she were a Manchu princess in her own right, James thought.

'I understand your feelings about age, Barrington. Your son will take your place.'

'My son, Majesty?'

'You have a son named Robert. How old is he?'

'He will be sixteen this year, Majesty.'

'Then he is ideal. You will send him to me, that I may see him for myself. And then he will become an officer in my navy.'

'Your Majesty, a boy of sixteen cannot command a navy.'

'I did not suppose he could. He must learn, so that when he is forty he will command. You will send Young Barrington to me, Barrington, that I may be sure he is your son. Then he will become an officer in my navy.'

James tried desperately to think of a way out: commanding the Chinese Navy had proved a disaster for his stepfather and had caused the death of his real father. 'With respect, majesty, my son Robert has been trained as a merchant, to succeed me as Master of the House of Barrington.'

'But he has also been trained as a seaman?' Tz'u-hsi asked anxiously.

'Well, of course, Your Majesty. All Barringtons are trained as seamen.'

'Then he will serve in my navy. You have another son, have you not?'

'Yes, Majesty. But—'

'He will succeed you as Master of the House.'

'I do not think he will be suitable, Majesty.'

'Your own son? Barrington, you are prevaricating. I will hear no more about it. Are you trying to tell me that you consider the House of Barrington to be more important than China?'

'Well, no, Your Majesty, of course not.'

'Then let us speak no more of it. Send your son to me, quickly.' She waved her fan to indicate that he was dismissed.

Chang Tsin waited in the antechamber, but James did not doubt that he had been able to listen to every word that had been spoken.

James Barrington and Chang Tsin had been friends for many years, since the days of Wuhu when Tz'u-hsi, or Lan Kuei – meaning Little Orchid – as she had then been called, had been simply the daughter of a Manchu *taotai* or Intendant, and Chang Tsin had been her servant. Since then they had both experienced a great deal of the ups and downs of life. Chang Tsin, in being sold for castration, had suffered far more than himself, James knew, but yet had he prospered, perhaps even more than himself. Chang Tsin's tunic and pants were of the finest pale blue silk, and his fingers were crowded with rings set with stones of enormous value.

His manner, too, had subtly changed. The subservience of the servant, although still very much a part of his public personality, was now too clearly submerged by the arrogant confidence of Tz'u-hsi's confidant, the person who filtered, and no doubt censored, all information that was placed before her, who shared her most intimate moments, and who shared, too, her enormous personal wealth.

Now he bowed to his old friend, his hands thrust deep into the sleeves of his tunic. 'You will dine with me, Barrington.' It was not a request, or even a suggestion.

*

To James's surprise, Chang Tsin took him out of the Forbidden City and into the Tatar City which lay south of it. At the Tien-an-men, the gateway to the imperial enclave, they picked up a squad of armed Bannermen, who marched before and behind them, clearing passers-by out of their way, driving away beggars with sweeps of their staves. People shouted curses at them as they picked themselves up from the gutters, but there could be no question that Chang Tsin was a very powerful man indeed.

Now he escorted James to a splendid house set back from the always crowded streets of Peking, in the midst of a luxuriant garden, a place of weeping willows and curved bridges, of little streams in which multi-coloured goldfish darted to and fro, of grassy verges on which peacocks strutted, filling the air with their raucous croaks.

'Do you like this place, Barrington?' Chang Tsin asked, as they strolled through the garden towards a little arbour, where two female servants were waiting to serve tea.

'It is delightful.'

'I have just purchased it.'

'You, Chang?'

'Should I not have a home of my own?'

'Well ... I would have supposed your home was in the Forbidden City.'

'That is where I work, and where I must spend a great deal of my time. But I need a place to which I can retire, from time to time.'

'Tz'u-hsi does not object to this?'

'Why should she, so long as I am there when she needs me?' Chang Tsin sat down, and gestured James also to a seat. He rang a little golden bell, and sipped his tea. 'Tell me of your sister. She is well?'

Chang Tsin was the man who had rescued Joanna Barrington from the T'ai-P'ing, and for that reason would always have a special place in the affections of the Barrington family.

'She is very well. Port Arthur is a beautiful city.'

'I have heard this. I have never been there. But you must give her my regards when next you write to her.'

'I shall do that. May I ask if there is any substance in the rumours which I hear on every side?'

'There are always rumours in Peking, Barrington. Is it not so in your great cities?'

'Absolutely. But ... do you not find these disturbing?'

Chang Tsin looked away from him, at the path to the house. 'What do you think of these girls?'

There were three females standing in front of him. They were well dressed and groomed, but while two were indeed girls, not yet in their teens, he estimated, the third was a mature young woman of perhaps thirty. 'Are they your servants?' James glanced at the two who had served the tea, and who had withdrawn to one side of the arbour, kneeling, heads bowed.

'No, no,' Chang Tsin said. 'The older one, I am contemplating taking to wife.'

'Ah,' James said. He knew that many well-to-do eunuchs had wives, although what they did with them was a mystery to him.

'She has been living with me these past few weeks,' Chang Tsin explained, 'that I may decide if I like her sufficiently.'

Now James was astonished. 'Her family permits this? What if you decide against her?'

Chang Tsin shrugged. 'Then I return her. Her family knows she will be a virgin. Come closer, Wu Lai.'

The woman approached, and bowed. 'This is my great friend, James Barrington,' Chang Tsin explained.

'I am honoured, sir.' The woman bowed again.

'As am I, Wu Lai,' James said, and looked at the two girls.

'They will be my daughters,' Chang Tsin said. 'They are orphans. Do you think they will do well, as my daughters?'

'I am sure of it,' James agreed. 'But do you not wish a son?'

Chang Tsin sighed. 'Yes. A son is what I wish more than anything else in the world. Save a long life and continued prosperity, of course. But finding one, that is the problem. A son must be loyal and courageous, and manly and strong. But above all, loyal. I have seen several boys, but I cannot feel in my heart that any of them is ideal.'

'Sons are seldom ideal,' James suggested.

'But you have two, and of your own loins. You are favoured above most men, Barrington.'

'It seems I am about to lose one,' James remarked.

*

James understood that there was no way that he could consider opposing Tz'u-hsi's express command – and remain in China. And there was nowhere for him to go. The House of Barrington had traded on the Yangtse now for seventy years, and he was the third generation to rule it. Robert had been going to be the fourth. But perhaps he still could be, in the course of time.

He consoled himself by reflecting that had Robert been born and living in England, and destined for the navy, he would already have departed to sea. On the other hand, joining the Royal Navy did not first entail a personal interview with Queen Victoria – with whatever good, or evil, that might follow from that.

Robert himself was delighted at the prospect, assuming that his visit to Peking was merely a formality. 'The navy,' he said, eyes gleaming. 'We Barringtons have always fought ships at sea.'

'I never have,' James pointed out. 'And this navy doesn't actually exist, as yet.'

'But it will. And I shall be in at the beginning.'

'Yes. I shall give you letters...' He wanted to say something about Tz'u-hsi. But he dared not. He had not dared even ask Chang Tsin some of the questions which were burning his tongue, which he had heard on every side in Peking; he had only been able to hint, and Chang Tsin had turned the question aside with polished ease.

Even before his conversation with Hart, James had never doubted Tz'u-hsi's determination to climb to the top and remain there; if any of the stories were true of the coup d'état she had pulled off when the Hsien-feng Emperor had died, the girl he had known and loved had grown into a very bold and ruthless woman. How great a step was it from being someone who had fought and won, against enormous odds, on more than one occasion, to becoming someone who would murder her own daughter-in-law, and even her closest female friend, if it were necessary to preserve her position?

She would say it was for the good of the state.

But he dared not say these things to his son. Robert would have to form his own opinions about the rumours. As for the woman herself . . .

'You must be very circumspect when in the presence of the Dowager Empress,' he said.

'Of course, Father. But is she not an old friend of the family?'

'Yes, or she would not have sent for you. However, obviously our relative circumstances have changed since we were friends in Wuhu back in 1850. She is now virtually sole ruler of all China. I am what I was then, really: a successful merchant. She has powers of life and death over everyone in China, and that includes us. Remember this.'

'I shall.' But clearly the boy anticipated no problems with a woman who had once loved his father. 'Do you suppose I will be able to see Chang Tsin?'

'I am certain of it. But there again . . . do not trust him with any of your private thoughts.'

'I thought he too was a friend, Father?'

'Oh, indeed. But his circumstances also have changed.'

Robert gave one of his easy grins. 'You are becoming suspicious of everyone in your old age, Father.'

'Maybe I am,' James acknowledged. 'Maybe I am.'

*

Lucy was terrified at the idea of Robert going off to serve in the navy, even a non-existent navy. 'Suppose China and Britain go to war again?' she demanded.

Unlike the Barringtons, Lucy Mayhew had been born in

England, and had only accompanied her parents to the Far East as a teenage girl.

'There is no possibility of that, at least at sea, for the foreseeable future,' James assured her. 'Robert will do very well, as long as he enjoys the favour of Tz'u-hsi.'

Lucy shivered. 'A murderess, it is being said.'

'That is something I would let other people say, if I were you,' James recommended.

*

'You must write every week and tell us what you are doing,' Lucy told her eldest son.

'And how many pirates you have executed,' Victoria said. At seven, with her long dark hair and bright blue eyes, she was every bit as beautiful as she had always promised to be, and she adored her elder brother.

'Every week,' Robert said. He clasped Adrian's hand.

'You go off, to fame and glory, and I remain here as a clerk,' Adrian said.

'You remain here to keep the House prospering,' Robert reminded him. 'Because I'm coming back. You don't want to forget that.' He went in to see his grandmother.

Jane was seventy-one, and crippled with arthritis. She spent much of her time in bed, only occasionally hobbling to the terrace to watch the ships passing up and down the river. But her brain was as active as ever. 'We earned our fortune on the sea,' she told Robert. 'We had our disasters as well, but it is the fortune that matters, now. Go and prosper.'

'And you keep safe till I come back, Grandma.'

Her eyes were misty.

*

Robert travelled with but a single servant. Lucy would have sent a perfect entourage, but James would not permit it. He did not wish there to be anything ostentatious about Robert's entry into either the navy or the cloistered world of the Forbidden City, which, as Tz'u-hsi had required, was his first destination.

Thus he also insisted that Robert wear Chinese clothes – tunic and pantaloons, boots and a flat hat to ward off the sun. But he gave the boy letters of introduction, both to Chang Tsin and to Captain Lang, and he allowed him to travel in transport belonging to the House. After some thought, he decided that this should be a sampan, and that the route taken should be the Grand Canal; it was late in the year, and the inland waterway promised a much safer journey than beating up the coast by junk, or even by steamer: there were now four steamships operating under the phoenix flag of the House of Barrington.

Robert had of course journeyed up and down the river several times before, on House business, as far as Nanking, but this was the first time he had entered the Canal itself. He had heard a great deal about it, and was not disappointed. The greatest man-made waterway in the world, it had been built more than a thousand years earlier, during the Tang Dynasty, remembered by the Chinese as a golden age of peace and prosperity. Since then it had several times been allowed to fall into disuse, as civil wars had swept across the Empire, but it had been largely restored by the Manchus, and although in places its banks were still crumbled, and in others the oarsmen had to fight their way through vast reed-beds or patches of water lilies, each plant several feet across, it remained on the whole easy going for all of the five hundred-odd miles to the Huang-ho, the Yellow River, another huge waterway of which Robert had previously only heard described.

There was little current in the Canal, and mooring up to the banks at night presented no problems. The crew was well armed, and Robert was equipped with both a revolver and a rifle, so they anticipated no trouble from any of the other sampans they passed, or the people on the banks, who were apt to change from apparently harmless tradesmen or farmers into bandits or river pirates whenever they saw the opportunity. But the country itself underwent a considerable transformation as the sampan travelled north: the flat rice paddies of the Yangtse valley gave way to more undulating countryside, now under wheat and barley, and the Canal itself, before reaching the Yellow River – so called from the quantities of yellow mud it brought down from the mountains to the west – lost itself in a string of large lakes, where sometimes they anchored out of sight of land on any side.

The Huang-ho itself was a huge, fast-running flood of water, larger than any other river in China, save the Yangtse, which tumbled down to the sea. Crossing it now was a considerable feat, for the river was in flood, and it was necessary to face obliquely upstream and row as hard as possible to prevent the boat from being swept past the opposite entrance of the Canal.

However, Captain Shung had made this journey before, often, and the Canal master also knew the hazards, and had stout warps ready to be hurled as soon as the sampan came close enough to the northern bank. Once secured, the boat could be guided into the still waters with the greatest ease.

The last stretch of the Grand Canal proper, from the Yellow River to where it joined the Pei-ho, was hardly more than a hundred miles, and they accomplished this in four days. As they approached Tientsin, situated at the junction of canal and river, Robert gazed at the rebuilt French Cathedral on the west bank, and then at the walls and towers and pagodas of the city itself. Tientsin was the first city of any size he had seen since leaving Chen-Kiang, but he was not interested in exploring cities, other than Peking.

The Canal, in a smaller form, proceeded beyond the Pei-ho, curving to the north-west now, to take the sampan right up to the walls of Peking. Robert stared at the approaching metropolis with mixed emotions; Peking did not appear very much larger or more populous than Shanghai or even

Nanking, but it was the centre of the Ch'ing Government, the hub of this vast empire, which by repute was now controlled by a single woman. Who had once been kissed by his father!

4

THE BRIDE

Robert's credentials obtained him entry to the city without difficulty, although his papers were thoroughly scrutinised before he was allowed to pass. However, he was again brought to a halt at the Tien-an-men, the gateway to the Forbidden City. No whole man could proceed further without the express command of the Emperor, or, in this case, the Dowager Empress, and he was forced to wait while the letters and credentials were sent in.

He was not kept waiting very long, however, before a eunuch arrived, a very grand looking fellow in his red robes. 'You are Young Barrington, the son of Great Barrington?' he inquired in his high, harsh tones.

'Yes.'

'You will come with me, please.'

Robert followed the eunuch through the gate. 'I am Wan Kai-san,' the eunuch said, importantly. 'I am second to Chang Tsin.'

'Chang Tsin,' Robert said. 'He is an old friend of my family.'

'Chang Tsin is very powerful,' Wan Kai-san said. 'It is good to have him as a friend.'

Robert looked left and right as they proceeded up a broad avenue, totally different from those in the city beyond the gate, simply because they were the only people on it, whereas outside he had had to force his way through the crowds.

There were buildings to left and right, but here again the difference to the outer city was marked. In the Chinese and Tatar cities there were any number of palatial houses, but they were situated cheek-by-jowl with shanty shacks and even tents. Here every building was made of gleaming white marble, raised on stilts to keep out flood waters during the wet season, and fronted with verandahs. Each was set well apart from its neighbour, and surrounded with green lawns and carefully topiaried hedges.

They were all occupied as well, and Robert realised he was being overlooked by a large number of women, who had come on to the verandahs to witness this unusual sight, a whole man who was neither a very old mandarin of the Great Council nor a member of the imperial clan.

Robert could hear their excited chatter as they pointed and his embarrassment grew. 'Ignore them, Young Barrington,' Wan Kai-san told him. 'They are so starved for sexual diversion they would tear you limb from limb to get at your manhood, if they could lay hands on you.'

That was not particularly reassuring. 'Are they allowed no men at all?'

'There is only one man resident in the Forbidden City, Young Barrington, and he is the Emperor. And the Emperor is but eleven years old. Nor,' he added, 'is he over-interested in matters of the flesh. Unlike his predecessor. No, no, most of these women must make do with fingers and dildoes. It is an unsatisfactory business.'

Now they were past the houses and Robert was gazing at the palace complex, the huge temples which rose in front of him, and in the distance to his left, the Imperial Dagoba, looming out of the trees surrounding the Ornamental Water, for all the world like a vast white marble bottle. 'This must be the most beautiful city on earth,' he ventured.

'It is beautiful,' Wan Kai-san agreed. 'You are privileged to see it, Young Barrington.'

Robert appreciated that more and more as they approached the temple complex, and he could see the famous Dragon Staircase, the steps leading up to the Altar of Heaven, on which a yellow imperial dragon had been painted with such skill that it gave the impression of actually moving, continuously writhing its way down the stairway. 'Only the Emperor may tread on the Dragon Staircase,' Wan Kai-san said.

To either side were other temples, but Wan Kai-san led Robert between them to the palace complex. Now there were more eunuchs and less women to be seen, but they too showed considerable interest in the intruder. Robert was more interested in the breathtaking beauty of the Ornamental Water, a large artificial lake, fed by a branch of the Canal which encircled the city, and studded with small islands which were connected by elaborately carved, curving marble bridges. The bridges, and the small pagodas which had been built on the islands, and the gleaming still water, were in themselves beautiful, but they were enhanced by the trees and shrubbery which surrounded and overhung them, a blaze of autumnal colour in every imaginable shade.

Wan Kai-san led Robert up to one of the bridges, and now he could hear the yapping of small dogs. They crossed the bridge and looked at a group of ladies, and several eunuchs, surrounding a somewhat small figure. Tz'u-hsi was seated before her easel, painting.

The ladies and the eunuchs turned to look at Robert, and the Pekingese dogs rushed forward, barking excitedly, but as Robert was not afraid of them, they did not actually attack him. Tz'u-hsi, however, did not turn her head, but continued making her firm, short brush strokes on the canvas.

One of the eunuchs detached himself from the now whispering throng and came forward to greet Robert. He was an elderly man, at least in appearance, and despite the heavy make-up he wore; James Barrington had told Robert that Chang Tsin was actually only in his fifties, but eunuchs always looked older than their years. And his clothes were the most splendid Robert had ever seen.

'Young Barrington.' He grasped Robert's hands. 'It is good to see you. You are much like your father.'

'You flatter me, Chang Tsin.'

'I speak the truth. Come.' Still holding Robert's hand, he led him forward, while the ladies fluttered their fans and gazed at him with huge eyes, and Robert remembered what Wan Kai-san had said, that they would tear him to pieces if given the opportunity. He found that difficult to believe of these delicate, graceful, painted creatures.

And in any event, they were irrelevant. For now he stood at the shoulder of Tz'u-hsi, and at last the Dowager Empress turned her head to look at him.

His father had told him of this woman's beauty as a girl, and certainly there were traces of it still to be seen in the well-formed bone structure of her face – heavily rouged – the deepness of her dark eyes, even the shape of the somewhat small mouth, and above all, the lustre of her black hair; only traces of this were visible beneath her huge winged head-dress, but it was nonetheless compelling. Of her figure it was impossible to guess beneath the voluminous yellow and red robes, but he gained the impression, from her face, that she was rather plump. 'I also like what I see, Young Barrington,' she said, her voice low.

Robert blushed, and stammered. 'Forgive me, Your Majesty.'

'Do you like my painting, Young Barrington?'

Robert swallowed. The painting was of an aspect of the Ornamental Water, and the use of colour was attractive; the trees themselves, however, and the buildings, were mere daubs.

'It is excellent, Your Majesty,' he lied.

Tz'u-hsi smiled. 'I sometimes wonder if my true talents do not lie in art. Then have I wasted my life. Your father has told you much about me, I know. But he has told me little about you. This is a fault you must rectify, Young Barrington. We will speak again.'

She turned back to her easel, and Robert looked at Chang Tsin in consternation; had he come all this way for so brief an exchange of words? Had he done something wrong? He had stared at the Empress. Presumably he was now damned forever.

But Chang Tsin was smiling as he came forward to escort him back to the bridge. 'Tz'u-hsi likes you,' he said softly. 'Your fortune is made, Young Barrington.'

'But . . . she has dismissed me.'

'And should she not? She will send for you again, when she is ready.' They reached the bridge, and Chang Tsin looked earnestly into his eyes. 'There are things you should know, Young Barrington. Tz'u-hsi has been a widow these past twenty years. This is lonely for a woman, and lonelier yet for an empress. Remember this, and remember, too, that the only person in this world who can now prevent you from reaching the stars . . . is yourself. Now go with Wan. I will see you later.'

*

Still uncertain whether he had enjoyed a triumph or a catastrophe, Robert followed Wan back out of the Forbidden City, and into the hustle and bustle of the Tatar City. It was quite late, and already dark, but the streets were busier than ever. 'I am starving,' Robert said, as they passed a meat-vendor. 'Can we not stop and eat?'

'No, no,' Wan said. 'You will eat when we reach our destination. It is not far.'

He led Robert through a few more streets and then stopped at a gate leading to a house set well back from the road. The gate was guarded by four Bannermen, who glowered at what to them was a Barbarian. 'This is where you will stay in Peking,' Wan told him. 'The house of Chang Tsin.'

Robert was impressed, and the more so when Wan led him through the porch and into the First Hall, to be greeted by a handsome, dignified woman. 'I am Wu Lai,' she told him.

'Chang Tsin's wife. These are my daughters, Chang Su and Chang Li.'

The girls were perhaps nine and ten, pretty and intelligent of features.

Robert glanced at Wan, suddenly at a loss for words. If his father had told him something about the domestic habits of successful eunuchs, he had never given the possible details of such an arrangement any thought, because he had never expected to encounter it.

'You will come with me, please,' Wu Lai told him, and led him through the Second Hall, the Ancestral Hall, where there was a shrine to Chang Tsin's forebears and an eternally burning candle – it would be Wu Lai's responsibility to make sure that it stayed alight – and so to a bedchamber at the back of the house. Here indeed he might have been in his own home, for the bed was a large tester and the furniture was solid, heavy wood, even down to a rocking chair.

'You will be comfortable here,' Wu Lai informed him.

*

Chang Tsin came home for supper that night. This was shared between himself, his wife, and their guest; the daughters were not present.

'When can I see Captain Lang and take up my duties?' Robert asked.

Chang Tsin smiled. 'You are impatient. This is good. Perhaps tomorrow you may leave for Tientsin. Captain Lang is at Taku; those are the forts that guard the mouth of the river.'

'But I passed by Tientsin on my way here,' Robert protested.

'That is true. It was your duty to come to Peking first. Here is still where your future lies. Now listen carefully, Young Barrington. Eat sparingly, and drink no wine at all: you will need all your senses about you this evening.'

'Who am I to meet?' Robert was intrigued.

'Why, when it is dark, you will return to the Forbidden City.'

Robert's apprehensions came back in a rush, but obviously there was nothing for it but to comply. When the meal was finished, Chang Tsin made him shave his chin, very carefully, and gave him a eunuch's robes to wear, as well as a round flat hat, such as he wore himself.

'You will not speak until you reach your destination,' he said. 'Leave that to me.'

'Should I be armed?'

Chang Tsin gazed at the revolver in dismay. 'Under no circumstances. Come.'

*

There were no delays for Chang Tsin, and if one or two of the guards looked twice at the unusually tall young eunuch accompanying him, no one was about to question so powerful a figure. They entered the Forbidden City and made their way along the avenue – even the verandahs of the houses to either side were now deserted, although lights gleamed in the windows.

They skirted the temple complex and reached the palaces, and Chang Tsin admitted Robert through a side door, then led him down a labyrinth of corridors. At last they reached an antechamber, guarded by a single eunuch, and here Chang Tsin paused. 'Take off your clothes,' he commanded.

'Eh?'

'Do as I say.'

Heart pounding as he suddenly realised why he was here, Robert undressed. He was aware of being both terrified and exhilarated. His only sexual experience had been a visit to a Shanghai brothel with his schoolfriends, a few months before. He had been a total failure. It had all been too public, too impersonal. His friends had laughed at him.

But now, was he being given to an Empress?

'Go through that door,' Chang Tsin commanded. 'And

remember what I told you earlier. Only you can interfere
with your future advancement, your future greatness, Young
Barrington. But remember this, as well: a man succeeds by
mixing daring with caution, aggression with humility, when
humility is called for, and above all, by understanding his
goal.'

He stepped back through the doorway, and it was sealed.
Robert looked at the eunuch, who looked back at him. Or
rather, perhaps, he thought, through him. Yet he still needed
instruction. He went up to the inner door, and there checked,
again glancing at the eunuch. The eunuch nodded, and
Robert drew a long breath, turned the handle, and stepped
through.

And again caught his breath. The chamber he had entered
was much larger than the anteroom, and contained a huge
tester bed in the very centre of the floor; this was the only
furniture apart from a chest set against the bottom of the bed
and the four sconces which illuminated the scene before
him. In the bed, seated cross-legged, was Tz'u-hsi.

The Dowager Empress was also naked; her hair loose and
shrouding her shoulders and back, gathering on the imperial
yellow sheet. And incredibly, if Robert realised his first
estimate had been correct, and Tz'u-hsi was inclined to
plumpness, she yet presented the picture of a young girl,
in her smallness, her suppleness ... almost her air of
innocence.

Behind him, the door closed, softly.

'Come forward, Young Barrington,' Tz'u-hsi said, her
voice quiet. 'Or are you afraid of me?'

Only you can ruin your own future, now, Chang Tsin had
told him. But that warning had included words as well as
deeds, he had no doubt. And he needed words, desperately:
Tz'u-hsi would not know he was a virgin. 'Should not a
fleeting moment fear eternity, Majesty?' he asked, as he
moved to the bed.

'That was prettily said.' She gazed at him, and then
allowed her eyes to drop, down his body; the suddenness as

well as the very nature of his circumstances had affected his manhood. 'Do you not know, of women?'

'I know a little of *women*, Majesty.' He was standing beside the bed.

'Almost perhaps you speak *too* prettily, Robert,' she admonished. 'Even empresses are also women. Do you know for how many years I have languished a widow?'

'Too many, Majesty.'

'All but twenty.' She stretched, and uncoiled, and lay back on the pillows, half on her side, her legs crossed, her chin now resting on her hand. 'A widow seeks solace. But where can it be found, in a world in which men seek only to boast of their triumphs?'

Robert's knees touched the bed, and slowly he climbed on to it, kneeling now, above her; the nearness of her, her subtle scent, her very real beauty, was at last having its proper effect. 'Only children boast, Majesty.'

'And you are the youngest man ever to enter this room, save for my son.'

Robert took a deep breath. 'I am here at your summons, Majesty. You must either trust me, or strike off my head, now.'

As he spoke, he stretched out his hand, to caress her shoulder, and then move the hair, before allowing his fingers to stroke down the flesh and on to her breast, just to touch the nipple, which was instantly erect. But then, the touch of her brought him fully erect as well: he was about to possess an empress.

A man succeeds by daring combined with caution, by aggression combined with a suitable humility when it is required, and above all, by an understanding of his goal. Thus Chang Tsin. He could only pray that the eunuch was right.

'Do you know the Chinese *Book of Love*?' Tz'u-hsi asked.

'Yes, Majesty.'

She moved her hand, to hold him, lightly. 'Your father

never knew this supreme moment, with me. We both wished it, but the time was never right. Yet once he touched me, in a way I had never known before. A way not in the *Book of Love*.'

She looked up at him, lips slightly parted. Robert understood what she wanted, leaned forward and kissed her, with more passion than he had anticipated being able to feel. This woman was old enough to be his mother. In Chinese terms, where thirteen was considered a marriageable age, she was old enough to be his *grand*mother! Yet he had never felt so eager.

She was surprised by his vehemence, and fell backwards, so that he lay on her. She allowed him to continue kissing her for several seconds, then tapped him on the shoulder. Immediately he rolled off her, rising to his knees, wondering if he had offended her.

She smiled. 'I remember when I was but a girl, and was first called to the bed of my master, the Hsien-feng Emperor, I was just as anxious as you, and just as afraid that I would give offence. Do you know, Robert, that I kissed the Emperor? He was surprised. But he enjoyed it. Nine months later I gave birth to the T'ung-chih Emperor, and thought my fortune was made.' Her fingers sought him again. 'I am a Jade Girl, and I would Play Upon the Flute.'

Robert immediately lay on his back, even if he could hardly believe that an Empress of China would wish to fellate anyone, much less a sixteen-year-old boy.

Her touch was exquisite; the caress of her lips made him shiver. 'Do not disappoint me, Robert,' she said softly, but apparently recognised that he could not hold on much longer, because a few moments later she knelt astride him, and lowered herself on to him. He reached up to hold her breasts, and watched her hair flailing to and fro as she rose and fell, giving little moans of pleasure, until she subsided on to his chest.

*

'Will you love me, forever, Young Barrington?' The voice whispered into his ear, and he realised that he had dosed off, after three hours of love play in which he had climaxed twice and she at least four times.

'Forever, Majesty.'

It seemed a needle had been thrust into his ear; she had bitten him. 'You are a liar,' she said. 'All men are liars, but young men are the biggest liars of all. You will forget me the moment another woman surrenders to your caress. Unless I were to keep you here, forever. Would you like that, Robert?'

'Ah ... if it pleases Your Majesty,' he muttered, uncertainly, although at that moment he did not see that it would be so terrible a fate.

She sat up. 'That would go against your destiny.' She straddled him, although at this moment clearly without any sexual motive. 'Listen to me, Robert Barrington. Your skin may be white, but you are Chinese. Or perhaps, you are Manchu, eh? That would be better. Your family have been Manchu since the first Robert Barrington agreed to serve my great forebears. You know this history?'

'Yes, Majesty.'

'Then you know that your future, and the future of all your descendants, depends upon the prosperity, the greatness, the power, of Manchu China.'

'Yes, Majesty.' Robert was becoming uneasy; he had listened to his father often enough expounding on the steady decline of both the Dynasty and the Empire.

'This prosperity, this greatness, this power, Robert, is my charge,' Tz'u-hsi said. 'It is impossible to trust my ministers. Even the princes of the House of Ch'ing plot against me. Thus I need men about me who I can trust, and who will come to my aid, to the aid of the Dynasty and of the Empire, should the occasion arise. And arise it will. Your father was such a man, Robert. Is such a man. But he is growing old. Will you replace him?'

'To the death, Majesty,' Robert said fervently.

'I was sure of it. To you I entrust my navy. This is a secret we share; no one else must know of it. Serve this Captain Lang, help him train my sailors, and in the course of time you will command them. Remember this. Betray me, and I will cut off your head. Nor will anyone believe you; the censors and pamphleteers spend their entire time writing scurrilous accusations of my immorality – one more will be of little account. Now go; it will soon be dawn, and at dawn I . . .' She smiled. 'I must attend a meeting of the Grand Council.'

'Will I see you again, Majesty?'

She stroked his chin. 'All things are possible, Robert. In your case, why, I would say all things are probable.'

*

Chang Tsin was waiting for him in the antechamber. A look confirmed what the eunuch had anticipated. 'You have touched greatness, Young Barrington,' he said. 'Now you must serve.'

'I have said that I will,' Robert protested. 'But I fear it will be some time before I am in a position to help Her Majesty.'

'It may well be sooner than you think,' Chang Tsin told him. 'Are you not aware that in another seven years the Emperor will be declared of age, and seek to rule?'

Robert had not considered that. 'Then what will become of Tz'u-hsi?'

Chang Tsin's eyes were hooded. 'Or the Dynasty. Or the Empire. You may well ask yourself these questions, Young Barrington. For be sure Tz'u-hsi will not let them go by default.'

As Robert stepped into the cold damp of a drizzling dawn, for the first time he wondered just what he had done to himself.

*

Captain Lang turned out to be a hatchet-faced Englishman with a temper soured by his experiences since arriving in China. 'A boy,' he remarked in disgust. 'They send me a boy. But I gather you at least have some knowledge of steamships, Mr Barrington.'

'Yes, sir. My father owns four side-wheelers.'

'That is to the good. You will probably have to undertake the duties of engineer until I can recruit one from England; these people do not understand the first principles of steam propulsion. As for the rest, I despair. But we must endeavour to carry out our instructions. I would have you meet this gentleman. His name is Ting Ju-ch'ang. I assume you speak Chinese?'

'Yes, sir.' Robert bowed to Ting, who was a very solid, hard-looking north Chinese in his early forties.

'I have appointed Mr Ting Admiral of the Fleet,' Lang said. 'Don't ask me what fleet as yet, because it is not yet in being. Admiral Ting, will you show Mr Barrington to his quarters.'

Robert reflected that it was a crazy world, where a captain gave orders to an admiral, and the admiral showed a sixteen-year-old who did not even as yet have a rank to his quarters. But Ting seemed oblivious of any possible breach of discipline; he was just happy to be rubbing shoulders with the bearer of so famous a name.

'I have met your father, Young Barrington,' he confided as they went down to the waterfront. Here the Pei-ho debouched into the Gulf of Chih-li, through extensive marshes. The marshes were fronted by a low sea wall to keep out the sea, not very successfully, and the forts themselves rose to either side of the entrance. These forts had been stormed by the British in 1861, at the cost of enormous Chinese casualties, and since then had been reinforced and armed with modern long-range artillery; they looked immensely strong. 'Now I am pleased to make your acquaintance,' Ting continued. 'This Captain Lang, he is impatient. Do we not already have a fleet?'

They had arrived at the docks, and Ting gestured towards

the dozen or so war-junks anchored just off-shore; with their shallow draft they could cross the bar in the event of bad weather.

'What the Captain wants are a dozen of those.' Robert pointed to the British and French men-of-war anchored further out in the gulf – steamships all.

'We will have them,' Ting said. 'Tz'u-hsi has promised this.'

Robert continued to gaze at the British squadron. He knew it represented about one per cent of Britain's naval strength. 'We shall never have enough ships to fight the British,' he commented.

Ting laughed. 'We are not going to fight the British. It is the Japanese we must worry about.'

*

Robert was surprised at Ting's anxiety about the Japanese, but as he came to understand more about Chinese politics – in Shanghai and the south the talk was only concerned with trade and gossip – he realised that the Admiral was probably very right.

For Japan too had felt the heavy hand of Western imperialism during the last thirty years, beginning with the landing of the American Admiral Perry in 1853, and the Japanese too had been forced to submit to bombardment by British squadrons and to grant trade concessions. But the Japanese had reacted differently to the Manchus, or the Chinese, who had attempted a national resistance and been roundly defeated. Once the proud samurai warriors had realised that their antiquated weapons and military systems could not hope to compete with the Barbarians, they had had a revolution. The Shogun, that Barbarian-Quelling-All-Powerful-General, who had ruled the island empire in the name of the Mikado – the Emperor – for six hundred years, had been overturned, and the Emperor restored to his powers and prerogatives.

And this had been no timid old man, but a bold youth

named Mutsuhito, no older than Robert himself, who had grasped his nation by the scruff of its neck and hurled it into the nineteenth century, scrutinising and then utilising the best, as he saw it, of European methods. He had taken his political system from Germany, his legal system from Italy, his naval tuition from Britain, and his military tuition from France – but he had not hesitated to replace his French instructors with German following the French defeat in 1870. Under Mutsuhito's leadership Japan had become a hive of industry and progress . . . and territorial ambition. By 1884 the Japanese had already effectively assumed a protectorate over the Ryukyu Islands, which had paid tribute to the Throne of Heaven since time began. Now they attempted to move into Korea, the hermit kingdom – again, since time immemorial, a client of the Chinese emperors.

Lang, together with Robert and Ting, was summoned to Peking, both to see Li Hung-chang and to be harangued by the Empress. For Robert this was an occasion to be reintroduced into the imperial bed, to his great pleasure, but Tz'u-hsi was not the relaxed lover of three years before. 'They wish war,' she declared. 'Well, so do I. We certainly cannot surrender to the Japanese. Is my fleet ready for war, Robert?'

'No, Your Majesty, it is not.' For although they had managed to obtain a couple of steamships, he knew the Japanese had more.

Her eyes flashed. 'You are a pacifist, like your father. Like Marshal Li.'

'I prefer to be a realist, Your Majesty. We need bigger and better ships than the Japanese, and more of them, to be able to meet them with any hope of success.'

She glared at him, then her eyes softened. 'Then you will have those ships, Robert. But for the time . . .'

He, and the other naval officers, were present at the meeting of the Grand Council to discuss the situation. Tz'u-hsi presided, looking from face to face.

'The Japanese have done nothing overt,' Li Hung-chang

said. 'But they are slowly building up their forces, and they are stirring up unrest, too. They are creating a classic scenario, Your Majesty. Before long there will be a riot, and a Japanese will be killed. They will then claim the right to intervene in the government of Korea.'

'Then we must send troops,' Tz'u-hsi said.

'They might regard that as a reason for war, Your Majesty,' Li said patiently. 'And we are not ready for war, even with the Japanese.'

'Are you telling me there is nothing we can do?'

'We can beat the Japanese at their own game,' said a quiet voice.

All heads turned to look at the speaker, a short, somewhat plump, and decidedly young army officer.

'Wait your turn, Yuan,' Li muttered.

'Let him speak,' Tz'u-hsi said. 'What is your name?'

The officer stood up. 'My name is Yuan Shih-k'ai, Your Majesty.'

Tz'u-hsi was frowning, as she realised that the forward young man was Chinese, as indicated both by his name and by his pigtail. She looked at Li.

'Colonel Yuan is one of our best officers, Your Majesty,' Li said. 'I brought him to this meeting because he has ideas which might prove useful.'

'Ideas?' Tz'u-hsi turned her gaze back to the colonel.

'Send me to Seoul, Your Majesty,' Yuan said. 'As commander of the Chinese garrison. I will deal with the Japanese.'

'You? And how many Bannermen?'

'I ask for no additional men, Your Majesty. Those we have already in Korea will suffice. With your permission, I will be their Bannerman.'

Tz'u-hsi's gaze swept the table as there was a rustle of both movement and whispered comment. The Manchu grandees were visibly irritated by the young man's effrontery.

'Tell me, Colonel Yuan,' Tz'u-hsi said. 'How old are you?'

'I am twenty-five, Your Majesty.'

'You aim very high, for one so young.'

'If a man does not aim high, Your Majesty, he will never rise at all.'

Tz'u-hsi almost smiled. 'When a man aims too high, Colonel, he has that much further to fall.' Once again her gaze swept the room. 'I shall grant your wish, and appoint you Commander-in-Chief and plenipotentiary at the court of the King of Korea. But mark me well, Colonel. Should you fail, and the Japanese gain control, you will be decapitated.'

Yuan bowed his head. While Robert wondered if the Empress, with her eye for young men, would now take *him* to bed.

*

Yuan Shih-k'ai did not fail his Empress. When Li Hung-chang was proved right early the next year, and the Japanese, having engineered an incident in which one of their nationals was killed, sought to seize power, the young soldier acted with ruthless brilliance, boldly kidnapping the Korean King and Queen and forcing them to sign a new treaty acknowledging the supremacy of China. When he wrote to Tz'u-hsi to tell her what he had done, he signed himself, 'The Last of the Bannermen'.

'The effrontery of it,' Chang Tsin growled; only Manchus could be Bannermen. Besides . . . 'He is implying that he is superior to any of your soldiers.'

But Tz'u-hsi smiled. 'Perhaps we have at last found a general to replace Li Hung-chang,' she said.

But that Japan was still seeking fresh ways of expansion at the expense of what they saw as the fading Dragon Empire could not be doubted, and without a strong navy, China was helpless effectively to deal with the impudent islanders.

'Her Majesty has the power,' Ting complained, 'to change China the way Japan has changed. As we are the most populous country in the world, she could make us into the most powerful country in the world. But she will not use this power.'

'I suspect Tz'u-hsi considers China already to be the most powerful nation in the world,' Robert suggested.

But the Empress's own position, Robert knew, was not as strong as that of Mutsuhito. In the eyes of many people, Tz'u-hsi held her power illegally, and the censors and leading mandarins were waiting with some anxiety, and in some cases secret plans, to see how she was going to cope with the Emperor's coming of age.

Meanwhile, in addition to the Japanese, there was trouble with the French. Despite the indemnities and the executions, the French had chafed ever since the Tientsin Massacre, longing for an opportunity to undertake some gunboat diplomacy and hack out for themselves a large chunk of Chinese territory. Since their disastrous defeat by Germany they had been steadily recovering their strength, and were now ready to flex their muscles. And now too they found an opportunity.

The French had long been trading with Cochin-China, the countries of Vietnam, Laos and Cambodia, situated in the very south-eastern corner of Asia. These again, from time immemorial, had been considered as part of the Chinese Empire, and had regularly sent tribute to the Throne of Heaven. The French now persuaded the local kings to conclude a treaty with them, acknowledging French supremacy. But infuriatingly, the Vietnamese continued to send tribute to Peking. As a result, in 1884 the French undertook a full-scale invasion of the country. All China was outraged, and Tz'u-hsi, as ever in the past, was the most warlike of her people. She ordered mobilisation and sent troops hither and yon. All to little purpose. Despite the brilliant efforts of Liu Yung-fu, the ex-T'ai-P'ing general whom Tz'u-hsi placed in command in Vietnam, the French steadily made progress.

The final disaster came when a French squadron entered Foochow Bay unopposed as there had as yet been no formal declaration of war between France and China, and after carefully positioning themselves, opened fire, destroying not only the Chinese ships which were in the harbour, but also the huge arsenal which was the hub of the Manchu rearmament programme, and which had actually been built with French assistance and financing in the first place.

All China was shocked, the navy more than anyone. But Tz'u-hsi cunningly turned the disaster to her own advantage. Declaring that she had been betrayed by her ministers, she dismissed them all, including Prince Kung, whom many had considered her right-hand man, but who had been suspicious of her ever since Alute's death, and replaced him with Prince Ch'un, the Emperor's father. This breach of Confucian ethics shocked the literati, and one of their most prominent scholars, Wen T'ing-shih, followed the earlier example of Wan Li-chung and committed suicide in protest.

Li Hung-chang remained as powerful and placatory as ever, however, and the usual indemnities were agreed to settle with the French and end the war.

'Without us being allowed to fire a shot,' Lang declared angrily to his officers. 'And now ... this!' He pounded his fist on the paper which lay in front of him on the table. 'Her Majesty has appropriated next year's naval estimates for the building of a new Summer Palace.'

The officers were struck dumb.

'Something must be done,' Lang insisted.

'It is not possible to remonstrate with Tz'u-hsi,' Admiral Ting said. 'She is a woman of iron will.'

'You mean she is a woman who has no sense of responsibility, no plan for the Empire, no plan!' Lang said angrily. 'Well, I can no longer attempt to create a modern navy in such circumstances. You!' He pointed. 'Mr Barrington. Your family is friendly with the Empress, I believe.'

Robert swallowed. 'Yes, sir.'

'Then you will go to Peking and inform Her Majesty that I will resign if these appropriations are tampered with. We need ships, and we need guns. Thus we need all the money we can procure. That money has been voted to be spent on the navy. To hive off whatever she requires for some

grandiose and irrelevant scheme is not merely irresponsible
. . . it is dishonest! You will leave tomorrow.'

*

Robert had received an order, and he was obliged to obey,
even if he felt he might be going to his own execution. In the
circumstances, he decided his best plan was to go direct to
Chang Tsin's house, and this he did, to be received most
hospitably by Wu Lai and her two daughters. 'I shall send
into the Forbidden City to acquaint my husband that you are
here,' Wu Lai said.

Chang Tsin came home that evening, sat with Robert, and
listened to what he had to say.

'This Captain Lang takes a great deal on himself,' he
remarked. 'And for such a mission he should have come
himself.'

'He was afraid that Tz'u-hsi would not receive him.'

'And he felt sure she would receive you? Young Barrington, do you suppose that because she once invited you to
share her bed she would not have you decapitated on the
instant should you anger her?'

'Even if I appeal to her on behalf of the navy which is
essential to the defence of China?'

Chang Tsin gave a grim smile. 'Many are those who have
appealed to the Dowager Empress in the name of the "good
of China". She follows her own council in all things. My
advice to you, Young Barrington, would be to abandon this
mission, and return to Taku.'

'I cannot, until I have seen the Empress. I have been
ordered to do this by my superior officer.'

Chang Tsin shrugged. 'You will remember what I told
you, that only you can bring an end to the prosperous life
that lies ahead of you. But if you will . . . you had best
accompany me. Her Majesty is a woman of moods; she may
well agree to see you, and then, by the time I have fetched
you, have changed her mind. If you are there, all things are

possible.' He grinned. 'Including your sudden demise.'

As before, he made Robert shave very carefully, dressed him in a eunuch's robes, and after dark led him into the Forbidden City. But this time he was not taken directly to Tz'u-hsi's bedchamber. Instead he was left in a small room, with no windows or access to the outside world, and told to wait there, knowing nothing of what might be happening, watching the door, for it might well open to admit his executioners.

Almost he dozed off, as weary hour succeeded weary hour, with hardly a sound to be heard outside his door. Then at last it opened, and Chang Tsin beckoned him. 'Do not speak, and be very careful.'

Robert followed him along a corridor, which had windows opening on to one of the inner gardens that marked this huge palace complex, and saw that it was close to dawn. 'Her Majesty is awake at this hour?' he asked.

'She takes her bath, so that she may be dressed in time to meet the Grand Council at sunrise,' Chang Tsin told him. 'This is when man's brain is at its best, is it not?'

'Of course,' Robert agreed, although he knew it was not so considered in Europe, and certainly Captain Lang was not an early riser.

They reached a doorway guarded by a eunuch, and were admitted into another antechamber, this one filled with sweet smells. Beyond another doorway Robert could hear the sound of voices. 'Wait here,' Chang Tsin told him, and went through this inner doorway. Robert gained the impression that there were several people in there, but the door had opened and shut very quickly.

Now his heart was pounding and he was sweating; the next few minutes might be his last on earth. He faced the doorway as it opened. Chang Tsin entered first, and held it for Tz'u-hsi, closing it immediately behind her.

Tz'u-hsi wore an undressing robe, and her hair was loose. She glowed from her bath, and had been drenched in perfume. Her face had not yet been made-up, and was again that of a young girl. But it was impossible to tell, from her expression, whether she was pleased to see him or not.

Her voice was quiet. 'Am I then your mistress, that you call upon me at your whim, Young Barrington?'

'It is a most urgent matter, Majesty.'

She inhaled, the breath rasping in her nostrils. 'Chang Tsin has told me of this *urgent* matter. Can I believe my ears that a boy of twenty dares to question the Dowager Empress as to the allocation of funds?'

'Your Majesty, Captain Lang wishes only to lead a Chinese fleet into battle against your enemies. A fleet capable of defeating your enemies.'

'Captain Lang! Does he know that you have visited me before?'

'No, Majesty. This I swear. He knows only that you and my father are friends.'

'Do not swear, Young Barrington. Only those who are lying, or preparing to lie, find it necessary to swear. I think Captain Lang has served his purpose. I find him displeasing to me. He is dismissed, as of this moment.'

'But your Majesty . . . all he wishes is to speak with you.'

'I do not wish to speak with him, Young Barrington.'

'But . . . who will command the fleet?'

'I have had good reports of Ting Ju-ch'ang. What do you say of him?'

'He is a fine seaman, Your Majesty. But he knows nothing of commanding steamships, or lines of battle.'

'Then you will have to teach him, Young Barrington. I make you . . .' She glanced at Chang Tsin.

'Flag-Captain to the Admiral would be most appropriate, Majesty.'

'As of this moment, you are Flag-Captain to Admiral Ting.'

'Your Majesty . . .'

'Are you not pleased, Robert?'

'I am overwhelmed, Majesty. But I fear my unfitness for such a post. I have never fought a battle at sea.' Or on land, he thought.

'Then call upon your father's knowledge and experience. He will not refuse his son.'

Robert was trying to understand what had just happened to him. 'And Captain Lang?'

'Captain Lang will be sent back to England, where he belongs. The Chinese Navy will be commanded by Chinese, and Manchus.' She smiled. 'And you.' She stared at him, a faint frown gathered between her eyes. 'Are you afraid to command?'

'Your Majesty . . .'

'Are you afraid to serve me?'

'It is all I desire, Majesty.'

'Remember that, always. But—' She half turned away from him, and then checked. 'I have in mind for you another reward, one of a more personal nature, which will reveal to the world the esteem in which I hold you, Robert. It is time you took a wife. I have selected the very one for you.'

Robert looked at Chang Tsin in consternation; Chang Tsin beamed at him.

'You will marry Chang Su.' Robert opened his mouth and then closed it again. 'She is a pretty thing,' Tz'u-hsi said. 'And she is intelligent. Chang Tsin has told me how fond you are of her.'

Again Robert looked at the eunuch: he had spent only half a dozen minutes in the company of Chang Su in all his life, was not even sure he could tell her apart from her sister. All he knew of her was that she was only thirteen years old.

And marriage? To the daughter of a eunuch? Even the most powerful eunuch in the Empire? Father would be aghast. As for what Mother would say . . . 'With respect, Majesty,' he said, 'I cannot marry without the consent of my parents.'

'Of course you cannot,' Tz'u-hsi said. 'I will send for them to come to Peking, in order that they may give their blessing. It will be a great occasion.'

*

'Robert! Married to a Chinese?' Lucy stared at her husband in consternation. 'And the daughter of a eunuch?'

'Well, of course she isn't the daughter of a eunuch,' James pointed out. 'She's adopted.'

'Eunuchs are despised by everyone,' Lucy declared. 'James, you cannot permit this.'

'I can do nothing about it, if it is indeed the wish of Tz'u-hsi.'

'You were friends with her once. Surely you can reason with her? James, this family, from the very beginning, has always kept itself racially pure.'

'Not entirely,' James argued. 'Grandfather Robert took a Chinese mistress after Grandmama died.'

'A mistress. He didn't marry her.'

'They were as married as any couple could be.'

'And what happened? They had a son who became a rebel, who raped your own sister, James, and was then executed. Do you want that to happen to Robert's family?'

'I see no reason why it should,' James said. 'This is an entirely different matter. The first Robert was a very old man when he took Tsen Tsing to his bed. He had no say in the upbringing of his son, and he made no attempt to teach John any of the Christian virtues. Robert is young. He will educate both his wife and his children to be true Barringtons.'

'Half-castes,' Lucy said bitterly.

'Lucy . . .' he held her hands. 'We are Chinese. Or at least, we are Manchus, by adoption. Our future lies in this country. It would be stupid of us to bang the drum of racial purity now. It would be even more stupid to antagonise Tz'u-hsi at this stage. Do you realise that Robert has been made a flag-captain, at the age of twenty? Not even Nelson accomplished that. He will be an admiral by the time he is thirty, as long as Tz'u-hsi is our friend.'

'Of a navy which only exists on paper,' Lucy said

contemptuously. 'As for Tz'u-hsi . . . what makes you think she is going to remain in power all that long?'

'I suspect she'll manage it for a while longer,' James said.

Eleven-year-old Victoria looked from one to the other; she had never heard her parents quarrelling before. 'Will we have to go to Peking, Papa?' she asked.

'Of course we will.'

'I've always wanted to go to Peking,' Victoria said.

5

THE MEN WHO WOULD
CHANGE THE WORLD

Murray Scott came down from Lo-shan to perform the Christian ceremony, which followed the Chinese one. Helen accompanied him. She still had the glow of a bride, and she seemed totally happy. They could speak only of the Mission, which they were apparently building with their own hands, aided by the forty converts they had already made.

'I worry so for you, up there in the interior, so far from us,' Lucy said.

'It is lonely, sometimes, Mama. But the converts are so sweet.'

'There is all this talk of how the Chinese hate the missionaries . . .'

'Well, I suppose some of them do. But they don't hate anyone up at Lo-shan. It's the most heavenly spot on earth.'

'A good place to have children,' James suggested.

Helen blushed. 'We've time, Papa. We've time.'

'What do you think about your brother marrying a Chinese?' Lucy asked.

'I think that's the best way to rid the country of its xenophobia. Intermarriage.'

Lucy looked at Murray Scott in despair, and he gave her

a sympathetic smile; he obviously didn't entirely share his wife's liberal point of view.

Joanna and Arthur Jenkins also attended the wedding, from Port Arthur; it was only a short voyage across the Gulf of Chih-li to Tientsin, and then up-river to Peking. Joanna was fifty-three now, but still possessed all of the Barrington looks to go with her Barrington height. Of the mental scars she must have suffered as a girl there was no visible trace. 'Where are you going to honeymoon?' she asked Robert. 'We should so like to entertain you at Port Arthur. It is really the most delightful spot on earth.'

'I'm afraid there won't be a honeymoon, Aunt Jo. My duties require me to rejoin the fleet immediately. But I shall visit you soon. I promise.'

She also seemed to find nothing wrong in a Barrington marrying a Chinese, Lucy thought angrily. She was isolated within her own family.

Except possibly for Adrian, who gazed at his brother with smouldering eyes. But perhaps Adrian was just jealous.

*

The marriage of his daughter to James Barrington's eldest son was the most important event of Chang Tsin's life, at least since Tz'u-hsi had taken him back into his employ. Tz'u-hsi could not attend the wedding of one of her subjects, but she sent handsome presents, of cloisonné work, and porcelain, and an enormous ruby ring for the bride, as well as a gold-inlaid sword for Robert. Chang knew, of course, that his adopted daughter was merely being used by the Empress. Tz'u-hsi was busily trying to create a cadre of loyal young men, men like Yuan Shih-k'ai and Robert Barrington, who, she hoped, would be the support of her old age, when Li Hung-chang might no longer be available. With Yuan perhaps in command of the army, Young Barrington in command of the navy, and both utterly loyal

to herself, for whatever reason . . . Yuan would always have
to be kept loyal by appointments and financial rewards – not
even Tz'u-hsi had been able to bend so far as to take a pig-
tailed Chinese to her bed – but Robert Barrington was
already secured by more intimate ties. Now she sought to
redouble his bonds.

But for Chang Tsin, it was a triumph. He was fond of
Chang Su, but he did not love her as if she had been his own
flesh and blood. She had been purchased to be a symbol of
his wealth and power. Now she was marrying into one of the
most powerful families in the Empire. This made his own
position the safer. Chang Tsin was well aware of how hated
he was, of how if Tz'u-hsi were ever to give the slightest
indication, even inadvertently, that he was no longer her
favourite, there would be a queue of vengeful people waiting
to get their hands on his throat. But there was no one in all
China outside of the Imperial Dynasty who would dare cross
swords with the House of Barrington.

He held his daughter's hands as she prepared for the
ceremony. 'You go to greatness, Su.'

'I am afraid,' she confessed.

'Of what?'

'Barrington is so huge. Will he not split me open?'

Chang Tsin smiled, and embraced her. 'He is no larger
than any other man, where it counts. And as his wife, you
will be one of the first ladies in the land.'

*

Fire-crackers popped, people shouted, food was eaten and
thrown aside, dogs snarled over the scraps, children
screamed for joy and wailed with exhaustion, and Chang
Tsin smiled.

'This day, Barrington,' he told James, 'I feel that all of our
adventures together have come to fruition.' He smiled at
Joanna, and held her hand. 'And ours, Joanna.'

For the first time since her arrival Joanna looked

embarrassed. No one had ever found out the truth of her escape from the T'ai-P'ing with Chang Tsin. No one had ever sought to inquire too deeply, because Chang Tsin had been already a eunuch.

'I share secrets with all of your family,' he told Robert. 'But most of all with you.'

Robert concluded that his new father-in-law was more than slightly drunk.

It was customary for a groom to carry off his bride to his own house, but Robert had no house in Peking. So it had been decided that he and Chang Su would spend their first night together in Chang Tsin's house. Wu Lai arranged it all and even placed a silver ewer in the bedroom, that her daughter might go to her husband correct in all essentials, according to Confucian law.

The celebrations were still at their height when the couple were escorted upstairs by their parents. Victoria, resplendent in pale blue satin and with her dark hair secured by an enormous satin bow, went too; she had never been so excited.

'It is strange, to have such a mixture of two ceremonies,' Wu Lai confessed to Lucy. 'I am not sure what to do.'

'I think the best thing we can do is leave them alone,' James suggested, as Lucy had throughout maintained a mood of rigid, disapproving politeness.

Wu Lai bowed. 'I leave you in good hands, my child,' she told Su.

The door closed, and Chang Su knelt before her husband. She wore a blue silk gown, and had already removed her shoes. Her hair was pinned on the top of her head with a porcelain brooch, decorated with paintings of tiny birds. She smelt of perfume and sweetness, and innocence.

Robert took the brooch from her hair, and the black tresses fell to her shoulders and beyond. Still she kept her head bowed and did not look at him, as she had not looked at him throughout the two ceremonies or the festivities afterwards. When he touched her cheek, and then cupped her chin to raise her face, she gave a little shiver. 'Are you afraid?' he asked.

She gazed at him from enormous black eyes.

'Of men? Or this man in particular?'

'I wish to be your wife, my lord.'

'And so you shall be, my wife.' He held her arms to raise her, then lowered his head to kiss her mouth. She stood still, immobile, only those slight tremors running up and down her frame. 'This is how we make love, in my country,' he told her.

She licked her lips; Chang Tsin had explained this to her. But she did not know what else Barbarian men did to their women: Chang Tsin had no first-hand knowledge of that.

She was so small; she barely reached the middle of Robert's chest. And she was as light as a feather, he discovered, when he lifted her from the floor and set her on the bed, standing on the mattress. There she hesitated, uncertain what he wished of her.

'Take off your gown.'

He was suddenly aware of desire, where there had been little before. But it was an odd desire, as Su unfastened her gown and shrugged it from her shoulders. The gown went straight down, only hanging for a moment at her hips before falling about her ankles.

She was so thin. Her breasts were the smallest buds, her hips narrow, her pubes shaded in the very lightest of downs, her buttocks small and tight. Yet all, with their complements of arms and legs, even the ribs which could clearly be seen through the thin flesh covering them, were exquisitely shaped.

But to lie on her would be to crush her to death. Even to hug her might be to shatter that fragile form.

He undressed in turn, and she gazed at him, her face expressionless, her eyes slowly widening. He knew she had only been Chang Tsin's daughter for half a dozen years, and presumably before he had purchased her there had been whole men and boys around her, but as she would then have

been six or seven perhaps she had not noticed. Obviously
she had not seen a naked man since, and certainly not one
erected, as he now was.

She was trembling again.

He knew what he wanted, but she would not be ready, and he
did not wish to hurt her more than was necessary. He stood
against her, took her in his arms, and kissed her again, holding
her lightly. He stroked her buttocks and her breasts, stooped to
kiss her groin. When he was satisfied, he straightened. 'I
would approach the Fragrant Bamboo,' he said.

She had certainly been taught the *Book of Love*, and her
eyes opened wider yet, as he brought her against him. She
put her arms round his neck, wound her legs round his
thighs, and clung there, as he adjusted her, and then held her
hips to bring her down to him. Her breath rushed against his
cheek with the pain of it.

But she was his, and he realised that she was going to give
him a great deal of happiness.

                                      *

The bride and groom departed, the feasting continued.
'Mother says that in England,' Adrian told Victoria, 'there
would be dancing at a wedding reception.'

'But the Chinese do not dance like Europeans,' Victoria
pointed out.

'Exactly. They're a dull lot.'

'You don't know how to dance, anyway.' At eleven,
Victoria was going through an age when logic was everything.

'I'd learn, goose, if there was anyone to dance with. I've
seen pictures of how they do it. None of this shuffling about
like the Chinese. In Europe, a man takes a woman in his
arms, and holds her . . .'

'Ugh!' Victoria commented.

'You'd probably enjoy it if you tried it.' Adrian had drunk

enough sake and plum wine to be feeling randy. In fact, he felt randy a good deal of the time. His principal recreation was accompanying one of the younger house servants into Shanghai to visit a brothel.

But such adventures always left him feeling dissatisfied. He invariably experienced a huge upsurge of violent passion which could not be alleviated by mere ejaculation. The girls were always willing enough, and some of them were quite pretty, but they could only perform as they had been taught, and the *Book of Love* did not extend beyond the parameters of sexual love.

Adrian did not love, or want to love, any of his partners. He wanted to possess a woman, as many women as possible, and make them do his bidding, watch them prostrate themselves before him, preferably in terror. He wanted to have the rights of an oriental despot, to be able to whip and beat, torture and even maim or kill, if he chose.

These were secret ambitions. He could not imagine what his father and mother, or indeed his elder brother and sister, would say if they knew of them. The Barringtons, whatever people might whisper behind their backs, prided themselves upon being islands of correct behaviour in a corrupt world.

But Robert now owned a woman. Chang Su was only thirteen. She could be moulded into anything Robert wanted. Not that attempting to mould her at all, certainly to enslave her, would ever cross Robert's mind, Adrian knew.

While he . . . he looked at his sister. Victoria was only two years younger than Chang Su – and she looked older. And she was his adoring sister; she was already his willing slave in most things.

And if he was nearly drunk on sake, she was even more so, as he could tell from the bright colour in her cheeks and the way she was smiling.

'Come outside,' he suggested.

Victoria followed him without hesitation. Several other guests had sought the fresh air, but Chang Tsin had a large garden, and Adrian soon managed to find a secluded spot, with a bench on which they could sit beside each other. 'What do you think Robert is doing now?' he asked.

Victoria rolled her eyes. 'He is lying with his wife.'

'Do you know what that means?'

'It's what husbands do with their wives,' Victoria explained, surprised that he didn't know this. 'Sing Shou has told me about it.'

Sing Shou was her nurse.

'What else did she tell you?' Adrian persisted.

Victoria hesitated.

'Come on,' Adrian coaxed. 'You can tell me.'

Victoria blushed. 'They take off all their clothes, and then they lie together.'

'And then?'

'She wouldn't tell me anything more than that.'

'Well, they do a lot more,' Adrian said. 'Would you like me to show you what they do?'

'Well . . .'

Adrian held her face between his hands and kissed her on the mouth while it was still open, pushing his tongue inside.

Victoria jerked her head away. 'Ugh!'

'Don't you like that? You'll have to like it from your husband.'

'Then I shan't get married.'

'Don't be a goose. Of course you have to get married. All women get married. I know, I'll choose your husband for you. Would you like that?'

'I think Papa would want to do that,' Victoria said.

'But Papa may be dead.'

'Don't say that,' Victoria snapped, her eyes filling with tears. 'Don't ever say that.'

Adrian grinned. 'Would you like me to show you what else a man does to a woman when they make love?'

'No,' Victoria said. 'I don't really want to know.'

'Of course you do. He'll want to feel your titties. Of course, you don't have any titties yet, do you?'

'I do so,' Victoria said angrily.

'Then let me feel them.' He pressed his hand against the bodice of her gown, and she sprang to her feet.

'Get off!'

Adrian grinned at her. 'And then he'd want to put his hand under your skirt, right up to your slit. Come here and let me show you.'

'Ugh! That's disgusting. *You're* disgusting! Just don't touch me ever again.'

She walked away, back into the throng. Adrian watched her go with smouldering eyes. One day, he thought, I am going to have you naked in my arms, little sister. But until then, he had to have someone.

*

He broached the subject to his father on their way back down the Grand Canal to Shanghai. James stroked his chin. 'A place of your own? At eighteen?'

'Robert was on his own at sixteen,' Adrian pointed out.

James had to agree. He could not tell his younger son that he could discern the differences in their characters, that Robert was obviously as solid as a rock, whereas Adrian . . . James could not be sure about Adrian. He only knew that he could see a darkness in Adrian's character which he could not understand, and had no idea how to deal with.

But perhaps the boy needed the responsibility of a place of his own. Properly supervised. 'Then we shall find you a house,' he said. 'Chiang Lu will see to it.'

Chiang Lu was a Chinese in his middle twenties, who had been in the Barrington employ since childhood. He was tall for a Chinese, and thin, and lugubrious. James reckoned he was the ideal supervisor of Adrian's household.

Lucy was as usual not very happy with the idea, but like her husband she had always found it difficult to get close to her younger son. So a small house was bought, in the International Concession, down-river from the Barrington

Mansion. 'You must come to visit me,' Adrian told Victoria, with a grin.

She stuck out her tongue at him.

But Adrian had more important things on his mind for the time being. 'The first thing we need, Chiang Lu, is suitable servants.'

'That will be my charge, Master Adrian.'

'I will choose my own servants, Chiang Lu. But you may assist me, if you wish. However, first I wish to ask you a question.'

'Yes, Master?'

'What do you desire more than anything else in the world?'

Chiang Lu considered. 'A long and prosperous life.'

'Do you think you will achieve your ambition?'

'If Fate wills such fortune, Master.'

'I am your fate, and your future, Chiang Lu, as of this moment. Remember this, and you will prosper. Forget it for a moment, and you will find yourself in the gutter.'

Chiang Lu digested this, then said, 'What do you wish of me, Master?'

'Simply that you obey me in all things. You no longer work for the House of Barrington. You work for me. Do you understand?'

'I understand, Master.'

'Then let us go out and get ourselves some servants. We will buy them, Chiang Lu. Do you know where this can be done, discreetly?'

'Yes, Master. I know of a house in Shanghai where the girls are for sale.'

'Take me there. And Chiang Lu, we will buy one for you, as well.'

*

Adrian and Chiang Lu entered the city, looking up at the row of grinning heads nailed over the gate, and glancing at the two men suspended in cages on either side of the entrance. These men were alive, but were soon to die; each cage was just big enough for the man, and his head was thrust through a gap in the bars forming the top of the cage. This gap had been closed around his neck – his chin rested on the bar across his throat and to keep himself from strangling he had to stand on tiptoe. From their lolling tongues and dreadful wheezing both men had been there for some time. They had not been fed or given water since sentencing, and they were tormented by girls and boys, who poked at them with sticks and made bets on which one would die first. But these were common sights in every Chinese city, where the Confucian ideal of the peaceful, literary gentleman went hand in hand with the most savage criminal code.

Chiang Lu led his master into the heart of the city, through crowds of people, past fortune tellers and roadside barbers; men selling meat and men selling manure – human and animal; rough and ready dentists and women buying silks; growling dogs and screaming children; before stopping at a doorway guarded by a eunuch. 'This fellow will assist us.'

The eunuch showed them into an antechamber, beyond which there was the sound of music and laughter. But the eunuch led them to a door in the side of the antechamber, and thence into a smaller room, where a woman was seated at a desk, using an abacus to do her accounts.

'This is Young Barrington, Madame Chin,' the eunuch said. 'Son of Great Barrington.'

The woman rose. To Adrian's eyes she appeared quite old, about twice his age, but was very well groomed and dressed. Her black hair was piled on top of her head; her complexion was clear; and her features, if not beautiful, were well formed and strong; while her figure, delineated by her skin-fitting blue gown, was obviously full. 'Young Barrington,' she said. 'My house is honoured by your presence.'

'My master seeks some women,' Chiang Lu explained.

Madame Chin gave him a contemptuous glance. 'Why else would he be here?' she asked.

'He wishes to buy,' Chiang told her. 'Two girls. Virgins. To take away.'

Madame Chin looked Adrian up and down, then parted a bead curtain behind her desk and opened an inner door. The eunuch had by now returned to his touting on the street. 'You sit,' Madame Chin invited, gesturing Adrian to a divan against the wall. Adrian sat down and Chiang Lu stood beside him. 'You wish to drink?' Madame Chin asked.

'Yes.' Adrian spoke for the first time. He was conscious of a growing excitement at what he was about to do, and his throat was dry.

Madame Chin rang a little bell, and another woman came in; she was also somewhat older than himself, Adrian estimated, was not the least attractive, and clearly only a maid. He watched her preparing hot water in which to immerse the bottle of sake while Madame Chin left the room. The maid served and Adrian sipped the hot, sherry-like liquor while he studied her, his excitement growing as he discerned the intelligence in her eyes, the serious concentration with which she went about her duties. He was here to buy whatever he liked, for whatever mistreatment he desired. But he wanted his slave to be able to feel.

The door opened, and Madame Chin returned. Behind her filed six girls. They all wore pantaloons, and nothing else; their black hair was loose and hung past their shoulders. From their small breasts Adrian estimated their ages as between thirteen and fifteen. They walked demurely, heads bowed, but each looked up as Madame Chin clapped her hands, and each little face broke into a smile, while they waggled their behinds and fingered their own breasts as seductively as they could.

'These are good girls,' Madame Chin said. 'They are clean, they have no disease, and they are skilled in music, cooking, gardening, and the *Book of Love*. I have schooled them myself. You will not find better girls anywhere in China. You may examine them if you wish. But remember they are virgins.'

Adrian looked along the row of faces. They were much alike. And he certainly wanted one of them, if only as a contrast to what he had in mind. 'That one.' He pointed at the girl with the largest breasts.

'Her name is Shu Lai-ti,' Madame Chin said. 'Go forward, girl.'

Shu Lai-ti moved into the centre of the room, smiled at Adrian, and then with a quick movement untied her pantaloons and let them drop around her ankles. Adrian licked his lips; her immature womanhood was compelling.

'Will you not examine her?' Madame Chin invited.

'She seems satisfactory,' Adrian said. He did not know enough about women to be sure he would not make a fool of himself; he would learn from this girl.

'I will examine her, Master.' Chiang Lu was eager. He made Shu Lai-ti spread her legs and bend, so that he could look between, pulling her buttocks apart. She continued to smile at Adrian, apparently not in the least embarrassed or humiliated. 'I think she will be satisfactory, Master,' Chiang Lu said, giving her several quick caresses. Shu Lai-ti straightened, and clapped her hands with joy.

'I have told her she is going to a great lord,' Madame Chin said.

Adrian and Shu Lai-ti gazed at each other, and she laughed. Possessing her promised a great deal of pleasure, but he had an idea she was so mentally conditioned to please and submit that she would even laugh when she was beaten.

'Go and prepare yourself,' Madame Chin commanded. 'You spoke of two, Young Barrington.'

Adrian pretended to look at the other girls. Even if his mind had not already been made up, there was little to choose between any of them and Shu Lai-ti. Not one of them had any intelligence, any ability to *feel*. 'I will take that one.' He pointed at the maid.

'You wish Wu Ping?' Madame Chin asked in surprise. 'She is a servant.'

'I wish a servant.'

'She is twenty-eight years old,' Madame Chin said.

Chiang Lu clapped his hand to his forehead in dismay.

'I have said I wish her,' Adrian told them. Wu Ping was almost old enough to have been his mother, but that made her more desirable.

'She is not able,' Madame Chin said, her voice almost a wail.

'She is diseased?' Chiang Lu asked eagerly; he wanted one of the others.

'None of my girls are diseased,' Madame Chin snapped. 'It is a physical deformity. No man can enter her naturally. It hurts them both.'

'Master,' Chiang Lu said urgently. 'Have done with this madness. Take one of these girls.'

Wu Ping was aware that she was being discussed, and stood in a corner of the room, her head drooping, the picture of misery.

'You can always sodomise her,' Madame Chin said, looking on the bright side. 'Does this please you, Young Barrington?'

'This pleases me,' Adrian said. 'How much?'

'The girls are each ten pieces of silver.' Madame Chin spoke hesitantly, anticipating some hard bargaining.

Adrian took out his wallet and counted out twenty pieces of silver. Madam Chin stared at the money in amazement for a moment, then scooped it up before he could change his mind. Wu Ping stared at Adrian, her mouth twitching with a mixture of fear and bewilderment.

'Will your excellency sample the girls now?' Madame Chin asked. 'Or any other girl in my establishment? There will be no further charge.'

'No,' Adrian said. 'We will take them with us now.'

Madame Chin bowed, and clapped her hands. 'Prepare yourself, Wu Ping,' she commanded. 'And you others, return to your room.' Wu Ping ran through the doorway; the others followed more slowly. 'They are sad not to have been selected by so great a lord,' Madame Chin explained. 'But you have chosen wisely, Young Barrington. Wu Ping will make a good servant. She is well trained. And Shu Lai-ti will give you much pleasure.'

'I have no doubt of it,' Adrian agreed, and glanced at a rather sad-looking Chiang Lu. 'Cheer up, Chiang. You can have them when I am not using them. Or we can have them together.'

Madame Chin's lips twisted.

*

Captain Lang duly departed from China, and Ting Ju-ch'ang became Admiral in fact as well as name. And slowly a navy was got together. By the end of the decade, Ting and Robert were the proud possessors of two battleships, the *Ting Yuen* and the *Chen Yuen*, both ironclad monsters of more than seven thousand tons, armed with four enormous twelve-inch guns, their hulls protected by a belt of armour fourteen inches thick; a twelve-inch belt also protected the guns, which were in separate barbettes. They were unquestionably the two most powerful vessels in the China Sea, and greatly increased the navy's morale, as it was felt a march had been stolen on the Japanese.

In addition the embryo fleet possessed several cruisers and smaller vessels, all steam-powered and made of steel. Perhaps best of all, they possessed a cadre of European officers, mainly Scots, who had volunteered to serve in this newest of navies. It was a proud day when Robert stood beside Ting on the bridge of the flagship, the *Ting Yuen*, to steam past the European squadrons anchored in the Gulf of Chih-li.

'The boy is doing excellently,' James reported to Lucy, after one of his visits to Tientsin. 'He is doing what he wishes, he is happy, and that wife of his is a little dream.'

'But not yet a mother,' Lucy remarked.

'Early days,' James said, and went off to go over the books with Adrian.

*

Robert was in fact happier than at any time in his life, for the fleet had also been found a proper base, in the vast, almost completely land-locked bay of Wei-hai-wei. Here Robert was able to buy himself a house and set up a home for Su, where he could visit her most nights of the week.

He was equally pleased with both the progress of the navy and his own part in it. Admiral Ting regarded him, rightly, as being his most trustworthy aide, and the two men had become good friends, even if Ting seemed quite unaware that Robert possessed an entrée to the centre of government. Tz'u-hsi had apparently accepted the inevitable and stepped aside on the Kuang-hsu Emperor arriving at his majority, but everyone knew, of course, that she continued to rule from 'behind the curtain', as she amply displayed when decreeing that the Kuang-hsu should marry upon taking over the government.

The Emperor, if no libertine like his immediate predecessors, was pleased with this idea, and Tz'u-hsi so far gave him his head as to permit him to make his own final choice of one of the girls as Empress, as had the T'ung-chih. But the Kuang-hsu chose a fourteen-year-old from the Tatala clan – the same as Alute. Tz'u-hsi immediately intervened. The girl was declared unsuitable, as was her sister, although they were both taken into the imperial harem, one as the Pearl Concubine and the other as the Lustrous Concubine. The Kuang-hsu then accepted his fate, and left the choice of wife up to his 'mother'. Tz'u-hsi chose the Princess Lung-yu, an unattractive girl – she had buckteeth – who was three years older than the Emperor. But she was also Tz'u-hsi's niece, the daughter of her one surviving brother, Kuei-hsiang, and her loyalty was assured.

Further to exert her control over the Emperor's relationship with his harem, Tz'u-hsi had the doorway between the Emperor's apartments and those of the Empress and the concubines blocked up, so that when the Emperor had one of them summoned to his bed, the girl had to pass over Tz'u-hsi's verandah, on a floor which creaked suitably at the least pressure. Thus Tz'u-hsi knew exactly whenever he slept with one of his women – and could easily discover the name.

If the Dowager Empress no longer attended the dawn meetings of the Great Council, Li Hung-chang still did so, and undoubtedly reported to her afterwards everything that was said or decided. There was thus no possibility of the Emperor being allowed to take any course against the wishes of his aunt and adoptive mother. But on the surface Tz'u-hsi appeared content to concentrate on her painting and on completing the I Ho Yuan, her new Summer Palace ... and, whenever she felt the urge, on entertaining her young men, those she intended should continue her power even after Li Hung-chung died – for he was now an old man.

But on the surface, at least, China appeared to prosper, and even to be moving, slowly, into the modern world.

*

In the spring of 1887, Jane Barrington died: she was seventy-seven. She had made her long anticipated visit to Port Arthur, been reassured of Joanna's health and contentment, and then seemed to lose interest in living. She no longer even took an interest in the affairs of the House. James and Joanna mourned their mother, but felt that she could have had few regrets over a long and adventurous life.

And certainly, interested or not, she must have died knowing her family's affairs were in good hands. James reckoned the House of Barrington had never been so established. Even Adrian had turned out better than he had once hoped. The boy was still given to moods of sullen introspection, when he would speak with no one, and he still took little part in the social life of Shanghai. James was fairly certain that he smoked opium, but decided against attempting to interfere or to inquire what went on in the privacy of his son's house; Adrian performed his duties adequately, and he had sufficient money never to need to descend to the depths of degradation which overtook so many addicts.

Of course, if Lucy were to find out . . .

But on the whole he was well satisfied with his family. Against all the odds Helen appeared happy, Robert was doing extremely well, and Victoria . . . as she entered her middle teens Victoria had become a quite outstandingly beautiful girl, with her long dark hair and lustrous eyes, coupled with a surprisingly voluptuous figure in one so young.

Heads turned when she walked the street, and young men were always calling at the Barrington Mansion in the International Concession, leaving their cards in the hopes that they would be invited to one of Lucy's soirées and perhaps have a chance to sit beside the daughter of the house.

The fame of her beauty even spread north. 'I hear you have a daughter of rare charm,' Tz'u-hsi commented when James visited Peking in the spring of 1892.

These visits were annual affairs. They were always at the command of the Empress, yet in keeping with custom James always had to take with him presents of considerable value, which duly went into the imperial coffers.

As she grew older, money appeared to be Tz'u-hsi's sole interest in life. James understood her weakness when he remembered how poor her father had been in his attempts to remain honest in such a graft-ridden society as that of China. Now, although by repute the wealthiest woman in the world, she continued to hoard money for her personal use and continually sought new titles, each of which brought her an additional income, while spending vast sums on adorning the I Ho Yuan. Her manner, too, was becoming increasingly arbitrary and contradictory. She might well veto an edict of the Emperor's one day and then agree to it the next, simply because her mood had changed, or, more likely, Chang Tsin had changed it for her.

The eunuch's power over her was disturbing. That he was genuinely fond of his old playmate could not be argued; in the privacy of his own house he called her the 'Old Buddha' as she grew more stout and slow in her movements. But his bottom line, like hers, was self interest and a perpetuation of his personal power. This was widely known, especially amongst the Grand Councillors and the literati, yet no one was prepared to do anything about it. Even if they had dared to conspire against the Dragon Throne, with instant decapitation their fate if discovered, they could think of no viable alternative. The Kuang-hsu remained an unknown quantity, locked away in the Forbidden City like the cousin he had succeeded, surrounded by eunuchs and women. His tutor, Wen T'ung-ho, one of the few whole men who ever saw him, gave out optimistic reports of his intelligence and claimed that he was interested only in books and learning, and had a good brain, but no one knew for sure.

At least, under the guiding hand of Tz'u-hsi, whatever the crimes of which she was suspected or the immorality of her own personal life, as it was whispered, the Empire was at peace; and if the Barbarians continued to encroach upon the everyday life of the Chinese, with their railway lines and their missions, their steamships and their arrogant, probing ways, they, like the Empress, had become fixtures.

As had the House of Barrington, James thought. More so, even, than Tz'u-hsi herself. But yet he remained at her mercy, and not only on account of either the House or Robert's career. His whole family was hostage to her moods.

Now he smiled, cautiously. 'Yes, Victoria is beautiful, Your Majesty.'

'And named after the Queen of Britain. Is the Queen very beautiful?'

For even in her middle fifties, Tz'u-hsi was as vain as ever.

'I do not think Queen Victoria could be described as beautiful, Majesty, except in so far as queens are always beautiful.'

Tz'u-hsi gave him a suspicious glance. 'I would see this beautiful daughter of yours.'

'Majesty?'

'It may be possible for me to find her a place amongst my ladies.'

'Your Majesty, that is not possible.'

Tz'u-hsi glared at him.

Desperately James sought to choose the right words. 'Victoria has been educated as an Englishwoman. She knows only freedom, of mind and body. To be shut up in a cloister would be to condemn her to death.'

'Do you not think I once enjoyed freedom, of mind and body? You should know these things, Barrington.'

'I remember, Majesty. You gave up those freedoms to become the greatest lady in the land. My daughter would not give them up, even for that.'

'Does she not do what you command her?'

'I would never command her to do such a thing, Majesty.'

Tz'u-hsi's eyes narrowed. 'You would dare to defy me?'

'A man's first duty is to his family, Majesty. That is the law of Confucius as it is the law of nature. His second is to his country. I have given you my eldest son, Majesty. You have no right to ask for any more of my children.'

They gazed at each other, and he saw a sudden rush of blood into her cheeks, discernible even under the caked white make-up and the heavy rouge. Her eyes gleamed, and her entire body seemed to swell.

He recalled that she had always possessed an ungovernable temper.

When she spoke, it was in a high shout. 'You dare to defy me, Barrington? Do you not know I could order your execution, now?'

James refused to lower his gaze. 'You have that power, Majesty.'

For a moment she was speechless. Then she pointed. 'Leave my presence. Leave it, and do not ever return. You are hateful to me. Hateful! Leave!'

James bowed, and backed from the room.

*

'You are a fool, Barrington,' Chang Tsin told him. 'It is a daughter's duty to serve her father, to marry whom he chooses, and until that choice is made, to go where he directs. Even if that involves that she should *not* marry. Is it not so in England?'

'I believe it is, in certain quarters,' James said. 'It is not a point of view I hold, or will ever practise.'

'Instead you will ruin yourself?'

'Do you really suppose so, old friend?'

Chang Tsin gazed at him for several seconds, and then smiled. 'No, I do not. The House of Barrington is too valuable to the Empire for Her Majesty ever to seek to curtail it, much less abolish it.'

'My only fear is for Robert.'

'There is no reason. Robert also is too valuable to Her Majesty. And to me, as he is my son now as well. But Barrington, be careful. Tz'u-hsi is capable of deep hatred to those who oppose her.'

'I will make it my business to keep out of her way,' James said, and went into the inner room to sit with Wu Lai, with whom he was now good friends.

*

Lucy was aghast when James returned to Shanghai and told her what had happened.

'My God! To think of Vicky, locked up in that den of iniquity . . . James, cannot we leave this place?'

'Now, you know that is impossible, Lucy.'

'I hate it. I hate all China. And most of all, I hate that terrible old woman.'

Victoria wasn't sure of how she felt about the situation. There was a part of her even wished Papa had given in to the

Dowager Empress and sent her to Peking. Of course, the thought of being shut up in the Forbidden City and never being able to see a man was dreadful ... but was it more dreadful than being shut up in the International Concession outside Shanghai?

Tz'u-hsi at least sounded an intensely interesting person. There were few interesting people in the Concession. Victoria felt trapped in the very small world of the English community. The Barringtons had little to do with the other nationalities who traded up the Yangtse, and even the British were inclined to regard them as freaks. Useful freaks, certainly, because of their knowledge of China and their influence with the local officials, 'local' meaning all the way up-river to Hankow and beyond. And they were no doubt a source of unending gossip to their compatriots because of their piratical past, their involvement in Chinese affairs and their known friendship with the Dowager Empress – but all of these things made them yet more freakish. There were several English families that had now lived in China for the better part of their lives, but none of them had any doubt that when their working days were over they would be returning to England. The Barringtons would be staying in China, as they had done now for nearly a hundred years.

Victoria knew that Mama was always talking about returning to England, and indeed she had several times suggested that she take Vicky with her, to find her a husband. Papa had refused to contemplate so lengthy a separation from his wife and favourite child, and in fact Victoria had soon come to agree with him. England sounded very nice from what she had heard of it, but also very boring, and she found all the Englishmen she met in Shanghai or on the odd visit to Hong Kong equally boring.

Her life seemed destined to be one long bore from beginning to end. When she thought of Helen, married to that po-faced missionary and living in some mud-hut village hundreds of miles up the Huang-ho, labouring like any skivvy while her complexion suffered and she rushed at a premature old age, Victoria's skin crawled. But the choice of husbands seemed to lie between missionaries or merchants or naval officers, and they were all po-faced. Why couldn't she marry a Barrington?

Adrian was a drag. She could never forget how he had tried to flirt with her – and touch her! – at Robert's wedding, even if she had never been sure how serious he had been. But she hated the way he looked at her, was always trying to be alone with her, always making snide remarks about her growing breasts or trying to squeeze her bottom, always inviting her to visit him at his house. She never complained to her parents, merely avoided him as much as possible, but she was actually a little afraid of him. As for going to see him . . . like everyone else she had heard the stories of how he beat his servants.

But weren't there other James Barringtons around, or even Roberts like her elder brother? She read and reread the stories of Frederick Ward and Charles Gordon, paladins who had been in China only just before her birth. Ward had been killed way back in 1862, but she had wept when the news arrived of Gordon's death in Khartoum.

There weren't any men like those around today – presumably because the Empire was at peace. No doubt this was a good thing for trade, but it was whispered that the reason there was no war was because there was no money to fight one, and heaven knew there were enough enemies to be dealt with – Japan, France, Russia – all lurking on the borders of the Empire, awaiting their chance to snip off another piece of Chinese territory.

She longed to know what Robert thought of it all, but Robert never visited Shanghai. He was too busy with his ships – and his Chinese toy bride.

She found that last concept fascinating, the idea of being given to a man one might only have seen once or twice before in one's life, of being utterly his possession. And what possession! One day when her mother was out she had found, in her parents' bedroom, a copy of the *Book of Love*, had turned the pages and gasped at the various recommendations, all graphically named, and graphically illustrated, too.

There was 'The Dragon Turns' – man on top of woman; 'The White Tiger Leaps' – man mounting woman from behind; 'The Fish Interlock Their Scales' – woman on top of man; 'The Fish Eye to Eye' – lying beside each other; 'Approaching the Fragrant Bamboo' – both standing; 'The Jade Girl Playing the Flute' – woman sucking male member; and a host of others. Most exciting of all, Victoria thought, was 'Twin Dragons Teasing the Phoenix' – the woman taken by two men at the same time, although hardly less so was the idea of 'The Blue Phoenixes Dance in Pairs'.

She had been fourteen when she had discovered that book, and had been in a state of febrile excitement for days afterwards, even as she had found it impossible to imagine her mother ever indulging in anything save 'The Dragon Turns' – the missionary position. Papa now, that was different.

As for what Adrian did with those doe-eyed serving girls of his – presumably when he was not flogging them . . .

But she had also realised, when she thought of the book and regarded the European men, young and old, who had come to call and sat on the verandah gazing at her with adoring eyes, that it was extremely unlikely any of *them* would indulge in unusual sexual activities of that sort.

To belong to a Chinese now . . . but of course Mama and Papa would never hear of such a thing; there had been enough of a to-do when Robert's marriage plans had been announced, and that had been an entirely different matter. Lots of European men kept Chinese mistresses, but somehow the idea of a white woman belonging to a Chinese man was regarded as quite unacceptable, that 'fate worse than death' which she read about in the novels of Marie Corelli.

The point was, she didn't want to belong to a Chinese man, to be treated virtually as a slave, to have no part of any worthwhile society – even if he might be a dream lover. But she found it sadly frustrating to wonder why it was not possible to have the two combined, a white man with the lusts and knowledge of a Chinese – such as her own father and brother – or, if such a thing were possible, a Chinese man with just those lusts and knowledge, who was yet a European in outlook and education ... and in his ideas of how to treat a wife when *not* in bed.

Looking at the people she met in the streets of Shanghai, when she visited the markets with her mother, or, as she grew older, by herself – although always accompanied by a servant – she felt such a dream was impossible of realisation. Until the morning in February 1894 when she was at the market buying silk, with Ching San the under butler, followed at the respectful distance by Kai Wong with his ricksha, and she saw an undeniably Chinese man a few feet away, but wearing European dress, from silk hat through morning coat to striped trousers and spats.

Victoria was so surprised she turned for a second look, and discovered that the man was both fairly young and devastatingly handsome. He was tall for a Chinese – about her own height – and had smooth, crisp features highlighted by a black pencil moustache; his chin was clean-shaven.

At that moment he looked round himself, and their eyes met; for a moment they gazed at each other, then he raised his hat while a small smile hovered around the edge of his mouth. Victoria inclined her head, then turned back to examine the silks being offered for her inspection, aware that her heart was pounding. Never had she been so instantly attracted to anyone. And he had smiled at her.

'Whoever is that man, Ching San?' she asked softly. 'Do you know his name?'

'Him? Oh, yes, Miss Victoria. I know his name. It is Tang Li-chun. He is a disreputable fellow.'

'Is he? He looks a very reputable fellow to me, Ching.'

'He is an associate of Sun Yat-sen,' Ching declared darkly. 'A revolutionary!'

Victoria decided not to press Ching San further; revolution was always in the air in the Chinese provinces and was always dangerous to those who became involved, even inadvertently, for one never knew who was an agent of the Viceroy, and thus of Tz'u-hsi herself. But that evening she asked her father if he had ever heard the name Sun Yat-sen.

'I have.'

'Tell me about him, Papa.'

'Why, he's one of those inevitable results of liberalising the regime, bringing it into contact with the West, you could say. Wealthy parents, educated in the States, qualified as a medical doctor, so he picked up a whole lot of "democratic" ideas, which he brought back with him to China.'

'You don't approve of democratic ideas?' she suggested.

'Oh, I do, in their proper place. The United States is a democracy. It is necessary for them. China is an autocracy. This is necessary for *them*. Can you imagine the total chaos that would result if anyone attempted to hold a general election in China? As for supposing that the Empire could be held together by an elected president rather than the Dynasty . . . my God!'

'Is that what this Sun man is suggesting?'

'Was suggesting. As you can imagine, he didn't suggest it very often before there was a warrant out for his arrest.'

'You mean he's been executed?'

'No. He fled the country. Now he operates from outside, mainly Hong Kong and Hawaii, stirring up trouble wherever he can.' He frowned at her. 'Where did you hear the name?'

'Oh . . . in the market.'

'Is that a fact? I didn't know any of his people were in Shanghai. I must have a word with Tseng Tsing-fan.'

The Viceroy! Victoria gulped; she might inadvertently have sentenced the handsome man to death. 'Why should you do that, Papa?'

'We don't want any trouble on the Yangtse, my dear. We had enough of that during the T'ai-P'ing.'

Victoria was appalled. She had grown up in China. The ghastly punishments meted out to criminals was something one hardly noticed, as a rule – one did not know the unfortunate people who were tortured to death. But to think of Tang Li-chun's handsome body suspended in a cage slowly to strangle, or even merely being decapitated . . .

Next morning she decided to go into the Shanghai market again. Ching San raised his eyebrows, that she should wish to do so two days running, but it was not his business to question the decisions of his imperious young mistress, and so Kai Wong was again summoned, and she rode into the city, Ching San jogging at her side. 'It is more silk you require, Miss Victoria?' he panted.

'No. I wish to talk with you.'

Ching San was so surprised he stopped jogging, and then had to run harder than ever to catch her up. Surely she could have talked with him at home?

'Stop here,' Victoria told Kai Wong, who immediately obeyed. They were just inside the old city gates, and people smiled and nodded at her as they passed through. Victoria Barrington was well known in Shanghai, but she was always worth a second glance.

Ching San caught them up, panting more heavily than ever.

'Ching San,' Victoria said. 'Can I trust you?'

'Me, Miss Victoria? You can trust me with anything.'

'I do not wish you to tell my parents what we are doing today.'

'No, no, Miss Victoria, I will not tell them.' Then he scratched his pigtail. 'What *are* we doing today?'

Victoria changed to English, which Ching San knew well enough; Kai Wong did not speak it at all. 'That man we saw yesterday. Tang Li-chun. You said you knew him.'

'Me, Miss Victoria? No, no. I said I new *of* him.'

'Do you know where he can be found?'

'Oh, Miss Victoria . . .'

'You do,' Victoria said. 'I wish you to take me there.'

Ching San goggled at her in consternation.

'Now,' Victoria added, and stepped down from the ricksha, settling her broad-brimmed straw hat more firmly on her head, and picking up her parasol.

'Miss Victoria, if the master found out, he would cane me. Or dismiss me.' The latter was far the more serious penalty.

'Now, how can he find out, Ching San, if you do not tell him?' Victoria asked.

Ching San scratched his pigtail again.

'You will remain here, Kai Wong,' Victoria told the ricksha boy, reverting to Chinese. 'Ching San and I have somewhere to go. We will return shortly.'

Kai Wong merely looked bored.

Victoria raised her parasol. 'Come along, Ching San.'

'This is very bad, Miss Victoria,' Ching grumbled in English. But he knew he would have to obey; there was no use arguing with Mistress Victoria.

He led her past the market and into the main avenue of the city, past the shops and through the beggars and the dogs, and then abruptly turned down a street leading off at right angles. This street was much narrower, but contained some substantial houses. And on this street people stopped to stare at the Barbarian girl. She was acceptable at the market and on the main avenues. Down here she was treading forbidden ground.

Victoria merely gave them an icy stare. They all knew she was a Barrington, and as far as she was concerned, the name provided a safe conduct anywhere in China.

Ching San was clearly very nervous as he turned another corner into a yet meaner alleyway, and the pair suddenly found themselves surrounded by half a dozen very rough-looking men.

'What do you want here?' one of them demanded. 'With her?'

Ching San stammered, and Victoria took over. 'I wish to speak with Mr Tang Li-chun. It is very important.'

'You are Barrington,' the man said. 'Your father is a friend of Tz'u-hsi. You have no business here.'

'I do. Most urgent business. It is a matter of life and death.'

The men exchanged glances, then the leader made a decision. 'You come.'

Victoria nodded, but Ching San caught at her arm, an unheard of gesture in a servant. 'You must not go, Miss Victoria. These men will not let you come back.'

'Don't be absurd, Ching,' Victoria said severely. 'If you are afraid, you may wait for me here. My father knows where I am,' she told the men.

They merely grinned, and she suffered a small pang of alarm herself. Then she remembered who she was and squared her shoulders. Besides, the man Tang had had such a nice smile. He would tell these louts where they got off.

Ching San, having reflected that if anything were to happen to his charge and he not be present he would certainly be sacked, elected to accompany her. They went further down the alley and one of the men opened a doorway into a substantial building with an upper floor. The interior was gloomy, lit by only a couple of lanterns, but there were several other men, as well as some women, in the room.

'You come in,' the leader of their escort told them.

Victoria closed her parasol and ducked her head to enter the room, then stood upright, making sure her hat was on straight.

'You wait,' the man said, and went up a flight of stairs on the right of the room. Behind her, Victoria heard the door being closed.

'They are going to kill us,' Ching San said dolefully.

'Oh, you are absurd, Ching,' Victoria declared, and tried smiling at the people staring at her, but none of them smiled back. Yet she noticed that although their surroundings were unsalubrious, they were mostly quite well dressed – and equally, that they looked more alarmed to see her than especially vicious.

The man reappeared on the landing at the head of the stairs. 'You come,' he said. 'Not you,' he snapped, as Ching San would have accompanied her.

Ching San made a kind of wailing sound, but Victoria

gave him a smile and climbed the stairs. The man opened the door at the top, and she found herself in a small room, facing Tang Li-chun. Behind her the door swung shut with a click.

Victoria glanced left and right; there was no one else in the room, which was furnished with a table – on which there were several papers and maps – and two straight chairs, and in the corner, a bed. A single lantern hung from the ceiling.

Her heart began pounding again at the sight of the bed, the understanding that she was alone with this man, but she managed a smile. 'Mr Tang?'

'Miss Barrington. I understand you wish to see me. Would you care to sit down?' His English was precise.

'Thank you.' She sat in the chair before the desk, and he sat on the far side, opposite her. 'You are in great danger.'

He waited, his face expressionless.

'My father knows you are in Shanghai, and he proposes to inform the Viceroy.'

'And who informed your father?'

'I . . .' she bit her lip. 'I did not mean to. I asked him about Sun Yat-sen.'

'What about Dr Sun?'

'Well . . . everything, I suppose.'

'This was after seeing me in the market yesterday?'

'Yes. My servant told me you worked for Dr Sun. I didn't know then that you were a revolutionary.'

'Is it revolutionary to wish freedom for your people?' he demanded, his voice suddenly hard.

Victoria licked her lips. 'You mean for the men of Han. I suppose to wish their freedom is revolutionary, to the Manchus.'

'An oppressive, conquering regime, which your father supports, Miss Barrington.'

Victoria felt she should be offended, but when she thought about it, she realised that the Manchus *were* an oppressive, conquering regime. 'My family has only known China under the Manchus,' she pointed out. 'As have you.'

'That does not mean any dictatorship must last forever.

They have failed the Empire. That means they have lost the Mandate of Heaven. Do you not realise this?'

Victoria was acquainted with Confucian ethics, which had a disconcerting, but convenient, way of allowing liberty of conscience. As in this case: it was the bounden duty of every man loyally to support the established government of his land, so long as that government was good and just and strong; where it failed in any of those directions, it was equally the bounden duty of every man to overthrow it, and replace it with a government which would rule in accordance with Confucian ideals. Unfortunately, it was largely left to the individual to determine what constituted good and just and strong rule.

'That must be your decision, Mr Tang,' she said, and stood up. 'I came here because I felt that it was my fault your presence was discovered. Now I must leave again.'

'What makes you think I will let you leave, Miss Barrington?'

Victoria's head jerked in mingled alarm and anger.

'You are a very foolish young woman,' Tang said. 'You are foolish because you are arrogant, and because you are beautiful. I understand you have told my men that your father knows where you have come. I do not believe this. If he did, he would not have allowed you to come; he would have come himself.'

Victoria glared at him. 'If anything were to happen to me, my father would find me, and you, if he had to take Shanghai apart. And the Viceroy would help him.'

'As I have said, you are very arrogant, Miss Barrington. When do you think your father will see the Viceroy?'

'He will do so this afternoon.'

'Then I must be out of Shanghai in a few hours. Once I have left, do you suppose it will matter to me if your father, as you say, takes Shanghai apart? Or if he finds your dead body in doing so?'

Victoria had a sensation of faintness; he spoke in such matter-of-fact tones.

'You see,' Tang went on. 'I do not think I can afford to let you go. You know where I am staying. And even if I have left, you would be able to incriminate my associates. Whereas, if you were not here, or unable to tell what you have seen, my people would go unharmed.'

Victoria swallowed, and sat down again.

'Tell me how you knew where to find me?' Tang asked.

'I . . . I was brought by my servant.' She knew she was betraying Ching San, but she was suddenly afraid.

'The fellow downstairs? How did he know?'

'I don't know. I asked him to bring me to you. He didn't know, for certain. He knew the street. Then we were accosted by your thugs.'

Tang smiled. 'My bodyguard, Miss Barrington. Well, you see, I cannot possibly let you go.' He got up and walked round the table; Victoria watched him as if mesmerised. He hitched one hip on to the table edge, immediately in front of her, reached out, and gently lifted her hat from her head. 'You are very beautiful. When I was in England, I saw many beautiful women. But none to equal you.'

'You have been to England?'

'Of course. Haven't you?'

'No.'

Another smile. 'You are more Chinese than myself. But should I not say, that as you cannot leave this place, I might as well possess you?'

Victoria found that she was pressing her back against the chair. 'I . . . I will not betray you. If I was going to betray you, would I have come to warn you?'

He held her chin, moved her face right and left. No one had ever touched her in so familiar a fashion before. Again she felt she should be angry, but she was not. His touch remained gentle. 'You have just told me that your servant did not know where I was to be found, only the area. When you came here, my men foolishly brought you to this house. Which is perhaps what you sought to discover.'

'No,' she said. 'I came to warn you. Only that.'

'Tell me why you should risk so much to warn a man you

had never met, seen only once in your life, and a man you obviously knew to be an enemy to the government your family supports, and thus to you.'

Victoria had to swallow again. 'I . . . I thought you looked nice. I do not want you to be arrested and executed.'

They stared at each other for several seconds. Then he said, 'A very European point of view, Miss Barrington. You have my gratitude.' He released her and stood up.

'Will . . . will you let me go?'

'My people would not like it. They also risk being arrested and executed.'

'I would swear . . .'

'On what? Your Christian Bible? That would hardly interest them.'

'I will swear on anything you wish.'

Once again he gazed at her for several seconds. 'You would have to join our tong,' he said.

Victoria licked her lips. Her knowledge of the tongs and triads was limited; no one ever spoke of them, not even James Barrington. Yet everyone knew they were there, secret societies dedicated to the overthrow of the Manchus . . . and also to every kind of criminal activity, some said. Actually to belong to one . . . but it promised to be a huge adventure, and she would be working for and with this man. 'I will join,' she said. 'If that is what you wish.'

'Are you certain? This is no light business, Miss Barrington. The tong will demand your soul.'

'Do I have an alternative?'

He smiled. 'No. But yet, you might prefer death to initiation.'

She threw back her head. 'I will join your tong, Mr Tang.'

'And serve Dr Sun until the day of your death?'

'Yes. If that is what you wish.'

She could hardly have put it more plainly than that, she thought: it was him she intended to serve. Was she mad? Or just exhilarated with this sudden step from total boredom to total commitment?

Again he considered her for some moments. 'It will take time. Have you time?'

Victoria looked at her lapel watch. It was still early, just after ten. 'I must be home for lunch.'

'Lunch,' he remarked. 'A great British institution. What time do you take lunch?'

'Normally at two o'clock.'

'Well, then, that should give us sufficient time. Perhaps you will not feel like lunch after you have been initiated.'

Again she tossed her head; he was poking fun at her. 'Try me, sir.'

A last appraising stare. Then he nodded. 'I intend to do that, Miss Barrington.'

He left her and went downstairs, presumably to make arrangements. She got up, walked to and fro. There was nothing in the room beyond a change of clothing.

She was at once excited and apprehensive. He had suggested that the initiation ceremony was something which would shock her, but she was determined not to be shocked. If she could not be shocked at the mere idea of belonging to a triad, why should the business of joining it disturb her?

The door opened behind her and she turned sharply, watched three women enter the room. They were all older than herself and their faces were serious, even grim.

'You speak Chinese, Barrington woman?' one asked in the local Shanghai dialect.

'Yes.'

'Undress.'

Victoria caught her breath. 'Why?'

'You join triad, you undress.'

'You come to us naked,' said one of the others.

Victoria licked her lips. 'I come to you here?'

'Downstairs.'

Victoria tried to think. There were men downstairs. Including Mr Tang. But she had agreed to do what he wished. Even to appear naked before him?

'There is little time,' the first woman said.

Victoria turned her back on them and undressed, laying her clothes on the bed. The women watched her, dispassionately. She wondered if they had ever seen Western-style underclothes before?

She laid her drawers on top of everything else, unlaced her boots and kicked them off, then rolled down her stockings. She could hear her own breathing and felt almost sick with apprehension: was she about to be raped, by a whole lot of men? But there could be no turning back now.

'You come downstairs,' one of the women said, and opened the door.

Victoria hesitated, then squared her shoulders and walked through the door on to the landing. She felt suddenly chill and had to exert all her mental strength to stop herself shivering.

Beneath her there were at least twenty men, gathered before a curtain. Tang Li-chun was there, as well as Chin San. She had forgotten about Ching, her own servant. Now she gasped as she saw that he too was naked. But, of course, he would have to join the tong as well. It was the first time she had ever seen a completely naked Chinese man, although Ching San was too clearly terrified to be the least attractive.

On the other hand, she was undoubtedly the first naked white woman any of those men had ever seen, except perhaps for Tang himself.

Then she realised that there were four other naked men standing beside Ching San. This was to be a group initiation.

'Go down,' one of the women commanded.

Victoria went down the steps, slowly, curling her toes over each riser. She was aware of emotions she had never felt before, and couldn't possibly identify. She looked straight in front of herself, refusing to meet any gaze, especially that of Ching San. She was aware that the women had followed her down, and stood to either side. Now they held her arms and marched her forward, between the men, to stand in front of Tang, who was waiting in front of the portion of the room that had been curtained off.

She had to look at him, and he was a splendid figure as he had changed his Western-style clothes for a yellow robe embroidered with crimson dragons; he looked every inch the Munchu prince he was deliberately copying.

He looked only at her face. 'Are you ready?' he asked.

'Yes,' she said.

Behind her she heard the shuffling of feet, and realised that Ching San was being brought into place as well. In fact, he was put to stand beside her; their shoulders touched, and he have her a quick glance, but she refused to return it. She dared not consider afterwards.

'Give me your hands,' Tang commanded.

They stretched out their right hands together, and he placed them between his. 'Do you swear eternal loyalty to the City of Willows, to Dr Sun Yat-sen, and to all he stands for?'

'I swear eternal loyalty to the City of Willows, to Dr Sun Yat-sen, and to all he stands for,' Ching San said.

Victoria did the same.

'And do you swear eternal enmity for the Manchus, and further swear to devote your life to their downfall?'

Again Ching San and Victoria repeated the words, while Victoria began to feel at once outraged and cheated. If she had been forced to expose herself to these men simply to take an oath . . .

But the ceremony had barely started. Now the curtain was pulled aside and she looked at the inner part of the room, where there were several strange objects and curiously arranged furniture, and beyond them, an altar on which were burning joss-sticks as well as various bowls from which odd scents were rising.

Tang walked through the waiting symbols to the counter, turned, and beckoned the first of the initiates. 'Commence your journey,' he commanded.

The man slowly went forward, pausing first to bow at the

'Mountain of Knives', which was literally several knives gathered into a pyramid; then to the 'Red Flower Pavilion', a flower arrangement; then the 'Circle of Heaven and Earth', where he had to climb through a bamboo hoop; then the 'Fiery Furnace', where he inhaled the scent of a vase of burning joss paper; then the 'Stepping Stones', where he climbed upon a chair and stepped across to the next; and lastly, the 'Two-Planked Bridge', where he walked across two narrow planks set between two chairs, before he got down to the floor immediately in front of the altar. His peculiar perambulation was almost like a children's game, and might have been amusing, but for the deadly seriousness of both the initiate and the people watching.

At the altar Tang had been joined by three other ceremonially clad members of the triad. Now they beckoned the next initiate. Chang Tsin was the fifth, Victoria the last. She felt unutterably foolish, and terribly exposed, as she had to lift her legs to climb through the hoop, and then on to the chairs, while everyone in the room watched her. But at last she stood before the altar, with the five men.

'Extend your right hands, palm upwards,' Tang commanded.

They obeyed. One of his assistants now lifted down the bowl from the altar, and held it before the initiates. It was empty, but another man emerged from behind the altar, carrying, to Victoria's dismay, a cock with had been tethered there, its wings fluttering and its eyes dancing to and fro at the sight of the people. He held the cock over the bowl, and the man beside him, with a single sweep of the knife he took from the altar, slit the creature's throat.

The people around Victoria hissed, and she felt like hissing herself, with horror, and the dying animal's blood drained into the bowl. Then the carcass was thrown to one side, and Tang went to the first man. He took a needle from the altar, held the man's hand, and pricked his middle finger. Blood welled, and Tang held the finger in turn over the bowl, and allowed several drops of blood to fall into it. Then it was

the turn of the second man, and then the third. Victoria
watched him coming closer in fascinated apprehension. He
did not look at the face of any of the men, nor did he look
at her face as he held her hand at the end and pricked her
finger, and then squeezed it over the bowl.

The bowl was then placed on the altar, and a cup was
dipped into it to bring up the mixture of human and
cockerel's blood. A broad-bladed knife was laid across the
bowl, and on this the cup was placed. The first man's wrists
were then bound behind his back, and he was told to drink.
This he could only do by bending over the altar and the cup,
and thrusting his tongue down into the noisome liquid.

Oh, my God, Victoria thought. But what disturbed her
most was that the initiate's hands remained bound as a
lighted joss-stick was held in front of his face, and suddenly
extinguished. 'Should I ever betray my oath of loyalty and
secrecy to the City of Willows,' he said, 'may my life be
snuffed out like this stick.'

Soon enough it was her turn. Wrists bound behind her, she
bent above the cup, and then had to arch her whole body
forward to reach it, terribly aware of the people behind her.
She nearly fell over, but steadied herself with an immense
effort, her hair tumbling down past her cheeks, as she pushed
her tongue downwards.

The blood tasted foul, and she gagged and thought she
would vomit. But she made herself swallow and then
straightened, gasping for breath. She hardly believed her
own voice, as she swore the oath.

But that was only the first oath. There were thirty-six in
all; oaths of friendship and hatred, oaths of loyalty and
disloyalty, oaths of death and oaths of life. Then at last their
wrists were freed, and their fellow members of the triad
crowded round, offering them cups of heated sake to to
drink. The room seemed to spin round Victoria's head, and
it seemed perfectly natural to stand naked in the midst of
some thirty people, only two of whom she had ever seen
before this morning. And none of whom made any attempt

to touch her sexually. But yet the atmosphere was redolent of sex.

Tang took her hand. 'Every woman member of the triad must belong to a man,' he said. 'Choose which of us it will be.' He pointed at the stairs. 'You may use the room upstairs.'

Victoria climbed the stairs in front of him. Everyone in the room, including Ching San, knew where she was going, and what was going to happen to her. But Ching San had taken the oath the same as herself.

Now she was going to be raped. No, she thought: I am doing this voluntarily. I have done everything today voluntarily. Because I want to belong to these people. Because I want to belong to this man!

She opened the door and stepped into the bedroom. Tang Li-chun closed the door behind them. Victoria turned to face him. 'Will you still leave Shanghai this afternoon?'

'I think it would be best.'

'Then when will I see you again?'

'When it is possible.'

'You mean to ... to take me, and then just leave me, perhaps forever?'

'It is not I taking you, Victoria,' he said. 'It is the triad. I am only its symbol.'

She gazed at him for several seconds. Sake still filled her brain, her mind. She dared not think about afterwards. She did not wish to. 'You will have to show me what you wish of me,' she said.

BOOK THE SECOND
The Foreign Devils

*'Sometimes she driveth o'er a soldier's neck,
And then dreams he of cutting foreign throats.'*

William Shakespeare, *Romeo & Juliet*

6

THE RISING SUN

Sing Shou was embarrassed. She had asked for this interview with the mistress, as she was entitled to do, as housekeeper and therefore responsible for the female staff at the Barrington mansion. In this regard, she had always considered herself also responsible for the two daughters of the house, having, during her thirty years as a Barrington servant, watched Helen and Victoria being born and having been their nurse during childhood.

Now her duty conflicted with her protective instincts – and with her fear of Lucy Barrington's reaction to what she had to say. But it had to be said. Lucy raised her head from the newspaper she had been reading. 'Well, Sing Shou? Don't tell me: one of the girls is pregnant.'

Sing Shou sighed. Lucy was of course referring to one of the servants. 'Yes, mistress.'

'Honestly, Sing Shou, the morals of your people astonish me. Or is it their lack of morals? Well, you know the rules, and so do they. She will have to go. And there will be no references.'

Sing Shou shuffled her feet.

'I will see the girl before she leaves,' Lucy said. 'Which one is it?'

Sing Shou took a long breath. 'It is Miss Victoria, mistress.'

Lucy had looked back down at her paper. Now she raised her head, a frown slowly gathering between her eyes. 'What did you say?'

Sing Shou licked her lips. 'Miss Victoria has not soiled her linen for three months, mistress.'

Lucy stood up, and then slowly sat down again. But Sing Shou was in charge of the laundry, and she took a detailed interest in all her tasks. 'Why did you not tell me this before?' she asked in a low voice.

'One month, mistress, could be fever, or perhaps bowel upset. Two months, perhaps also. But three months . . .'

And there was certainly nothing wrong with Victoria, Lucy knew. Indeed, never had the girl been so lively and contented as during the past three months. Never had she looked so beautiful.

Lucy felt pain, and looked down at her hands; they were clenched so tightly her nails had cut her palm.

'You are bleeding, mistress,' Sing Shou said solicitously. 'Let me fetch ointment.'

'It is nothing. Who knows about this?'

'Nobody mistress.'

'Yet,' Lucy said. 'Very well, Sing Shou. Thank you for telling me. Would you ask Miss Victoria to come to me, please?'

'She is riding, mistress.'

Lucy raised her head, sharply, and her tight features slightly relaxed. 'Well, when she comes in. The moment she comes in.'

Sing Shou bowed and hurried from the room. She wondered if Miss Victoria was going to 'have to go'.

*

Lucy walked up and down the sewing room in an attempt to calm her nerves. She was tempted to send down to the office for James to come home, but decided against it until she had spoken with the girl. How she wished Jane were still alive – and she had not wished that since the old lady's death!

What could possibly have possessed the girl to do such a thing? She blamed the lack of proper supervision, of course. It had been James's attitude. He should have known better. It had been his parents' decision that he and his sister should, at a very early age, shoulder the responsibility of managing the Wuhu office of the House. The result had been Joanna's kidnapping and rape. So perhaps the older Barringtons had not foreseen the T'ai-P'ing; it had still been a most unwise course.

But James had not learned. He had always given all of his children too much freedom. And what were the results? Helen married to some hot-headed missionary and disappeared up the Yellow River – Lucy might have approved of the marriage at the time, but she had not expected her eldest daughter to disappear so completely; Robert married to a Chinese; Adrian living like some Oriental despot – she hated visiting him, because she always felt he and his servants shared some secret of which she knew nothing, and was afraid to find out. And now... She gazed at her youngest daughter as Victoria knocked and entered the room. She had taken off her hat but still wore her habit, and carried her whip. Her hair was caught in a snood, and her blouse was damp with sweat; there were little beads of perspiration on her cheeks. She was absolutely redolent of good health.

'Mama? Is something the matter?'

Lucy sat down. 'Don't you think it is unwise to ride in your condition? Or are you hoping for a miscarriage?'

Victoria gulped.

'A miscarriage would certainly seem to be the answer,' Lucy went on.

Victoria sat down as well, unasked. 'How did you find out?'

'Stupid girl! Do you not suppose that Sing Shou knows whenever we menstruate? Or do not, as the case may be?'

Victoria bit her lip. 'Then everyone knows!'

'Sing Shou swears not. And I believe her. For the moment. We need to act very fast. What is the name of the father?'

Victoria raised her head. There were red spots in her cheeks, but no other evidence of emotion. 'That is my business.'

'Do you really suppose so? Is he going to marry you?'

'No. He cannot.'

'You have given yourself to a married man?' Lucy was aghast.

'I do not know if he is married,' Victoria said. She had not thought to ask.

'My God!' Lucy clapped her hands to her forehead.

Victoria stood up, took a turn about the room, her boots quiet on the carpet. 'I am sorry, Mama.'

'Sorry?' Lucy shouted. 'You have given yourself to some . . . some clerk who will not marry you . . .' She frowned, as she caught a quick change of expression in Victoria's face. 'At least tell me his profession.'

'No,' Victoria said.

'Very well,' Lucy said. 'You will go to your room and remain there until your father gets in. He will make the necessary arrangements for the abortion . . .'

'No,' Victoria said again, her voice sharp.

Lucy glared at her. 'You cannot mean to have this child?'

'I wish you to understand, Mama. I belong to this man.'

'What nonsense. You mean you think you are in love with him. While he is very evidently not in love with you.'

'I *belong* to him,' Victoria said, her voice low but determined. 'Nothing can ever alter that fact, now. And I am going to have his child.'

*

'What are you going to do?' Lucy demanded.

James lit a cheroot; it was a defensive action, to give himself time to think.

'She seems entirely to have lost her senses,' Lucy went on. 'She talks of committing suicide if we force her to abort. My God! I wonder you do not whip some sense into her.'

'I doubt that would accomplish anything but a permanent estrangement,' James said quietly. 'Victoria is not a girl to accept punishment; she is too strong-willed.'

'Ha!' Lucy commented.

'It is what will be best for her that we must consider. Obviously the ideal thing would be for her to marry this man, even if we arranged a divorce as soon as possible afterwards. But as she will not, or cannot, tell us his name, it seems that is not a possible option. I do not think destroying the babe will do anything more than destroy Victoria as well.'

'You mean to let her have it?' Lucy was again aghast.

'In all the circumstances, I think that would be best, yes. Once it is born, Victoria may take a more responsible attitude. It may be possible to have the babe adopted.'

'Her reputation will be ruined. So will ours.'

'I don't think that need be necessary. She will go away, before she starts to show, and return after it is all over.'

'To England?' Lucy was suddenly eager.

'No. That would be rather obvious.'

Lucy's face fell. 'Then where?'

'We have two alternatives. One is to send her up the Huang-ho to Helen. But I am against that. Helen, or at least that husband of hers, may take a rather strict attitude to the situation and cause an estrangement.'

'Is that all you can think about, an estrangement?'

'So I think the best approach is Joanna,' James said, as if she had not interrupted. 'We can be quite sure that Joanna will sympathise, and that Victoria will be happy there.'

'Joanna!' Lucy got as much contempt into her voice as she dared. Of course Joanna, in view of her own murky past, would sympathise.

'I shall make the arrangements immediately,' James said.

'And suppose Victoria does not wish to visit Joanna?'

'Victoria will be delighted,' James declared. 'She has always wanted to see Port Arthur.'

*

'It is the most heavenly spot,' Joanna had written, more than once. And as the SS *Kowshing* approached the entrance to the huge, land-locked harbour, known as the Tiger's Tail, Victoria was inclined to agree with her aunt. But then, anywhere on earth would have seemed as heaven, after Shanghai. Especially a Shanghai without Tang. She belonged. She had not told her mother a lie in making that declaration. Mama, poor, narrow-minded Mama, assumed she was a foolish young girl who had fallen in love. Mama knew nothing about obscene ceremonies in darkened rooms, and if she did, would dismiss them as unpleasant rubbish. Papa, more steeped in Chinese mores, might well have understood. But he might not have forgiven.

That belonging had been utter. The giving of herself to Tang had been still more complete. She had not known so much of herself – perhaps she had known nothing of herself – until his gentle fingers had stimulated her into total passion, a desire only to give and be taken, to be flooded by his manhood.

She had certainly been flooded by his manhood. Presumably pregnancy had been almost inevitable, although its probability had not occurred to her at the time. But it had been no more than incidental. Even when she had realised her condition, well before Sing Shou had played the tattle, she had continued to live her normal life, confident that Tang would return to her in time to save her from disaster.

He had not. In fact, she did not even know if he was alive or dead. When he had finished with her, she had left Shanghai, with Ching San, and returned to the International Concession and the almost unreal gentility of European civilisation. She and Ching San had hardly spoken. They had hardly spoken since. They shared a dreadful secret; there was nothing left to talk about. Indeed, silence was all important. For Papa *had* been to the Viceroy that day three months ago, and the servants had spent the next few days muttering about raids by Manchu Bannermen, and arrests . . . and executions.

'You must find out,' Victoria had told Ching, and he had come back to her to say that Tang had escaped the city before the raids. He had disappeared. That had been several months ago, and she had heard nothing more of him. Or of the tong. Perhaps it had been destroyed. She could not suppress a secret wish that it had – so long as Tang had escaped – that her secret was now limited to Tang and Ching San. And now she was even escaping Ching San. But she carried Tang's child. And would rear his child too. And teach him to bring down the Ch'ing!

To do that, as there was no prospect of hiding the child's ancestry once it was born, she needed an ally. Robert, married to a Chinese woman, was of course her best prospect. But she had not been allowed the time to see Robert, and to write him was too great a risk. Adrian, over-obviously scandalised at the news, would probably help her – at a price. And Adrian's price she was not prepared to pay; she both feared and distrusted him. Thus, failing her brothers, there was only Aunt Joanna. Papa could not, however inadvertently, have made a better choice. Yet even Aunt Joanna needed to be approached with the greatest caution – she had never borne a Chinese child, only been raped by various Chinese men.

She was waiting on the dock as the steamer nosed its way alongside. Victoria had been gazing in wonder at the breathtaking aspect of the place, for once the twisted entrance of the Tiger's Tail had been negotiated, there opened up a huge land-locked inland sea, with branches disappearing into little coves and inlets in every direction, the whole fed by a small river which meandered down the centre of the sloping coastline to plunge into the harbour.

The main part of the city was built to either side of this stream; the houses rose up the slopes behind, and were fronted at the waterside by the docks and godowns of the merchants for whom Port Arthur was an important entrepot – it remained ice-free all winter. Behind the town, stark on the hilltop, Victoria could make out the squat shapes of several forts, as there were forts on either side of the Tiger's Tail behind her; Port Arthur was reputed to be impregnable.

The harbour contained several warships – it was indeed one of Victoria's hopes that Robert might visit in his battleship during her stay here – and was a bustle of ships of all sizes, some under sail and some steam-powered, coming and going, unloading against the dockside, or lying at anchor awaiting their turn. Yet despite the combined first impression of a place devoted to business and defence, there was much beauty in the woods which covered the slopes; and outside of the city itself, on either side, could be seen large houses tucked away between their tree-screens.

There was a berth waiting for the *Kowshing*, which was British registered and officered, and she went alongside immediately. The gangplank was run out, and Victoria hurried down it; she had spotted her aunt in the waiting throng. Having reached the land, however, she hesitated, uncertain of her reception. 'Vicky, my dear girl!' Joanna embraced her. 'I have the trap waiting.'

'What about my boxes?'

'Chan, you will see that Miss Victoria's luggage is brought up to the house,' Joanna commanded. The servant saluted, and went on board himself to make the arrangements. Joanna led Victoria through the crowd to where a pony and trap waited, held by two small boys. Joanna tipped them, and climbed on to the driving seat. 'I always drive myself,' she said, 'although some people find it unseemly. You may sit in the back if you wish.'

'I'd rather sit up here with you,' Victoria said, climbing up beside her aunt and feeling a warm glow spreading over herself. Here surely was total support.

Joanna glanced at her to make sure she was securely seated, then released the brake and flicked the whip. The pony broke into an immediate trot, bouncing over the uneven cobblestones, while dogs barked and children scattered from in front of them.

'Am I going too fast for you?' Joanna asked.

'No, honestly.'

'You need to be careful,' Joanna remarked. 'If you are serious. About having the babe, I mean.'

'I am serious, Aunt Jo.'

Joanna changed the subject. 'What do you think of Port Arthur?'

'It's beautiful.'

'I have always thought so. When you are settled, I will take you for a ride over the hills to the Neck. That is where the Liao-tung Peninsular joins the mainland. It is only a few yards wide at its narrowest point. It is dominated by a fort, which makes the Peninsular, and therefore Port Arthur, impregnable from the land. And, of course, it is already impregnable from the sea.'

'Who would ever attack it?' Victoria asked.

'The Japanese, my dear. They have long coveted it. But you did not come here to speak of war. As I said, you are probably safer here than anywhere else in China. Here is the house.'

They had been climbing the hill, above the town and away from it to the east. Now they turned down a brief drive between swaying cypresses, and found themselves in a small courtyard, fronting a neat little two-storied house. 'Not one of the grand mandarinal palaces you find further out, I'm afraid,' Joanna remarked. 'But we are comfortable here, and it is near the Mission.'

'I think it's absolutely charming,' Victoria cried, leaping down from her seat and running up the steps to the front porch, before turning to look out, through the trees, at the distant waters of the harbour. 'Just sweet.'

Servants had appeared, and to these Joanna handed over the trap. She escorted her niece up the stairs to the spare room. This was at the back of the house and had no sea view, but overlooked a hardly less attractive vista of tree-covered slopes stretching upwards. 'I hope this will be all right.'

'It's perfect.'

'When your boxes arrive, I'll come up and help you unpack.' Joanna turned to the door, and there checked. 'Your father didn't actually say, well . . .'

'I'm four months, Aunt Jo.'

'I see.'

'So I'm sorry, but I shall be here for a while.'

'My dear, you're most welcome.'

Victoria took an envelope from her reticule. 'Papa sent you this . . .'

Joanna slit the envelope, took out the piece of stiff paper. 'It is an order on the House. Really, this wasn't necessary.'

Joanna, of course, although married to a missionary, received a regular income from the House in any event, and was really quite well off.

'It's actually not so much for my board,' Victoria explained. 'Mama didn't want anyone in Shanghai to know what had happened so . . . there's no layette, you see.'

'Of course, how stupid of me. Don't worry, my dear, my seamstress will run you up everything you may need. And for the baby.' She opened the door.

'I would like to thank you, Aunt Jo,' Victoria said.

'For having you to stay? My dear, it is my pleasure.'

'I meant, for not . . . saying anything.'

'We shall have a talk, when you're settled,' Joanna said. 'Arthur comes in about six.'

'Ah . . . does Uncle Arthur know about . . .'

'Yes,' Joanna said. 'Well, he would have to, wouldn't he? Don't be afraid, Vicky. We're here to help you, not scold you.'

*

Going downstairs that evening was nonetheless an ordeal. Uncle Arthur was in his seventies now, utterly bald save for a white fringe over his ears, and was a trifle deaf. Victoria had always been vaguely afraid of him. But as Joanna had promised, Arthur Jenkins never mentioned the reason for Victoria's visit at all; he was clearly content to follow his wife's lead. Over the next few days Victoria found her nerves gradually settling down. Joanna kept her busy, as they went into town to visit the seamstress and explain what they wanted, and as she showed Victoria over the peninsular. They went up to the Neck and gazed across it at the mountains rising to the north. 'It's all still China,' Joanna said.

'And ruled by the Manchus,' Victoria remarked.

'Well, yes, it is.' She glanced at her niece. 'Don't you like the Manchus?'

'They are tyrants. The Ch'ing, anyway.'

'Politics?' Joanna asked with a smile. 'Are they yours, or borrowed?'

Victoria bit her lip. But she had to talk to this woman some time, and her aunt had been unfailingly kind thus far. She waited while Joanna turned the trap and began driving over the road back to the town, invisible beyond the hills surrounding the harbour. 'They were borrowed. But they are mine now,' she said.

'Then they were best kept to yourself.'

'The Ch'ing cannot rule forever,' Victoria insisted.

'Probably not. But we at least should hope that they rule for as long as possible. Without the Ch'ing there would be no House of Barrington. As for Chinese revolutions . . .' She gave a little shiver, and Victoria knew she was remembering her own experiences at the hands of the T'ai-P'ing.

'This revolution will be different,' Victoria said.

Another glance, but this time Joanna was frowning. 'You almost sound as if you know something about it.'

'I do.'

Joanna gazed at the road. 'Does your father?'

'Well, everyone knows there is a movement against the Ch'ing.'

'And he approves?'

'Oh, no. He would suppress it.'

'But you wouldn't,' Joanna said thoughtfully. 'Again, I'd keep that to yourself. What does your . . . the father of your child think about it?'

The cue Victoria had been waiting for. 'He is dedicated to it. The overthrow of Ch'ing. As am I.'

Joanna stopped the trap and turned to face her. They were entirely alone on the road, with no one in sight in any direction. 'I think you should tell me about it. About him. He sounds a dangerous man. Barbarians have no business meddling in Chinese politics. Your father has always followed that rule, unless commanded to break it by the Empress.'

Victoria drew a long breath. 'The man I am speaking about is not Barbarian, Aunt Jo.'

Joanna gazed at her for several seconds, and Victoria braced herself for an explosion of revulsion that she should be carrying a Chinese child. But Joanna accepted the news without visible reaction. 'I see,' she said at last. 'Is this why you refused to tell your parents his name?'

'Yes. Aunt Jo, he isn't . . . well, anyone ordinary. He was educated in America, and speaks perfect English. He dresses like a Barbarian. Most of the time.'

'And he plots the overthrow of the Ch'ing. You'll be telling me next that he is a follower of Sun Yat-sen.'

Victoria could not believe her ears. 'You know of Dr Sun?'

'Word gets around. Vicky, you must see this is madness. I don't know how you and this man got together, but he is going to be captured and executed eventually. They always are. And if you are involved . . .'

'I am involved. Irrevocably. I have sworn an oath . . . Will you promise never to repeat what I am going to tell you?'

Joanna had lived all her life in China: Victoria had already told her enough by mentioning the word 'oath'. 'Oh, my God,' she said. 'Oh, my God! No, I do not promise, and you must not tell me. That way protects us both.'

Victoria bit her lip.

'And the child?' Joanna asked.

'If you will not help me . . .'

'How can I help you?' Joanna asked. 'Do you seriously suppose you are not going to be betrayed, some time, by someone? Do you seriously suppose you can raise a Chinese child, in those circumstances? The only advice I can give you is to leave China just as quickly as possible. And do not ever come back.'

'I cannot do that. Not while Tang lives.'

'Tang,' Joanna said.

'That, at least, I would beg you to keep a secret, Aunt Jo.'

'Yes,' Joanna said. 'I can keep that secret.'

'Will you let me stay here, and have the baby?'

Joanna picked up the reins, and the trap began to move again. 'I have agreed to do that, Vicky.'

'And after?'

'May God have mercy on your soul.'

*

'Marshal Li wishes to speak with Your Majesty,' Chang Tsin said, as he completed Tz'u-hsi's toilette.

'What does he wish with me at this hour?' Tz'u-hsi asked.

It was just dawn, and the Grand Council would as usual be assembling in a few minutes. Li usually came to her, after the meeting, to bring her up to date on what was going on, what had been decided. Presumably the Kuang-hsu Emperor knew of this. When *he* visited her, he always assumed that she knew all the recent decisions of the Council, even if he never formally asked for her approval.

She was content enough. The I Ho Yuan was officially completed by now, but for her it would never be completed.

There was always something to be added. It, and her other amusements, her theatricals and her gambling, occupied her entire time, or at least, she pretended so. But even had she still ruled, there would have been little to distract her. The Empire was as much at peace as it ever had been, or perhaps ever could be. She felt she could trust those around her, however far removed they were from her person, however much they seemed to serve the Emperor; James Barrington's prompt action in alerting the Viceroy of Chekiang Province to the presence of a revolutionary cell in Shanghai only a few months ago was proof enough of that.

According to the report the cell was dominated by Western-educated men. That angered her. The business of allowing bright young men to travel to Europe and America, officially to be educated in Western culture but in reality to imbibe revolutionary ideas, had obviously been a mistake. Li's mistake. But they were really of very little importance while her viceroys remained vigilant.

But Li's wish to see her, *before* a meeting of the Council, suggested some kind of a crisis. Chang Tsin wrapped her in an imperial yellow robe, and she went into the antechamber. Due to the weight she had put on over the past few years, she was inclined to waddle, with a great swishing of silk. But she never doubted that she was still beautiful to those who served her.

Li Hung-chang looked both old and tired as he bowed to his mistress. He had served her now, with total loyalty, for more than thirty years, had preserved the Empire in the face of the threats, and indeed the invasions, of the Western Barbarians, had resisted all this woman's demands for war, while endeavouring always to prepare for it . . . and now had to concede failure.

'You look unhappy,' Tz'u-hsi commented as she sat down, Chang Tsin taking his usual place at her shoulder. 'Why are you unhappy, Li?'

'Your Majesty, I bring grave tidings. I have heard from Yuan Shih-k'ai. He has positive information that the

Japanese are about to launch an invasion of Korea.'

Tz'u-hsi frowned. 'Can they do this?'

'They have the men, certainly, Majesty. They have the ships. It is a matter of the will, not only to face us, but to face the certain condemnation of the Western Powers.'

'What does Yuan advise?'

'General Yuan is of the opinion that, because of the factors I have just mentioned, the Japanese will probably follow the same tactics as in 1885: have their agents foment a disturbance in which some Japanese nationals will be killed, and thus have reason to send an army to protect their people and their interests. They will then say that this is what the Western Powers would have done, as they have done so often in the past.'

'They are devils.'

'General Yuan therefore offers the opinion that we should forestall the plan by reinforcing our garrison in Korea. This he feels would make the Japanese think again, as it will also make the Koreans they hope to goad into revolt think again.'

'Are we allowed to do this, under the terms of our treaty with Japan?'

'We are allowed to do so if there is serious unrest. We will say that we have certain knowledge of such unrest brewing. In any event, if our men are in Korea before the Japanese know of it, there will be nothing they can do, save protest. Then we can negotiate their withdrawal. But the mere fact that we have acted, decisively, will give them pause.'

'That is wishful thinking,' Tz'u-hsi said. 'How long will it take an army to march from Peking to Seoul? Three months across the mountains of Manchuria. The whole world will know of it before our troops pass the Great Wall.'

'Not if we were to transport our men by sea, Majesty. From Tientsin across the Gulf of Chih-li, past Port Arthur to Inchon, would be a matter of less than a week. Even if Japanese agents saw the men embarking, they could still not get word back to Tokyo in time.'

'Have we the ships available?'

'The SS *Kowshing* is anchored in the Gulf now; she has recently returned from Port Arthur. I have issued orders for her to remain at anchor, pending instructions from Peking. This is a large ship, Majesty, which will take two thousand men with all their equipment, including artillery. What is better, it is British owned and registered, and the officers are British. The Japanese will have to consider the reaction of Great Britain should they attempt to stop her.'

Tz'u-hsi smiled. 'You are a cunning rogue, Li. But why have you come to me? I have no say in these matters, now.'

'I am about to put this news and my proposal before the Emperor, Majesty. I wished you to know of it first, so that should His Majesty come to you for advice, you will be able to help him.'

'Yes,' Tz'u-hsi said thoughtfully. 'I believe in such a crisis he may well come to me for advice. You have acted wisely, as always, Marshal Li.'

Li beamed, and bowed.

'I have one more word of advice,' Tz'u-hsi said. 'It is that you send word to Wei-hai-wei, to put the fleet on alert.'

Li bowed again.

*

A week later, the SS *Kowshing* raised her anchor and proceeded to sea. On board were two thousand Chinese troops, with their officers and full equipment. She was two days out, and virtually abeam of Port Arthur, although out of sight of the port, when she was hailed by a Japanese squadron and commanded to stop.

The English master of the *Kowshing* refused to do so, pointing to the Red Ensign flying from his stern. The captain of the lead Japanese cruiser, Togo Heihachiro, issued a direct warning that non-compliance would mean the sinking of the ship. Again the master of the *Kowshing* ignored the summons. A few minutes later the Japanese warship opened fire. Struck in several places, the *Kowshing* capsized and sank.

The Japanese cruiser put down boats and rescued the English officers. The Chinese soldiers were left to drown.

7

THE WOUNDED DRAGON

The news of the sinking of the *Kowshing* crashed on to China like an enormous bomb. 'War!' Tz'u-hsi shouted. 'They want war, they shall have war. Send General Yuan whatever he needs. And tell Admiral Ting to put to sea.'

'Your Majesty,' Chang Tsin ventured.

Tz'u-hsi snorted. 'I know. I no longer rule China. But even the Emperor must accept that war is now inevitable. I will see him immediately. Prepare him for my coming.'

*

'Oh, my God!' Lucy said. 'Oh, my God! Robert! What is to be done?'

'I imagine Robert will be quite safe,' James aid. 'The Chinese fleet is immeasurably superior to the Japanese. The Japanese have no battleships; the Chinese have two. No, it is Vicky I am thinking about.'

'Port Arthur? Port Arthur is impregnable!'

'I still think she is going to be rather close to the theatre. I'm going to bring her home.'

Lucy was appalled. 'But . . .'

'I know. She won't have had the baby yet. We'll just have to put up with the scandal, my dear. I'm not going to risk her life.'

*

'War,' Admiral Ting said happily. 'I had feared that I might die without ever leading my fleet into action. Now, against the Japanese! You will issue orders for us to put to sea immediately, Captain. We sail for the Sea of Japan!'

'Yes, sir!' Robert answered enthusiastically. He too had doubted these two splendid ships would ever go into action.

'We cannot fight without ammunition,' Commander von Hanneken remarked. 'We must have more shells for the twelve-inch.'

The German commander was officially employed as Inspector of the Chinese Coastal Defences, but he was a gunner, and spent most of his time on the two battleships. Certainly he had raised the guncrews to a high level of proficiency, but he was always complaining about shortage of ammunition.

Robert grinned at him. 'The best way to get some more shells, Commander, is to fire a few.'

He hurried to make the ship ready for sea. As he reached the deck, however, he saw a steam pinnace approaching from the shore, flying the flag of the Viceroy of Chih-li Province, and experienced a sudden tightening of his stomach muscles. It could be a final inspection before they sailed, or it could be . . . He went back into the Admiral's day cabin, where Ting was poring over his charts. 'The Viceroy, sir.'

Ting accompanied him on to the bridge wing. The duty lieutenant was already summoning the watch, and the boatswain's whistle was co-eeing. Engineer-Commander Mackintosh emerged from his boiler room to see what was going on, and joined Robert and the Admiral and Von Hanneken on the quarter-deck to salute Li Hung-chang as he came on board, moving slowly and a trifle hesitantly. Li was very old, and he had never cared for ships. 'Your excellency.' Ting bowed. 'Welcome aboard *Ting Yuen*. We are preparing for sea, in accordance with our orders.'

Li nodded, then to Robert – he had known Robert since he had been a small boy – and then gazed with distaste at the ladders he would have to climb to reach the bridge. He went up, followed by the senior officers, and seated himself in Ting's day cabin, Ting and Robert standing anxiously before him. Von Hanneken and Mackintosh – both incongruous in their blue uniforms and peaked caps amidst the gaudily clad Chinese, including Robert – waited just outside the door, as impatient as any of them to learn the reason for this disconcerting visit. 'What I have to say must remain absolutely confidential,' the Viceroy said.

Robert's stomach muscles tightened even more.

Ting was also concerned. 'Our orders are countermanded?'

'No,' Li said. 'I have not come to countermand your orders, Admiral. But I have come to . . .' he hesitated. 'Explain them.'

Ting and Robert exchanged apprehensive glances.

'The fleet will put to sea as instructed,' Li went on. 'But it is the decision of the Grand Council, endorsed by the Emperor, that you will at all times act upon the defensive. Your base will be Port Arthur, and from there you will not only protect the Liao-tung Peninsular, you will cover the Gulf of Chih-li and any attempt by the enemy to launch a seaborne invasion of the Shantung Peninsular, or indeed, further to the south. Is this understood?'

'But . . . the theatre of war is in Korea, your excellency,' Ting protested. 'The Japanese must ferry their army across the sea. If we defeat their fleet in the Sea of Japan, they cannot do this.'

'The Grand Council has no fear of a Japanese army landing in Korea,' Li said. 'General Yuan Shih-k'ai is being supplied with sufficient troops to defeat them. Your business is to prevent the Japanese from using the sea to launch any flank attacks upon the Chinese mainland.'

Robert could tell the ageing statesman did not himself believe what he was saying. 'With respect, your excellency,' he ventured. 'How is General Yuan being reinforced?'

'Through Manchuria. The army is already on the march.'

'But, your excellency, if we defeated the Japanese fleet, it would be possible to send the troops by sea, in a fraction of the time.'

'And if you were defeated, Captain Barrington?'

Robert looked at Ting. 'We have the two most powerful ships in Asia, your excellency,' Ting protested.

'A sea battle is an imponderable,' Li pointed out. 'You will obey your orders, Admiral. What is more, should you be attacked by the Japanese, you will again act upon the defensive at all times. Let them come to you, and rely upon your big guns to destroy them. Do not engage them in a running battle. Your ships may be more powerful, but theirs are faster. Let them come to you, Admiral.' He stood up. 'I will wish you good fortune.'

*

Robert went ashore to say goodbye to Chang Su. Over the years she had put on weight, and was now decidedly plump. She had long since abandoned any hope of having children, at least partly because Robert seldom slept with her any more. This did not seem to disturb her. She could even joke about it. 'You have married the daughter of a eunuch,' she would say. 'Who has turned out to be a eunuch herself.'

But she could still weep at the thought of her husband going off to war. 'You will be killed,' she moaned, hugging him.

'I do not think there is much possibility of that,' Robert said. He could not explain his remark, but if the fleet was going to wait for the Japanese to attack them, then he would probably not even see action.

Next day the Chinese fleet sailed. The ten cruisers, varying in size between one and three thousand tons, and armed with old-fashioned cannon and new-fashioned machine-guns, led the way; only two of them, the *Ping Yuen* and the *Tsi Yuen*, had any armour, but then, the Japanese heavy guns were expected to concentrate on the battleships, as unless they were sunk or put out of action no victory could be won. Behind the cruisers steamed the two battleships, their four huge twelve-inch gun turrets – each turret contained a single gun, one forward, one aft, and two amidships – filling the onlookers with a sense of awe. Large crowds turned out to cheer the fleet to sea.

*

'Oh, aren't they splendid!' Joanna stood on the verandah of her home, with Arthur and Victoria, and peered through the trees at the Chinese fleet approaching the Tiger's Tail.

Even Victoria had to admit that the fleet was rather splendid to watch. It represented the might of the Ch'ing. And on board the flagship was her own brother. How she longed to see him again. And not merely because she had not seen him in several years; he would also, she hoped, be the solution to her problem, as well as being able to tell her what to do.

The letter from Papa, requiring her to return to Shanghai, had arrived only a few days previously. It had come by a small coasting junk whose captain had related how he had seen Japanese cruisers moving to and fro in the mist. How true that was nobody could be sure, although the lookouts on the forts on top of the Tiger's Tail also claimed to have seen the grey shapes of Japanese cruisers and patrol boats. Reports were also coming in of an engagement between a Chinese squadron and some Japanese ships, which had resulted in severe damage to the cruiser *Kwang Yih*; she had only narrowly escaped destruction. All of which meant that sea travel was a dangerous business, while to consider going through the mountains of Jehol in Victoria's condition was out of the question – she was now six months pregnant, and showing it.

Joanna had been equally uncertain as to the best course to take. They had never discussed the future since that day returning from the Neck. Joanna remained unfailingly kind, but Victoria knew that her aunt was deeply concerned and would indeed have very much liked to be rid of her responsibility. But she too had considered the idea of a return to Shanghai, in all the circumstances, to be too great a risk. She also wanted to discuss the matter with her nephew. 'Chan,' she called to the servant. 'Get out the trap.'

Joanna drove, Arthur and Victoria sat in the back; Victoria could no longer risk sitting up on the driving bench. It took them some time to reach the docks, because everyone in Port Arthur was moving in the same direction, eager to greet the great ships as they brought up. The noise was tremendous, as the rasp of the anchor chains plunging into the still water was matched by the cheers and exploding fire-crackers on the shore, as the forts fired a salute, and the ships responded; the sound reverberated from the cliffs land-locking the harbour, and seabirds rose in great numbers. Joanna clapped her hands as she watched the dragon and phoenix flags fluttering from the mastheads, and gazed through Uncle Arthur's telescope at the ornate woodwork decorating the bows of the battleships, the huge guns staring grimly fore and aft.

Boats were put down, and the crews came ashore. Robert was amongst the first: Admiral Ting of course knew that he had relatives in the port.

'Robert, you darling boy!' Joanna embraced him. Then he shook hands with Arthur, while Victoria gazed at him in admiration. He wore Chinese dress, a red robe over blue tunic and pants, with red boots. His hat was red. He looked nothing like any of the British naval officers who had come calling in Shanghai. But he was more than six feet tall and powerfully built, and he was her brother – and he was

Captain of the greatest warship in the Chinese fleet. And, as a servant of the Manchus, he was her enemy. But he was not to know that. Yet.

He left his aunt and uncle and came towards her, his expression a strange mixture of pleasure and sadness: she had always been his favourite sister. 'Vicky!'

She clung to him. 'It is so good to see you.'

'It is very good to see you ... looking so well.' He could not stop his gaze dropping to her belly as he stepped back.

'We must talk,' she said.

'You can come home for a meal?' Joanna asked.

'I should love to. But you are going to be seeing a lot of me, you know. Port Arthur is to be our base for the next few weeks. Well, until the Japanese are defeated, anyway.'

'Are they going to be defeated, Robert?' Joanna asked.

'Of course, Aunt Joanna,' he assured her.

*

Victoria showed Robert James's letter, and he studied it with a frown. 'I can understand Father's concern, of course,' he said. 'But I agree with you. You will be far safer here than attempting to regain Shanghai. There *are* Japanese cruisers out there, and as we saw with the *Kowshing*, they're not averse to sinking merchantmen.'

'Those poor men,' Joanna said. 'The fishing boats went out and said the sea was just a mass of corpses. And the sharks ...'

'I agree, it was a dastardly act, especially as there had been no declaration of war.'

'Papa seems to feel there may be fighting here on the peninsular,' Victoria said.

'I'm not saying you won't hear the sound of gunfire, from time to time,' Robert admitted. 'The Japanese will probably make a demonstration. But that's why we're here, to cover the Liao-tung Peninsular and the whole Gulf of Chih-li. You're not afraid of a little gunfire, are you, Vicky?'

'No, I'm not. So, if it's all right with you, Aunt Jo, we'll stick to the original plan.'

'Of course, my dear,' Joanna agreed. 'But I do think you and Robert should have a little chat.'

After dinner Joanna took Arthur for a stroll in the garden, very deliberately, so that the two young people could be alone. 'Help yourself to port,' she told Robert as they left.

Robert did so. 'Father wrote to me,' he said. 'And explained. Well, in so far as he knew. Seems hard, I know.' He sat beside his sister. 'If I get a girl pregnant, I'm patted on the head and told, you naughty lad ... but everyone's secretly proud of me. You get pregnant, and there's a tremendous to-do. It seems a shame you wouldn't marry the man. Or is it a case of couldn't?'

'Maybe a bit of both.'

'You wouldn't care to tell me why?'

'I'd love to tell you why, Bobbie. But if I do, you will feel obliged either to go after the man yourself, or to tell Papa. I can't have that.'

'You don't feel this man has rather done you dirt?'

'No, I don't.'

'Well ... nothing more to be said. What did you want to chat about?'

He was setting up to be hostile. It had in any event been madness to consider telling him the truth. And yet, she desperately needed his support, with at least a half-truth. 'I need your help,' she said.

'I can't give it to you unless you're prepared to give me some, Vicky.'

Vicky inhaled, slowly. 'My child will be half-Chinese, Bobbie.' He gazed at her for several seconds, then got up and refilled his glass. 'Perhaps I should have one too,' she suggested.

'Should you?'

'One glass of port isn't going to harm him.'

He poured, handed her the crystal goblet. 'Now I think you *have* to tell me his name.' He sat beside her again.

'His name doesn't matter. It is not someone you know, or will ever know.' God willing, she thought.

'You mean . . . it was just some itinerant Chinese? Or is he a Manchu?'

'No. He is Chinese. And itinerant . . .' She shrugged. 'Perhaps it was an act of madness. That doesn't alter anything. When it happened, I wanted it. Desperately. Call me a wanton if you like. It's my child I'm concerned with.'

'Mother and Father do not know?'

'Of course not. But I thought you—'

'Oh, I'm not going to throw up my hands in horror at the idea of your having sex with a Chinese, Vicky. But you are taking a very hard road if you are thinking of bringing up this child as your own. Mother and Father will never speak to you again. You'll be an outcast in the European community . . .'

'Robert . . .' She drank her port, her hands trembling so that she needed both to steady the glass. 'Would you have him?'

Robert frowned.

'You haven't a son of your own. You could adopt him. You have a Chinese wife. No one could complain if you adopted a Chinese child.' Robert finished his drink. 'He'd have Barrington blood in his veins,' Victoria pressed.

'And whose else?' Victoria put down her glass. 'I think I am entitled to know that, Vicky, if I am to take the child as my own.'

Victoria hesitated. But after all it was the only way out.

Robert listened in silence. Then he got up and refilled both of their glasses. 'I should place you under arrest.'

'I have committed no crime.'

'You have joined a tong, Vicky. An illegal organisation. And you have taken an illegal oath.'

'Then arrest me.'

'Do you really wish the downfall of the Ch'ing? It will mean the downfall of the House of Barrington, as well, you know. And me. I am sworn to die, if need be, defending the Dynasty.'

'It need not be like that. If Dr Sun can command sufficient support, he can force the Emperor to abdicate.'

'That might be possible. He could never force the Dowager Empress to quit.'

'She is retired. She is no longer important, surely.'

'Tz'u-hsi is as important as she ever was. And for anyone to think otherwise would be a great mistake.'

'What are you going to do?'

He sighed, finished his drink. 'Forget what you have told me, I suppose. But you do realise that this man Tang, and his master, are very likely to be caught, and executed?'

'I know there is that risk.'

'And if your name comes out ... well, at the very least you will bring disgrace upon us all and have us expelled from China.'

'No one is going to betray me, Bobbie. That was the reason for the oath we all took.'

'Oh, Vicky, Vicky, how childish can you be? Haven't you just betrayed them all, to me?'

Victoria opened her mouth and closed it again. 'I knew you could be trusted.'

'You have still broken your oath. And how many members of your tong, do you suppose, have a brother or a sister, or a wife or a lover whom they *know* can be trusted?'

'Will you take the child?' Victoria didn't want to think about what he was saying – it was too unpleasant.

Robert shrugged. 'Yes, I will take your child, if that is what you wish.'

She hugged and kissed him: her relief was tremendous. It meant she could look forward to the birth with total confidence.

She was also glad she had told him. Now they were true intimates. As for a member of the tong betraying her, supposing any of them had survived, she refused to allow herself to consider it, or the fact that she had so lightly broken her sacred word. In doing that, she had invited her own death. But she had not truly betrayed them, surely. She *knew* Robert could be trusted, absolutely.

Joanna could tell that Victoria and Robert had resolved something, from the lightening of Victoria's spirits. But in fact she had very little time for considering Victoria's problems in the light of her own, and of the problems of everyone in north China. For the Chinese strategy of refusing to risk its fleet in an offensive campaign was very rapidly proved to be utterly mistaken. The Japanese landed a huge army in Korea, virtually unopposed, and soon controlled most of the country. General Yuan Shih-k'ai did his best with the men at his disposal, but by the beginning of September the enemy were advancing in several columns upon the strategic city of Ping-Yang, which controlled the approaches to the River Yalu, the boundary between Korea and Manchuria. It was obvious to everyone that if Ping-Yang fell, Korea was lost.

Belatedly the Chinese Government realised its error. Reinforcements had to be got to Ping-Yang just as quickly as possible, and the only way that could be done was to send them by sea. Orders therefore arrived at Port Arthur for the fleet to take up its position off the mouth of the Yalu in order to cover the transports. Few could doubt that the Japanese fleet would attempt to prevent fresh troops from reaching the beleaguered city, and the prospects of a sea battle at last seemed likely.

Throughout its month in Port Arthur the fleet had been working hard preparing for sea, making last-minute adjustments. Von Hanneken continued to worry about his shell supply. 'We need at least a hundred shells per barrel,' he complained. 'And we have forty.'

'That is one hundred and sixty for the ship,' Robert pointed out. 'Then *Chen Yuen* is equally armed. Three hundred and twenty twelve-inch shells. Between us we can destroy the entire Japanese fleet.'

'It will not be as easy as you think,' the German grumbled.

But there was no way the defect could be remedied in Port

Arthur, and now that the order had come to engage the enemy a possible shell shortage had to be forgotten. Robert concentrated on more immediate matters. The reports from the *Kwang Yih* had indicated that the thin steel screens protecting the guns had been worse than useless; they had merely been cut to pieces by the Japanese fire and the steel splinters had done as much harm as the enemy shells. He thus had them removed from the rest of the ships, and instead erected barricades of full coal sacks, which he felt would absorb incoming shot. He also had all the ships' boats sent ashore, with the exception of one per vessel. 'There will be no abandoning ship,' he told his officers. Equally he had hoses rigged to soak the decks immediately before any battle, and buckets of sand made ready.

'It would probably be a good idea to strip off all that decorative lacquerwork in the bows,' he suggested to Ting. 'That stuff will burn like tar-paper.'

'It can do no damage,' the Admiral objected. 'And to remove it may lower the men's morale.' So the lacquerwork remained.

Ting himself was concentrating on getting his people into the right spirit. 'There will be no quarter,' he announced in a circular to the fleet. 'Even if an enemy ship hoists the white flag, you will continue firing until it is sunk.'

Robert felt like objecting to that ruthless philosophy as well, but decided against it.

*

On Saturday, 15 September 1894, the twelve ships of the Chinese fleet put to sea, cheered out of the harbour by the entire population of Port Arthur, and accompanied by several gunboats and six torpedo-boats. In the bay of Ta-lien-wan, just north of Port Arthur, they rendezvoused with the six transports, carrying four and a half thousand men and eighty field guns. There was also a squadron of colliers, and the next morning was spent in coaling, so that every ship would have its maximum range over the next few days.

That Sunday evening they put to sea again, and next morning were off the mouth of the Yalu. The transports immediately began unloading their men and material, while Ting disposed his ships, anchored in a long line across the estuary, the two battleships in the centre, the cruisers and smaller vessels to either side. Orders were given for the men to exercise at the guns, and the crews were just being piped to dinner, when the lookouts on several of the mastheads reported considerable smoke to the south-east.

Ting and Robert both levelled their telescopes, but only the smoke was at present visible, although this was growing in volume every moment. 'It has to be the enemy, sir,' Robert said.

'Agreed. Issue the command, Captain. The fleet will raise anchor and proceed to sea. Hoist all battle flags.'

'And the order of battle, sir? Line ahead?'

'No, no. Our orders are to let the enemy come to us. We will proceed in the exact formation that we have now. All ships will steam slow ahead in line abreast; six knots will be sufficient.'

Robert would have liked to argue; the only fleet he had ever heard of which had gone into action in line abreast had been the Spanish Armada, and that hadn't done too well. But he reflected that no matter what formation Ting adopted, all they really wanted was to have the Japanese squadron within range of their twelve-inch guns.

The anchors came up, and the ships put to sea. Just after noon the Japanese vessels came into view, in line ahead, a brilliant sight in the midday sun; each ship was painted white, with the golden crysanthemum of Japan emblazoned on its bows, while the red sun decorated the battle flags which streamed in the wind. Robert checked his watch and sent a lieutenant up the mast to take off the distance with his sextant. Von Hanneken was in the forward turret with the gun-crew. Ting walked up and down the bridge.

The sea was calm, the skies clear. It was a perfect September day. And twenty-two ships were hurtling at each other in what was going to be the first major battle between ironclad steamships in the history of the world. The Chinese, steaming slowly ahead, endeavoured to maintain their line, but inevitably the outside ships began to fall back, so that, again like the Armada, Robert thought, they insensibly formed a crescent. On board the *Ting Yuen* at least everyone seemed calm; the flagship, and her consort, were so large that there was no reason not to be totally confident of the coming fight.

'The range is six thousand metres,' called the lieutenant on the conning tower above the bridge. 'Five thousand six hundred. Five thousand four hundred . . .'

'Tell Commander von Hanneken he may open fire, Captain Barrington,' Ting said, and with the insatiable curiosity of the Chinese, himself went down the ladder to observe the firing of the guns from close at hand. Robert relayed the command, and a moment later the forward barbette exploded in flame and smoke, while the entire ship shuddered as the shell, weighing eight hundred and fifty pounds, hurtled on its way. Robert made an entry in the log; it was ten minutes to one, and the Battle of the Yalu River had commenced.

*

The first shot fell just short of the leading Japanese cruiser, sending up a tall pillar of white water. Now the *Chen Yuen* also opened fire, as did the cruisers, although the range was far too great for their lighter guns. The Japanese did not reply, but came on at full speed. Robert's signal lieutenant was busily identifying the ships, and giving the names and characteristics to his midshipman. 'Lead ship is *Yoshino*, four thousand tons. She can make twenty-three knots; that is faster than any on our side. Then *Takachico* and *Naniwa Kan*, sister ships, three and a half thousand tons each;

Naniwa Kan sank the *Kowshing*. Then *Akitshushima*, three thousand tons; she is armed with one long French thirteen-inch. Then the flagship, *Matsushima*, and two sisters, *Itsukushima* and *Hasidate*, four thousand-plus tons. They also have one thirteen-inch each, and twelve-inch armour protecting their batteries.' They were the most formidable of their opponents. But it was clear that the Japanese cruisers were all far larger than any on the Chinese side. It would be the battleships, of which the Japanese had none, that would decide the conflict, barring some unforeseen disaster.

Robert watched *Yoshino* alter course as she came within three thousand yards, so as to pass obliquely along the Chinese line. The other Japanese ships followed her lead, and at the same time opened fire. Instantly the sea was a seethe of white water and flying spray, and enormous booming explosions. Robert was taken aback by the speed and accuracy of the Japanese fire, and while their first shots fell short and merely deluged the battleships with water, they very rapidly got the range, while now that the two fleets were so close all the smaller guns, the Hotchkiss and Nordenfelt quick-firers and the many machine-guns, opened up as well. 'A hit!' Ting shouted, as flame and smoke exploded on *Yoshino*'s foredeck. But the damage made little difference to her speed or fire power. And a moment later there came a shout from forward. 'The Admiral is hurt!'

Feeling sick with dismay, Robert scrambled down to the main-deck. He could see no evidence of an enemy shell having struck the ship, but Ting was stretched on the deck, unconscious and bleeding from the nose, while Von Hanneken stood above him. 'What happened?' Robert shouted.

'He got too close to the gun when it was fired, and was struck down by the blast,' Von Hanneken replied.

Robert bent over the unconscious man. Ting was not dead, and was probably suffering more from shock than any injury. Robert summoned two men. 'Take the Admiral to his cabin, and stay with him,' he said. Then he looked at Von Hanneken.

'You must take command,' the German said. 'There is no
one else.'

'What of McGiffen?' The captain of *Chen Yuen*.

'You are Chinese,' Von Hanneken said. 'Whatever the
colour of your skin. McGiffen is a Scot. It is your duty,
Barrington.'

I am only just thirty years of age, Robert thought
desperately. And I have never fought a battle at sea, before
today. But then he remembered that neither had Ting, or any
other man in the fleet. He squared his shoulders.

Von Hanneken grinned and saluted. 'What are your
orders, Admiral?'

'Why, the same as Admiral Ting's. Maintain course and
speed, and keep firing.'

Robert dashed back up to the bridge. Now the Japanese
were striking home as well. *Ting Yuen* was smothered in
shot; as he had feared would be the case, the lacquerwork
forward was already burning, and there were regular heavy
thuds as shells crashed into the armour protecting the
superstructure. Amazingly, however, and most reassuringly,
none of the Japanese projectiles seemed able actually to
penetrate the steel.

On the other hand, as far as Robert could calculate in the
unending din as the entire Japanese squadron steered across
the Chinese bows, the enemy were delivering about twelve
rounds for each of their own, and maintaining this remarkable rate as they steamed round the right wing of the Chinese
squadron, and attacked its rear, thus placing themselves
between the Chinese and the land – and the transports.

Von Hanneken hurried up to the bridge, seeking orders.
But Robert knew that he had no hope of turning his fleet
without inviting chaos. 'Use your stern guns, Commander,'
he said.

Von Hanneken ran aft to resume firing, while Robert sent
for a damage report, and went out on to the bridge wing
himself to look at the situation. The superstructure of the
Ting Yuen was dented in many places but was otherwise

undamaged, and the coal bags protecting the heavy guns had also done their bit, although several of them had been pierced and coal was scattered over the deck. But where there was no armour the Japanese quick-firers had cut the thin steel to ribbons, and a large number of men had been hit, while from right forward the burning lacquerwork was sending clouds of smoke aft to obscure their vision.

Looking right and left, Robert could make out that the *Chen Yuen* was similarly bruised but equally undamaged, while the smaller vessels, although they had inevitably suffered more severely, were also fully capable of continuing the fight. He felt a surge of confidence, which had diminished under the hail of Japanese fire, now recommencing from astern. But they had already thrown everything they had at the Chinese, without sinking or disabling any of them, and several of the Japanese vessels were on fire. It seemed certain that as the battle continued the heavier metal of the Chinese was bound to tell.

But then he heard a shout of dismay from Commander Sung, his executive officer, and hurrying to stand beside him, watched the outside left-hand Chinese vessel, the *Tsi Yuen*, one of the two armoured cruisers, increasing speed to leave the battle line and make off to the south. At that moment Admiral Ting reappeared on the bridge, looking little the worse for his accident, and in a towering rage as he saw what was happening. 'The wretch!' he bellowed. 'The cowardly wretch! I will have his head, Barrington. I will have his head!'

Robert gulped, for now the ship beside the *Tsi Yuen*, the *Kwang Chia*, also increased speed and ran for her life. 'We have lost two ships,' Von Hanneken said, panting as he arrived on the bridge.

'The cowards will suffer,' Ting vowed.

Von Hanneken looked after the fleeing ships. 'I meant, over there.'

They peered through the smoke, and saw that on the extreme right of the fleet, where the Japanese pressure had been heaviest as they rounded the Chinese squadron, the *Chao Yung* and the *Yang Wei* were both blazing, it seemed from stem to stern, and had also dropped out of the line. 'We have still six ships left,' Ting declared. 'Keep firing.'

It was well on in the afternoon, and several of the Japanese ships had also taken severe damage; Robert, greatly relieved that Ting was once again in command, felt that the battle could still go either way. But now there was real catastrophe for the Chinese squadron as the cruiser *Chi Yuen*, on the right of the greatly diminished Chinese line, was struck on the waterline by a thirteen-inch shell. Before anyone had properly understood what had happened, the two-thousand-ton ship heeled over and disappeared. The men on the bridge of the *Ting Yuen* stared in horror, and on both sides the firing slackened.

'Resume firing,' Ting shouted. 'Resume firing! Where is Von Hanneken?'

Even as he spoke, the German reappeared through the smoke.

'You are wounded,' Robert told him.

Blood was streaming down Von Hanneken's right arm, and his jacket was torn. 'It is only a scratch. I have some serious news: we are out of ammunition for the twelve-inch guns.'

Robert and Ting both stared at him in consternation.

'I told you this would happen,' Von Hanneken said. 'We were inadequately supplied. Now we must just sit here and be battered to pieces.'

Ting ran on to the bridge wing to look at the Japanese, who were coming round the left-wing of the attenuated Chinese squadron, having performed a complete circle, their guns still blazing away. 'The *Chen Yuen* still fights,' he cried. 'Oh, brave McGiffen.'

But even as he spoke, the *Chen Yuen*'s heavy guns also fell silent. 'We are lost,' Ting declared, returning inside the bridge, his face the picture of dismay.

'We need a miracle,' Von Hanneken agreed.

Robert went down to the main-deck to order the torpedoes to be fired. No Japanese ship had been sunk. If he could just make one hit ... but even as the deadly tubes struck the surface, he realised that there was indeed a miracle taking place. Having completely circled the Chinese fleet, reduced its strength by half, and silenced their main armaments, the Japanese were steaming back to the south-east as fast as they could.

The firing ceased. The torpedoes ploughed aimlessly out to sea. The Chinese looked at each other in amazement.

Robert returned to the bridge. 'What are your orders, Admiral?'

Ting pulled at his moustache; he was as bewildered as anyone by what had happened. 'We will return to Wei-hai-wei,' he said, 'to drop off our wounded and replenish. And to deal with those cowards who ran away.'

*

The cruiser *Tsi Yuen* entered Port Arthur that night. She had been struck once, by a thirteen-inch shell, and her after-deck was a shambles, although she was by no means disabled. 'The battle is lost,' Captain Sen told the crowds on the dock. 'Our fleet is destroyed.'

The news spread through the town and up the hill. Late as it was, Joanna and Victoria drove into the town to see what they could learn about casualties. Both felt sick. But by the time they got there the cruiser had already left again, and in her place there was a torpedo boat, which denied Sen's story, and claimed a victory. 'The Japanese retired in disorder,' her captain declared. 'Admiral Ting is master of the Gulf of Chih-li.'

'Were there many casualties?' Victoria asked. 'How did the flagship fare?'

'It was struck many times, Miss Barrington. Many times. I do not know how many men were killed. But there must have been many.'

Which ended their brief euphoria. They hardly slept, and next morning Joanna called Victoria on to the verandah to show her the fleet, or what remained of it: five ships steaming south, some miles offshore. The battleships were easily identifiable, but even through the telescope it was difficult to make out how badly they had been damaged. 'Why aren't they coming here?' Victoria asked. 'They were to protect us, weren't they?'

Never had she felt so utterly lonely. It was more than the possibility of a Japanese attack upon Port Arthur. It was the departure of Robert's ship, when she did not even know if he was alive or dead.

But the Japanese were the more serious problem. The Battle of Ping-Yang had actually been fought before the two fleets had met at the Yalu, and the Japanese had been victorious. Now they claimed all of Korea, and only a month after the naval battle, Marshal Oyama's Second Army began landing north of Port Arthur.

*

'November is always a wet month in Port Arthur,' Joanna said, sitting beside Victoria on the verandah, and watching the rain pouring down immediately in front of them. There was no wind, and so the verandah remained free of the rain itself, but the dampness pervaded everywhere. And always in the background there was the rumble of thunder. But it was not thunder. The sound was made by the Japanese guns, bombarding the Neck.

Joanna was now eight months pregnant, and in her own opinion as big as a house. Movement was painful and slow; bodily functions were an ongoing misery. But the biggest misery of all was the total isolation in which she, and all the ten thousand inhabitants of Port Arthur, existed. No news had come to the town since the departure of the last gunboat, on 19 September, six weeks before. The Japanese fleet, having recovered from the still unexplained aberration which had allowed Ting to withdraw his battered ships to the safety of Wei-hai-wei, could now be constantly seen, ranging up and down beyond the Tiger's Tail. It was they who controlled the Gulf of Chih-li, not the Chinese. Sometimes they even came close enough inshore to fire into the harbour; they were apparently under orders not to aim at the town itself. The guns on the Tiger's Tail seldom replied. Partly this was to conserve ammunition, but partly, as Victoria well understood, it was a result of low morale.

Because the town was cut off to the north as well. The Japanese troops were encamped just across the Neck, awaiting the orders to assault, while their guns kept booming away. Of course, as everyone from the Governor down kept repeating, Port Arthur was impregnable. But did anyone really believe that any more? When even the fleet had abandoned it?

Arthur Jenkins came in from a visit into town. It was necessary for either Joanna or Arthur to go to town every day, because various supplies were already running short, and the townspeople were more likely to sell to one of the Barbarians, who had more money, than their own kind. But today Arthur looked worried. 'The town is full of pamphlets,' he said. 'Signed by Marshal Oyama, calling upon Port Arthur to surrender.'

'Pamphlets?' Joanna inquired. 'How did they get there?'

'Nobody knows. It has set up a panic about Japanese agents actually being in the town. It's what the pamphlets say that is disturbing, in my opinion. They say there is no hope of relief, that both the Chinese Army and Navy have been utterly defeated. They say that if we surrender, no harm will be done to anyone, and private property will be respected. But if we do not . . . the town will be given up to the sack.'

Victoria listened to air being sucked into her aunt's nostrils. Joanna had already experienced a sack, when Wuhu had fallen to the T'ai-P'ing. But that had been more than forty years ago, when she had been a girl no older than

Victoria herself, and young and strong ... 'What has been the Governor's response?' Joanna asked in a low tone.

'That he will defend the fortress to the end,' Arthur said. 'Poor fellow, if he defends and loses, he'll be killed by the Japanese. If he surrenders, and is returned to Peking, he'll be executed by the Ch'ing. He really has no choice.' He sat beside his wife and held her hand. 'These are civilised people we are talking about, Jo. Talk of a sack is just to frighten the defence.'

Both women looked at him. They were remembering the sinking of the *Kowshing*, the two thousand men left to drown. The Japanese might be civilised, but they were also utterly ruthless when it came to achieving their ends. Arthur knew what they were thinking. 'They rescued the British officers, didn't they? They're not going to harm any white women.'

*

'Something must be done,' James Barrington insisted. 'You cannot just abandon the port.'

Li Hung-chang looked at the excited Barbarian. He had known this man for many years, had watched him grow from an uncertain boy into the dominant personality he now was. His heart bled for him. But he had several children, and in any event ... 'Port Arthur is impregnable, Barrington.'

'Do you really believe that, Li? Do you?'

Li spread his hands on his desk. 'We must believe that. And even it it does fall, every day it holds out gives us room to breathe. It is consuming an entire Japanese army. In any event, Barrington, there is nothing we can do. General Yuan Shih-k'ai is in full retreat through Manchuria. Our fleet lacks the munitions to go to war. There is nothing we can do, save hold on, and hope the Japanese overreach themselves.'

'I wish to see Tz'u-hsi,' James said.

'She does not wish to see you. She is as upset as anyone by what is happening. And what good would it do? She no longer commands events. It is the Emperor you should wish to see.' He gave a sour smile. 'And he does not wish to see you either.'

'You know, Li, and I know, that she does still control events.'

'That is not so, Barrington. Her Majesty has retired from public life.'

'Then tell me it isn't true that she appropriated navy funds to build herself the stone replica of a Mississippi Paddle Steamer on the Ornamental Water. Funds which would have bought the munitions our ships lack.'

'I know nothing of such matters,' Li said. 'Prince Ch'un is in charge of the Navy Board. You should apply to him.'

'And he won't see me either. And you are prevaricating, Li.'

Li's eyes were hooded. 'Port Arthur is impregnable,' he said again. 'Put your faith in that, Barrington.'

*

Victoria awoke with a start. That she could sleep at all was remarkable, for the noise was tremendous, and continuous. In addition to the constant bombardment from the north, the ships of the Japanese fleet had now moved close inshore, and they too kept up a constant fusillade of shots, aiming to pass over the town and hit the forts on the hills beyond. The whine of the shells, the dull explosions, and the distant seethe of a restless and frightened people all merged into one giant cacophony, unceasing and unsparing. But simply because it was unceasing she had become used to it. It was like suffering a continual headache. Then what had awakened her so sharply?

She sat up, listened to a gigantic wail emanating from the town below the house. She got out of bed, went to the window, and the wail grew louder. Behind her the door opened, and Joanna came in. 'The Japanese are across the Neck.'

Victoria faced her. 'Then we are lost!'

'There are still the forts on the hill . . .'

'If they couldn't keep them from crossing the Neck, those forts won't keep them out of Port Arthur, Aunt Jo.'

'Listen,' Joanna said. 'We are in no danger. Remember that. We'll just have to stay at home the next few days, until the battle is decided.'

Stay at home, Victoria thought. Yet the Jenkinses' house was a haven, if not of peace and quiet, at least of non-war. None of the Japanese shells had landed nearby; they were in any event aiming above and beyond the town. That was reassuring; it indicated that the Japanese commanders, for all of their fearsome pronunciamentos and their apparent determination to take Port Arthur by storm if need be, were not into the business of killing civilians.

Nestling amidst the trees as it was, the house was even divorced from any physical evidence of the conflict, save for the noise. It was possible to believe that perhaps the war would simply flow round this little piece of England – Arthur Jenkins kept the Union Jack flying above the house – and leave it untouched. But it was coming closer every day. On the third morning after the Neck had fallen, Victoria sat on the verandah and almost thought she could hear the shrieks of the combatants. Although even Uncle Arthur no longer went out, and the servants no longer came in, leaving Joanna to do all the housework, they knew that the Japanese had fought their way to the hills, and were poised for the final assault. How she wished the Governor would surrender. Surely he had done sufficient, so that even his masters in Peking would allow his survival, and those of the men he commanded – but still the gunfire continued.

She saw movement in the trees, and stood up in concern. There were men, running down the hillside just beyond the limits of the property. Even at a distance she could recognise them as Chinese soldiers. They looked decrepit, dirt-stained and frightened, and few retained their rifles, although several still kept their parasols, which they raised above their heads to keep off the rain. She thought that this perhaps summed up their fighting qualities. Now they represented defeat, like the first trickle of water seeping through a cracked dam, and threatening to become a flood. Aunt Jo had seen the men too. 'Cowards! They will be shot,' she commented, as she came on to the verandah.

'They know they have no hope of victory,' Victoria argued. 'I think the sooner it is over, the better.'

All morning the men streamed by. At first none of them paid the slightest attention to the house in the trees; all the inhabitants of Port Arthur knew that it belonged to the Reverend Jenkins, and over the years he had become a much respected figure in the community, not least because he was married to a Barrington woman.

But while three of them were having a frugal lunch, as their food supplies were beginning to shorten, three men climbed through the fence and came up to the steps. Joanna went out to speak to them. 'What do you want?' she asked.

'We stay here,' one of the men, a corporal, said.

'Your place is in the town,' Joanna admonished.

'We cannot go there. In the town we will be killed. We will stay here. The Japanese will not trouble us here.' He pointed at the Union Jack. 'They will not fight the British.'

Joanna hesitated, and looked at Arthur, who had come on to the verandah to discover what was going on. 'Technically we would be sheltering troops in time of war,' she said.

'They are our people,' Arthur told her.

'And if the entire army decides to camp in our grounds?'

'One bridge at a time,' Arthur said equably. 'You must keep out of sight,' he told the soldiers. 'You must come into the house and go down into the cellars.'

'Yes, we will do that,' the corporal agreed.

They filed through the house, casting curious glances at Victoria.

'I hope you know what you are doing,' Joanna said.

'We are representatives of the Christian Church, and therefore of the teachings of Christ,' Arthur said severely.

The afternoon wore on, and now the shouts of those who

were still fighting were very close, as well as the cracks of
the rifles, distinct from the booming of the guns. They were
surrounded by death and destruction. Joanna took water and
some food down to the three soldiers, and Victoria returned
to the verandah in an effort to see what was happening.
Through the trees she could see the waters of the harbour,
but there were no ships in sight, and no men. Then she saw
four women hurrying through the trees, and recognised their
leader as Joanna's cook, Chu-te.

They all looked very frightened; Chu-te's hair, normally
carefully coiled on the nape of her neck, was loose, and their
clothes were torn and untidy from coming through the
woods. One of them was quite old and was clearly exhausted. 'These are my mother and sisters. The Japanese are in
the town, missee,' Chu-te told Victoria. 'They are killing
everybody.'

Victoria didn't believe her. But she couldn't send them
away. 'You'd best come in,' she said. 'But keep out of
sight.'

Joanna sent them down to the cellar to stay with the
soldiers. 'Do you think she was telling the truth?' Victoria
asked.

Joanna looked vague. 'They're supposed to be civilised . . .' She looked past her niece at the gate. 'Oh, God,'
she said.

There was a group of men there, arguing. They weren't
wearing the smart blue and white uniforms with the
matching peaked caps of Japanese soldiers, but rather loose
robes. And instead of rifles and bayonets they were armed
with fearsome double-handed swords thrust through their
sashes. But they were clearly Japanese.

'They're pointing at the flag,' Victoria said confidently.

To her surprise and alarm, Joanna fell to her knees and
began to pray. Victoria ran inside. 'Uncle Arthur! Aunt
Jo . . .' Arthur Jenkins hurried on to the verandah with her,
and gazed at his wife. 'All I said was, they're pointing at the
flag,' Victoria said.

'That's what the T'ai-P'ing did, just before they took her,' Arthur muttered.

'Oh, my God! I'm sorry, Uncle Arthur. I didn't know.'

'How were you to?' Arthur held his wife's shoulders and slowly raised her to her feet. 'Come along, dear. Come . . .' He watched the gate being thrown open, and the Japanese – there were about a dozen of them – coming into the yard. 'Take your aunt inside,' Arthur said in a low voice, as he faced the intruders.

Victoria wanted to stay with him, but she helped Joanna into the house. Tears were streaming down Joanna's face, but she didn't say anything. Victoria sat her down and turned back to the door, listening to her uncle's voice.

'What do you want?' Arthur was asking in Chinese. 'Can you not see the flag? This is British. British!'

'You got Chinese inside?' asked one of the Japanese, speaking very bad Mandarin.

'There are no Chinese here,' Arthur insisted. 'You . . .'

Victoria heard a sound beside her, and turned. One of the Chinese soldiers had heard the voices, and was peering from the cellar doorway. 'Go back,' she snapped. 'Close the door.'

But the Japanese had seen him through the open front door. They gave a roar, thrust Arthur to one side so that he fell heavily, and burst into the house, drawing their fearsome swords as they did so. 'Wait!' Victoria shouted. 'Stop!' They did stop, to look at her, and she saw the gleam of lust in their eyes. Not only was she very pregnant, she was also unmistakably a long-nosed, hairy Barbarian. 'Stop,' she repeated, supposing she had won the day.

They hesitated, and the soldier in the doorway ran for it, trying to get out of the house and into the woods. The Japanese gave another shout, and turned together. Victoria clasped both hands to her neck as one of the great blades swept sideways and cut the fleeing man's head cleanly from his shoulders. He had no time even to shriek as his skull went spinning across the room to hit an occasional table, while his trunk collapsed on the floor, spewing blood.

Victoria's knees gave way and she sank into a chair. Dimly she was aware of Joanna retching on the settee beside her. She watched the Japanese run at the cellar door, and then down the stairs. She heard cries of terror, bestial shouts and laughter, pleas for mercy. One of the Chinese women burst out of the doorway and ran across the lounge. But two of the Japanese were behind her; they had discarded their kimonos and the loin cloths they wore beneath, and revealed rampant masculinity as they caught the girl, threw her to the floor, and ripped off her clothes in turn. Victoria wanted to close her eyes, but could not. She stared in horror, wondering if she and Tang had looked remotely like that in the throes of their mutual passion.

But there was no passion for the Chinese girl; when the men were finished with her, they cut and slashed at her body with their swords, and left her mutilated and lifeless on the floor. Victoria wanted to try to stop them, but couldn't move. She wanted to scream, but her throat was dry. She sat and stared, her stomach churning.

The other Japanese came up the stairs from the cellar, dragging on their clothes. Their sword blades were wet, and they were excited, chattering at each other as they relived what they had just done. They wiped their swords clean on the torn clothing of the girl who had been raped and murdered. Then, to Victoria's consternation, they replaced their swords in their sashes, lined up before her, and bowed. 'No more Chinee,' said the man who spoke the language. 'We go. No more Chinee.'

They filed from the room, down the verandah steps, and out of the yard. Victoria could hear her own breathing even above Joanna's sobs. She stood up and staggered to the door. The Japanese had disappeared into the trees, and there was only Uncle Arthur, lying where they had pushed him.

Victoria knelt beside him, tried to raise his head, realised he was dead. She remained kneeling for some moments, unable to move, while the churning in her stomach gradually turned to pain.

*

'Come in, Robert.' Ting Ju-ch'ang sat at his desk in the Admiral's day cabin on the *Ting Yuen*. 'Sit down.' Robert saluted, then sat before him. 'Port Arthur has fallen,' Ting told him.

Robert swallowed. He had known it had to happen. But so soon?

'The town was sacked,' Ting went on. 'According to the reports, there was a massacre. I have no further details. But I am sure the lives of Europeans would have been spared. This is a war between China and Japan. I can give you no information on your sister, or your aunt and uncle. Nor can I give you any leave, Robert.'

'I understand that, sir.' The two men had always been friends. Over the past few disastrous months their friendship had grown. Robert had stood at Ting's shoulder when the captain of the *Tsi Yuen* had been condemned for cowardice and sentenced to instant decapitation. But he knew, as Ting knew, that their defeat at the Yalu had not been caused by any defections on the part of their cruisers; it had been caused by the criminal negligence which had let them run out of ammunition . . . and had since let them remain without food for their guns. 'I was going to ask if there was any chance of us being sufficiently replenished to put to sea.'

'None that I can see.'

Robert had never been sure how much this man knew of his private life. 'My family have some influence with the Dowager Empress. Perhaps if I were to go to Peking . . .'

Ting gave a grim smile. 'Do you not suppose I have considered that course of action, Robert? I have written to Viceroy Li Hung-chang suggesting it. And he has replied to say it would do no good. Her Majesty is no longer in control in Peking. The Emperor pursues his own course. And he is no friend of anyone who once had the ear of his aunt. We must hope for better times. That is all we can do.'

Ting, Robert felt, had given up trying. He could hardly be blamed, having been so badly let down by his employers. But *he* had no intention of giving up. Besides, he was desperate for information. He went ashore and wrote to his father, but it was well into December, and snowing, before he received a reply.

'Victoria and Joanna are back in Shanghai, courtesy of the Japanese,' James wrote. 'If it can be called that. They only saw a little of the sack, but it was sufficient to give Arthur Jenkins a heart attack from which he died, and that and what she saw has driven Joanna into a state of shock from which we are not at all sure she will ever recover.

'The Japanese are apologising on all sides. They are claiming, and this is to a certain extent borne out by eye-witnesses such as *The Times* correspondent, Villiers, that their regular troops behaved impeccably. Unfortunately Oyama's army seems to have included irregulars, members of the so-called *samurai* class. This class has officially been broken up in Japan, but there are still many adherents to the old code of *bushido*, which I understand has many virtues, but which also embodies the concept that the vanquished deserve no mercy. These rogue *samurai*, impossible to discipline and thus to include in any properly constituted force, are employed as bearers and orderlies by the army. Traditionally they always carry fearsome swords, and with these hideous weapons they were loosed upon the unhappy inhabitants of Port Arthur. It is said that they have been punished for their excesses, but that can only be small consolation to the dead and maimed.

'But you will wish to hear about Victoria. She survived her ordeal with all the strength and courage I would expect of a daughter of mine, even though the events of that day brought on a premature delivery, with which, in the absence of any help – your aunt being prostrate with grief and shock – she had to cope entirely upon her own.

'For this, and the safe birth of a healthy child, I salute her, but I am bound to say that the fact that the babe is a half-caste has upset your mother to an alarming degree. She can hardly bring herself to look at the child, and Victoria still refuses to divulge the name of the father; we are left with the unpleasant supposition that it is one of our own servants. However, she also tells us that you have signified a willingness to adopt the boy. If this is true, I should like to hear from you as soon as possible, as this would of course greatly alleviate the situation . . .'

The letter had been addressed to Robert's house in Wei-hai-wei, and he had gone ashore to receive it. Now he smiled across the room at Chang Su. 'We are to adopt a son,' he said.

'You did not tell me of this.'

'I wished to surprise you. It was not definite before. Now it is. A son. Is that not splendid? As soon as the war is over, we will go to Shanghai to receive the child.'

'I do not understand,' Chang Su protested.

'There is nothing to understand. When the war is over, you will be a mother. You should be pleased.'

*

'You,' Adrian told his sister, 'are shit!'

Victoria turned away. She had endeavoured not to be alone with him since her return. This had been easy to do, as in her condition she had been put to bed, with her baby, and had stayed there for some weeks. Now she was as strong as she had ever been. And he had seized the first opportunity to find her alone in the garden, with her son.

'To get yourself pregnant is bad enough,' Adrian said. 'But by a Chinese . . . do you know what I would do, if I were Father? I'd have you and that bastard strangled and dropped into the river.'

'Then I must be relieved that you are not my father,' Victoria said quietly. She could tell it was not family pride that was outraging him. It was the thought that she had allowed another man into her bed. Any man would have been bad, but for it to be Chinese ... At least he knew nothing else about her child's father. Ching San had mysteriously disappeared from the Barrington household while Victoria was at Port Arthur, so Adrian had no way of finding out her secret.

'Yes,' he agreed. 'Count your blessings. Because I may well be in Father's position, one of these days. He isn't getting any younger.'

'You are *obscene*. And what makes you think you'll *ever* be Master of the House? Robert—'

'Robert,' he sneered. 'Robert is a long way away, dearest Sis. Fighting a war that will probably never end. And which he probably won't survive.'

*

In fact, that the end was not going to be long delayed was obvious to everyone. Everyone, it seemed, save those in control in Peking. Perhaps they relied upon the onset of winter to bring a cessation of the Japanese advance, and certainly hostilities in Manchuria ground to a halt. But although the weather in the Gulf of Chih-li and beyond in the China Sea was very bad as the year ended, the Japanese, with their now total naval supremacy, had no intention of allowing their enemies any breathing space.

Despite heavy falls of snow and biting gale force winds, an army was put ashore on the Shantung Peninsular, and soon made itself secure; Wei-hai-wei, supposedly even more impregnable than Port Arthur, was now open to attack from the land. 'We should put to sea, whether we have ammunition or not, and see if we cannot destroy the Japanese by ramming,' Robert said. Von Hanneken had taken himself off, as there were no more big guns to serve.

'I have no orders to do that,' Admiral Ting replied. 'My orders are to remain in Wei-hai-wei, and defend it to the last.

We still have ammunition for our Hotchkiss guns. We are floating forts. And we cannot be attacked from the sea.'

Certainly the harbour seemed secure enough. It was fronted by two islands, one of which, Liu-kung-tao, was quite large and contained two forts. Between it and the mainland to the north, and from it to the small fortified island of I-tao and then to the southern end of the bay, there stretched a stout boom. Inside these defences there were some eighteen square miles of protected water.

Protected from the sea. But the Japanese advanced steadily on the land, and within a few days shells were plummeting over the hills and into the harbour itself. The guns on the forts – there were several on the mainland as well as on the islands – replied vigorously, while the ships remained at their anchors and waited to be hit.

Soon the Japanese were shelling the town of Wei-hai-wei as well, and Robert made a hasty trip ashore to see how his people were getting on. Chang Su and her women were terrified, especially as everyone by now knew the story of what had happened in Port Arthur. 'Just because of that, you are safe from a sack,' Robert told them as reassuringly as he could. 'The Japanese will never risk another affront to world opinion like that. Stay in the cellars. I will come to you as soon as I can.'

He returned to the *Ting Yuen*, with some difficulty, for as the sun went down the temperature plummeted to well below zero, and ice was forming on the sea. But his quarters on the battleship at least were warm, and the cold seemed to have had its effect on the Japanese as well, for the guns were silent. He dined with Ting, as he usually did, and having checked that a proper lookout was being kept, went to bed early. To be awakened, just after midnight on 4 February, by the jangling of alarm bells.

Robert leapt out of bed, pulled on his clothes, and dashed on to the bridge. It was even more bitterly cold, but the night had exploded into a kaleidoscope of flashing lights and searing sound, with machine-guns blasting in every direction and alarm rockets streaking skywards.

'They are attempting to break the boom, sir,' Commander Sung panted.

Robert levelled his telescope, but could see nothing in the darkness beyond a succession of lights gleaming and then disappearing again.

'Torpedo boats,' Ting muttered, joining him. 'If they get in . . .' Robert understood Ting's implication. While the bay of Wei-hai-wei was some six miles long by three wide, much of it was shoal water, and in any event, that was insufficient room for a battleship to manoeuvre.

'We *must* put to sea, Admiral.' Robert was almost begging.

'Let us see if they can get through. Let us . . .' There was a succession of explosions. The Japanese torpedo boats were through the boom, and letting off their deadly fish in every direction.

'Commander Sung,' Robert snapped. 'Raise as much steam as possible, and then weigh anchor.'

'Yes, sir.' Sung ran for the ladder, and there checked, pointing. Out of the darkness there loomed the shape of a two-funnelled Japanese torpedo boat.

'Open fire!' Robert shouted. 'Everything you've got.'

The Hotchkiss guns and the machine-guns spouted flame and lead, but they were not powerful enough to stop the Japanese craft, which came on until she was about three hundred yards away, and then swung hard to port. Robert stared at her while his heart sank. She had been hit, and was on fire forward, but she had been able to release her torpedoes. He found himself counting, and had reached six when there was a huge, dull thud from aft, and a column of water shot high into the air.

The battleship did no more than tremble, as if, at sea in a storm, she had struck a particularly solid wave. But no wave would have had the ability to penetrate her hull.

'Have the bugles sound to close all watertight doors,' Robert told Sung, relieved at the quiet calm of his voice.

Then he went below himself, to encounter Engineer Commander Mackintosh coming up. 'The port engine room is flooding, sir,' the Scot reported. 'Water is pouring in aft.'

'Have you power for the starboard engine?'

'At the moment, sir. But the bulkheads are leaking.'

'Raise whatever steam you can, and standby for orders.'

Robert returned to the bridge, where Ting was waiting. He made his report, and Ting pulled his moustache. 'Slip your cable, Captain. We will attack these gunboats.'

Robert felt sick. 'I am bound to tell you, sir, that this ship has not ten minutes to live.'

Ting stared at him. 'Then what do you suggest?'

'That we use what power we have, while we have it, to beach her. On the island, sir. Then our guns will still be useful.'

Ting hesitated, walked to the rail to look out at the exploding night; the battleship was already commencing to list. 'Very well, Captain Barrington,' he said. 'Use what means you can to save your ship.' He turned back to his friend, and held out his hand. 'I fear we have fought our last fight together, Robert.'

8

THE HUNDRED DAYS

'The fleet is destroyed, Majesty,' Chang Tsin said. 'The battleship *Ting Yuen* is a rotting wreck, already being dismantled by the Japanese since they have taken Wei-hai-wei.'

'We had two battleships,' Tz'u-hsi said coldly. Her whole demeanour was so angry that her ladies, clustered as usual behind her as she painted on the banks of the Ornamental Water, shuddered and huddled closer together.

'The *Chen Yuen* was captured as part of the surrender of the port, Majesty.'

'I have never heard of a battleship surrendering.'

'There was no more ammunition, Majesty.'

'We have suffered from treachery. Fetch Admiral Ting to Peking. I will have his head.'

'Admiral Ting is dead, Majesty. He committed suicide after surrendering the fleet. All the senior officers committed suicide.'

Tz'u-hsi shot him a suddenly alarmed glance. 'All?'

'All except Commodore Barrington, Majesty.'

'Ha!' She was clearly relieved. 'He preferred dishonour!'

'It is not the Christian way, to commit suicide, Majesty.'

'Not the Christian way,' Tz'u-hsi muttered. 'The war is going badly.'

'I am afraid it is lost, Majesty. Li Hung-chang says we must sue for peace, before the Japanese conquer Manchuria itself, and advance against the Great Wall.'

'Never,' Tz'u-hsi declared. 'Sue for peace from the Japanese? I will not have it. It will mean the end of our domination in Asia.'

Chang Tsin cleared his throat; had he not been mortally afraid of his mistress he would have reminded her that Chinese domination in Asia had been lost with the Anglo-French invasion of thirty-five years before. Instead he said, 'The Emperor has already sent to seek the Japanese terms, Majesty.'

'Without referring to me?'

Chang Tsin watched with alarm the too well-remembered signs of rage beginning in Tz'u-hsi's face, the enlarged eyes, the mottled veins in her forehead, the twitching fingers. She had not truly lost her temper since her retirement. Actually he feared her anger less than he feared that she would give herself a stroke with the intensity of her emotions.

Now she suddenly turned to face her ladies, who shrank back even more. 'You!' She pointed. 'And you! Come here!'

The two young women went to stand before her, visibly trembling. 'Now, you,' Tz'u-hsi said. 'Slap her face!' The girl goggled at her. 'Did you not hear me?' Tz'u-hsi demanded. 'Slap her face!'

The girl licked her lips, took a long breath, then swung her open hand against her friend's cheek. The second girl staggered and made a strangled exclamation of pain and dismay.

'Can you not slap harder than that?' Tz'u-hsi demanded. She pointed at the second girl. 'Slap her back. Use your strength!'

The second girl hesitated but a moment, then returned the blow, with such force that she turned both her victim and herself sideways. 'Again!' Tz'u-hsi commanded. 'Slap each other's faces, again and again.'

The girls obeyed, swinging both left and right hands against each other's cheeks. They panted. Sweat and tears flew, heavy make-up disintegrated, and elaborate coiffures came tumbling down in black streaks about their ears. Soon their lips were cut and bleeding to add to the mess. The other women clung to each other in terror, while Chang Tsin looked on as impassively as he could. Exhausted, the girls could hardly swing their arms any more. Now they both cried loudly.

'Oh, be off with you,' Tz'u-hsi snapped. 'You look dreadful. Wash your faces.' She turned back to her easel. 'Where is young Barrington?' she asked Chang Tsin in a low voice.

'He has returned to his parents' home in Shanghai, Majesty.'

'You mean he has deserted his post?'

'There is no longer a navy, Majesty. All who survived have returned to their homes.'

'They are all deserters. I will have their heads. Send a messenger to Shanghai, and command Young Barrington to come to Peking.'

Chang Tsin hesitated. 'You intend to execute Young Barrington, Majesty?'

'What I intend to do is no business of yours, rascal!' Tz'u-hsi shouted. 'Send for Young Barrington!'

*

'He is a fine boy,' Chang Su said, cradling the babe in her arms. 'What is his name?'

'Martin,' Victoria said. 'It is the name of my grandfather.'

'Not your real grandfather,' Lucy pointed out, coldly. If she was becoming more reconciled to her grandchild now that it was about to be adopted, she had still not forgiven

Victoria for what she had 'done to the family', by returning
home before disposing of the child. That the Japanese might
have interfered with all of their plans, or that Victoria had
revealed exceptional courage in delivering herself and
surviving, was irrelevant to her. Nor was she relieved that
Victoria had concocted a story about the babe being an
orphan she had rescued from its dying mother's arms during
the sack of Port Arthur – there were rumours enough.

As for having to cope with her sister-in-law, Joanna, who
appeared to be in the middle of a prolonged nervous
breakdown . . .

'His name is Martin,' Victoria repeated, with that stub-
bornness her mother was coming to know . . . and fear. 'You
will take good care of him, Su.'

'Oh, yes,' Su said. 'I will look after him as if he were my
own.'

*

Her presence made Lucy uneasy. But then, so did Robert's
presence, with his entourage of male and female servants,
with whom, she had no doubt, he slept as the mood took him.
He had become more sinicised than any of his forebears –
because they had allowed him to marry a Chinese. She hated
the very thought of it. As for what they were going to do with
Victoria, who now that she had finished feeding the child
could presumably be expected to leap into bed with any
Chinese who crooked his finger at her . . . these were matters
she longed to discuss with James. But James was a much
preoccupied man as he attempted to digest the news both of
the war and, coming out of Peking, of the Treaty of
Shimonoseki.

'The terms are quite staggering,' he told his sons. 'China
must recognise Korean independence, which virtually
means she must accept Japanese hegemony there, and in
addition she must cede outright Formosa, the Pescadore
Islands, and the Liao-tung Peninsular. That means the

Japanese will retain control of the Gulf of Chih-li and therefore the sea approaches to Peking, as well as possessing a huge base lying just off the Chinese coast, from which they can strike at the mainland as and when they choose. This is all in addition to an indemnity of three hundred million taels of silver. These make the terms Germany gave France twenty-five years ago seem positively generous.'

'Can we survive?' Adrian asked. Adrian Barrington was twenty-eight now. James would have been happy to admit that the boy had proved a success as manager of the House. But he had still never married, still smoked opium in the privacy of his own home, and still had his moods, no doubt induced by the drug, of black depression.

James had always endeavoured to love all of his children equally, but he could not hide from himself his pleasure at having Robert back. If only it were possible for him to stay . . .

'What are your plans?' he asked, as they sat together on the verandah and looked out at the river and the shipping, so much of it flying the Barrington House flag.

'I only came to put Su in safety,' Robert said. 'Now I should return to Peking, and discover what the Tsung-li-yamen has next in mind. With Ting and all his senior officers dead, I suppose I am Commander of the Chinese Navy.'

'Which no longer exists.'

Robert sighed. 'Should I have died with Ting?'

'It would have been a senseless gesture. He stood to lose his head.'

'That would have been criminal. He fought magnificently. But we were starved of everything we needed to fight successfully.'

'It is the Chinese way. I am not even sure about *your* head, Robert. It might be an idea for you to leave China.'

'Run away? What of Su, and the boy?'

'Take them with you.'

'And leave you all behind to pay for my crime? Not to

mention Chang Tsin and his family.'

'Well, at the least you'll stay here, until the smoke settles.'

*

Shanghai was like an oasis of stability in a shifting world. Down here there was no evidence of Japanese triumphs. No guns exploded, and no people died. No more than usual, anyway, and those had never included Barringtons.

Robert even renewed much of his earlier affection for Su, as she obviously warmed to the elegant, relaxed way of life in the Barrington mansion, and as she equally obviously came to adore the baby she had so oddly accumulated. She and Victoria spent all day with the babe, fussing over him, changing him, talking to him ... perhaps the most pleasing aspect of the entire situation was the friendship which had sprung up between the two women.

There was tremendous gossip, of course. But Robert felt his mother had vastly overrated the situation. The first Robert Barrington had broken all the rules, both by his piracy and by then accepting Chinese citizenship and Manchu law. Nothing his descendants might do could possibly change that: the real gossip in Shanghai was when there was *no* gossip about the Barringtons. A crisis could only arise if they were ever forced to abandon China.

This he was determined would never happen. Thus he must sit out this period of disarray in the north. Yet he could not just disappear. He wrote to both Li Hung-chang and Chang Tsin announcing that he was again fit for duty, and that he awaited orders. But his letters had barely been sent when he received one from Chang Tsin, summoning him to Peking.

'What do you think it means?' Robert asked his father.

James read the letter for the second time. 'It is from Chang, writing on behalf of the Dowager Empress. The Empress is officially retired. So I don't think this is a summons to answer for your defeat. It is a private matter.'

'Shall I refuse?'

'I think that would be unwise, Robert. If you intend to go to Peking anyway, it might be a good idea to see her. I don't accept that she has voluntarily walked off the stage. It just isn't in her character. Will you leave Su and the boy here? It might be safest.'

*

But Su refused to remain in Shanghai. 'You are my husband, and you go to see my father,' she pointed out.

'And the boy?'

'He is my son, Robert.'

Robert looked at Victoria. But she had always known this moment would arrive. 'May I come to see him?' she asked.

'Of course,' Su assured her. 'I will write and tell you of him.'

*

They went by way of the Grand Canal, which Robert considered safest, even if peace had been signed at Shimonoseki. As it turned out, he was wrong. On the third night after leaving Chin-kiang, they tied up for the night close to a small town where the Canal entered the Yangtse. He went ashore as usual for a walk. Chang Su preferred not to accompany him, so he took his principal servant, Chou Li-ting.

They began strolling towards the town, and stopped to look at a large group of young men, apparently performing calisthenics in a field outside the walls. They stood in orderly ranks, and at a command from their leader, went through a series of movements which consisted of thrusting a leg forward and stamping it down, swinging the other leg in a circle so as to advance the whole body, which was held rigidly upright, and then thrusting their arms and closed fists forward in turn, while uttering fierce cries.

'They are called the I Ho Ch'uan, the Society of Righteous Harmony Fists,' the Captain on the gate explained. 'They are dedicated to avenging our defeat at the hands of the Japanese.'

'Well, they'll certainly be fit if it comes to another fight,' Robert remarked.

'They are a troublesome lot,' the Captain commented. 'They believe the way to defeat the Japanese is to weed out all the elements in Chinese society which weaken the nation, and return to the pristine purity of the past.'

'When was China ever pristinely pure?' Chou Li-ting sneered.

'The Righteous Harmony Fists declare that it is the coming of the foreign devils that has weakened China. They say the first duty of all Chinese is to expel the Barbarians.' He gulped as he remembered who he was talking to, even if Robert was wearing Chinese clothes.

Robert was not terribly interested. All his life there had been odd groups of fanatics seeking the expulsion of the long-nosed, hairy Barbarians, a term now abbreviated down to 'foreign devils'. They came and they went. He did not suppose these young men who gave the impression of training to be boxers would prove any different.

As he went to pass through the gate, however, one of the young men looked at him and saw the colour of his skin, as well as discerning from his size that he was no Chinese. 'Look!' he yelled, pointing. 'A foreign devil, in our midst.'

'Spying!' someone else shouted.

'Death to all foreign devils!' shrieked a third.

The exercising stopped, and the entire body, some forty strong, turned to stare at Robert and Chou Li-ting. And now it appeared that they were armed, as several stooped to pick up long poles to which were tied either knives or sickles.

'We must leave, Master,' Chou said urgently.

'You mean to run away from these louts?' Robert had had all the running away he could stomach. 'You had best disperse those people, Captain, before someone gets hurt.'

The young men were now stamping on the ground and waving their weapons, clearly working themselves up. 'Your servant is right. You should leave,' the Captain muttered.

'You mean you refuse to maintain the law?'

'I dare not, Barrington. I do not think my men will fire on those boys. Most of them are related.'

'I am damned if I am going to run away from a bunch of thugs,' Robert told him. 'If your men will not defend us, will they stop us from defending ourselves?'

'I do not think so.'

'You had better see to it,' Robert said, and stepped forward. 'Stay at my shoulder, Chou.'

The little mob was now very close. Robert went towards them. 'Death to all foreign devils,' they screamed.

'You are foolish young men,' Robert told them. 'You will all wind up in prison. Now get away to your homes.'

The men stared at him in surprise. Presumably no one had had the temerity so to address them before. Then one gave a howl and ran at Robert, his home-made pike thrust forward. Robert did not hesitate. From beneath his tunic he drew his Colt revolver, aimed, and shot the man in the leg. He sprawled headlong, shrieking in agony, his pike flying from his hands.

Those behind him checked.

'Draw your gun, Chou,' Robert said in a low voice, then spoke more loudly to the now quiet men. 'The next man who charges me is dead. Take your friend to a surgeon. Be off with you.'

They hesitated, then one, bolder than the rest, again shouted, 'Death to the foreign devil!' and ran forward, followed by several of his friends.

'Fire, Chou,' Robert said, and did so himself. They fired six shots between them, and five of their assailants lay on the ground, only a few feet away. Two were dead, the others moaned and twisted in their blood.

Behind Robert, the soldiers of the guard muttered at each

other and shuffled their feet. They knew Robert to be a commodore in the navy, and also that he was reputed to have the ear of the Dynasty. But as the Captain had said, these people were their friends and relatives. 'In the name of Heaven, return to your ship,' the Captain said. 'You cannot kill them all.'

'I think he is right, Master,' Chou said. 'Soon we will be out of bullets.'

There was nothing for it, Robert realised. Facing the men, he and Chou backed along the path. The mob followed them, shouting and chanting, 'Death to the foreign devil,' but lacking firearms themselves they dared not risk another charge.

At the sampan, the crew had heard the shooting and armed themselves with rifles, while the women huddled inside the centre tent in terror. 'Cast off, Shung,' Robert told the captain as soon as they were on board. 'We shall have to find somewhere else for the night.'

*

'Robert!' Chang Tsin embraced his son-in-law. 'It has been too long. And this is my grandson?' He peered at Martin, cradled in Su's arms. Wu Lai hovered, eager to hold the baby.

Chang Tsin grasped Robert's arm, and led him aside. 'These are sad times.'

'I would have said that looking over our shoulders is a waste of time,' Robert said. 'Now we must concern ourselves with the future.'

'Agreed. But in which direction? Her Majesty is very angry at our defeat. And by the Japanese! She says, had she retained power, no such disaster could have occurred.'

'I'd like to believe her,' Robert commented. 'But I can't.'

'And now the Emperor is behaving oddly. He is surrounding himself with scholars and savants, when he should be spending his time with the generals; with men like you, who have fought the enemy. And all the time, the country degenerates into anarchy.'

'I saw some of it on my way here,' Robert acknowledged. 'Have you heard of these Righteous Harmony Fists?'

'Yes, I have heard of them.' Chang frowned. 'Did you encounter some?' Robert told him of the incident on the Canal. 'They will bring much trouble upon us,' Chang said sombrely. 'At a time when we can afford no trouble. Robert, I beg of you, be discreet when you see Tz'u-hsi.'

*

It was no longer necessary to use disguise to enter the Forbidden City; Robert had been summoned to an interview with the Dowager Empress as Commodore of the Navy. Once within the palace complex, he was taken directly to Tz'u-hsi's apartment, where the Dowager Empress was sitting down to her midday meal, surrounded by her ladies and eunuchs, who were of course all standing. And immediately behind her chair there stood Jung-lu, recalled from exile in her hour of need, and looking as warlike as ever. Robert wasn't sure whether to be relieved or alarmed at the old warrior's presence.

It was the first time since his first meeting with Tz'u-hsi that Robert had been received by her in state, as it were. But his attention was more taken by the meal with which she was confronted. There were far more than a hundred dishes, of every possible variety. He bowed, and she waved her hand at him. 'Young Barrington,' she remarked with satisfaction. 'Come and stand beside me.'

He obeyed, then waited while she picked up a piece of bread, moulded into the shape of a butterfly, and slowly masticated it. 'I am beset with catastrophe, as usual. Drink some wine.'

One of the eunuchs hastily filled a golden goblet and presented it to him, while he realised that it was not sake, but *samshu*, a very strong drink. But he obediently sipped.

'Tell me of Wei-hai-wei,' Tz'u-hsi commanded. 'The truth.'

Robert did so, while she surveyed the various dishes and finally selected a special kind of mushroom, called a Monkey's Head, which swelled when cooked in water; Robert knew it was not obtainable in Chih-li Province, but only in the south of the country, from whence it must have been sent specially for her table. 'Not enough ammunition. That is criminal,' Tz'u-hsi commented when he had finished. 'Who do you blame? I shall have his head.'

Robert opened his mouth and then closed it again.

'Eat,' Tz'u-hsi commanded, and herself selected a magnolia leaf which had been fried in batter and gave it to him.

Robert chewed and swallowed. 'I am a sailor, Majesty. I know nothing of who commands our supplies.'

'I shall find out,' Tz'u-hsi said darkly, nibbling some pork rind which had been cut into tiny pieces and fried – it was called 'tinkling bells'. 'Go now.' She waved a hand, and a eunuch hurried forward to present her with a cup of tea flavoured with rose petals. Others began clearing the table, as Robert was escorted through the door.

'What happens to all that food?' he asked Chang Tsin. 'Her Majesty ate but five or six mouthfuls.'

'Some of it will be thrown away. After we have taken our share,' Chang Tsin said with a grin. 'What is left will be served up again tomorrow. But you ... I feared for you, Barrington. I am very relieved.'

Robert grinned in turn. 'I also was a trifle anxious.'

Chang led him towards the main thoroughfare. 'But all is forgiven, at least for you. She expects you tonight.' He glanced at Robert as the younger man stopped, and gave a sly smile. 'She is sixty years old. Did you not know that a woman of sixty can be as lecherous as one of twenty? Indeed, more so, as she has more experience, and therefore more desire for experience.'

*

Robert had not expected such a summons. He was fairly sure that his mother, who was the same age as Tz'u-hsi, no longer wished or expected his father to visit her bed. But then, even if four times a mother, perhaps Lucy Barrington had never been that enthusiastic about sex. There could be no doubt that his father maintained several Chinese mistresses, even if, not being Chinese himself or married to a Chinese wife, he did not introduce them into his own household.

But a woman of sixty . . . He had no idea what to expect, and in the event was astounded to discover Tz'u-hsi waiting for him as she had always done in the past, sitting naked and cross-legged in her bed as he was admitted by the eunuch on duty. Now she was definitely fat rather than plump, yet, if her face was lined and could almost be described as gnarled, the flesh covering the still full breasts and the even fuller thighs was as firm as he remembered it; no doubt Chang Tsin's massages kept it so. 'It has been too long, Robert,' she said. 'Come here and kiss me. Hug me. Make me feel, Robert.'

Her very desire made her beautiful, and holding so much eager, voluptuous flesh renewed his own youthful vigour. They loved each other with tumultuous passion for several violent minutes, then she fell back exhausted, and he lay beside her.

'You are my own true love,' she said.

'You flatter me, Majesty.'

'And do you not like being flattered?' she asked with one of her roguish chuckles. And then was suddenly serious. 'You have been defeated. China has been defeated.'

'China has been defeated before, Majesty.'

'By Barbarians such as yourself. But by Japanese . . . When last the Japanese invaded Korea, they were beaten.'

'That was four hundred years ago, Majesty.'

'Are we weaker now than then?' She sat up, restlessly. 'My nephew surrendered without my permission.'

'He is the Emperor, Majesty.'

Tz'u-hsi snorted. 'He is a simpleton who thinks the world

can be controlled by words rather than deeds.'

'He is the Emperor, Majesty,' Robert repeated, carefully.

Tz'u-hsi swung her leg over his thighs and sat astride him, as she liked to do. 'When you fought the Japanese, Robert, did you fight for me, or for the Emperor?'

'For the Empire, Majesty.'

'I am the Empire.'

He could risk temporising no longer. 'Thus I fought for you, Majesty.'

'Then you will do so again. When the time comes. I wish you to return to Wei-hai-wei, and commence building a new navy. I make you Admiral. Whatever you wish you will receive. Proceed as if nothing had happened. But be ready for my summons. Yet first . . .' She smiled and lowered her body on to his.

*

'I am sure she means nothing less than to resume full control of the Government,' Robert told his father-in-law. Chang Tsin was the one person with whom he could share his dreadful secret. 'And that will surely mean civil war.'

'I cannot believe even Tz'u-hsi would risk that,' Chang argued. 'She knows how well hated she is by too many of the mandarins. It would be too dangerous.'

'Then what did she mean?'

'I do not know, Robert. It would be best for you simply to obey her.'

*

Robert wrote to his father and Adrian to explain the situation, and returned to Wei-hai-wei, where his house remained, shuttered but intact. Chou Li-ting opened it up, and the women settled in.

For Robert it was a matter of attempting to encourage the crews to return – they had all scattered to their homes – and of attempting to discover what ships had survived the war and where they might now be. He wrote letters and sent messengers in every direction, and was visited by Li Hung-chang himself. The Viceroy was now seventy-three years old, but he seemed to have doubled in age from the last time they had met, on the outbreak of hostilities two years before. 'Things could be worse,' he said. 'The Barbarian Powers have forced the Japanese to give up the Liao-tung Peninsular, and Port Arthur, in exchange for a further indemnity.'

'But that is splendid news,' Robert said. 'Had they held Port Arthur, it would have been a pistol pointed into the Gulf of Chih-li.'

'Agreed. But the news is not that good. Instead we have leased it to the Russians for twenty-five years.' Li gave a little shrug. 'They "requested" it.'

'And we are in no position to refuse. Are we ever going to be in a position to refuse anything, your excellency?'

Li spread his hands. 'We must watch, and work, and hope.' He gave one of his brief smiles. 'And perhaps pray. I have much confidence in His Majesty.'

Robert frowned at him. 'The Emperor?'

'Yes. I know many think that he made a pusillanimous peace with Japan. But it was necessary. I recommended it.'

Robert recalled that Li Hung-chang had always been anxious to make peace, whatever the cost, rather than fight; the terrible excesses of the T'ai-P'ing rebellion had left their mark on his personality. 'Now I think he is taking a real grasp of affairs,' Li went on. 'He is still very young, but with the Dowager Empress retired, and no longer interfering in the Government, I think he may emerge more and more. His Majesty is intent upon reforming the country, and he is right to believe that any future strength we may accumulate can only be a result of internal stability, of good finances, which means good and just government. This way undoubtedly lies our future prosperity.' He glanced at Robert. 'Her Majesty does not agree, of course.'

Robert was not to be drawn. 'But she is retired, as you say, your excellency.'

*

Over the next year the situation worsened, as Germany, France, Britain and even small countries like Belgium sought concessions from the moribund dragon. Robert even had to evacuate Wei-hai-wei and take himself to Tientsin, as Britain claimed the harbour as a naval base. Following the murder of two German missionaries in Shantung, the Kaiser also demanded a naval base, at Tsing-tao, and indeed, most of the peninsular. 'It hardly looks as if China can survive as an independent country,' Robert wrote to his father. 'Certainly along the coast. What is so distressing is that no one seems able to do anything about it. Yet the people are aware of what is happening. I very much fear that there will be a great explosion of anger and resentment against the Dynasty some time in the not too distant future.'

James Barrington quite understood his son's concern. James was now sixty-seven years old, and with Lucy constantly importuning him, was about ready to retire ... and even to go to England, a country he had never visited, but which he had to consider as home. Yet he was not prepared to abandon the House, and was still not convinced that Adrian could possibly be placed in overall charge. 'Would it not be possible,' he wrote in reply, 'for you to return here and take over the management of the House? Surely everyone can see that there is never going to be another Chinese Navy. I doubt if the powers would agree to it, even if there was a suitable port in which to put it.'

*

As Robert had indicated to his father, the nation as a whole was very aware of what was happening. Its mood was represented by the famous *Letter of Ten Thousand Words*, written by a radical scholar, K'ang Yu-wei. In it K'ang called for nothing less than a political revolution, while always declaring his steadfast loyalty to the Dynasty: among many recommendations, he demanded an abrogation of the Treaty of Shimonoseki, even if it meant a resumption of the war; the abolition of the traditional, stifling, examinations for office; and the removal of the capital from Peking, so vulnerable to invasion from the north and so old-fashioned and inhibiting, to modern, bustling Shanghai.

Many people dismissed K'ang, and his ardent disciple, Liang Ch'i-ch'ao, as irrelevant hacks. K'ang, in particular, had delivered a prodigious literary output during the past few years, his work covering a gamut of material from such things as *Chinese Progress*, mainly reprints of missionary tracts, through the *Laws and Timetables of British Railways* to a translation of *The Adventures of Sherlock Holmes*, in fact, everything he could lay hands upon which was fundamentally different to the accepted Chinese way of life. But rumour had it that his *Ten Thousand Words* had been studied by the Emperor, and it was known that K'ang had been summoned to Peking to join the coterie of literary men who now surrounded the Dragon Throne.

Other rumours followed one after the other during the next year, as well as some very interesting events. Principal amongst these was the retirement of Li Hung-chang, and his replacement as Viceroy of Chih-li Province by ... Jung-lu. This was astonishing, as no one, and certainly not Robert, could have any doubt that the veteran soldier remained Tz'u-hsi's favourite favourite, as it were. Robert could only imagine the in-fighting and jockeying that was going on in Peking, as the Kuang-hsu sought to take complete control of the state, and kept encountering his aunt's men, and his aunt's ideas, wherever he turned. At all events, Li Hung-chang had evidently fallen from her favour: doubtless because of the part he had played in the peace with Japan.

Then Prince Kung died. If for more than ten years he had been less in evidence as the throne's right-hand man, he had nonetheless been head of the Tsung-li-yamen, the Foreign Ministry, and his influence, often in opposition to the Dowager Empress, had remained high.

That a decisive situation, in which Tz'u-hsi must either assert herself or truly retire into private life, was fast approaching, seemed obvious. And to others than just Robert. News kept arriving in the comparative calm of Tientsin of unrest throughout the Empire, with those who supported the Emperor's dream of reforms opposed to those traditionalists who thought that China need never change. And the numbers of those who preached damnation to all 'foreign devils' seemed to be growing, judging by the increasing reports of attacks upon Christian missions or Chinese converts, more often than not carried out by the ever-spreading Society of Righteous Harmony Fists, contemptuously dubbed 'Boxers' by the foreign press. This was very disturbing, when Robert thought of Helen and her husband stuck on the upper reaches of the Huang-ho, but letters from the mission gave no hint of alarm, and there appeared to be no question of their abandoning their post.

As, he supposed, there could be no question of him abandoning his, despite his father's wishes. In any event, he did not see how the present slowly developing crisis could long endure, as proved to be the case when on 11 June 1898 the Emperor suddenly announced a whole series of very far-reaching reforms indeed.

The first proposals were entirely admirable, and met with universal approval. The Emperor was determined to hasten the construction of a railway from Peking to Hankow, several hundred miles up the Yangtse-Kiang, thus truly opening up the interior of the country to rapid travel; he declared his intention of arming the Banner Army with the very latest in Western weapons, and of establishing a naval college for the training of officers, as well as a University of Peking, to be coupled with a vast expansion of the education system throughout the country. 'Just what we have all been advocating,' Robert wrote to his father.

But the second half of the programme, announced on 30 August, struck more directly at the very roots of Chinese Confucian society. It was declared that all sinecures were to be abolished and the examination system was to be overhauled, as recommended by K'ang Yu-wei; that the Green Flag irregular troops who had always supported the Bannermen in past wars – and were the principal military force at the command of the provincial viceroys – were to be disbanded; and that a budget system of financing was to be introduced. Now it was a matter of waiting to see how the great mandarins and provincial viceroys, and more importantly the Dowager Empress herself, reacted. But Robert was yet taken by surprise when on the morning of 16 September, Yuan Shih-k'ai was announced.

*

Robert stood up to greet the famous soldier, who, despite his defeat by the Japanese in Korea three years before remained a national hero for his courageous fighting retreat through Manchuria. Yuan was now thirty-nine years old, short, more heavy-set than ever, with close-cropped hair which gave him a bullet-head, from which the obligatory pigtail emerged incongruously.

His present post was Viceroy of Shantung Province, and he therefore had every right to be in Tientsin, but he had never found it necessary to call upon Admiral Barrington before.

Now he bowed, then shook hands. The door to Robert's office had remained open, and Yuan looked at it meaningfully.

'Close the door,' Robert told his secretary.

Yuan sat down. 'I am told, Barrington, that you greatly esteem Tz'u-hsi,' he remarked without any preamble.

Robert sat also. 'Her Majesty has held my family in esteem for many years, your excellency.'

'I am speaking of you personally, Barrington.'

'Her Majesty has been gracious enough to grant me her favour,' Robert said carefully.

'This is well known. Her Majesty expects the utmost loyalty and devotion from those she has favoured.'

'This is also well known,' Robert countered.

'What would your reaction be were I to tell you she is in danger?'

Robert frowned. He found it difficult to imagine the Old Buddha ever permitting such a situation to arise.

'She opposes the reforms being promulgated by the Emperor,' Yuan told him. 'The Emperor fears his aunt. He feels that he cannot be safe unless her power is removed.'

'How do you know this?'

'Because I have been approached by members of his clique and invited to assist them in placing the Dowager Empress under restraint.'

'And you are telling *me* this?' Robert asked. 'Are you sure these toadies of the Emperor are not trying to act on their own?'

'That thought did occur to me,' Yuan agreed. 'So I pretended to go along with their plans, but I told them I could not act unless instructed to do so by the Emperor himself. Two days ago I received his instructions to use my army to place his aunt and her supporters under arrest.' From his pocket he took a folded piece of parchment and laid it on Robert's desk.

Robert opened the paper, and read it. It had clearly been written by a court calligrapher. But it was signed by the Kuang-hsu. Except . . . He raised his head. 'The Emperor has signed this in black ink.'

Yuan nodded. 'And an imperial decree is always signed in vermilion ink.'

'Then it is a forgery?'

'No. That is the Kuang-hsu's signature. It is an example of the uncertainty of the Emperor's mind. He wishes Tz'u-hsi removed, but he cannot bring himself to make it an imperial decree.'

'We are discussing treason.'

'What is treason, Barrington? Disloyalty to the Throne, or disloyalty to the Empire?'

'A very Confucian conundrum, your excellency.'

'It is time for me, for us, to make a decision, Barrington. If I carry out the Emperor's "request", Her Majesty will be gone, swept away, forever. I have no doubt that once she has been conveyed to a suitable place of imprisonment, a means of having her die, rapidly, will be found. After all, she is an ageing woman. Sixty-three years, in another three months. No one would be surprised. Then the Emperor will be sole ruler of the Empire. But I do not believe he is fit to rule. I believe we will then be ruled by scholars like K'ang and his clique. I believe it will mean the dismemberment of the Dragon Empire.'

'Of the Ch'ing Empire, certainly. Do you, a Chinese, your excellency, seriously wish to perpetuate the Ch'ing?'

'I seek to save the Empire, Barrington. And it is only the Ch'ing holding it together. At least at the moment,' he added as an afterthought. 'Now as to the alternative. If we go to the Dowager Empress and tell her what we know, and she decides to act, as she undoubtedly will, then the Emperor may well die. Certainly he will be deposed. We will then have to find a new Emperor, but I am sure Tz'u-hsi will be able to do this. The point is that whoever she chooses will be at best a small boy, and thus she will resume her personal rule, for the next dozen years at least. That could be a fateful step for the Empire. For the whole Far East.' He gazed at Robert. 'The Empress, for example, would never have made peace with Japan.'

'Why are you telling me this?' Robert asked. 'I have no armed force with which to support either party.'

'I am telling you this because you are Barrington. Because you have the House of Barrington at your disposal.'

'The House of Barrington is at the disposal of my father.'

Yuan's eyes were hooded. 'Does he not constantly importune you to return and take over the management?' A quick smile. 'It is my business to know what goes on about me, Barrington, even to the extent of having my people tamper with the mails. If we support the Dowager Empress, it will be your task to assume control of the House and throw its weight behind the new regime. Or shall I say, the old regime? More, it will be your task, as an Anglo-Chinese, to convince the Western Powers that China seeks only peace – at least until we are ready for war.'

'And you expect me to play this two-faced role? Why?'

Another brief smile. 'Because you have stood high in the favour of the Empress. Or should I say that you have *lain* in her favour.'

Now was not the time to take offence. 'Then what you are saying is that you have made your decision, your excellency.'

'Yes,' Yuan said. 'Are you with me?'

9

THE BOXERS

Yuan Shih-k'ai had his plans all laid. For the time being he pretended to be in the Emperor's camp; in accordance with this, and with the conspiracy he had unearthed, he travelled to Peking, accompanied by a strong personal bodyguard.

Ahead of him went Robert, travelling alone, entering the city clandestinely and going straight to Chang Tsin's house. The old eunuch was in the Forbidden City, but Wu Lai entertained her son-in-law until her husband came home. Chang Tsin frowned. 'You look like a man with a great deal on his mind. Su is well? And the boy?'

'They are very well. Chang, I must speak with the Empress tonight without fail.'

Chang's frown deepened. 'I do not know if that will be possible.'

No doubt because Tz'u-hsi is planning to entertain some other young man she would bind to her cause, Robert thought. 'Without fail, Chang,' he repeated. 'It is a matter of life and death, for us all. Including yourself and your family.'

That persuaded Chang, and Robert entered the Forbidden City in disguise that evening. But Chang did not dare disturb

Tz'u-hsi while she was watching a play being acted out for her by her ladies and younger eunuchs, or while she was eating her supper. It was close to midnight before the door swung in to allow Robert into the Empress's bedchamber, when he was disturbed to see how much additional weight his old mistress had gained, and how she had lost some of her teeth. But her character was as vehement as ever. 'You take too much upon yourself, Barrington. Are you that anxious to gain admission to my bed?'

'Did not Chang Tsin tell you that the matter is most urgent, Majesty?'

'What can be more urgent than love? But I am not in the mood tonight.'

'Life is more urgent than love, Majesty.'

Tz'u-hsi frowned at him. 'Your life has been threatened, Robert?'

'I am concerned with *your* life, Majesty.'

Tz'u-hsi's head jerked. 'Speak!'

Robert repeated what Yuan Shih-k'ai had told him.

Tz'u-hsi did not interrupt. 'Yuan,' she said softly, when he had finished. 'And Barrington. My people.'

'We await your instructions, Majesty.'

She glanced at him. 'Can you doubt what they will be?'

'They must be written, Majesty.'

Tz'u-hsi got out of bed. 'Summon Chang Tsin,' she commanded. 'He will be in the next room.' Robert opened the door, and found that Chang was indeed waiting, anxiously pacing up and down. Tz'u-hsi wrapped herself in an undressing robe. 'Fetch me paper,' she told the eunuch. 'I have an order to issue.'

Chang hesitated. 'And the ink, Majesty?'

'It will be an imperial decree,' Tz'u-hsi said. 'I wish the vermilion ink. And then summon Jung-lu.'

*

Tz'u-hsi herself led Jung-lu, Robert and Yuan Shih-k'ai into the Emperor's apartment, the moment Yuan assured her that all the city gates were in the hands of his men. Eunuchs scurried to and fro in consternation, but Jung-lu was supported by a squad of his personal guards, and they could do nothing. The Kuang-hsu gazed at his aunt in consternation; he had been dragged from his bed.

'Do you know,' Tz'u-hsi demanded, 'the law of the Imperial Household for one who raises his hand against his mother?' She slapped him across the face so hard that he staggered. 'Arrest this cur,' Tz'u-hsi said. 'Take him to the Ying T'ai.' This was an island on the south lake of the Sea Palaces, with only one bridge to the mainland, and that a drawbridge, which could be raised to seal the island completely. 'He will remain there,' Tz'u-hsi said. 'At my pleasure.' She surveyed the shivering eunuchs. 'Execute these carrion,' she said.

They were hurried from the room.

'You are committing a crime,' the Kuang-hsu protested.

'I am saving the Empire, and the Dynasty,' Tz'u-hsi told him. 'You may take Lung-yu with you to your prison.'

The Emperor's women, alerted by the noise, had accumulated in the doorway. Now Lung-yu gave a squeal of pleasure.

'What of me?' begged the Pearl Concubine. 'You cannot send His Majesty away from me.'

'Arrest that woman,' Tz'u-hsi said. 'She is distasteful to me.'

*

It was also time to deal with the Emperor's 'clique'. These had mostly fled, but six of them, to be known as 'The Six Gentlemen of the Reform Movement', were seized, summarily tried by a court convened by Jung-lu, and beheaded. K'ang Yu-wei, however, escaped on a British ship to Hong Kong.

The coup d'état was completed when a decree was issued

in the Emperor's name: 'From this day forth Her Majesty will transact the business of the Government in the Side Hall of the Palace, and on the day after tomorrow We ourselves at the head of Our Princes and Ministers shall perform obeisance before Her in the Hall of Diligent Government . . .'

'There is still much to be done,' Tz'u-hsi told her faithful. The coup seemed to have reawakened her youth, and she sparkled with energy. 'Jung-lu, you will be responsible for Peking and Chih-li Province, as before, but with greater responsibility. I wish no riots.'

'There will be none, Your Majesty,' the old soldier promised.

'Yuan Shih-k'ai.' She smiled. 'My last, and most famous and loyal Bannerman. I leave you to deal with the provinces.'

Yuan bowed.

'And you, Barrington . . .' She paused to consider.

'Let me return to Shanghai, Majesty.'

'For what purpose?'

'Ostensibly, to take my place as Master of the House of Barrington, Majesty. But more importantly,' he hurried on as she snorted, 'to interpret what has happened to the English, and indeed, the entire Barbarian community.'

'That community is represented by their legations here in Peking,' Tz'u-hsi argued.

'The Barbarians will listen to my explanation rather than that of the Tsung-li-yamen, and even more, if I am seen to be free to leave Peking.'

'And me,' she grumbled.

'Can you doubt that should you ever need me, Majesty, I shall be at your side?'

She smiled. 'No. I can never doubt that now. Go and prosper, Barrington. And make sure that I do also.'

*

A few days later the body of the Pearl Concubine was found at the bottom of a well in the Forbidden City. The official verdict was that she had committed suicide on being separated from her master, but no one doubted that she had been thrown down the well on Tz'u-hsi's order.

*

The news of the coup d'état rocked the world, but there was nothing anyone could do about it, or wanted to do about it. The important factor, from the point of view of the trade-hungry Barbarians, was that the Empire was again seen to be held in strong hands, and their various concessions and privileges were confirmed. No one raised a word of protest when it was announced, early in 1899, that due to his ill-health the Kuang-hsu Emperor was no longer even to sign imperial decrees, or appear in public. The Dowager Empress would do the signing, and where the Emperor was required to perform religious duties as the Son of Heaven, his place would be taken by Prince P'u-chun, the teenage son of Prince Tuan, a Ch'ing prince who also happened to be Tz'u-hsi's nephew.

'Do you suppose she is grooming the next emperor?' James Barrington asked his eldest son.

'I doubt it,' Robert said. 'Certainly not P'u-chun. He would be able to rule personally in three of four years, and I don't believe Tz'u-hsi is intending to give up power again in that short a time.'

'From our point of view, let us hope she goes on forever.'

Robert grinned. 'Even knowing her to be an unbridled despot who has committed God alone knows how many murders?'

'You do not know her as I do, Robert.'

His father, so proud of once having proposed marriage to the Little Orchid, and kissed her on the lips, had no inkling of *his* relationship with the Dowager Empress, nor would he ever – Robert was determined. Besides, he agreed with the

old man, even if he knew just what a dragon lady Tz'u-hsi
had become. As she had said so proudly, he was her man,
now and always. There was no way he could alter that, even
if he wished.

Thus he defended her to the Europeans who now clustered
in the International Concession outside Shanghai, and
assured them that the Empire was entering a period of
stability and goodwill. At the same time he concentrated
upon relearning the arts of peace, after having for so long
practised only the art of war.

In fact, he found an empire of his own waiting for him.
During all the fuss and fury which had been going on in the
north, the House of Barrington had grown. There were now
seven steamships flying the phoenix flag, and some twenty
junks, not to mention nearly a hundred sampans. The House
traded up the Yangtse, its own special preserve, and of
course the Grand Canal, and along the coast down to Hong
Kong and Macao and Canton. But its ships also plied
between Shanghai and Singapore, Manila, and even Aus-
tralia and New Zealand, while there was a regular monthly
sailing between Shanghai and San Francisco.

'You are to be congratulated,' Robert told his brother.

He had anticipated some jealousy and even rancour when
he had returned as Master. But Adrian had made no demur.
And Robert was not about to replace him in any way, even
if he wished he could discover what truly went on behind
those dark eyes. Popular gossip had it that Adrian indulged
himself in every vice known to man within the confines of
his own home, but then popular gossip was always rampant
about the Barringtons; certainly whenever Robert had reason
to visit his brother he could find nothing amiss.

On the other hand, Adrian, who was now thirty-two, never
entertained, and showed not the slightest interest in finding
himself a European bride, or even a Chinese one; it had been
so long since he had accepted a social invitation that he no
longer ever received one. Now he seemed perfectly content
that his older brother should return to take over control of the

House. James was clearly delighted. At sixty-nine, he was very anxious to feel that the future was secure.

Robert was happy to be back for another reason: to keep an eye on Victoria, for their mother was ailing, and, indeed, within a few months of his return Lucy died. It was doubly sad, he thought, how, although she had never been particularly close to any of them, her passing affected them all, deeply. Helen came down from Lo-Shan to visit, and Robert was equally disturbed to see how his still beautiful elder sister had aged. Nor did she seem as happy or even contented as when last they had been together. But she would not discuss her domestic affairs and after the memorial service she went home to her distant mission.

*

Robert assumed that he was the only member of the family – save possibly Aunt Joanna – who knew that Vicky belonged to a tong. And the entire European community appeared to accept the story that the child adopted by himself and Su was an orphan his younger sister had rescued from the shambles that had been Port Arthur after the Japanese sack.

Vicky, of course, was delighted to be reunited with her son, even if Martin, who was now four, was very definitely Chang Su's son, and naturally far more Chinese in his upbringing than English. But Vicky could visit Robert's apartments every day.

This also gave them opportunities to have private talks. 'What are you doing with your life?' he felt compelled to ask.

'I read a lot, and do some charitable work in Shanghai . . .' She glanced at him.

'No thoughts on marriage?'

'I have a husband.'

'Oh, really, Vicky, can't you see that's absurd? Do you intend to sit here for the rest of your life waiting for that scoundrel to return?'

'He is not a scoundrel. He is a dedicated man. Yes. I am

waiting for him to return. He will, one day.'

'I wonder. For two reasons. If he is, as you say, a dedicated man, then his dedication is to revolution, not you. I'm sorry, but you must accept that.'

'I do accept that, Robert. But that is no reason why I cannot be dedicated to *him*. You were offering another reason.'

'Well, this Sun Yat-sen has rather fallen out of sight, hasn't he?'

'That's not surprising. Do you know the agents of your beloved Empress tried to kidnap him in England? They *did* kidnap him, in fact, and were holding him a prisoner in the Chinese Embassy in London until he could be put on a ship back here. Can you imagine what would have happened to him had he been returned to China?'

'He would have been executed.'

'After no doubt being horribly tortured. Anyway, he managed to drop a note from the window of the room where he was being held, and the British police got him out. Thank God for the British police.'

'You do realise that if he had been brought back here, and, as you put it, been horribly tortured, it would have been to make him reveal his associates? Your name might well have been one of them.'

'Dr Sun would never have betrayed anyone,' Victoria asserted. 'No matter what they did to him. Even supposing he knows I exist, which I doubt.'

Robert decided to divert the subject. 'It is still absurd for a beautiful girl like yourself to waste her life away, waiting for some dream which can never come true. Surely there is some worthwhile man here in Shanghai you could marry.'

'There are several "worthwhile" men here in Shanghai who have proposed to me, in the hope of achieving the cachet of having secured the most notorious of the Barrington women as their wife. And probably sheltering behind the Barrington name as well. I'm happy the way I am. And with you home . . .'

'And little Martin.'
She smiled. 'I'll not deny that.'

*

Robert had to leave it like that, at least for the time being. And before the end of the year his attention was entirely distracted. Adrian came into the office one morning distinctly put out. 'These Boxer people are getting beyond a joke,' he said. 'Do you know they have attacked one of our sampans? Seems there was quite a fight. Our people got away, but two men were killed. And this is within twenty miles of Shanghai.'

Robert frowned at him. 'Boxers? Here in Shanghai.'

'You live like an ostrich, Bobby. They're spreading everywhere.'

'Well, we're not having them on the coast.' He went to see Chao Chin-lu, the Viceroy.

'I know, Barrington.' Chao was a small, thin man with an habitually worried expression. 'They are utter scoundrels.'

'Who for some reason are being allowed to get away, quite literally, with murder,' Robert pointed out. 'Don't get me wrong. I have nothing against young men keeping fit, so long as they confine themselves to that. But when they start attacking my people ... I was attacked by them once, you know, Chao. I shot a couple of them.'

'Yes,' Chao said unhappily.

'Well, I want this lot rounded up and at least brought to trial.'

Chao spread his hands on his desk. 'I cannot do that, Barrington.'

'Cannot? If you feel you lack the men, don't worry about it. I'll supply the men. Just give me a warrant, and I'll deal with the matter myself.'

'There can be no warrant, Barrington.' Chao looked as if he were in physical pain. 'The Boxers are not to be interfered with. There has been a directive from Peking.' He frowned. 'Did you not know this?'

Robert could not believe his ears. 'A directive from Peking? No, I did not know this. Nor can I believe it.'

'You must believe it, Barrington. The directive is signed by the Dowager Empress, in vermilion ink.'

Robert hurried back to the office and wrote to Chang Tsin. 'I do not know what is happening,' he penned. 'I can only suppose the Empress has been tricked into making a judgement on a matter of which she knows nothing. In which case I would beg you, Chang, to have her correct her instructions. These people are dangerous, and their numbers are growing. If they are not checked now, and suppressed now, we may well have another T'ai-P'ing on our hands. We have discussed this before, and you agreed with me. Now you must act before it is too late.'

Then it was a matter of waiting for a reply, which arrived early in the new year. The Barbarians celebrated the new year, which was also the last of the old century, with enormous parties, and even challenged the Chinese in their use of fireworks. The Chinese, of course, as they followed an entirely different numbering system for history, were politely unimpressed. In any event, Chang Tsin's letter quite ended the festivities as far as Robert was concerned. 'I am afraid that Her Majesty is well informed concerning the Boxers and their inclinations,' Chang wrote. 'In so far as their principal aspect appears to be xenophobia, Her Majesty feels that to attempt to suppress them would be to attempt to negate a very natural feeling of antagonism towards the Barbarians who have made so free with our country, a feeling which is also shared by a great number of Manchus. But you may rest assured, Barrington, that the situation is being carefully monitored, and that should action become necessary, it will be taken.'

Robert showed the letter to his father. James had now entirely retired from the business, but since the death of his wife could think of no reason to leave the China he loved and in which he had lived all of his life. He frowned as he read. 'You understand the real meaning of this?'

'Of course. Tz'u-hsi has always hated the Barbarians. She has never forgiven them for burning the Yuan Ming Yuan back in 1861. Now she has a fresh cause for her personal xenophobia: the way they have all grabbed as much Chinese territory as the others would permit. But she knows she cannot openly oppose them and throw them out: she lacks the strength.'

'So she is encouraging local anti-Barbarian movements,' James said. 'Does she really think she can get away with it? All it takes is for one European to be murdered . . .'

'I am going to Peking to see her,' Robert declared. 'Before we have another catastrophic war on our hands.'

*

When Robert told his household that he was going to Peking, Chang Su announced that she wanted to accompany him; it was some time since she had seen her 'parents'. Robert was quite agreeable to this, as he did not want anyone to suspect the reason for his journey until after he had reached the capital. That he and his wife should wish to visit her parents was entirely natural, while Victoria happily moved in to babysit Martin.

They used a sampan and the familiar route up the Grand Canal. In addition to the crew, Robert took Chou Li-ting and six other male servants – men he had trained to use rifles – and felt quite confident that they could deal with any would-be attackers. And in fact their obvious strength, for they did not attempt to hide their weapons, allowed them to travel unmolested. But he was disturbed at the numbers of Boxers they saw on the banks, performing their apparently harmless calisthenics, to be sure, but also on occasion waving a variety of home-made weapons.

Their numbers seemed to grow as they travelled north, and when Robert stopped at Tientsin, the Governor, Lao-ching, was grave. 'You must be careful, Barrington,' he said.

'There are many of these people between here and Peking. They are a great nuisance.'

'And I suppose you have orders not to interfere with them,' Robert said grimly. 'What do the Barbarians think about it?'

'They are very concerned. They come to me and speak of it continually. But there is nothing I can do. I have my orders.'

*

Next morning Robert continued his journey, crossing the Pei-ho and proceeding up the continuation of the Canal which ran parallel to the river. But they had not proceeded very far when they heard gunfire. 'It comes from over there, excellency,' said the sampan skipper, Shung Li-chu.

Robert surveyed the bank. There was a village in the distance, which looked deserted. To their right, the direction from which the sound of firing was coming, were several low hills; whatever was happening was beyond that. 'What lies over there?' Robert asked.

'It is a Barbarian construction camp,' Shung said; he made this journey every month with Barrington goods for sale in the capital. 'They are building a railroad.'

'The Belgian company,' Robert remembered. Now he could hear a huge sound, like that of waves beating on a rocky shore – people shouting, accompanied by the explosions of fire-crackers, and punctuated by the sharp cracks of rifles and revolvers. 'Pull in to the bank, Shung,' he commanded.

'You aren't going ashore?' Su asked in consternation.

'I wish to discover what is going on.' If, as he suspected, the Boxers were attacking the railway camp, then he would have some concrete evidence to give to the Empress, perhaps to force her hand before the Barbarians decided to take action themselves. 'Once we're ashore, Shung,' he told the captain, 'you'll take the sampan out into the middle of the Canal, and anchor. Do not approach the bank until I return. And should anyone attempt to get out to you, shoot them.' Shung nodded, while Su and her maids retired beneath the centre tent.

Robert took Chou and his six-man bodyguard with him. They disembarked, every man carrying a full bandolier, while Robert had a revolver as well as a rifle, and hurried towards the rise. The noise was growing louder every moment, and was now filled with a kind of triumphant paean. But before they reached the top of the rise it suddenly abated. Robert stood on the hill and looked down into the shallow valley beyond. To his right the iron rails gleamed as they led back towards the river and Tientsin – such of them as were still in place, for a good number had been dug up and thrown away from the track.

To his left he saw to his astonishment quite a large body of mounted men, obviously Bannermen, from their flags and weapons. But this force was motionless, like him watching what was happening beneath them. For in front of him the railway encampment had been overrun. Several of the buildings were on fire, and the many-coloured tunics of the Boxers, together with their waving, equally multi-coloured flags, were to be seen everywhere as they searched for loot.

Most of them were gathered in front of the largest building, however, where some kind of a negotiation seemed to be going on. Robert levelled his binoculars and made out three white men talking to the leaders of the mob. There was much arm-waving and gesticulating, on both sides, and he guessed that the Belgians, having defended themselves as well as they could, were surrendering against a promise of safe-conduct.

A few minutes later he was proved right. Several more men, and to his concern, three women, also came out of the house. He watched the men throw their arms on the ground, as had apparently been demanded by the Boxer leaders. Then the entire party, some dozen Europeans, began to make their way away from the house and towards the hill on which he waited; they obviously reckoned their best bet was to reach the Canal rather than attempt to walk back along the railway line, and perhaps encounter another band of Boxers.

The Boxers parted to let them through, but Robert's glasses as well as his ears indicated that they were shouting at the Barbarians, shaking their fists in their faces. He chewed his lip as the group came closer, still accompanied by a considerable number of the Boxers, and the noise grew. Then the inevitable happened. One of the Boxers reached out and grabbed the hair of one of the Belgian women. It was long auburn hair, and had been floating behind her on the breeze as she hurried with her companions. The woman gave a little shriek of terror, and the man beside her struck at the offending hand.

Instantly the crowd closed on the little band. The mutter of sound grew into a roar, punctuated by the screams of the women, and knives flashed in the afternoon sunlight.

The Bannermen continued to watch, without interfering. Robert drew a long breath. He was about to risk his life. But he could not watch the Europeans being cut to pieces before his eyes. 'Pick your targets,' he told his men. 'It is the Boxers you must hit.' He waved them into line, aimed himself, and fired into the mob. His men followed his example, then they ran forward together, uttering tremendous shouts. Taken by surprise, the Boxers fell back. They had no firearms themselves; those surrendered by the Belgians had been left at the encampment.

Robert halted his men with a wave of his arm. 'Aim! Fire!' he shouted, and another volley tore into the crowd. Now the Boxers scattered in every direction, and Robert could lead his men forward again. To gaze at catastrophe. The Belgians lay in a heap, scored and slashed by the knives and scythes of their assailants; several of the wounds were ghastly, and most of the Barbarians were already dead.

'Cover me!' Robert pulled and tugged at bloodstained clothing, listened to moans, and a shriek of pain from one man who had lost an arm. 'Can anyone walk?' he demanded.

A woman struggled to her feet. Only a girl, certainly not yet twenty years old, with long auburn hair. The girl whose hair had started the massacre! Her face was pale, lightly dusted with freckles, her eyes wide with horror. Her clothes were torn and bloodstained, but from the way she moved she did not seem seriously injured. 'Stay by me,' Robert told her, and dragged one of the men to his feet. He had received a knife thrust in the belly, but was at least alive, although he was bleeding profusely and moaning with pain. The man who had lost his arm was clearly about to die, for even as Robert bent over him he fainted from loss of blood, which was still streaming from the stump. Of the other women, one was dead – her skull was split open. The third was alive, just; there was a knife still embedded in her back. When Robert pulled her to her feet she uttered the most unearthly scream of agony.

'Mama!' the girl shouted, and caught the woman as she would have fallen again. Instantly the bodice of her dress turned red, and the woman slumped through her arms to the earth.

Robert had found one other living man, although he too was badly wounded. 'They are coming again, Master,' Chou said.

'To the Canal.' Each of the wounded men was lifted up by one of the servants. Robert stooped over the girl, who was kneeling beside her dead mother. 'You cannot help her now,' he said. 'If you would live, you must come with me.'

She raised her head, and he realised she was incapable of making that decision at this moment. He swung her from the ground. She struck at him with her fists, but he threw her over his shoulder, slung his rifle on the other shoulder, and drew his revolver. The Boxers were very close now, waving their weapons.

'Fire,' Robert told his men, at the same time casting a glance towards the distant, watching Bannermen. Still they did not move, but the Boxers checked again. With three more of their number sprawled on the ground, the mob were

now showing a disinclination to press the determined band
too closely in favour of mutilating the already dead Belgians, or returning to the railway encampment in search of
loot. Robert and his people were able to regain the Canal
bank, where Shung, listening to the various sounds, had
brought the sampan into the side as soon as they came in
sight.

'You are covered in blood!' Su shrieked.

'It is not my own,' Robert assured her, and took the girl
from his shoulder. She had apparently fainted and could not
stand, and he had to lift her on board the boat and place her
on the divan in the cabin.

'Who is she?' Su asked, peering under his arm.

'I have no idea. But she is at least alive.'

Su snorted. 'She is very pretty.' Where it had never
occurred to her to be jealous of a Chinese servant, she was
instantly hostile to the Barbarian girl.

'Is that a fact?' Robert had not considered the matter
before, but now he realised that his wife was quite right. The
face was small and compact, the figure youthfully mature,
and the hair absolutely glorious. And the girl's eyelids were
fluttering as she seemed to regain consciousness, to reveal
huge green eyes. 'Get her something to drink, and stay with
her.'

He returned to the bank, but Chou greeted him with a long
face. 'These men are dead, Master.'

Robert gazed at the still bodies, then up the hill, where
several Boxers had appeared. Even as he looked at them, one
of them fired a captured rifle. It was a wild shot, but he could
no longer expose his people. 'Then let us be on our way,' he
said.

*

Once they were beyond the reach of the Boxers, who
showed no wish to follow them, Robert was able to visit the
girl he had rescued. He found her sitting up, having been

given sake to drink by a watchful Su.

'You saved my life, sir,' the girl said, in halting Mandarin. 'But . . .' looking from his Chinese clothes to his face. 'You are not Chinese?'

'My name is Robert Barrington,' Robert said, in English.

The girl gulped, and replied in that language, although with a strong accent. 'I have heard of you. My father . . .' Her lip quivered. 'My father!'

'Was he at the railhead?' She nodded. 'Then I am afraid he is dead. As is the lady you called mother.'

Tears welled from the huge green eyes and trickled down her cheeks. Robert knew that the true understanding of her position had not yet sunk in; she was only aware of grief. But he had to discover what was to be done with her. 'Will you tell me your name?' he asked.

She sniffed. 'Monique. Monique Carremans.'

'And have you any other relatives in China?' She shook her head. 'Well, then, in Belgium?'

'I have uncles in Brussels, monsieur.'

'Well, Monique, I am on my way to Peking now. There I will deliver you to the Belgian Legation, and you will be taken care of by the Baron de Vinck and his wife, until they can make arrangements for you to be returned to your family in Belgium.' She gazed at him from enormous, tear-filled eyes. 'I can do nothing else,' he explained.

'The men who murdered my father and mother, monsieur . . . will they be punished?'

'Oh, yes,' Robert promised her. 'They will be punished.'

*

To his consternation, however, he found that there were a large number of Boxers, gathered in different groups, outside the very walls of the capital. Having entered the city, he went direct to the Belgian Legation and delivered Monique Carremans to the minister. 'But this is very serious,' Baron de Vinck de Deux-Orp said. 'I mean, we have all heard of these Boxers, and put them down as mere rogues. But to attack a railway company ... and you say there were Bannermen looking on? There will be repercussions. The guilty must be punished, and there will have to be an indemnity ...'

'Yes,' Robert agreed wearily. 'I am on my way to see the Dowager Empress now.'

'But you understand I must make an immediate report to my government. And also to the other Legations here in Peking.'

'Of course,' Robert said. 'You must do as you think best. I would only beg you to care for that unfortunate girl. Her parents were murdered before her very eyes.'

'My wife and I will care for her as if she were our own daughter,' the Baron promised.

Robert next went to see Chang Tsin, and told him what had happened. Chang listened as gravely as had de Vinck. 'This was bound to happen,' he said when Robert was finished.

'As I warned you several months ago,' Robert reminded him. 'Now the only hope Tz'u-hsi has is to denounce these people as rebels and bandits, which they are, turn out the army, and crush them out of existence before the European Powers take matters out of her hands. Who commands here in Peking?'

'Jung-lu still commands the Peking Field Force,' Chang said. 'But the commander of the Banner Army in Chih-li Province is General Niem. You will have to discuss it with Tz'u-hsi, Barrington. But Barrington ... be careful, I beg of you. These are dangerous times.'

*

Chang was always offering words of advice, Robert reflected. To him, all times were dangerous. Well, in this case he was right. But the danger was to the Dynasty, the very foundations of Manchu rule in China.

There were no disguises required for the Master of the House of Barrington. He was escorted up the main thoroughfare of the Forbidden City by eunuchs. Those they encountered, women and other eunuchs, bowed to him. He had the status of a senior mandarin of the Empire.

Tz'u-hsi received him in state, seated on her throne, in all the glory of her winged head-dress and her imperial yellow tabard with its crimson dragons, worn over a gown of green silk. The nail protectors on the third and fourth fingers of each hand were at least twelve inches long, and her face was a mask of caked white make-up. But those magnificent eyes seemed not a whit less brilliant than the first time they had ever looked into his.

She was alone, save for four of her ladies, two eunuchs, beside whom Chang Tsin went to stand ... and Jung-lu. Robert wasn't sure whether he was pleased to see the old Manchu paladin at her shoulder or not. 'Barrington,' she said. 'It is good to see you. Tell me what presents you have brought me.'

'I have no presents, Your Majesty.' Beneath the make-up it was difficult to read any change of Tz'u-hsi's expression. But her eyes had grown opaque. 'I brought no presents, Majesty, because I had not anticipated visiting you. My purpose in coming to Peking was a private visit to my father-in-law, Chang Tsin. But a most grave matter has arisen. Majesty, the Boxers are becoming a rebellious force as dangerous as were the T'ai-P'ing.'

If he had hoped to arouse her old antagonism to the revolt which had brought disgrace to her father and all but toppled the Dynasty, he was disappointed; Tz'u-hsi merely snorted.

'Majesty, these villains are running wild throughout the country, attacking anyone connected with foreigners. They have even appeared in Chekiang, and have attacked sampans flying the flag of the House of Barrington. Majesty, my people can defend themselves, although some have been killed. But yesterday I came across a band of these people attacking the Belgian railway encampment only a few miles from Peking. Several of the Belgians were killed. Majesty, you will remember what happened only three years ago when two German missionaries were killed; that cost the Empire nearly all of the Shantung Peninsular. What do you suppose will happen now, if these people are not seen to be punished by the Barbarians?'

Tz'u-hsi gazed at him for several seconds. Then she said, 'I am told that Belgium is a very small country.'

'That is true, Majesty. But they may well invoke the help of their fellow Europeans.'

'I am told the British are embroiled in a war in South Africa, in which they are being defeated.'

'Yes, Majesty, that is also true. But—'

'Once upon a time, the British and the French invaded our country. The Emperor, my husband, was weak and was defeated. The Barbarians burned the Yuan Ming Yuan.' Tz'u-hsi's eyes flashed, but her voice remained quiet. 'Since then the Empire has undergone many vicissitudes. It seems that our armies, and our navy, are not able to beat the Barbarians. And for too long has the conduct of our foreign affairs been in the hands of men like Prince Kung and Li Hung-chang. That is no longer so. Prince Tuan is now the head of the Tsung-li-yamen, and he has advised me of many things.' She paused and Robert waited, aware of a slowly growing sense of despair; he knew Prince Tuan to hate the 'foreign devils' as much as the most rabid Boxer.

'Prince Tuan has made a great study of the Barbarians,' Tz'u-hsi said. 'He has told me that they all hate each other. Forty years ago, the British and the French fought against us together, because they both wished to impose their will upon us and seize parts of our territory for themselves. Now the Russians and the Germans and even the Belgians, not to mention the Japanese, have seized parts of our territories. But Prince Tuan tells me that all of these people hate each other. He tells me that only two years ago there was nearly a war between Britain and France. I have just reminded you that Britain is now at war in any event with the people in

South Africa. Prince Tuan tells me that France and Germany hate each other, and will soon again go to war with each other, and that Belgium is a very small country. He tells me that the Russians are hated by all, and that the Russians hate the Japanese. He tells me that there is no possibility, today, of the Barbarians acting together against the Empire. Are these things not true, Barrington?'

'Well, Majesty, yes, in the main they are true. But—'

'You wish me to suppress the Boxers? But the Boxers are patriotic young men who would rid the Empire of the disgrace and humiliation heaped upon it during the past forty years. Do you not wish those humiliations avenged, Barrington? It is our will that the Boxers should be allowed to do what they can, and that we will wait and see the response of the Barbarians. The Boxers are not forces of the Empire. They are not commanded by Manchus. Indeed, I do not believe there are any Manchus with them. We will wait and see, Barrington. I am sorry your people have been attacked. You have my permission to defend yourself, and I will reimburse you for any losses you may suffer.'

Robert looked at Jung-lu, and then at Chang Tsin, but both of those stalwart supporters of the Dynasty kept their faces rigid. 'Then the attacks on Barbarians will continue?'

'How can I say? I do not control the Boxers. I have never spoken with a Boxer, to my knowledge. But I believe they will continue,' Tz'u-hsi said. 'Prince Tuan has discussed this with the Barbarian ministers in the Legations. He has advised them that what is happening is a great upswelling of xenophobia, caused by their exactions, and that it would be wisest for them to abandon Peking and withdraw to the coast, indeed, to leave China altogether. They have refused to accept the Prince's advice. Instead, we have been informed that they have sent to the coast for additional Legation guards. I have forbidden them to do this; it is against the terms of the treaties agreed by the Kuang-hsu Emperor. If they send more soldiers into Peking, it will be an act of war. I have told them this. And I have told my army commander, General Niem, and the commander of the Peking Garrison . . .' she glanced at Jung-lu, '. . . that such a move on the part of the Barbarians must be resisted.'

Robert drew a long breath. 'Majesty, the Barbarians will defend their Legations. They will send troops, even if it means having to fight the Chinese Army.'

'Then they will be defeated,' Tz'u-hsi said confidently. 'This is not forty years ago, Barrington. Forty years ago the Barbarians had modern weapons, my people had none. But now my people have modern weapons as well. They will know how to deal with these insolent foreign devils.'

Robert tried another tack. 'Majesty, it is the duty of your government to protect the Legations against damage, and their inhabitants against harm. This is accepted international law.'

'Protect them?' Tz'u-hsi demanded. 'How am I to protect them, Barrington? There are too many Boxers.'

'The Boxers have no discipline, no proper weapons, Majesty. Marshal Jung-lu would disperse them in an hour.'

'Barrington,' Tz'u-hsi said. 'You have served me long and well. But I can never forget that you are a Barbarian yourself. Now you would have me wage war upon my own people, who are doing nothing more than follow their natural instincts? Shame on you. I have told the Barbarian ministers what to do: leave Peking until these disturbances die down. If they refuse to follow my advice, I can accept no responsibility for them. Their blood will be on their own heads.'

10

THE EMPRESS RAMPANT

Both Jung-lu and Chang Tsin accompanied Robert into the antechamber. 'You must see this is madness,' he told them. 'Tz'u-hsi is deluding herself if she thinks the Barbarians will suppose she has no control over the Boxers.'

'She is right when she says there are few Barbarian soldiers in China,' Jung-lu said.

'Do you not suppose they will summon soldiers, and ships, as is necessary?' Robert asked.

'Her Majesty is determined that the Legations shall be closed,' Chang Tsin said. 'She has long regarded this as the ultimate insult to the Dynasty.'

'And if they will not go? Because they will not go.'

The Manchu general and the old eunuch looked at each other.

'Then may God have mercy on us all,' Robert said.

*

'You take it too hard,' Chang Tsin said, when they were seated for dinner at his house. 'The Barbarians understood that the Dynasty could not be held responsible for the T'ai-P'ing.

Indeed, eventually they joined with the Dynasty in suppressing that rebellion. Why should they not do so again?'

'Father, that was forty years ago.'

'What is forty years? The T'ai-P'ing waged war upon Barbarian and Manchu alike.'

'This is a different generation. The Barbarians know more about China now than they did forty years ago. They know more about Tz'u-hsi. Do you suppose they do not know that the viceroys have been told not to suppress the Boxers? That they do not know those orders have come from Peking? I should like to know what Yuan Shih-k'ai thinks about it.'

'Marshal Yuan is a provincial viceroy,' Chang Tsin said. 'It is not his business to have opinions.'

'You mean Yuan has also protested against this policy.'

'He is obeying his orders.' Chang Tsin peered at his son-in-law. 'What are you going to do?'

'I will have to consider that.'

'You should return to Shanghai and the House of Barrington. Her Majesty has said you may defend yourself.'

'I had intended to do so anyway. But, if you don't mind, Father, I will remain in Peking for the next couple of months. I may be of more use here than in Shanghai. However, I would like to write a couple of letters.'

*

Helen Scott entered Murray Scott's office somewhat diffidently. After fifteen years of marriage she had a healthy respect for his irascible temper and knew how much he hated being disturbed, especially when composing his sermon. Although Murray had learned to write Mandarin fluently, he still found difficulty in speaking the language, and the words in his sermons had to be carefully selected for ease of pronunciation.

But this was too important to wait until he was finished. Now he looked up from his desk and frowned at her. 'What is the matter, woman?'

'Mail has arrived. There is a letter from Robert.'

Murray Scott snorted. 'Another family crisis? What, has your sister given birth to another half-caste?'

Helen flushed; how often had she wished she had never confided that secret. But she kept her temper, as she had learned to do throughout her marriage. 'This is a more serious matter. Have you heard of the I Ho Ch'uan?'

'The Society of Righteous Harmony Fists? Yes, I have heard of them. They are some pseudo-religious group on the coast.'

'According to Robert, they have become a rather political group, and they are spreading all over the country. He says Europeans are being attacked.'

'I am afraid, my dear, that Europeans generally bring these misfortunes on themselves, by their utter arrogance.'

'I know,' Helen conceded. 'But now the attacks are spreading to missions. Robert feels we should go down to the coast. Rejoin the family in Shanghai for a while. Until this blows over.'

'You astonish me,' Murray declared. 'You've had it too good, that's your trouble. All of these years, you've had it too good.'

Helen regarded him from under raised eyebrows, and then looked at the plain wooden floors; the walls, whose only decorations were religious tracts; and her own dress, which had been darned a dozen times. She had had it too good? As a Barrington, she received an income from the House – but Murray had always refused to let her spend any of it on improving either the beauty or the comfort of their home. 'We did not come here to live in luxury,' he would say. 'We came here to work for God.' Now he said, 'This has been one of the least troublesome of all missions. Our converts have been good, hard-working people. Here, up the Huang-ho, we have been able to divorce ourselves from the hurly-burly that goes on down at the coast. And now you wish to run away, because your brother is afraid of some minor heathen religious movement?'

'Robert is afraid for *us*,' Helen snapped. Murray really had no right to accuse anyone else of arrogance. 'He says that the Boxers are spreading everywhere, and that, remotely placed as we are here, we could be in danger.'

'So you propose to pack up and leave. And what about the home we have made here? What about our converts? Are you going to abandon them?'

'They would come with us. As for this "home" . . . well, have we ever really made a home here?'

'I see. I am beginning to understand,' Murray said, his tone icy. 'I know you have always hated it here . . .'

'That is not true, Murray.'

'That for the past few years you have been seeking any excuse to leave,' Murray went on as if she had not spoken. 'Now you have at last found one, provided by your brother. Tell me honestly, Helen: if I let you leave, will you ever return?'

'Let *me* leave?'

'You don't suppose I am going, do you? This is my life. These are my people. I am not deserting them. And,' he went on as she would have spoken, 'I am not letting you take them away with you, either, down to the coast to be corrupted. Here we are, and here we stay.'

Helen glared at him for several seconds, then turned and left the office.

*

The Mission was situated some five miles from the nearest village, and indeed they had little to do with the village, as Murray had always been determined that they should be as self-sufficient as possible. They had their own small herd of goats, which gave them milk and provided them with furs, and even, on special occasions, meat; they grew their own maize and green vegetables; they bought their own cloth and made their own clothes. Murray had studied medicine and was able to deal with any minor ailments – when it was something major, the Chinese accepted that death was a probable concomitant.

He was a dedicated man, and Helen respected him for it. Any physical or emotional love she had once felt for him had long been dissipated, probably because he had never been greatly interested in either; he had seen a beautiful young woman with a famous name, made a play for her . . . and she had fallen for his enthusiasm and transparent moral goodness.

Father, she recalled, had had his doubts from the very beginning. Fathers, she suspected, were very often right, as they were men themselves, and more able to judge their sex than were their immature daughters. Yet, Helen felt, the marriage would have been very successful had she been able to have children. There was of course no evidence that *she* was not able. The pair of them had simply not been blessed.

Now . . . it was too late. It was not that at thirty-seven she was definitely too old for motherhood. Far from it. Neither was it that at thirty-seven she was no longer beautiful. But Murray would condemn her as sinful even for thinking such thoughts. And would he not be right? In her heart, Helen knew she *had* seized on Robert's letter as an excuse to get away; to return to the coast; and parties and laughter, fashionable clothes and vivacious people. Being a missionary was a vocation; she lacked the application.

Things had not been so bad when old Appleby had been alive. In many ways he had been every bit as difficult to get on with as Murray. But she had not been Appleby's wife. She had merely been an extraordinarily attractive woman, with whom events had thrown him together. He had sought to please her as much as he could, and whatever his faults, he had had a vast capacity for enjoying himself, the ability to forget that he was a man of God and relax with a bottle and laughter. Murray never forgot that he was a man of God, and he did not drink.

And yet, he had not actually refused her permission to leave. She lay awake, listening to him snoring beside her,

and stared at the darkness. Robert had said they should
leave. She would surely be committing no crime by
following the advice of her brother, who was so close to the
councils of the Dowager Empress. If Robert said she should
leave, she would be a fool not to. To return to Shanghai, to
the International Concession, without Murray . . .

*

'I have decided to take Robert's advice and go to Shanghai
until this trouble is over,' she said at breakfast on the
Monday morning.

They sat on the verandah of the Mission House and
looked out, past the stockade and down the hill where the
goats grazed. Immediately beneath them the chickens
clucked as they were fed, and indeed all around them there
was a slow hum of awakening energy: Murray Scott liked
his people to work, and to be seen to be working. 'You mean
you are abandoning me and the Mission,' he remarked.

'I am taking Robert's advice. And I strongly recommend
that you do so also.'

'And I have told you that I will not.'

'Then I am sorry. But I wish to go.'

'I would be within my rights to refuse permission.'

'Then you would be keeping me a prisoner here against
my will. Be sure my family will know of it.'

'Your family,' he sneered. 'The great Barringtons. Oh,
indeed, no doubt they would send an army up the river to
claim you. Well, if you wish to desert the Mission, then go
and be damned to you.' He got up and stamped down the
steps.

Helen felt almost light-headed as she packed her two bags
– there was little enough to take – and summoned Sung Chu,
the convert girl who acted as her maid. 'I am going to the
coast,' she said. 'Will you come with me?'

'Oh, yes, missee.' Sung Chu's eyes shone. She had
overheard the altercation at the breakfast table.

*

'I can give you no money and no escort,' Murray told her.

'I am sure I will manage without either,' she said. 'I would but beg the use of two mules as far as the village.'

He snorted, but made no demur.

The whole Mission turned out to see her on her way. For fifteen years she had been a part of their lives. Now they knew she was going, perhaps not to return. Helen had tears in her eyes as she bade farewell to the women and the children, quite a few of whom she had helped to deliver. The women wept openly.

Murray waited by the gate. She paused beside him. 'I will come back,' she said. 'If you wish me.'

'You must suit yourself,' he replied, his face rigid.

Did he feel nothing at all, at the end of fifteen years? But then, did she? It had happened too suddenly, too inconsequentially, for her to feel anything at the moment. That would come later.

She mounted her mule, riding astride in her Chinese pantaloons, and Sung Chu followed her example. Then they rode through the gate, accompanied by a single young man, who would return with the animals. The gates closed behind them.

Helen did not look back as she rode down the hill towards the village and the river. If she did, she was not sure that she wouldn't have gone back. But she had nothing more to give, either to her husband or to the Mission.

She was well known in the village, just as it was well known that she was actually a Barrington. She wrote an order to the Headman, against the House, on a page torn from her notebook, and he was happy to accept it, and allow her the use of a sampan, with crew, down to the nearest town.

'You be careful, Missee Scott,' he told her. 'There is trouble down the river. You no wish an escort?'

'I do not need an escort,' she told him. Because I am

Helen Barrington, she reminded herself. Everyone in China knew, and feared, that name. For too long she had been hiding under a falsehood.

*

Helen and Sung Chu journeyed without mishap for four days, although wherever they stopped for the night or for food there were rumours of what the Boxers were doing, and of massacres of Chinese converts, as well as attacks on missions.

'It is very dangerous for a Barbarian to travel, especially a woman alone,' said the Headman at a village some two hundred miles down-river from the Mission, and within a day's journey of the junction with the Grand Canal, which meant it was no more than a week from Peking or Tientsin. It was a place where Helen and Murray had stayed on previous trips up and down the Huang-ho, and Wong Chun was almost a friend. 'Why do you not stay here, Mrs Scott, until the troubles are over?'

'When will that be?' Helen asked.

Wong Chun spread his hands. 'Who can say? But these people must be suppressed.'

Helen had no intention of waiting, but she pinned up her hair beneath her broad-brimmed Chinese hat. Her complexion was too fair for a Chinese, even sun-burned as it was, but she would have to be approached quite close for anyone to make a judgement on that. However, next morning her boatmen refused to go any further, at least with her on board. 'I am not a Barbarian,' she argued. 'I am as Chinese as any of you. I was born here, as my father and grandfather were born here.'

But they would not change their minds. Nor would any of Wong Chun's people take the risk of encountering a band of Boxers with a white woman on board. 'You must stay here,' Wong Chun insisted.

'Sell me two horses,' Helen said. 'I will give you an order on the House.'

'I have no horses to spare,' Wong said. 'Anyway, it would be too dangerous for you to travel alone across country with only one servant.'

Helen knew she was beaten, at least for the moment. 'Then let me send a message,' she said.

Wong Chun was agreeable to that, and she wrote letters to Robert in Shanghai and to Chang Tsin in Peking, telling them where she was and asking them to send a sampan, adequately armed, up-river to collect her, and despatched her boatmen, who appeared willing to take a message. Then it was a matter of waiting, as day after day went by. But only three days had passed when two sampans were sighted coming up-river, crammed with men: the morning sunlight glinted from their swords and spearheads.

'Bannermen?' Helen asked, standing on the bank with Wong Chun, hardly able to believe her good fortune.

'Boxers,' Wong snapped. 'You must get inside.'

He hurried Sung Chu and Helen into his house, then went down to the dock to confer with the visitors. Helen watched through the window, as much arguing and gesticulating took place. But she also watched more and more Boxers coming ashore, every one armed with some kind of weapon, even if she saw no firearms. But there were no firearms in the village either.

She was aware of a slow tightening of her stomach muscles. Wong Chun did not seem to be winning the argument. And as she watched he turned away from the Boxers and began hurrying up the street towards her. Sung Chu grasped her mistress's arm. 'I think we should run, Missee Helen.'

'Run?' Helen demanded. She was Helen Barrington. She was not going to run away from a crowd of yokels. Besides, they would very easily be caught and brought back, and the humiliation of it would be unbearable.

The Boxers advanced into the village, although they remained some distance behind Wong Chun, while the people of the village stood to either side, watching the scene, but making no attempt to interfere. The door opened.

'Well?' Helen demanded. 'What do these people want?'

Wong Chun was the picture of both terror and dismay. 'They want you, Mrs Scott.'

'Me? How do they know I am here?'

'They stopped the sampan, Mrs Scott, and the men told them you were here. They took possession of the message to your brother. Now they want you. They say, if I do not give you to them, they will burn the village and kill all my people.'

Helen could hardly believe what he had just told her. 'Do you not know what they mean to do to me?'

Wong Chun hung his head. 'They will burn my village.'

Helen felt an urgent need to scream and shout, in sheer mental agony. But she was Helen Barrington. 'Then you must delay them while we leave from the back.'

'They will burn the village,' Wong Chun repeated again.

'Will you not at least give my maid time to escape?'

'They wish her too. She is a Christian.'

Sung Chu burst into tears and fell to her knees.

'You . . . you are unspeakable,' Helen told him.

From outside she could hear a voice shouting.

'They want you, now, Mrs Scott. You must go out to them.'

Helen looked at Wong Chun's wife and daughters, clutching at a last straw. But the women merely retreated to the far side of the room, huddled together. Helen squared her shoulders and went to the door. She was Helen Barrington.

*

Having written to Helen and his brother to acquaint them with the situation, Robert also wrote to Yuan Shih-k'ai, to obtain his opinion on what was going on. He did not doubt that Yuan could be the most formidable man in China, if he chose to be. Then he had to wait, and watch, and be increasingly disturbed, not only at the news which came in from the country districts, but at the increasing numbers of Boxers who arrived in Peking. Many pitched their encampments outside the walls, but a large number entered the gates and camped in the parks in the Chinese city. It would have been a simple matter for the various gate captains to close the doors and refuse entry; there was no way a rabble armed only with knives and spears could take Peking by assault. That no attempt was made to do so could leave no doubt in anyone's mind that the Bannermen were acting under orders from the Forbidden City, but when Robert demanded an explanation from Chang Tsin, with whom he was naturally staying, the old eunuch merely bowed and smiled and said, 'No ruler should go against the will of his people, Barrington. Or in this case, her people.' The bare-faced hypocrisy of it was sickening, and this from his own father-in-law.

To compound matters, a reply came from Yuan, couched in the most non-committal terms; it was very obvious that the famous soldier was as determined as everyone else to sit on the fence and see just what would happen, what the Boxers would do, and more important, what the response of the Barbarians would be.

Robert had no doubts on either score. He could only try to avoid the coming catastrophe. He called at the British Legation and asked to see the Minister, Sir Claude Macdonald. The name of Barrington counted for a great deal, and he was quickly admitted to a large, airy office, and greeted by a somewhat slight man with aquiline features and a thin, wide, military moustache. Robert knew that Macdonald had had a distinguished career as a soldier in his youth, but he very much feared that the word slight entirely summed him up. The Minister gestured Robert to a seat, gazing at his Chinese clothes with interest. 'I haven't had the pleasure before, Mr Barrington,' he remarked. 'Although of course I have heard a great deal about you. Now tell me what I can do to help you.'

'Why, nothing, your excellency,' Robert said. 'I have come to help you. I wish to speak about the I Ho Ch'uan.'

'Ah, the Boxers. Yes, they are becoming quite a nuisance. I'm afraid that Her Majesty is góing to have to take steps against them. That Belgian business was an outrage.'

'You are aware that there have been other incidents since, some involving British subjects?'

Macdonald nodded. 'Yes. I have made an official protest to the Tsung-li-yamen.'

'Sir Claude,' Robert said earnestly. 'There are tens of thousands of Boxers encamped outside the city. For God's sake, there are some twenty thousand now *inside* the city. Why do you suppose they are there?'

'Really, Mr Barrington, there is no need for blasphemy. I have no idea why they are here, save, I assume, to present some kind of a petition to the Throne of Heaven.'

'Sir Claude, they are here to fulfil their avowed purpose, of driving every Barbarian out of China. They intend to begin with the Legation staffs.'

Macdonald frowned at him. 'I really cannot believe that. We are the accredited representatives of our sovereign governments. We are protected by international law.'

'Do you suppose the Boxers care a damn for international law, if they have even heard of it?' Robert almost shouted.

'The Tsung-li-yamen understands the situation.'

'The Tsung-li-yamen does what it's told, by the Dowager Empress. And in this instance it has been told to allow matters to take their course.'

Macdonald pulled at the ends of his moustache. 'I consider you are being quite unduly alarmist. In any event, what course of action do you recommend we should follow?'

'I recommend you should pack up and go down to the coast, where you can be protected by your own people.'

'Abandon my post? That I could never do. My dear fellow, don't you realise, it took us nearly forty years of war and negotiation to establish our right to representation in Peking? We could not possibly consider abandoning such a point of principle.'

'Then at least send your women and children away.'
Robert was almost begging.

'I shouldn't think they'd go. Anyway, that would indicate
we were uneasy about the situation.'

'And you are not uneasy about the situation?' Robert
asked in despair.

'Uneasy about a mob? My dear fellow, I should not care
to attempt to count the number of times a British Embassy
or Legation has been assailed by a mob. Don't think I am
taking this lightly. I have sent down to the coast for
additional guards. There are seventy-five men on their way.'

'Seventy-five men,' Robert remarked. 'I told you, there
are not less than twenty thousand Boxers in the city, and ten
times that number between here and Tientsin.'

'Seventy-five English soldiers, Mr Barrington. And a
similar number of other European troops for most of the
other Legations as well. I assure you, sir, that the mob may
do what it wishes, but this happens to be British territory,
and it will remain so, by Heaven.'

*

Robert couldn't make up his mind whether or not the man
was a fool, or the stuff of which heroes are made. Perhaps
the two traits were intermingled. Unfortunately, it wasn't
just his own life Macdonald was risking. But his concern for
the lives of the Legation staff and their families disappeared
when he returned to Chang Tsin's home and found the
eunuch wearing a very long face. 'There is trouble up the
Huang-ho,' he said. 'And this has arrived.'

Robert read the letter with icy fingers clutching at the nape
of his neck. It was from Helen, addressed to Chang Tsin,
asking for assistance as she was being held in a village some
fifty miles up-river from the junction with the Grand Canal.
In it she said she had also written to him . . . He looked at
Chang Tsin. The letter was dated ten days previously.

'The sampan was stopped by Boxers, and the men

searched. Your sister's letter to you was found. This one was overlooked as it was addressed to me. But when they found the letter, the Boxers continued up the river.'

'I need fifty men, armed with rifles. And I need them now. I am leaving in an hour.'

'Robert, there is nothing you can do now. It is too late. Whatever has happened, has happened.'

'How do you know that? In any event, if anything has happened to my sister, I intend to avenge her.'

'Robert . . . Her Majesty will be very angry.'

'Her Majesty gave me *carte blanche* to defend myself. That includes any member of my family. Go to Jung-lu and tell him I need those men, or I shall recruit them for myself.'

*

Robert didn't know whether Jung-lu had referred to Tz'u-hsi before detailing the force to accompany him, but he was very rapidly supplied with the men he wished, while Chang Tsin telegraphed ahead to have two steam pinnaces standing by at the junction of the Huang-ho and the Grand Canal. He also took with him Chou Li-ting and his own six servants, as men upon whom he could absolutely rely.

He reached the junction only four days after receiving Helen's letter, commandeering the necessary sampans to transport his men. Even on this short journey he came across too much evidence of the way the Boxers seemed to have taken over the entire country, but as outside of Peking they travelled in groups of one to two hundred, they were not disposed to tackle fifty very well-armed Bannermen, while Robert was pleased with the way his people seemed eager for a fight.

The pinnaces were waiting, and they made rapid progress up the river, reaching the burned-out village the next morning. Robert's heart did a great roll as they nosed into the bank, where the dock had been destroyed. There was no sign of human life. The houses were blackened piles of timber, and only half-starved stray dogs scratched about the debris.

Robert sent out search parties, one of which returned just before dusk with a woman they had found hiding in the woods behind the village. The woman looked as half-starved as any of the dogs, and was terrified. They fed her and gave her sake to drink, and she relaxed somewhat.

'What happened here?' Robert asked her. 'Were you Christians?'

'No, no,' she protested. 'No Christians here. Except for the white woman and her servant. But the Boxers punished us for sheltering the Christians.'

'Tell me what happened to the Christian women,' Robert said.

The woman rolled her eyes, and they gave her more sake to drink. 'The white woman was staying in the house of our Headman, Wong Chun, when the Boxers came,' she said. 'She had her servant with her. When the Boxers told Wong Chun that he must surrender her or they would burn the village, he went up to the house and spoke with her. I do not know what was said, but after a few minutes the woman came out of the house and walked down to the Boxers.'

'She walked to them?' Sen-ch'o-lin, the Banner Captain, was amazed.

But it had been Helen. Helen Barrington, Robert thought. 'Was her servant with her?' he asked; he had to say something, to subdue the raging torment in his mind.

'No, she was alone. I was standing close by, and I heard what was said. The woman walked up to the Boxers and she asked them what they wanted of her. They replied by shouting, death to all Christians and all Barbarians. And she replied, I am no Barbarian. I was born here. But you are a Christian, they shouted. You must die. I am Helen Barrington, she told them. She was not afraid. I am Helen Barrington. If you harm me you will have to fight the House of Barrington.' She paused for breath and some more sake, while Robert waited, not daring to anticipate what she might say next.

'They stared at her,' the woman went on. 'And she turned away from them to go back up to the house. Then one of the Boxers knocked off her hat, and her hair fell down. It was like gold, falling from a sack. The man held her hair and threw her to the ground. They took away her clothes, and they dragged her round and round and round this compound by her hair, laughing and calling her a Barbarian pig.'

'Did they rape her?' Robert asked in a low voice.

'When they had dragged her round the village several times by her hair, and she was covered in dust and blood, then they mounted her. Then they took their knives and they cut her. They cut off her breasts, and her toes and fingers, and they gouged out her eyes and they cut out her tongue.'

'But she was dead,' Sen-ch'o-lin suggested.

'I think she was dead when they had finished,' the woman said. 'But not when they began. Anyway,' she added, 'when they had finished they cut off her head.'

'Did no one attempt to help her?' Robert asked.

'The men were too afraid, excellency.'

'And so they burned your village anyway.'

'They made the young men join them, and they raped the young women, and then they burned the village.'

'What happened to the servant?' Sen-ch'o-lin asked.

'They treated her as they treated the Barbarian woman. Then they took away both the heads,' the woman said.

'And your Headman, this Wong Chun? Did he escape?'

'They castrated him, and then they cut of his head too.'

'Which he richly deserved,' Sen-ch'o-lin said severely.

'How long ago was this?' Robert asked.

'Many days, excellency.'

'Shall we go after them, Barrington?' Sen-ch'o-lin asked.

Robert inhaled until he thought his lungs might burst. How he wanted to go after them, to spend the rest of his life chasing them, hunting them down, one after the other. But he would never succeed. He did not even have a single name to work with. And there were more important things to be done.

'We will continue up the river,' he said.

*

They continued as far as the Mission; here there had been no sign of the Boxers. Murray Scott listened to what Robert had to say, his face expressionless. 'She would go,' he said when Robert was finished. 'Because you told her to. I said it was madness.'

'Your wife had just been horribly murdered,' Robert said. 'Have you nothing to say about that?'

Scott's shoulders hunched. 'I told her not to,' he repeated. 'But she would go.'

'Have we more business here, Barrington?' asked Sench'o-lin.

'No,' Robert said.

*

Robert regained Peking at the end of the first week in June, to find that the situation had vastly deteriorated in his absence. The reinforcements for the Legation guards, four hundred and eighty-five men of various nationalities – British, American, Japanese, French, German, Belgian – had arrived safely, but no sooner had they done so than the Boxers had not only torn up the railway line by which they had travelled from Tientsin, but also torn down the telegraph line connecting the capital with the coast.

Robert learned that an Imperial Edict had been issued condemning these actions, but still General Niem was taking no steps to suppress the Boxers, or even to prevent their continuing attacks upon any Barbarians or known Christian converts found on the streets; several of these had been murdered. Amongst the slain, close to the capital, were the German Minister and several other Europeans, including a woman who, like Helen, had been savagely mutilated.

He requested an interview with Tz'u-hsi, but she refused

to see him. He therefore called on Jung-lu. 'It is a serious situation,' the old Manchu paladin acknowledged.

'It is a situation that can be ended at a stroke of Her Majesty's pen,' Robert argued.

'It has gone beyond that,' Jung-lu said. 'Did you know that there is a Barbarian fleet in the Gulf of Chih-li? That they have bombarded the Taku Forts and taken them by assault? That is an act of war. Did you know that there is a military expedition on its way here from Tientsin, commanded by an English admiral? That too is an act of war.'

'You have declared war?' Robert was aghast.

'No, we have not. This military action is in breach of international law. Her Majesty has protested most strongly to the Barbarians.'

'What do you suppose will happen when they get here?'

'If they get here.'

'You mean to oppose them with the Banner Army?'

'No, I do not. It is they who are breaking the law.'

'Well, then . . .' Robert frowned at the general. 'My God! You mean to let the Boxers fight them?'

Jung-lu's eyes were hooded. 'If it is the will of the people to oppose this Barbarian invasion, there is nothing we can do to stop it.'

'You would send unarmed peasants against regular troops?'

'The Boxers are not entirely unarmed, and there are many thousands of them. Our information is that there are only some two thousand Barbarian soldiers and sailors in Admiral Seymour's command.'

'Either way, there could be a massacre. And you do not care?'

'My opinion is irrelevant, Barrington. The Barbarians have brought this upon themselves. They are stirring up the entire Empire against themselves. They must take the consequences.'

'Well, you must at least deploy your Peking Field Force

to protect the Legations. *That* is international law.'

'I can do nothing to help the Legations, Barrington. They were advised to leave. They have been *ordered* to leave. They have refused to do so. Now they too must take the consequences.'

Robert leaned forward. 'General Jung-lu,' he said earnestly. 'It happened before I was born, but you were alive. Do you remember when the British sent a negotiating team to Peking in 1861, and they were seized, and some of them murdered? The British and the French defeated the Banner Army, took Peking by storm, exacted a huge indemnity, and burned the Summer Palace. That was the result of the murder of three or four men. Can you imagine what they will do if the Legation staffs are murdered? There are several hundred people in those Legations. And a good number of them are women and children. The Barbarians have a very special regard for their women and children. I will tell you this: if you allow those people to be murdered, the Barbarians will burn Peking about Her Majesty's ears.'

'The Barbarians will never act together.'

'I believe they will, in this case. They may fight amongst themselves, constantly, but they will always unite against a threat from another race. In any event, if they will not, then the British will act alone.'

'The British are entirely occupied in South Africa. They have not the men to send an army against us.'

'General, the British will always find the men, if they have to. Forget what you read about the Germans and the French and the Japanese. However hypocritical they are about it, the British are the most warlike people on earth. You allow those Legations to be destroyed, and you will have a British army in Peking. And then may God have mercy on your soul. And that of the Dowager Empress.' And my own, he thought.

Jung-lu pulled his moustache.

*

Robert didn't know whether he had made an impression or not. He went on to the street to see what was happening for himself, and strode through a crowd of Boxers, who were performing their weird calisthenics and shouting their blood-curdling slogans. Robert looked left and right, daring any one of them to meet his eye. Oh, to be given command of the Peking Field Force for a single day, to destroy this vermin and avenge Helen.

The Boxers regarded him with obvious hatred. But it was a passive hatred at the moment. Here in Peking he was well known to be a member of the ruling clique – and he was accompanied by his seven well-armed servants. Having left the Forbidden City he made his way back to Chang Tsin's house. His route took him close to the Legation Quarter, which was situated against the south-eastern wall of the Tatar City. All the Legations were clustered together, dominated by the British, which was by far the largest and had the most exten-sive grounds.

Here there were more Boxers than ever, and Robert had not walked very far when he heard the sounds of uproar and even of shots being fired. He hurried round the corner, and saw that a group of Europeans, who had obviously been out shopping, were surrounded by a shrieking mob, who were seeking to pre-vent them regaining the safety of the nearest Legation, above which flew the red, black and gold tricolour of Belgium.

Instantly he remembered that unfortunate girl, Monique Carremans, whose parents had been murdered before her very eyes, and felt a sense of great relief that she must have got down to Tientsin before the railway had been destroyed. But these were her countrymen, again in danger of their lives. He looked behind him and saw a group of armed Bannermen, watching what was happening, but making no effort to interfere.

'Do you know me?' he shouted.

'You are Barrington,' their sergeant said.

'Then you know I have to be obeyed. You will follow me, and disperse that mob.'

'We have no orders—'

'I am giving you orders now,' Robert told them. 'Haste!'

They fell in behind his seven men, and advanced into the streets. By now the Europeans had formed a group, backed against a wall, close to the Embassy, from where some guards had issued, hesitating as they were faced with a pitched battle on the Peking streets. The mob of Boxers had grown larger, and the noise was tremendous. 'Present,' Robert told his men; his force was some forty strong. 'Aim over their heads.' The Bannermen obeyed. 'Fire!'

The volley rippled into the afternoon, and the Boxers checked, looking over their shoulders at this unexpected interruption. 'Advance,' Robert commanded, and the Bannermen moved forward; he had taken his place in their front rank. The Boxers stared at them, and began shrieking threats and imprecations against them. 'Disperse!' Robert shouted. 'Or we will fire into you.'

The Boxers retreated, uncertainly, as the Bannermen continued to advance, and Robert reached the Europeans. 'Quickly,' he said. 'Into the Legation.'

There were several women in the party, and these were hurried away by their menfolk, who had been using revolvers to keep the Boxers at bay, although they had not actually fired into them. But one of the women pulled free. 'Monsieur Barrington!' she cried. It was Monique.

'Why are you still here?' he demanded. He had forgotten what a lovely child she was, with her flowing auburn hair and lustrous green eyes. 'You were to be sent to the coast.'

'Monsieur le Baron would not hear of it, Mr Barrington. He said it would show weakness. Monsieur . . .' She held his arm. 'I did want to go. I am so afraid.'

One of the men had followed her and now held her arm as well, speaking to her in Walloon. 'I must go inside, monsieur.'

'Do you speak English?' Robert demanded of the man.

'Why, yes. Ah! You are Admiral Barrington. You saved this young woman's life, I believe. We are grateful, monsieur. We would be more grateful if you would use your influence with the Dowager Empress to call off these hounds of hell.'

'You should have left when you had the chance,' Robert told him. He looked down at Monique, and had a vision of her being dragged naked along a village street by her hair, before being mounted by a Boxer and then having her breasts cut off before her still living eyes. The thought made him feel sick. 'Do you wish to leave Peking, Monique?'

'Monsieur?' Her eyes lit up. And then the fire died again. 'We cannot.'

'The girl is right,' the man said. 'Baron de Vinck has announced that we shall stay. There can be no exceptions.'

'You, sir, and your baron, may do what you choose,' Robert told him. 'I brought this young lady to you to be protected. As it seems you are incapable of doing that, I shall resume my care of her. Good day to you, sir.'

The man stared at him with his mouth open, as did Monique.

'Would you like to come with me, mademoiselle?' Robert asked. 'To safety?'

'Oh, yes, of course. But—'

'Do you have any belongings in the Legation?'

'I have nothing. These are borrowed clothes.'

'Then you will come with me now. You will have to wear Chinese clothes in any event, when we leave the city.'

'Monsieur, you are kidnapping this young woman,' the Belgian official declared.

'She wishes to come with me, monsieur,' Robert told him.

'She is not old enough to know what is best.'

'I think she is far more sensible than any of you.'

'There will be a report of this outrage,' the Belgian shouted. 'You are worse than the Boxers.'

'I am leaving now, with my people,' Robert said, and pointed at the end of the street, where the Boxers had gathered, still shouting their threats. 'I would get inside your Legation before those fellows, who *are* Boxers, come back.'

*

Robert regained Chang Tsin's house without difficulty, and there formally introduced Monique to Wu Lai and Chang Su, both of whom looked at the Belgian girl with some suspicion.

'She was to go to the coast,' Chang Su commented.

'Exactly. But they did not send her. So we will take her ourselves, when we leave.'

'You cannot leave,' Wu Lai pointed out. 'There is fighting down the river.'

'I have every intention of leaving,' Robert told her. 'Just as soon as can be arranged.'

And be damned to the whole lot of them, he thought, Barbarians, Boxers, and Ch'ing alike; his only desire was to regain the comparative peace and security of Shanghai – and tell his father what had happened to his eldest daughter.

'Will this mean trouble for you, monsieur?' Monique asked.

'Nothing I can't handle,' Robert assured her.

Chang Tsin was less sanguine. 'What have you done?' he demanded, when he returned that evening from the Forbidden City. 'There is an uproar, from both the Boxers and the Belgians. The Boxers have sent to tell Her Majesty that you fired upon them. The Belgians have sent to tell her that you have kidnapped a woman. This is very bad, Barrington. You are a married man. Your wife is my daughter.'

Robert wondered which of the two aspects of the situation he regarded with more concern. But he explained that Monique was the girl he had rescued the previous month, and that after that earlier ordeal he intended to make sure that she at least was taken out of Peking to safety. Chang Tsin was not greatly relieved, although he stroked his chin when he was again introduced to Monique. 'She is very pretty,' he commented.

'So if you will arrange transport for me,' Robert told him,

'I should be grateful. I need those fifty Bannermen again. With Sen-ch'o-lin; he is a most reliable fellow. Thus six sampans. Organise that, and we shall leave immediately.'

Chang Tsin went off grumbling, just as Chang Su grumbled whenever she saw Monique, who for her part, sat in the garden and looked apprehensive, her face only lighting up whenever Robert approached her. The blow fell when Chang Tsin returned that evening. 'You are under arrest,' he told Robert. 'By order of Her Majesty.'

11

THE EMPRESS REPENTANT

Robert looked past his father-in-law for the file of Banner-men who would march him off to prison and probable execution. His own servants were having a well-earned rest. But there was no one else in the room.

Chang Tsin observed his concern, and smiled. 'You are not to be imprisoned, Barrington. What, you, head of the House of Barrington, and one of Her Majesty's oldest ... companions in honour? No, no. Tz'u-hsi merely feels that your heart is not with her in this business, and that if you are left to roam free you will cause discord. You are therefore placed in my care for the duration of this crisis.'

'You mean until the Legations have been destroyed and their inhabitants murdered,' Robert said angrily.

Chang Tsin spread his hands. 'What will happen, will happen. It is in the lap of the gods. Once the crisis is over, you shall be free to resume your life. And prosperity.'

*

'At least,' Chang Su told him, 'I shall have you to myself for a while.'

Robert made no reply; he was already considering his best course of action. This was obviously to wait for the arrival of the relief column from Tientsin, which he had no doubt would disperse the Boxers. Monique was distressed to have been the cause of trouble for him, but he reassured her that his arrest had probably been inevitable, as he had opposed the Boxers from the beginning, and promised her that he would hand her back to the Belgian Legation once it had been relieved.

She didn't appear very pleased about that, and he gathered that her enforced stay with her compatriots had not been a happy time, quite apart from her grief at the death of her parents.

But only a few days later news arrived that Admiral Seymour's column had been defeated and was retreating to Tientsin with heavy casualties. Robert could not believe it at first; no Barbarian army had been defeated by the Chinese since the two sides had first encountered each other in 1840, saving only when, in 1861, the British had been, briefly, repelled from their assault on the Taku forts at the mouth of the Pei-ho. But there could be no doubt that it was true when European heads and uniforms were paraded through Peking to the joy of cheering and jeering crowds. On that same day the Boxers launched an attack on the Legations and quickly overran the smaller buildings. The Barbarians retreated to the British compound, and there prepared to make a stand.

'What of the Banner Army?' Robert asked Chang Tsin.

'They have no part in this,' Chang told him. 'At the moment.' He smiled. 'They are not needed, at the moment.'

Robert felt absolutely helpless; he had no doubt that there was soon going to be a massacre which would make the worst excesses of the Indian Mutiny seem like a tea party. And what would happen then? He could not believe the European powers would just accept the situation. He asked Chang Tsin to arrange a meeting with Tz'u-hsi, but once again she refused to see him. Nor would Jung-lu receive him. They had apparently set their course and were not to be dissuaded.

It was a course, he knew, Tz'u-hsi had had in her heart for nearly forty years, ever since the British and French had destroyed the Yuan Ming Yuan. His own resolve was hardening. He could do nothing to help the Legations, but neither could he just sit in Chang Tsin's garden and watch events unfold.

He summoned Chou Li-ting, the head of his servants, and told him what he meant to do. Chou pulled his moustache, but his loyalty was to the House of Barrington first and Manchu China second, as Robert well knew.

It had never occurred to Chang Tsin that Robert Barrington, his own son-in-law and the Dowager Empress's erstwhile lover, as well as a man whose entire fortune was bound up with the Ch'ing Dynasty, would even consider disobeying an imperial decree. Thus Chou Li-ting and his men had not been disarmed or restrained in any way, any more than Robert was restrained, except in so far as he could not leave Chang Tsin's house.

Chou could come and go as he chose, however, and he made the necessary arrangements, alerting old Captain Shung to prepare the sampan and its crew and to stock the boat with provisions. When these were completed, he reported to Robert, and the plan was put into effect. That night, after Chang Tsin had returned from the Forbidden City and he and Robert were sitting down to their evening meal, Chou and two of his men entered the room.

Chang looked up in irritation, but Chou addressed Robert. 'All is ready, Master. The house is in our hands.'

Chang looked from one to the other, only now realising that the servants were armed. 'What is the meaning of this?'

'I have decided to return to Shanghai, Father,' Robert told him. 'Your servants have been taken prisoner by my men. Now, I wish you to write me a pass to leave the city tonight.'

'Are you mad? Tz'u-hsi will have our heads.'

'She will have to catch me to obtain mine,' Robert said. 'As for you, you are acting under duress. If you do not give me the pass I shall kill you, and forge it. Your seal is in the house; it will not be difficult.'

Chang Tsin's mouth opened and shut like that of a stranded fish. 'This is outrageous,' he spluttered. 'You are my son-in-law. Would you break every Confucian ethic? A son who kills his father is doomed to an eternity of hell.'

'Write the pass, or die,' Robert said, sounding absolutely resolute, even while he knew he could never kill this poor old man who had been a friend of his family for years before he had even been born. But he also knew that Chang, for all his outward arrogance, possessed the basic cowardice of every eunuch. Chang wrote out the pass. 'Now come.' Robert escorted him to where the women had been eating, and where two more of Chou's people stood guard over Wu Lai, Chang Su, and Monique, all of whom were looking totally bewildered.

'What is happening?' Su inquired.

'We are leaving. Chang Tsin, I am going to have to tie you up, with Wu Lai, to enable us to make good our escape. You will be able to get free in due course.'

'You will die,' Wu Lai declared.

'I think we are all going to do that, sooner or later. Su, collect your things.'

Chang Su looked at her father.

'I forbid you to go with him,' Chang Tsin said.

'The decision must be yours,' Robert agreed. 'Monique, you will come with me.'

Monique licked her lips as she looked from face to face, uncertainly.

'You will go off with that woman?' Su demanded. 'I am your wife.'

'If you do not come with me now, you are no longer my wife,' Robert told her.

'You will stay here,' Chang Tsin insisted.

'My husband . . .'

'He is a Barrington,' Chang Tsin said. 'He will perish with the Barringtons. Do you wish to perish with them?'

Chang Su bit her lip.

'You must make up your mind, now,' Robert said.

'I must obey my father.'

'Very well,' Robert said. He beckoned his servants. 'Bind them up.' Chang Tsin and the two women were made to lie on the floor, and their wrists were tied behind them and then tied to their ankles. 'Now gag them,' Robert said.

'I will laugh when they kick your head away from your body,' Chang Tsin snarled.

Then his mouth was stopped and he could only stare at Robert with venomous eyes, as did Wu Lai. Chang Su was weeping.

Robert escorted Monique to the door. 'Will you not be in serious trouble, monsieur, as he said?' the girl asked.

Robert's smile was grim. 'I am already in serious trouble, Monique. It would be a waste of time to get cold feet now.'

Chang Tsin's servants had all also been bound and gagged, Robert reckoned it would be several hours before any of them would get free and sound the alarm, and by then, with the telegraph destroyed, he intended to be beyond pursuit. There was the usual group of Bannermen on the street outside the Head Eunuch's House, but when Robert showed them his pass they let the little party through. It was the same at the gate, and within half an hour of leaving Chang Tsin's house they were in their sampan on the Grand Canal.

They pushed off immediately, rowing at a good speed, while Robert set the imperial dragon standard in the bow to leave no one in any doubt they were travelling on Tz'u-hsi's business.

'Will we escape?' Monique asked, when he joined her inside the tent.

'Yes,' he promised. 'You may lie down and get some rest.'

'I would rather stay awake, with you, monsieur.'

By the glow of the lantern he saw a slight flush suffuse her cheeks. And realised he was also embarrassed. If from their

first meeting he had admired this girl's beauty and really
remarkable composure, she had up till now been only
someone he had been fortunate enough to rescue from an
unthinkable fate. He had not dared consider her as anything
more than that. Apart from being married, he was old enough
to be her father. He had not expected to be thrown together
with her, like this, while his life – certainly his marriage –
was in a state of crisis.

It was obvious that she was suffering from an extreme
case of hero-worship, as well as feeling guilty for having
caused him so much trouble. And she had no one else to turn
to.

If he could get her back to Shanghai, to Vicky . . . but that
was a long way away. 'Well,' he said. 'I think I will lie
down, just in case there is no opportunity later.'

*

He slept, although he was very conscious of the girl beside
him. At dawn he was awakened by Chou, who reported that
there was a considerable body of Boxers on the bank. 'The
men are tired, Master,' Chou explained. 'They would like to
stop and rest.'

'Well, we must continue past those fellows,' Robert told
him, and himself went on deck. The Boxers gazed at the
sampan, but they could make out the imperial dragon, and
although they shouted at them, no attempt was made to stop
them – clear indication that the rebels were confident of
imperial support. Robert was able to moor up to the bank
some distance further on and let his people sleep for a few
hours before they continued on their way, into the town of
Tung-Chow.

Here there were even more crowds, and Robert responded
to the various greetings, but did not stop. In Tung-Chow it
was possible to leave the Canal and enter the Pei-ho, and this
they did. The Canal was where any pursuers would look for
them, and the river promised better speed, although there

was the risk of encountering sandbanks. But Shung had navigated these waters throughout his life, and in fact they made good time, through country which was largely empty.

Robert tied up to the bank for that night. The following day they would reach the junction with the Han-ho, and Tientsin, but before that they would have to pass through the town of Yangtsun, and he did not know whether it was occupied by Boxers or Barbarians. As far as he was aware the Barbarians were holding Tientsin itself, as well as an outpost in the Arsenal on the north bank. If the Boxers were in Yangtsun they would therefore almost certainly wish to question why an imperial sampan was proceeding towards the enemy. As he did not intend to be checked now, there was every prospect of a fight, and he wanted his people fresh.

He explained the situation to Monique. 'You will give me a gun,' she said. 'I have shot a rifle before.'

'I think it would be best if you lay in the bottom of the boat,' he said.

'While you fight for me? Why should you do this, monsieur?'

'I shall be fighting for myself as well, Monique. My safety as much as yours depends on our reaching Tientsin.'

Chou's people cooked their evening meal, and then sentries were posted, although the neighbourhood appeared clear of any inhabitants at all; they had passed the smouldering wreckage of a village earlier that day – presumably the inhabitants had attempted to resist Boxer demands for food – and it seemed probable that the whole area had been evacuated because of the fighting. Robert slept heavily, but was again aroused by Chou, this time while it was still dark. 'Horsemen,' Chou said.

Robert sat up and listened, to both the jingle of harnesses and the occasional rasp of weapons. The sentry who had first reported the noise pointed down the river. 'The Boxers have no cavalry,' Robert said. 'It must be a Barbarian patrol.'

'I do not think so, Master,' Chou said. 'I think they are Bannermen.'

'Then we must talk our way past them.' Robert alerted all his people, but warned them to maintain a peaceable appearance unless it actually did come to a fight. Then they ate, and awaited daylight.

When it came, they saw a force of mounted Bannermen some half a mile away, also apparently waiting on the dawn. Now half a dozen of the soldiers approached, led by a captain. 'Barrington!' Robert stood on deck. 'You are under arrest,' the Captain said. 'You must return with us to Peking.'

'By whose order?' Robert inquired.

'By order of the Dowager Empress.' Robert frowned while he tried to think. Could a messenger possibly have got past them in the night? The Banner Captain gave a grim smile. 'The telegraph line has been repaired, Barrington. At least as far as Yangtsun. Did you not know this?'

It had not even occurred to Robert that it might be. 'I have twelve men on board this sampan,' he said. 'Each one is armed with a repeating rifle. I would ask you to let us pass.'

The Captain looked astounded. 'You would defy Tz'u-hsi?'

'In this instance, yes. You'll cast off, Shung.'

The sampan captain called his men, and they came on deck to release the mooring warps. Robert signalled Chou and his people to show themselves, and their weapons.

'You must die, if you defy Tz'u-hsi,' the Captain said.

'Not this morning, Captain. Unless you wish to die first.'

The Captain hesitated only briefly, then turned his mount and walked it back to his men, followed by his escort.

'They will attack us now,' Chou suggested.

Robert nodded. 'Get out into the stream, Shung, and put your men to work.'

The sweeps went in, and the sampan surged forward. Monique came out of the tent and gazed at the horsemen. 'Is there going to be a fight?'

'I suspect so. Stay under cover.' He watched the Banner-men mounting their horses, and told Chou and his men to stand by. But for the time being the sampan was making very good time. Then, to his surprise, the Bannermen, having formed columns of four, cantered off, parallel with the river, to be sure, but making no effort to approach the bank. In a few minutes they had disappeared over a rise.

'They mean to stop us in Yangtsun,' Chou said. 'There is the railway bridge under which we have to pass.'

'Yes,' Robert said thoughtfully. 'There is a tributary stream bearing off to the left a few miles from here, is there not?'

'That is true. But it only leads to a lake, not back to the river.'

'It will still throw them off our scent,' Robert said. 'We will go down to the lake, abandon the sampan, and from there make our way across country to the river. It is only a few miles to the Arsenal opposite Tientsin.'

Chou again looked doubtful, but he was not going to argue with his employer. They swept on down the river, and an hour later saw the subsidiary stream leading away to the left from the east bank. Shung heaved on the steering oar, and the sampan began to turn. As it did so, a line of Bannermen appeared, standing up on the far bank of the stream, rifles aimed, and exploding even as Robert realised that the Banner Captain had guessed what might be his plan.

'Back your sweeps,' he shouted, for on the narrow stream they would be too close to their opponents to make a fight of it. Already one of Chou's men had been hit and had fallen into the bottom of the boat, shrieking in agony. But even as Shung bellowed his orders Robert heard the chatter of a Hotchkiss gun, and felt the sampan shudder as a stream of bullets poured into the wooden hull. Immediately the boat began to fill and list. Two more of his men had been hit; one was dead, and floated off down the river, on his face.

'We are sinking!' Shung shouted, unnecessarily.

'Make the far shore,' Robert snapped.

Monique looked out of the tent. 'There is a lot of water in here.'

'Are you hit?'

'No. I am all right.'

'Well, keep your head down.'

The Hotchkiss continued to chatter, as the waterlogged sampan turned right round. Carried by the current, it had drifted out into the centre of the stream. Chou and his remaining two men were kneeling behind the gunwale and gallantly returning fire, but Shung's boatmen had all leapt overboard. They knew the sampan would never make the west bank.

Robert holstered his revolver. 'Abandon the boat,' he told his men. 'Make for the shore.' He crawled into the cabin, where Monique, kneeling up to her thighs in water, gazed at him with huge eyes; oddly, she did not seem to be afraid. 'We will have to swim for it,' he told her.

'I cannot swim. Leave me, monsieur, and save yourself.'

'Come on.' He grabbed her hand, and before she could protest, had gained the rail and jumped in, the girl in his arms. They struck the water with a huge splash, and he immediately turned on his back, holding Monique by the shoulders and using his legs to kick them towards the shore, allowing himself to be swept along by the current so long as he was making progress to the west bank. For the moment the sampan was between them and the Bannermen, who continued to fire at the sinking craft, but she was going very rapidly now and a few moments later disappeared with a gurgle, leaving only a whirl of disturbed water; the tent broke away and drifted down-river.

By now the current had carried Robert below the Bannermen's position, and they were in any event preoccupied with those members of the crew who had swum to the near bank and were being rounded up and arrested. The poor devils would almost certainly be executed, but Robert could do nothing to assist them now: he had Monique to think of. She remained as still as possible, once again demonstrating her complete confidence in him, even if thus far his attempts to ensure her safety had been in the main unsuccessful. Now his feet struck the bottom, and a moment later they were in the bushes which clustered along the riverbank, just in time, as someone had seen them and several shots were sent in their direction.

Robert hugged the girl against him and the bank; any movement could betray them. And after a few more shots the Bannermen turned their attention to the rest of the crew. 'We must get up the bank,' he told her. He could just see over the top, and it was a wooded and bushy area. 'If they see you they will shoot at you. Get into the trees and lie there until I come to you.' He looked down at her. 'Ready?'

'Please come to me,' she said.

He grinned. 'I mean to. Go.' He grasped her thighs to give her a push up; she reached the top of the bank and sensibly making no attempt to get to her feet, rolled away from it as fast as she could. He watched her disappear into the trees. There was no response from the opposite bank, where the Bannermen, having secured those prisoners they had captured, were making ready to march off; their horses had been brought up.

Robert followed Monique's example, and rolled into the trees behind her. 'Those poor men,' she said. 'Are they all dead?'

'I think they very probably are. Or they soon will be.'

'All because of me,' she said.

'All because of me. They were my servants.'

'What will become of us?' she asked.

'We must try to get down to the Han-ho. We're on the wrong side of both rivers for Tientsin, but we should be able to obtain some kind of a craft. I don't think we should move again until dark, however.' She looked up at the sun, coming through the trees; it was still only mid-morning. 'Yes,' he agreed. 'We may well become a little hungry. First thing, I suggest we get out of our wet clothes. I will go over there.'

He crawled away from her for some distance, removed his tunic and pantaloons, and found a patch of sunlight in which to spread them and sit himself to allow his body to dry. Then

he checked his revolver and cartridge belt; they both seemed
in good order – he could protect himself and the girl, for a
while. Much would depend on whether the Bannermen
opted to cross the river at Yangtsun, and then come up the
west bank looking for survivors. But that would take some
time. Meanwhile . . .

'Monsieur,' Monique whispered from behind the bushes
separating them. 'There is someone coming.'

He had heard the movement as well. 'Lie down and keep
out of sight,' he told her, and himself knelt in the bushes,
holstering the revolver and drawing his knife instead – he
didn't want to risk a shot until he was sure there were neither
Boxers nor Bannermen in the vicinity.

He heard movement behind him and turned sharply; a
nude Monique was wriggling through the bushes towards
him. 'Over there!' she whispered, apparently unconcerned
about his nakedness. But then, if she thought of him as a
father . . .

He concentrated on the direction in which she had
pointed, and estimated there was only one intruder. 'Show
yourself,' he commanded. 'Or die.'

'Master!' Chou stood up in relief. Then he saw the girl,
and his eyes rolled. He was still fully dressed in his wet
clothes, and even carried a satchel.

'Thank God it's you,' Robert said. 'Are there any
others?'

'No. They were in too much haste. The Bannermen got
them all. We are fugitives, Master.' He came closer,
endeavouring not to look at Monique, who had risen to her
knees.

'We shall try to make the river when it gets dark,' Robert
told him. 'What have you got in that bag? Not food?'

'Bread. I snatched it when we were going down.'

'Chou, you are a hero.' Now Robert did look at the girl.
'Are your clothes dry?'

'No, monsieur. May I have something to eat?'

'Go behind those bushes.'

She crawled away again, an unforgettable sight, for she was a very mature sixteen-year-old, with full breasts and strong legs and thighs. Robert looked at Chou, who took out some of the bread. It was soggy, but was still edible. Robert broke off half a loaf and tossed it to the girl, who caught it, then sank out of sight. Robert and Chou ate together. 'I am sorry about your people,' Robert said.

'No man can go against fate,' Chou remarked, enigmatically. 'What is your plan?'

'To gain the river, a boat, the Grand Canal, and the Yangtse.'

'I have lost my rifle,' Chou said. 'And we will need more food.'

'We shall have to do the best we can,' Robert told him.

*

Monique dressed herself, as did Robert, and the three of them sat together in the bushes. The day was quiet now. Robert thought of poor old Shung, who had been a faithful servant of the House for so very long – he remembered their first journey up the Grand Canal together. 'What will happen between you and your wife?' Monique asked.

'That depends on what happens with this entire business.'

'But you would like to be reconciled with her, if you can,' she persisted.

He looked at her, but she would not lower her gaze. 'Don't you want to go home to your uncles in Belgium?' he asked.

'I would rather stay here. With you.'

'With a married man who is a fugitive from justice and who is also old enough to be your father?'

'With a man who has saved my life perhaps three times, and who has been kind to me.'

'You are an uncommonly bold young woman, Monique.'

'These are uncommonly bold times, monsieur.'

He wanted her desperately. It was a tremendous awakening to realise that he had never loved a European woman, that up to a few minutes before he had never seen a European woman naked. He had liked what he saw. To have sex with Monique, he would be virtually virginal again, at least in his mind. And Monique had never loved anyone, but was clearly supposing that his sex would be of the Chinese variety . . . No doubt she had heard sufficient about the 'obscenity' of that – from prurient Europeans.

But to take her, just because they both wanted, when her want was composed of so many things, but above all, he estimated, by a fear that she might not have a tomorrow, and his by a purely sexual desire, would be criminal.

Yet he knew it was going to happen.

*

In the middle of the afternoon they heard voices. Chou crawled to the edge of the copse, and came back to report. 'Boxers,' he said. 'It is a small party; seven men. But they have two horses.'

Robert stroked his chin. 'How far is it from here to Yangtsun?'

'I would say about forty miles.'

Robert nodded. 'Then they cannot possibly make it tonight. They will camp. They will have food.'

Chou looked doubtful. 'Seven men? And we have no rifle.'

'We have our knives, and my revolver. Did they have any firearms?'

'I saw a rifle.'

'We must hope there is only one, and deal with it first. But we will have the advantage of surprise.'

Monique had been listening to the conversation. 'You mean to attack those men?'

Robert nodded. 'We need their horses, we need their arms, and we need their food.'

'You mean to kill them?'

'Yes. I am sorry, Monique, but there is no alternative.

If the Boxers take us prisoner, they will certainly kill us. And if any one of those men escapes, they will rouse the entire countryside against us.'

Monique bit her lip, most attractively.

*

They moved out at dusk. Because of the horse manure, the trail was easy to follow, and in any event the Boxers appeared to be using a well-worn track. Robert's only real fear was that they would link up with a larger group, but when, just before midnight, they saw the glow of a camp fire, it was easy to determine that the party remained small.

'You stay here,' he told Monique. 'I can offer you nothing. I need the gun.'

'I understand.' She sat down, her legs drawn up beneath her. Her fate, if something did happen to him, was unthinkable. But this was their only hope of survival.

He and Chou crawled forward until they were within fifty feet of the camp. The horses were tethered on the far side of the fire, and six of the men were sleeping, wrapped in blankets. The seventh was keeping watch, but from the way his head nodded he was clearly half asleep; a rifle leaned against his legs. Obviously they did not suppose there were any enemies within a hundred miles – they would know that the ordinary Chinese were too afraid of them ever to attack them. 'Are you ready?' Robert asked Chou. 'It must be very quick, and very complete.' Chou nodded. 'Then . . . now!'

He had given Chou his knife as well. The Chinese leapt to his feet and ran forward, Robert beside him. The noise of their approach alerted the horses, which whinnied. The guard sat up, looking left and right in alarm, and reaching for his rifle. Robert already had him in his sights, and squeezed the trigger. The explosion startled the remaining men, although the guard fell without a sound. Chou was still running forward, and reached the dead man and the rifle before any of the others was properly awake.

Robert had by now turned his revolver on them, taking careful aim; every shot had to tell. He brought down two men before the other four were on their feet. But by then Chou had levelled the rifle, and his first shot cut down another. Robert dropped a fifth. Neither of the surviving two gave any thought to escaping; they both drew their swords and charged, one at Chou and one at Robert. And both fell before they could reach their objectives. The sounds of the shots echoed into the night, which was then once again quiet. The fire continued to burn. The horses moved restlessly, excited by the firing. And seven men lay on the ground. Not all had been killed outright, but Chou moved amongst them, cutting the throats of the living.

How simple it was to commit a massacre, Robert thought. In an unsatisfactory manner, Helen had been partially avenged. He heard movement and turned sharply, reaching for the cartridges to reload his revolver. But it was Monique. 'I told you to wait for me to come to you,' he said.

She came up to him, and gazed at the Boxers. 'Are they all dead?'

'Yes.'

Chou was searching the bodies and finding money, judging by the clink of coin as he emptied their satchels into one. 'There are two rifles,' he said. 'And two bandoliers.'

'Give me one,' Monique said.

Chou looked at Robert, who nodded. The girl slung the rifle and one of the bandoliers on her shoulder.

'What of food?'

'The remains of their dinner, in this pot, and a sack of beanshoots, with some uncooked meat.'

Robert sniffed the meat. It was high, but edible.

'I am so hungry,' Monique said.

'Yes, but we cannot stay here. Someone may have heard the shots.'

They saddled the horses, packed up everything from the Boxers they thought they could use, and left, Chou riding one horse with the satchels, Robert the other. Monique sat behind him with her arms round his waist. 'I suppose you have killed many men,' she murmured, resting her head on his shoulder.

'I have been a soldier since the age of sixteen. Or at least a fighting seaman.'

'Now I have become a soldier, at the age of sixteen,' she remarked.

'But you have not yet killed anyone. Try to keep it that way.' Then he remembered that at the age of sixteen, he had not yet killed a man, either. She had time.

They rode away from the encampment to the west. This was actually the wrong direction, but it would throw any pursuers off their scent, at least until they got down to tracking in earnest. They rode for about three hours, then Robert called a halt in a little dip, where they were sheltered from any casual passers-by. Chou hobbled the horses and lit a small fire; they ate, and felt immensely better. There was even a pool of muddy water in the dip and they were able to drink, and let the horses drink also.

'How many hours to dawn, do you suppose?' Robert asked Chou.

'Not many now. The air is chill.'

'And we do not know for sure where we are. We will rest until sun-up, and then head for the river.'

Chou grinned. 'And become pirates as well as robbers, if necessary.'

'If necessary,' Robert agreed.

He wrapped himself in one of the blankets they had taken from the Boxers, and lay down. But did not sleep. He was waiting, and after a few minutes, Monique came to him.

*

She had brought two of the blankets, and spread one on the ground with determined housewifery. It was not a time for asking if she knew what she did. Robert had certainly killed men before, but never had he carried out quite so lethal an execution. His mind and body were disturbed with a mixture of exhilaration and guilt, and a curious satisfaction that he had proved himself so ruthless, so much a reincarnation of his immortal great-grandfather. That the girl should come to him seemed hardly less than his due as a conqueror. That she should *wish* to come to him turned their connection into a delight.

She was eager to be held naked in his arms, to kiss him and snuggle against him, to lose all of her fears and her loneliness in his strong embrace. Equally was she anxious to be possessed, to feel his hands on her breasts and buttocks and between her legs, his mouth on hers, their tongues throbbing against each other. Clearly she knew a great deal about sexual matters, even if she was a virgin, but Robert took her as any European might have done on this first occasion, and he hoped she found this reassuring. She was a treasure, in the muscle-hardness that lay beneath the outer softness, in the length and straightness of her legs, the silky texture of her hair, so unlike the stiff Chinese variety. 'I shall never let you go,' he told her. 'I shall keep you at my side, forever.'

'Forever,' she whispered, hugging him against her.

*

They gained the river by dusk, undetected by any Boxers, who they realised were massing their forces to assault Tientsin, a concentration being, as usual, overlooked by the Bannermen. As for the Bannermen, they seemed to have decided that Barrington had drowned in the river; there was no sign of any search parties.

Once at the Han-ho, they did indeed become pirates. Well armed now, it was a simple matter to commandeer a sampan and its crew, and go hurrying down the river; they left the horses in exchange. Shots were fired at them from the banks, but they had not travelled very far when they realised the shots to their right were coming from modern rifles, in greater numbers than any possessed by the Boxers. Robert immediately set a white blouse as a flag, and closed the bank. The shooting ceased, and soon they were in the hands of a company of Japanese marines, an advance guard thrown forward from Tientsin. 'Barrington,' remarked their captain, who spoke Mandarin. 'I have heard of you.'

'We are escaping from Peking,' Robert explained.

The Captain made no comment, although undoubtedly he knew that Robert Barrington was one of Tz'u-hsi's commanders, but sent them down-river with an escort. That evening Robert found himself in the military encampment outside the city, where the flags of half-a-dozen nations flew, and large numbers of soldiers and marines of every nationality hurried to and fro. Tientsin had clearly recently been the scene of a battle – in fact Robert learned that it had been held by the Boxers and then stormed by the Barbarians; there were burned houses and rotting corpses everywhere.

He was taken before Major-General Gaselee, a heavy-set man with a bald head but a thick moustache. 'Robert Barrington,' Gaselee remarked. 'Yours is a familiar name, sir. You are head of the House of Barrington.'

'That is correct,' Robert said. 'Now, General, I need all the assistance you can give me to regain Shanghai and my proper responsibilities.'

'I am informed that you have a young woman with you.'

'She is Belgian, and escaped with me from Peking.'

'May I ask how old this woman is?'

'Sixteen, I believe.'

'And you have armed her with a rifle? Really, Mr Barrington. Where are her parents?'

Robert found himself beginning to dislike the General. 'Her parents were murdered by the Boxers.'

'From whom you rescued her. How heroic,' Gaselee remarked. 'Now you say you have come from Peking. Can you tell me the situation there?'

'It is desperate, for the Legations. Some of them have already been overrun. The various staffs and guards are making a stand in the British Legation. But I very much doubt they can hold out much longer.'

'A few hundred men against the entire Chinese Army? I agree that is unlikely.'

'As far as I know,' Robert said evenly, 'the Banner Army is not part of the force besieging the Legations.'

'And you should know, because you serve in it, eh?'

'No, General, I am not a Bannerman.'

'Will you deny that you are a part of the coterie which surrounds and advises the Dowager Empress?'

'I wish I were. I was an officer in the Chinese Navy, once.'

'Barrington, everyone knows you are a renegade who serves the Manchus, as has your family for the past hundred years.'

'General, I do not know what you are trying to prove. Yes, my family has served the Manchus for a hundred years. That does not mean I have to approve of everything they do. For opposing their support of the Boxers I was placed under arrest in Peking. I have escaped that arrest and am now on my way back to Shanghai. Any assistance you can give me will be much appreciated.'

'Do you expect me to believe that?'

'You had better, as it is the truth. It is also the truth that the Legations are going to fall within a very short space of time. I would advise you to negotiate a safe withdrawal of their inhabitants with the Tsung-li-yamen just as quickly as you can.'

'Aha!' Gaselee said. 'Now we have it. You were sent here to negotiate a surrender.'

Robert was amazed. 'Do I look like an envoy, General?'

'There is no end to the cunning of these yellow devils,' Gaselee declared. 'They well know we will never negotiate. Not after the way they fired on poor Seymour's column. So they have sent you, apparently a fugitive, to warn us that there will be a massacre in Peking if we do not agree to their terms. Oh, yes, I see it all. Well, it won't work, Barrington.

It may interest you to know that we have assembled an army of approximately fifteen thousand men here in Tientsin. Every nation with a Legation in Peking is represented. We commence our march tomorrow. This time we are really going to settle with those devils, and with the biggest devil of all – Tz'u-hsi. She is going to hang from the highest tree in her Forbidden City. What do you think of that?'

'I think you are going needlessly to sacrifice a great number of lives, General Gaselee. You may be able to fight your way up to Peking. But there is no way you can possibly get there in time to save the Legations. Then the blood of some seven hundred Europeans will be on your head. I have told you the situation. If you intend to persist in this madness, I wish no part of it. I am going back to Shanghai, with or without your assistance. Good day to you, General.'

He got up, and looked down the barrel of a revolver, which Gaselee had taken from his desk drawer.

'You are going nowhere, Barrington, except into a cell,' the General said. 'As far as I am concerned you are as guilty as any Manchu mandarin. I am holding you until we take Peking, and if any European lives have been lost in the Legations, why, you'll stand on the scaffold alongside your mistress. Guards!'

Robert was too surprised to react. Not that there was much he could do in any event, for the room was immediately filled with armed men, and within seconds he found himself in a recently built cell block, apparently intended for recalcitrant soldiers. He was at least given a room to himself, but his request to send a message to Chou was refused by the commandant, Captain Lister. 'Prisoners are not permitted to communicate with the enemy,' Lister pointed out. 'Anyway, the rascal has disappeared. He fled when he heard what had happened to you.'

'With Mademoiselle Carremans?' Robert asked eagerly.

'Why, no, fortunately. Mademoiselle Carremans has been taken into care by the Belgian staff here, until arrangements can be made for her repatriation.'

'Then at least let me send a message to her,' Robert said.

'I think you want to forget about that young lady, Barrington,' Lister said. 'It's not unlikely that amongst the charges against you will be those of abduction and rape.'

'Do you seriously suppose Mademoiselle Carremans will support such charges?'

Lister grinned. 'Probably not. She had the temerity to threaten us with a rifle. But she has been disarmed . . .'

'If she has been hurt—'

'You are in no position to utter threats, Barrington. Whether or not the young lady wishes to bring charges is not relevant to whether or not you will be charged; she is obviously not entirely of sound mind.'

Robert decided against taking offence, in his circumstances. 'Am I not even allowed to write to my family?' he demanded. 'By God, man, I am China's leading merchant. Do you really suppose you can treat me like some common criminal?'

'In our eyes, Barrington, that is what you are,' Lister told him, and closed the door.

*

'You say Barrington is dead?' Tz'u-hsi asked, her voice low.

'I am afraid that is the case, Majesty,' Chang Tsin said. 'His sampan sank on the river, and his body was not amongst those recovered. Neither,' he added with some satisfaction, 'was that of his mistress.'

'Barrington,' Tz'u-hsi muttered. 'I did not wish this to happen. How did this happen, Tsin?'

'I am as sorry as you, Majesty. But the fact is that he was a traitor to the Dynasty. He was a traitor to us all, even my poor daughter . . .' He paused, because Tz'u-hsi did not appear to be listening. 'If Your Majesty would care to consider the situation . . .'

Tz'u-hsi turned her head to look at him.

'A Barbarian army has definitely moved out of Tientsin, Majesty,' Chang said, 'and is advancing.'

Tz'u-hsi looked at Jung-lu. 'Is this true?'

'It would appear so, Majesty.'

'They are fifteen thousand strong, Majesty,' Chang Tsin said.

Tz'u-hsi glared at Jung-lu. 'Why was this business not finished weeks ago?'

Jung-lu shuffled his feet. 'The resistance has been very determined, Majesty.'

'What of the artillery? Those Legations should be a mass of rubble by now.'

Jung-lu looked even more embarrassed. 'It has been difficult to emplace, Majesty. There are so many houses, narrow streets . . . We have been unable to obtain a clear field of fire.'

'Well, now we seem to have a full-scale war on our hands. It must be settled, Jung-lu. The Barbarians must be destroyed. Every one must be killed. Once there is no one left to rescue, this Barbarian army will turn back.'

*

James Barrington looked up from the report which Adrian had placed on his desk. James was seventy, and looked even older than that. The news of Helen's death, and the manner of it, had seemed to add ten years to his life, a life which in any event had not recovered from Lucy's death. 'What is happening to us, Adrian? My family is being destroyed.'

'I want you to know how sorry I am, Father. I . . . I can only try to take his place.'

'I know you will, boy.' James heaved himself to his feet. 'I must go down to the cemetery. Will you come?'

'There's a shipment unloading, Father. I must be there.' He grinned. 'Life, and work, must go on.'

'Of course, boy. Of course. Thank God you're here.'

Adrian stood at the window to watch his father go down the steps beneath him and out into the garden; Lucy's grave was beyond the willows. Where Father wanted to be buried too. Adrian wondered where Robert had been buried – supposing he was buried at all.

He left his father's study and went to Victoria's apartment. The servants bowed as he passed them. Master Adrian was not a very regular visitor to his father's house; for him to come early in the morning had to mean something important had happened, even if they did not as yet know what. 'Miss Victoria is not dressed,' the maid protested, as he entered the apartment.

'Still in bed?'

'No, no, Master. But she eats breakfast.'

She looked as if she would have liked to stop him, but did not dare. He stepped past her, and went on to the verandah, where Victoria sat in a dressing gown before her breakfast tray. Victoria's apartment looked out over the front of the house and the river; she would not have seen her father go to his wife's grave. Now she frowned at her brother. 'What brings you here so early in the morning?'

He sat opposite her, snapped his fingers. The maid, hovering in the doorway, hurried forward with a fresh cup and poured coffee. 'You have this objectionable habit of treating everything, and everyone, as if they belong to you,' Victoria remarked, munching toast.

'Everything does,' Adrian said equably. 'Or soon will. I have just received a message from our agent in Peking. Robert is dead.' Victoria's head jerked, and the half-eaten piece of toast fell from her fingers. 'I'm afraid it's true,' Adrian said gently. 'I have told Father. He is very upset.'

Victoria stared at him as if he were a snake. 'As are you, I can tell.' Adrian finished his coffee and stood up. 'I will leave you with your grief. When you have recovered, we must have a chat. After all, we are the last remaining Barringtons, you and I . . . and that bastard brat of yours.'

'If you touch Martin . . .'

'I wouldn't touch him with a ten-foot pole. But Vicky...'
He paused by her chair, and let his hand rest on her shoulder;
he could feel the tension beneath his fingers. 'When Father
dies, as I am terribly afraid may not now be long delayed, I
intend to run the House *my* way.' He grinned at her. 'I may
require assistance from you. I may even *demand* it. Do
remember that, Vicky.' As he left the verandah, he heard the
shattering of crockery behind him.

*

The noise of the firing at the Legations could be heard all
over Peking, even in the depths of the Forbidden City. There
was no other topic of conversation. Even the ladies of the
court, for all their lives cut off from any news of the outside
world, knew all about the day-to-day situation, which
alternated between rumour that Sir Claude Macdonald was
about to surrender, and the hard fact of the renewed firing.

Tz'u-hsi attempted to live her normal life, but she was too
distracted. She knew in her heart that this business was
turning out badly, because she had relied upon the native
Chinese to do her work for her. They were a spineless lot.
It had become worse because even her Manchus would not
support her. Even faithful Jung-lu, the friend and lover of her
girlhood, the great prop of her old age, was temporising.
Tz'u-hsi had no doubt that had he marshalled and emplaced
all the artillery in the capital he could have blown the
Legations to bits in a matter of days. But whatever he agreed
to do when in her presence, he had not been able to bring
himself to command his Peking Field Force, all Manchu
Bannermen, to fight alongside the Boxer rabble. Equally he
could not convince himself that it was possible to exterminate the Barbarians; as fast as one lot were driven away,
another lot appeared, even more warlike and grasping.

She should have his head. In her youth, perhaps she would
have executed him for failing her. But with Barrington dead,
Jung-lu was the last man in China on whom she could utterly

rely. And even Barrington had opposed her over the Boxers.

She was furious. But having her maids fight each other was merely frustrating. Sometimes she beat them herself, when her temper got the better of her. And now she had to listen to a new sound of gunfire, slowly growing louder . . . from the east.

She sat in her garden, at her easel, pretending to paint, but hardly adding a stroke. Her ladies clustered as ever behind her, and the dogs yapped. Someone was crossing the bridge, and of course it would be Chang Tsin. He arrived beside her, trembling and sweating. 'Speak.'

'The Barbarians are approaching the city, Majesty. The Boxers have fled before them.'

Tz'u-hsi turned her head. 'What of General Niem and my Bannermen?'

'They too have fled, Majesty.'

'Jung-lu?'

'The General remains in the city and will defend it, Majesty. But he says he cannot answer for your safety. He says you must leave Peking and go north, to Jehol. But I think he is wrong, Majesty. I think the Barbarians will follow you into Jehol, and besides, that would be to go too close to Korea, and the Japanese. I think you should go west, beyond the Great Wall, into Shansi Province. They will not follow you there.'

'Because Shansi is a desert,' Tz'u-hsi observed.

'It will provide you with a refuge, Majesty, until the Barbarians go away again.'

'If they ever do,' Tz'u-hsi said.

Chang Tsin was greatly relieved that she should be taking the news so calmly. 'We must hope, Majesty.'

'I have been betrayed,' Tz'u-hsi said, and Chang Tsin trembled, as he realised he had been too optimistic. 'I am surrounded by weaklings and traitors.' She got up from her stool and glared at her ladies. 'Well, you have heard. Go and pack our things. We must leave this place. Hurry.'

The ladies swarmed over the bridge, chattering at each

other. The dogs barked even louder. 'The Emperor ...' Chang Tsin ventured.

'Oh, he will have to come too. If he falls into the hands of the Barbarians he will give them everything they wish.'

'I will see to it,' Chang Tsin said.

'You will see to nothing,' Tz'u-hsi snapped. 'You ...' She pointed at one of the other waiting eunuchs. 'Attend His Majesty and inform him that we are leaving Peking within the hour. You ...' She pointed at another. 'Summon General Jung-lu to me here.'

'Majesty, do not despair,' Chang Tsin said. 'Were you and the Hsien-feng Emperor not forced to flee Peking in 1861, only to return, stronger than ever? *You* returned, Majesty, as Tz'u-hsi, as the most powerful woman in the world.'

Tz'u-hsi looked at him; to his dismay, he saw that her face had not softened. 'Yes, I remember fleeing here in 1861,' she said. 'And you were not with me. You abandoned me, Chang Tsin, because you feared for your head.'

'I was carrying out your orders, to save James Barrington from execution. I returned to you as soon as I could.'

Tz'u-hsi's lip curled. 'You returned to me when you found out I had become Dowager Empress. Had I sunk beneath the weight of those terrible times you would have found a new mistress. I know you for what you are, Chang Tsin. And you may have saved James Barrington's life, but now you have let his son perish.'

Chang Tsin gave up. While she was in this mood there would be no reasoning with her. He would have to be patient. 'Majesty, have I your permission to go to my family and bring them to join your party?'

Tz'u-hsi pointed at him in turn. 'It is your advice has brought me to this,' she said.

'Majesty ...' He was trembling again.

'You told me to support these Boxers,' Tz'u-hsi said. 'You told me the Barbarians would evacuate Peking. You, Chang.'

Chang Tsin fell to his knees. 'I advised as I thought best, Majesty.'

'Now you tell me I have nothing left but flight,' Tz'u-hsi said. 'And you would bring your "family" to watch my humiliation?' She flung out her other hand, pointing at the remaining eunuchs, who were smiling at Chang Tsin's disgrace. 'This carrion wishes to return to his "family",' Tz'u-hsi said. 'Take him to them. And there strike off his head.'

'Majesty!' Chang Tsin raised his hands in supplication. 'Have mercy. Am I not your oldest friend? Majesty, whatever I have done throughout my life has been with you in mind. I have sought nothing but your power, your wealth, your success . . .'

'You have been like a millstone around my neck,' Tz'u-hsi told him. 'Because once I felt sorry for you. Do you suppose I am not aware of how you have been stealing from me all of these years? Are you not the wealthiest eunuch in China?'

'It is all yours, Majesty,' Chang Tsin wailed. 'All yours. Everything I have is yours.'

'Enough,' Tz'u-hsi said. 'I do not wish to look at him again.' The eunuchs closed on Chang Tsin and dragged him away, still screaming.

*

'Good morning, Mr Barrington,' said Captain Lister, as the door of the cell swung open. Robert blinked at him. Although he was taken out for exercise once a day he still found sudden sunlight hard on his eyes. But this was the first time he had seen Lister in several weeks, weeks in which he had sat in his cell and seethed, while listening only to the wildest rumours, which had varied from the complete massacre of everyone in the Legations to the utter defeat of the Barbarian Army. 'Will you not step outside?' Lister invited.

Cautiously Robert left the cell. 'You mean you are releasing me?'

'I am under orders to send you to Peking. You will be accompanied by a guard.'

'Who has sent for me? The Dowager Empress?'

In which case it might be necessary to make a break for it.

'Not so far as I am aware, Mr Barrington,' Lister said. 'You are to see Sir Claude Macdonald.'

Lister would say nothing more than that, and Robert could find out nothing about either Monique or Chou. He was as completely in the dark as if he had still been in prison, although he did gather that the relief column had reached Peking and taken it by storm, while, miraculously, the Legations had still been holding out. However, suddenly his treatment could not have been better. He was allowed to bathe, given the best to eat and drink, and presented with a new suit of Chinese clothes to wear. Then he left, by sampan, with an escort of British soldiers, for the capital; the railway line had not yet been rebuilt.

But there could be no arguing that the Barbarians had taken control of Chih-li Province. Every town was garrisoned by a detachment of troops, mainly Japanese, and the Canal banks were constantly patrolled by Indian lancers, while sampans manned by British seamen and armed with machine-guns moved up and down both the rivers and the Canal.

Robert had little to say to his escort. He had a great deal on his mind, not least being the whereabouts of Monique, but he could do nothing until he discovered what Macdonald wanted, and what the immediate future held for him.

*

The destruction in the Legation Quarter was greater than Robert had supposed possible for the defenders to have been holding out when the relief column arrived. Soldiers were still digging into the rubble in their search for corpses, and women and children were still in the process of being evacuated; few did more than give the big man in the Chinese tunic and pantaloons a passing glance. No Manchu soldiers were to be seen, and indeed, very few people at all, a strong contrast to the usually crowded streets of the great city. Many of the Chinese houses, even well away from the Legation Quarter, showed signs of having been ransacked, and Robert gathered that the Barbarian soldiers had even penetrated and looted the Forbidden City.

Sir Claude Macdonald received him in the same office as a few months earlier, although the room was now bullet scarred. But the British official was as dapper as ever. 'Well, Mr Barrington,' he said. 'It seems you were right and I was wrong, in our prognostications of the future.'

'But it also seems you were justified in your decision to hang on here,' Robert acknowledged. 'Or were you?'

Macdonald gestured him to a chair. 'If you mean, was I justified in obeying orders, of course I was. If you mean, did the cost justify the issuing of those orders . . .' He sighed. 'That you will have to ask my superiors.'

'Just what was the cost?'

'Sixty-two people have died, defending these Legations.'

'And the missionaries who have been murdered? The Chinese converts?'

'I can give you no figure for those. I believe they were considerable. But you must remember those atrocities would have happened even if we had all marched out of Peking back in June.'

'Perhaps you should not have been here in the first place,' Robert suggested.

Macdonald stared at him for several seconds. Then he said, 'We are here, Mr Barrington, and we intend to stay. And we intend to exact the requisite penalties for the outrages that have been committed. However, it is not our intention to overthrow the Dynasty or to interfere in the internal affairs of China. I assume you know that the Dowager Empress, together with the Emperor, has fled the city? We want them back.'

'Do you really suppose Tz'u-hsi is going to surrender herself to your jurisdiction?'

'There is nothing like that in question. We wish the Ch'ing to resume their prerogatives and rule this country. Oh, as I have said, we will exact penalties for what has happened. There will have to be an indemnity, and certain heads will have to roll. However, I am informed that the true instigator of what happened, the Chief Eunuch, Chang Tsin, has already been executed.'

'Chang Tsin?' Robert sat upright.

'Yes. I assume you knew the fellow?'

'He was my father-in-law.'

'Your . . .' Macdonald digested that for some seconds. 'Then you have my sympathy. I had no idea.' Suddenly he looked quite disconcerted. 'Your wife, his daughter . . . she is in Shanghai?'

'No,' Robert said. 'She was with her family here in Peking. She will be very upset. With your permission, Sir Claude, I would like to go to her.'

'Ah . . .' Macdonald took out his handkerchief and patted his forehead. 'Was her name Chang Su?'

'Yes.' Robert frowned. 'Just what has happened?'

'I'm afraid I have some very bad news for you, Barrington. Chang Tsin was taken to his own house, by orders of the Dowager Empress, apparently, and there beheaded. His wife and daughters, on being left alone with the body, hanged themselves.' His shoulders sagged. 'I am most awfully sorry, but there it is.'

Chang Su, Robert thought. He had long ceased loving her, but she had always been a good and faithful wife to him. And a loving mother to little Martin. He should have taken her with him, by force. But would she not have committed suicide anyway, on learning of Chang Tsin's death?

And Chang Tsin! Chang Tsin had survived so much, always so that he could stand at his mistress's shoulder; seek to control her; have her, from her emotional needs, in his power, at least from time to time. Knowing all the while that he was at the mercy of her mood. And the Old Buddha had got him in the end.

'I imagine this puts a different complexion upon things,' Macdonald said.

'What things?'

'Well ... as I have been saying, we do not seek to bring down the Dynasty. Heaven forbid. That way lies chaos. It is essential that the Emperor, or at least the Dowager Empress, returns to Peking to resume ruling. Our problem is how to accomplish this, as she appears to be in fear of her life and refuses to receive our envoys in her desert fastness. When the conundrum was put to me, I could think of only one solution: you. You are British, Barrington, but you serve the Manchus. Yet I know you did not support them in their attempt to use the Boxers to accomplish our expulsion. But I also know that you are a confidant of the Dowager Empress, perhaps the one non-Chinese person in the whole world to whom she would listen. And I am equally sure that you desire peace and stability within this great country as much as anyone. But if she has executed your father-in-law...'

'There is also the small matter that I was placed under arrest by the Empress for opposing her over the Boxers, and escaped, and that having escaped, I was promptly arrested by the British for being a supporter of the Ch'ing.'

Macdonald pulled his moustache. 'It's a tangled world. But ... is it possible that despite all you will undertake this mission?'

'It could mean my head. Tz'u-hsi has a long memory for those she considers have opposed her or deserted her.'

'You would travel as an accredited British envoy, of course.'

'Do you think that would make a halfpenny's worth of difference to Tz'u-hsi?' But he knew he had to go. No matter what happened to him, he had to think of the House and its prosperity. As for Chang Tsin and Chang Su, and Wu Lai, well, Chang was certainly as guilty as anyone for encouraging

Tz'u-hsi to support the Boxers. Besides, this was China, the most pragmatic society in the world. Only tomorrow mattered. And it was just possible to do some arranging of tomorrow for himself.

'I will accept your commission, Sir Claude,' he said.

'Will you? Oh, I say, good show, old man. You won't regret it, I promise you. Her Majesty's Government do not forget their friends.'

'I am sure they do not,' Robert agreed, drily. 'However, there are conditions. Or one condition, anyway.'

'Name it.'

'When I left Peking I had a girl with me, a Belgian, named Monique Carremans. Her parents were killed by the Boxers. She was with me when we reached Tientsin, but there we were separated by your people.'

'I assume this is the young lady you took by force from the Belgian Legation before the start of hostilities.'

'I took her because she asked me to, Sir Claude.'

'Still, really, Mr Barrington, a sixteen-year-old girl . . . You have lived in China too long, I suspect.'

'I have lived in China all of my life, Sir Claude, which is why you are now assuming I may be of some use to you. I wish the young lady found.'

'The young lady is safe in Tientsin, Barrington. She will be returned to Belgium as soon as a passage can be arranged. It is a matter of finding a chaperone.'

'She is not going back to Belgium. I wish her to be here when I return. Should I not return, I wish her to be sent to the House of Barrington in Shanghai. I will write letters to my brother, who in my absence is Master of the House, and to my sister, who will look after her.'

'My dear fellow . . .'

'The House of Barrington will take care of her future and see to a suitable marriage in the course of time,' Robert continued.

'I see.' Macdonald looked somewhat relieved, then his head jerked. 'But if you do return . . .'

'I intend to marry her myself.'

'I really don't think I can agree to this, Barrington. Your proposal is quite outrageous.'

Robert smiled. 'So is yours, Sir Claude. The only reason you want Tz'u-hsi back running things is so that you can avoid an unending guerilla war and hopefully collect your indemnity. Is that not true? But I will give you a loophole. You may ask Mademoiselle Carremans if she wishes to marry me. If she says no, then you may return her to Belgium.'

'I am quite willing to accept that you have turned the girl's head. That is beside the point. You do realise that this may well cause an international incident.'

'International incidents are your affair, Sir Claude. Results are mine. Is your answer yes, or no?'

'I have the power to place you back under arrest, you know.'

'And whistle for your indemnity. Or wind up trying to run China for yourself, and watch Great Britain go bankrupt.'

Macdonald did some more moustache stroking. 'I agree, under protest. And I wish you to know that your behaviour is not what I consider that of an English gentleman.'

'I know,' Robert said. 'But then, you see, I never went to Eton. I will leave immediately I have arranged an escort. And after I have seen my wife's grave.'

*

'Barrington,' Tz'u-hsi said. 'They told me you were dead.'

How are the mighty fallen, Robert thought. He had done a great deal of travelling about China in his time, but always, because of his name and wealth, in considerable comfort. His trek west in the shadow of the Great Wall had been the most difficult journey he had ever undertaken. He had climbed mountain passes, with peaks towering to either side above him, and he had crossed a desert. Now that autumn was far advanced, he had suffered endless rainstorms. Of his original party of sixteen, two had died, as well as four horses. And here he was, in a scrubby little town, face to face with the ruler of all China.

Tz'u-hsi wore plain clothes and little make-up, and was attended by just two ladies and four eunuchs, and Jung-lu. There was no sign of the Emperor, although Robert knew he had accompanied his adoptive mother. But she was protected by a regiment of the Peking Field Force, whose colonel had peered long and hard at Barrington and had him searched before admitting him into the Dowager Empress's presence. Now he straightened from the kowtow. 'As a famous American once said, Majesty, the reports of my death were greatly exaggerated.'

'That pleases me. Even if you angered me, I would not have you die, Barrington.'

'Did Chang Tsin anger you, Majesty?'

Tz'u-hsi's eyes flashed. 'He brought this calamity upon us. I know his daughter was your wife. But he was not truly her father.'

'My wife is also dead, Majesty. She could not survive her father's execution. Even if he was not truly her father.'

'Have you come all this way to reproach me, Barrington? If so, you had better leave again.'

'I have come to take you back to Peking, Majesty.'

'Have you an army out there in the mountains, Barrington? Or do you take me for a fool?'

'I have come at the request of the British, acting on behalf of the other Barbarians, Majesty. China must be governed. And you are the Government.'

Tz'u-hsi smiled. 'You mean they admit defeat?' She looked at Jung-lu. 'Did I not tell you they would admit defeat?'

'Yes, Majesty.' Jung-lu gazed at Robert, seeking the truth.

'They admit defeat, Majesty,' Robert agreed; it was his business to succeed in his mission and get home, not to indulge in semantics. 'There is a matter of an indemnity . . .'

'How much this time?'

'Four hundred and fifty million taels.' Tz'u-hsi stared at him. 'Over forty years,' Robert added. Breath whistled through Tz'u-hsi's nostrils as she gave a sigh of relief. 'With interest,' Robert said.

'Forty years,' Tz'u-hsi said contemptuously. 'We will give the business to Hart. He is good at collecting indemnities.' She smiled. 'In forty years we will all be dead. Is there nothing else?'

'There is a list of ninety-six officials who the Barbarians require to be punished. I have it here.'

Tz'u-hsi took the list and studied it. 'They are all guilty, save for Jung-lu. I will not surrender Jung-lu.' The old general stood stiffly to attention. 'Jung-lu could have destroyed the Legations in twenty-four hours,' Tz'u-hsi said. 'But he did not use his artillery. He says you recommended this, Barrington.'

'I did, Majesty.'

'Then his name must come off the list, or yours must go on it.'

'I will see what can be done, Majesty. Will you return with me to Peking?'

'The Emperor will be pleased to go home,' Tz'u-hsi said.

BOOK THE THIRD
Fall of a Dynasty

'Where the ... banners flout the sky
And fan our people cold.'

William Shakespeare, *Macbeth*

12

THE GATHERING CLOUDS

'It is good to be home,' Tz'u-hsi said.

Even if it was a somewhat topsy-turvy home, for the Barbarian soldiers had thoroughly looted the Forbidden City.

'It was the Japanese did this,' Jung-lu said darkly.

'We shall rebuild and refurbish,' Tz'u-hsi said equably. 'The Barbarians have come to our door, and gone away again. Have we not won a great victory?'

*

'You are officially dismissed from my Navy, as of this moment,' Tz'u-hsi said. 'I am not displeased with you, Barrington. You and I have shared some happy times, and I will not forget how faithful you were in the matter of the Hundred Days. But I cannot accept the possibility that you may again oppose my wishes in the future.'

'I understand that, Majesty.'

'Then come closer, and let me touch you for the last time.' Robert approached and knelt before her. She stretched out her hand to rest her fingers against his cheek. 'I once said to

your father, go and prosper. Now I saw the same to you,
Young Barrington.'

*

'Well, Barrington,' Sir Claude Macdonald said. 'You are to
be congratulated. Is the Emperor pleased?'

'I have no idea,' Robert said. 'I have not seen His Majesty.
However, Her Majesty looks forward to receiving you in
audience, as soon as she is settled in.'

'She will actually receive another. I have been relieved. I
am officially exhausted,' Macdonald explained. 'I suspect
the truth of the matter is that not everyone has approved of
my handling of this whole affair. Not the least criticism, I
may add, has been of my decision to employ you to bring
about an end to the conflict.'

'Still, as you have said, it is a satisfactory end to all
concerned. Except perhaps the dead. And now, Sir
Claude . . .'

'You wish your reward.' Macdonald's tone was thoughtful. 'That too has not been approved by my superiors.'

Robert frowned at him. 'What are you trying to say?'

'What I have just said. But I do keep my word,
Barrington. Mademoiselle Carremans is beyond that door.'

Robert's heart gave a bound as he crossed the room.

'I assume you are taking her to Shanghai?' Macdonald
asked.

Robert checked. 'That is my intention.'

Macdonald nodded. 'Then I shall not see you again.'

He did not offer to shake hands.

*

'I'm afraid my family is still regarded as a bunch of
renegades, hardly reformed pirates, utter villains,' Robert
remarked. 'Even by Tz'u-hsi. I hope you know what you are
doing.'

They sat in the stern of the sampan as they were carried down the Grand Canal, and Monique was constantly amazed at the changing scenery; she had previously known only that small part of Chih-li Province in which her father had worked. Now she rested her head on his shoulder. 'I have never been so sure of anything in my life.'

Then what of him? He was thirty-five years old, more than double her age. No wonder the Europeans regarded him as an ogre. But he was also the luckiest man in the world, to have survived so much, with all his possessions intact, and a whole new future to anticipate. It was his business to make her the luckiest woman. But first, the family. He had sent a message ahead, and Adrian was on the dock to greet him. 'Thank God you are back,' he said. 'We had given you up for lost.'

Robert introduced Monique, but he could tell something was wrong. 'Father?'

Adrian nodded. 'He never recovered from the shock of learning what happened to Helen. But then, I do not believe he ever really recovered from Mother's death. I know they were not close at the end, but I suppose she represented continuity. The news of your death was the last straw. We are down to three.' Adrian shrugged. 'There is also Aunt Jo. She doesn't say much.'

'I have brought you misfortune,' Monique said.

'On the contrary. You are the only fortunate aspect of this whole affair.' Robert looked past his brother. 'Chou!'

'Master!' Chou embraced him.

That at least was reassuring. Chou greeted Monique warmly, and listened with huge eyes to the story of Chang Su's death.

'Where is Martin?' Robert demanded.

'He is with Victoria,' Adrian explained. 'It seemed the obvious thing to do.'

'Yes,' Robert agreed, and clasped his brother's hand. 'I owe you a great deal for holding the fort here in my absence.'

'I am your brother,' Adrian reminded him.

*

Adrian went home and threw his hat in the corner as he
stalked through the door. His girls and Chiang Lu bowed
before him. 'He is back,' he snarled. 'Back, when he should
be dead. And with a woman he means to marry.' The girls
trembled and began to cry as he took out his cane.

*

Robert took Monique to his sister's apartment. 'I did not come
to meet you,' Victoria explained, 'because I seldom go out.
But I am so glad to see you back, safe and sound. Are you going
to stay?' He nodded. And she gave a sigh of relief, then
embraced Monique. 'Welcome. I need a sister.' At twenty-six
she was perhaps more beautiful than ever, but there was no
happiness in her face. Robert had more than a suspicion that
she and Adrian had not been getting on amidst the collapse of
the family. And yet, she was not miserable, either. She was still
waiting. As she had been waiting for seven years.

He returned to be alone with her while Monique settled in.
'Are you still determined to waste your life?'

'I am still determined to spend it usefully, you mean,' she
countered. 'Are you still determined to support the Ch'ing?'

He sighed. 'I'm afraid that, like the Barbarians, I can think
of no alternative. Certainly to hand China over to a bunch of
revolutionary dreamers would be a disaster.'

'You know nothing about it.'

'And you do. Have you heard from your tong recently?'

'I do not think the Shanghai tong still exists. I think it
must have been wiped out, while I was in Port Arthur. Have
you seen Aunt Jo?'

'Yes. I'm very sorry for her.'

'She's alive,' Victoria said, and he saw that her eyes were
filled with tears.

He reverted to the point. 'But you think your friend Tang
is still alive.'

'Tang is my husband, Robert,' she said. 'Yes. I *know* he is still alive.'

'You've heard from him?'

'No, I have not heard from him. But if he were dead, I would have known.'

There seemed little point in arguing with her. Robert began to feel that the only totally sane, and living, member of his family, apart from himself, was Adrian, for so long derided as a misfit. And of course Monique. They were married in the spring, by which time Monique was pregnant. They named their son James, after his grandfather.

Robert was equally pleased with the financial position of the House of Barrington. He knew that the Empire as a whole was labouring under the imposition of the enormous indemnity demanded by the Barbarians. But that had little to do with his business; the House paid its customs dues and other taxes as it had always done; what happened to the money after it left his office he refused to make his concern. And there were encouraging signs that the Barbarians, or at least some of them, were beginning to take a more civilised view of the prospect that was China; the Americans announced that they would use their share of the indemnity to found a university college for Chinese.

As for the Dynasty, that too seemed to have settled into civilised old age. The Boxers had been Tz'u-hsi's last attempt to assert herself and drive out the Barbarians. Robert knew he would never again be her intimate, but from all the reports coming out of Peking, the Old Buddha had mellowed to an unbelievable degree. Of course it was possible that she was engaged in some new plot, conceived within the deep recesses of her cunning brain, but somehow he doubted it. He felt China was entering a new era, in which, he hoped, it would gradually move into the twentieth century.

The changing times were signified firstly by the death of Li Hung-chang, not long after the end of the rebellion, and then of Jung-lu, of asthma, early in 1903. Li had of course been very old, and exhausted by his unremitting labours on behalf of the Dynasty; Robert had a suspicion that Tz'u-hsi might have breathed a sigh of relief at his departure, as they had seldom agreed on how to handle the various crises that had affected her reign, although she had always bowed to his wisdom in the end.

No doubt she was far more disturbed by the death of her old friend and lover, the man who had saved her life back in 1862 when the Hsien-feng Emperor's uncles would have had her murdered. But Jung-lu had also been getting on in years, even if he had been no older than the Empress herself. *She* seemed indestructible, but she could not replace her old paladins. From all reports her new chief minister, Prince Ch'ing – Prince Tuan had been required to commit suicide as a sop to the Barbarians – although a member of the Imperial Household, was a man of neither decision nor talent.

Robert indeed half expected a summons to Peking himself, especially when Robert Hart retired. But it did not come. Tz'u-hsi could not bring herself to forgive – or perhaps she feared his influence. But he was content to be left alone to live his life as he chose, and to find much pleasure and happiness in doing so. He adored his child-bride, who as the years went by became a mature and beautiful woman, and a perfect mother, even if she did not conceive again.

She had corresponded, briefly, with her remaining family in Belgium, and reassured them that she was well and happy; they had been content to accept what had happened rather than attempt to create a diplomatic incident.

He felt a growing confidence in Adrian and ignored the whispered rumours of what went on behind the closed shutters of his brother's house. If only he could persuade Victoria to take a husband and settle down to a proper life, he would not have a care in the world. But in the meantime he could watch Martin grow into a handsome teenager, who was very fond of his young cousin James. Robert would not have been human if he did not remember the stories he had heard of the previous half-caste Barrington, who had commanded the T'ai-P'ing armies against his own family, and relate them to Martin's father. But that character had totally disappeared, and Martin gave no sign of possessing a rebellious nature.

Even if his mother apparently never gave up hope of being reunited with her lover.

*

At the beginning of 1907 Joanna died. She was seventy-five years old, the very last link with the tumultuous days of the mid-nineteenth century. But she had been more than that to Victoria. Not only had Joanna been the first person with whom she had shared her secret, they had also shared that dreadful experience when Port Arthur had fallen. Since then Joanna, her mind dulled by the loss of her beloved Arthur, had seemed to spark into life only when in the company of her niece.

But her death made Victoria think. She knew Robert was right, and she had to start considering the future. She had waited for thirteen years for Tang to come back into her life, or indeed to hear something from or about Sun Yat-sen. She did hear of him from time to time, but never in China. Now she was thirty-three. Her youth was gone. As was her youthful adventure. It had all been so romantic, so daring, so revolutionary ... and so brief! Now Martin was almost thirteen. The boy had never asked any questions about his heritage. He did not need to. He was the son and heir of Robert Barrington ... he assumed. He remembered his 'mother' and grieved for her death. He had never asked any questions about that, either, but he was going to, eventually.

As for his 'aunt' ... Victoria had no doubt that he loved her, because they had been so close in recent years. How she wanted more than that! How many times had she been tempted to tell him the truth, and had had the sense and the self-control not to? But his future worried her. Robert had as

yet given no inkling of what might be in his mind and the
two boys were treated with exact equality, even by Monique.
Victoria was not even sure if Monique knew the truth,
although given the continuous evidence of how much Robert
adored his wife and shared everything with her, she had to
suppose she did. But in any event Monique and Robert had
a son who was pure white and who was equally Robert's
own, as opposed to an adopted son whose father was a
revolutionary. They could have no doubt as to which of the
boys was the true Barrington heir.

Victoria had no desire to oppose her brother, or to oust
little James from his rights. After the death of her father she
had survived only because of the news, received immediately after the funeral, to Adrian's consternation, that
Robert was after all alive and would be coming home. All
she sought was for Martin to have a full and prosperous life.

It was something she was going to have to discuss with
Robert, soon enough. But she knew that would involve a
discussion of her future as well. So . . . back to square one.
Was he right, and her life totally wasted? Was it too late to
begin again? The scandal was a long time in the past . . . but
she could not be sure it would not start up all over again
should she take up with any prospective husband.

Supposing there could ever be one. Men might still turn
their heads to look at her when they passed her on the street,
but none ever came calling any more. Miss Victoria
Barrington was known to be an odd one; no doubt there were
as many rumours spread about the depravity of her private
life as there had ever been about Adrian – or about Robert
in recent years: an endless topic of conversation was of how
the Master of the House had used the Boxer upheaval to
kidnap for himself a Belgian bride who had been nothing
more than a schoolgirl.

But obviously there were decisions to be made, if she
could just manage to arrive at one. In the meantime she
proceeded on her way, keeping house for her brother –
Monique had made no attempt to usurp her prerogatives –

and dreaming her dreams. Until the morning when she went to the market in Shanghai, unaccompanied as she had not felt the need of an attendant servant since joining the tong, and, looking across a meat stall, saw Ching San.

*

Victoria's heart seemed to give a little jump; for a moment she could not think. Ching San waited to be sure she had both seen him and identified him, then he turned and walked into the crowd. He knew she would follow him. She paid for her purchase with trembling fingers, then set off, as casually as she could, smiling and nodding to people, but moving towards that so well-remembered street.

The street was empty save for a few dogs and urchins, who stared at the Barbarian woman in amazement; none of them would have been born when last she walked here. She went past them, reached the corner, and looked down the alleyway. Ching San waited a few feet away. 'I thought you were dead,' Victoria said.

He grinned. 'I serve the tong. As do you, Miss Victoria. There is one would speak with you.' He opened the door and stepped inside.

Heart pounding, Victoria followed. The tong house remained the wreck the viceregal Bannermen had left it following their raid; the door hung on its hinges and the shuttered windows were also smashed. She closed her parasol and peered into the gloom beyond, at cobwebs and dust, heard the scurrying of rats. She pushed the broken timbers aside and stepped through, waiting for her eyes to become accustomed to the gloom. She could not see Ching San. But there, at the head of the stairs, was Tang Li-chun.

Immediately the thirteen years since she had first seen him, just like this, need never have been. The only difference was that today he wore Chinese clothes; that apart he did not seem to have altered in any way. 'I see you have not changed, Victoria,' Tang said. 'You are as foolhardy as you always were.'

'Did you not wish me to come to you?'

'Of course. But you were still very foolish to do so.'

'Am I not a member of your tong?' She crossed the floor, her boots echoing on the wooden boards. A rat ran in front of her, but Victoria was not afraid of rats. She looked up the steps, and he turned and went into the bedroom. She hesitated only a moment before going up. Perhaps she had never really expected any more effusive a greeting than this, however much she might have hoped. The steps were rotting and she had to tread carefully, but she reached the top and pushed open the door. He sat on the bed, which was made up with a new mattress, a blanket, and a pillow; he had been using it for some time.

'Why are you not married?' he demanded.

'I am married. To you.' She pushed the door shut.

'That is very foolish of you, Victoria.'

'So I have been told.' She sat beside him. 'But it is what I wish. You are looking well.'

'And you ...' At last he touched her, taking off her hat and releasing the pins which held her hair, so that it tumbled in dark profusion past her shoulders. 'You are more beautiful than ever.' She turned, into his arms.

*

'We have a son,' she told him, as they lay naked together. She had been like a virgin again, but the experience had been no less delicious. She wondered how many women he had had in the past thirteen years. But he had come back to her, at last. However briefly.

'I know.'

'You mean you have known about me, all of these years, and not come to me?'

'I would have been unsafe, after the destruction of the tong.'

'I would never have betrayed you.'

'I could not be certain of that.'

'So you employed Ching San to spy on me.'

'Not at all. When you left Shanghai for Port Arthur, Ching San felt unsafe. I think before then he had counted on your presence, as a fellow tong member, to protect him. But with you gone, he fled to me. He has proved a very faithful servant.'

'You mean you have been in China all of these years and never attempted to see me?'

'I have not been in China all of these years,' Tang said patiently. 'Much of our work is done outside of China.'

Victoria realised she was wasting time in senseless recriminations. 'But you have come to see me now. Do you wish to see your son?'

Tang sat up. 'You have told him about me?'

'No. But I wish to. Will you give me permission?'

'He is too young to understand. Perhaps afterwards.'

Victoria frowned. 'After what?'

'After the triumph of Dr Sun.'

Now she sat up as well, her shoulder against his. 'Now?'

'As soon as the Dowager Empress dies. It cannot be long now. She is seventy-two years old, and we have heard that she is not in the best of health.'

'Then why must you wait until she is dead? Are you so afraid of that old woman?'

Tang did not take offence. 'When she dies there will be much uncertainty.'

'Will not the Kuang-hsu Emperor resume his reign?'

'It will be his duty to do so,' Tang agreed. 'But he has not reigned for nearly ten years. In that time he has been mostly a prisoner. As I have said, there will be much uncertainty. Dr Sun is of the opinion that our time may then be ripe. But we must be prepared. We will need your help.'

She turned her head. 'Is that the only reason why you have come back to me?'

He put his arms round her, cupped her breasts, drew her down to him as he lay down. 'Do you not think I would have come before, if I could?'

She sighed. He was here. That was all that mattered. 'What help can I give you? Have you a new tong?'

'It is too dangerous here on the coast. We are going to establish our Yangtse headquarters at Hankow. Have you been there? The House of Barrington has warehouses there.'

'I have been there. Many years ago. Do you wish me to go there again? Will you be there?'

'When the time is right.'

'When will that be?'

'When we are ready. To be ready, we need arms and ammunition. Modern rifles. Machine-guns. We wish you to obtain these for us. We do not expect you to be able to supply cannon. These we will have to capture for ourselves. There is an arsenal at Hankow. If we can seize that, we will have an unlimited supply of weapons. But first, we need the guns to capture the arsenal.'

Victoria pushed herself off his chest to look at him. 'Just how am I supposed to procure rifles and machine-guns?'

'The House of Barrington imports many things. Why should it not import arms and ammunition?'

'There is no reason. Save that I am not Mistress of the House.'

'You will appeal to your brother.'

'That would be worse than useless. Robert stands for the Ch'ing even more than did my father.'

Tang's eyes became opaque. 'Then you refuse to help us?'

'For God's sake, Tang, do you not think I would if I could? But for me to mention a word of this, even your name, to Robert would be a disaster for us all. Including Dr Sun.'

His hands fell away. 'That is a pity.' Gently he moved her off him, got up and began to dress. 'I must leave. Before your brother discovers that I am here.'

She gazed at him in total dismay. He had come back, not for love of her, but to enlist her aid. Now, as she would not help him, he was going to leave, and she would never see him again. And would that not be good riddance? He did not love her. He considered her some kind of chattel. She was Victoria Barrington. Was she to be treated like dirt, by a man her brother would not even allow in the front door?

But he was the only man she had ever loved, or ever would love. And he was the father of her child. Nothing else mattered than that. Tang was dressed. 'Do not leave for fifteen minutes.' Even when abandoning her, he was giving her orders.

She drew a deep breath. To help him would mean an almost impossible sacrifice. But was not thirteen years an impossible sacrifice? And to help him would mean she would be at his side. If she made certain of it. He was at the door. 'Wait,' she said. 'I will get you your guns and ammunition.'

He turned. 'You have just said you cannot.'

'I have two brothers.'

'And the younger one will help you? We hear bad stories of this brother.'

'He will help me,' Victoria said.

Tang came back towards her. 'Then listen. The guns and bullets must be shipped up to Hankow. You must arrange to have someone trustworthy there to see that they are available for our use. When they are there, you will inform me.'

'Will you be in Hankow?'

'I will be close by.'

Victoria licked her lips. 'I will help you on one condition, Tang.'

'You will make conditions with me?'

'If you wish the guns, yes.'

He looked at her for several seconds. Then he asked, 'What is this condition?'

'I will deliver the guns to Hankow personally. I will see that they are kept for your use. But I will also remain in Hankow. I wish to be with you. Whatever happens after I have delivered the guns, I wish to be with you.'

He frowned. 'Victoria, when we get the guns we will

make war on the Ch'ing. Many people will be killed. Perhaps I will be killed.'

'That is all the more reason that I wish to be with you.'

'Perhaps *you* will be killed.'

'I am not afraid of that.'

'We will have to live in the mountains. Life will be very hard.'

'I am not afraid of that, either.'

He looked at her pink and white beauty, the manicured perfection of her hands. But he could see, too, perhaps for the first time, the strength of her mind. 'You will never see your family again.'

'Of course I will see my family again, Tang,' she said. 'When we have won, and the Ch'ing are overthrown, and we enter cities like Peking and Shanghai in triumph.'

'And if we do not overthrow the Ch'ing, you may find yourself being publicly executed. Not even your brother will be able to save your life, if you are discovered to be an agent of the Kuomintang.'

'Do you not believe we will triumph, Tang?'

'Of course I do. But it is necessary to look at both sides of a coin.'

'You have done so. Now agree to my terms, and I will get you your weapons.'

*

Wu Ping bowed low before her master. 'Miss Victoria is here,' she said.

Adrian frowned, stepped past the woman, and stood in the open doorway of his sitting room. Victoria was seated on the window-seat, her back to the pane. Never, he thought, had she looked so beautiful, with her hair unusually arranged in a Western-style pompadour. She wore the latest Western fashion, her waist pulled in to accentuate at once the swell of her breasts and her hips, and her skirts had ridden up over her knees to reveal her boots and stockings. She made him feel almost sick with desire for her. But he allowed no trace of his feelings to enter his tone. 'I am privileged,' he remarked.

'I need your help.' Her tone was brusque, business-like. There was no other way to approach the situation.

He sat opposite her, one leg carelessly thrown across the other. 'You need my help,' he echoed, and observed that for all her air of studied calm, she was very nervous. Her fingers, twined together, could not keep still, and she was sweating more heavily than the warmth of the day occasioned.

'Does that not please you?' she asked.

'I am sure it does, or will. Tell me what I can do for you?'

'What I have to say must remain a secret between you and me.' He got up and closed the door. 'I am about to place my life in your hands,' Victoria said.

Adrian sat beside her on the window-seat. He separated her hands, and took one between his. Still holding it, he placed the back of his hand against the bodice of her gown. 'How it swells as you breathe. I promise you, dear sister, that I shall take the greatest care of your life.'

*

The butler stammered with excitement. 'The Marshal is here, master,' he said. 'The Marshal.'

Robert looked up from his newspaper, while Monique did the same from her sewing. It was a Sunday morning, and she had only recently returned from church; Robert did not attend. Now he stood up to greet the short, heavy-set man who was waiting in the hall of the Barrington Mansion – wearing civilian clothes and looking like nothing so much as a prosperous merchant.

Robert could not remember ever seeing Yuan Shih-k'ai out of uniform. Since Chang Tsin's execution, he had lacked an ear in the Forbidden City, but from the reports of his various agents he was well aware how the famous soldier had prospered since he had refused to become involved in the Boxer fiasco. He remained Viceroy of Shantung Province, and there he had created almost a miniature kingdom for himself, with an army which it was said was the equal of any in China, trained on the Japanese model and clad in Western uniforms as well. Tz'u-hsi accepted this, apparently, as she still regarded Yuan as her first line of defence against the Japanese. He was her Last Bannerman.

But to see him here in Shanghai . . . Obviously, when one viceroy entered the territory of another, it was necessary for him to do so privately. But Robert would never forget the last time Yuan Shih-k'ai had called on him privately. 'Yuan!' He extended both his hands, and had them clasped firmly while the Marshal looked up into his eyes, searchingly, as was his custom.

'Barrington! I happened to be on a journey to visit one of my relatives, and felt I could not allow the opportunity to pass of calling on my old comrade-in-arms.'

'Then welcome indeed,' Robert said, even though he knew the Marshal was lying. 'You have not met my wife.'

At twenty-three Monique had reached a breathtaking maturity and was the more beautiful with her Western-style pompadour, and the slight breathlessness with which she greeted her guest. 'I have heard so much about you,' Yuan said. 'Of how Barrington carried you off from beneath the very hands of the Boxers. There is true romance.'

Monique glanced at her husband, still shy whenever that episode was recalled. 'He saved my life.'

'And now you make him happy. That is as it should be.'

'Will you take tea, your excellency?'

'That would be very nice.' Yuan stepped on to the verandah and looked out at the garden, the flowing stream the gently rustling willows.

'Leave us,' Robert mouthed at Monique.

'Then I will go and have it prepared,' Monique said, and swept from the room in a seethe of silk.

Yuan continued to look at the garden. 'You are singularly

blessed, Barrington. All of this . . . Is it permitted to inspect your flowers more closely?'

'I should like you to.' Robert accompanied him down the steps. He could only be patient, until Yuan decided to say whatever he had in mind.

'The House of Barrington,' Yuan mused, strolling along the path. 'More than a hundred years of prosperity.'

'We have had our ups and downs,' Robert reminded him.

'That is the way of life. But I have no doubt that you look forward to another hundred years of prosperity, for your dependents.'

'In so far as any man dare look that far ahead.'

Yuan found a bench down one of the side paths, and seated himself, fanning himself with his hat. 'Do you still see much of Tz'u-hsi?'

Robert sat beside him. 'I have not seen Tz'u-hsi for nearly seven years. I did not support her over the Boxers, and she has not forgiven me.'

Yuan gave a brief smile. 'I doubt that she has forgiven me, either, for pleading illness. However, as we have both served her in our time,' – he did not seem aware of the double entendre – 'we must both be prepared to forgive her. No doubt we will both mourn at her passing.'

'Is this imminent?'

'She is an old woman. Her death must be imminent. Have you given any thought to what happens after she is gone, Barrington?'

'I assume the Kuang-hsu Emperor will resume his reign.'

'You say that very casually. Do you imagine that the Kuang-hsu has forgotten that it was you and I and Jung-lu who overthrew him in 1898? Jung-lu is dead. We are alive. And I for one intend to stay that way. Do you keep in touch with what is happening in the country as well as in Peking?'

'In so far as I can.'

'Have you ever heard of the Kuomintang? It is a revolutionary society dedicated to driving out the Manchu, founded by a man called Sun Yat-sen.'

'I have heard of Sun Yat-sen,' Robert said, suddenly tense. 'But not recently.'

'I can tell you that he has paid several visits to China recently. Without being caught. This is because he has a considerable network of tongs working for him, willing to take risks to preserve him and his republican ideals. Sun Yat-sen is also aware of the Dowager Empress's age. It is my belief that he is only awaiting her death to promote his revolution. So you will see that Tz'u-hsi's death will cause us many problems, both from above and below, as it were.'

'And you have a solution to these problems?'

'Of course. Have we not worked together before, successfully? Now it is more than ever important that we work together. China is about to enter a period of great uncertainty. The only way to overcome uncertainty is to be strong. I have the strength. But an army needs to be paid, regardless of what is happening to the national economy. You have the financial strength to back me. You will have my word that you will be repaid, every tael.'

'To help you to do what, exactly?'

'To overcome chaos, and create a strong China.'

'To replace the Ch'ing, you mean. I am sorry, Yuan. There are many things about the Dynasty I abhor. But I am sworn to uphold them.'

Yuan gave a gentle smile. 'I have said nothing of overthrowing the Ch'ing, Barrington. What I have said is that with Tz'u-hsi dead, we cannot permit the Kuang-hsu Emperor to reign, or he will have our heads. But there are other princes, suitably young princes, who could become the Son of Heaven.'

'With you as regent?'

'I do not think I am suited for such a position. I would be army commander.'

'So you would control the regent.'

'I would *advise* him,' Yuan said. 'He will need me, to crush this Kuomintang and maintain order.'

Robert studied him. But he knew that Yuan was uttering

sound common sense. The Kuang-hsu would indeed not have forgiven the men responsible for his overthrow. And after Tz'u-hsi's death there would most certainly be chaos, especially if Sun Yat-sen was allowed a free hand; what Robert had seen of revolutions and revolutionaries was more than enough to last him a lifetime. But he would not be a party to murder. 'And the Kuang-hsu?'

'Honourable retirement, in close confinement?'

'I have your word?'

'Of course,' Yuan said. 'I see your charming wife on the verandah. Shall we not go and take tea?'

13

THE END OF AN ERA

Robert entertained Yuan Shih-k'ai to dinner. It was a glittering occasion, with several of Shanghai's principal foreign merchants and their ladies present. But most of the guests had eyes only for the two Barrington women.

Victoria wore a shoulderless black gown, revealing gleaming white skin in a plunging décolletage; her black hair was loose on her shoulders. Sparkling rings adorned her fingers, but her eyes, like her smile, were guarded, except when she looked at her handsome thirteen-year-old son.

Monique's dark green gown had shoulders, but hardly less décolletage. Her auburn hair was as usual upswept in a pompadour, and she wore but a single wedding ring, although round her neck there was the pearl choker Robert had given her as a wedding present. But her entire face was alive as she smiled and entertained her guests, paying particular attention to the famous soldier who sat on her right.

'Your brother is a lucky man, to possess two such magnificent women,' one of the guests remarked to Adrian, who had also been persuaded to attend this most special occasion.

Adrian gave one of his secretive smiles. 'Why, I doubt he *possesses* either of them. Robert is not a possessive man.'

*

Next day Yuan was on his way, and Robert called on Victoria. 'Thank you for attending the dinner.'

She inclined her head. 'I suppose it does no one any harm to remember I am still alive.'

He sat beside her. Over the past week he had noticed a certain change in her demeanour. She had looked more alert, more interested in what was happening around her ... and at the same time, more defiant. And that was disturbing. As disturbing as what Yuan had had to say. 'Vicky, I want to ask you a question, and I want you to promise to answer me truthfully.' She bent her head over her sewing. 'Have you heard anything from Tang recently?'

'I thought you said I would never hear from him again.'

'I would like you to answer my question.'

She raised her head and looked at him with her enormous blue eyes. 'Have you heard of him? That he is in Shanghai?'

He bit his lip; he was being outmanoeuvred. 'I have heard nothing of Tang. But I have heard of his master. Why do you think Yuan came here? It was to warn me that Sun means to foment a revolution, probably the moment Tz'u-hsi dies.'

Victoria bent over her sewing again. 'That rumour has been going the rounds for fifteen years.'

'Yuan is taking it seriously. Because Tz'u-hsi *is* probably going to die some time soon. Vicky, should you be approached by the tong ...'

'What tong, Robert? It was wiped out years ago.'

'Perhaps, here in Shanghai. But I have no doubt it still exists. I want you to promise me that should you be approached to help them in any way, you will tell me immediately.'

'Of course. If you wish me to.'

'Do you swear that, Vicky, by everything you hold sacred?'

'Does anything I may hold sacred mean anything to you, Robert?'

He sighed. 'Vicky, it could mean your life. If there were to be a revolution, and you were found to have helped Sun Yat-sen in any way, I am not sure even I could save you from execution.'

She half smiled. 'Very well, Robert. If I am approached by any member of the tong, in the future, I will come and tell you about it.'

He wasn't sure he was any further ahead; certainly she had not actually given any promise. But he did not suppose he would obtain anything better.

*

Victoria went for a walk that evening, in the cool, and when she knew Adrian would have returned from the office. She felt a strange mixture of exhilaration and self-disgust, of satisfaction mingled with fear.

Her upbringing in the midst of the startling cultural contrasts that was China had left her morally aseptic. Her mother's endeavours to educate her as a Christian had seemed meaningless when she had always been surrounded by a complete negation of all Christian principles. Faith, hope and charity had little part in the Chinese philosophy. But even the Chinese regarded incest as a crime, punishable, indeed, by death. She did not suppose the fact that she hated her brother and herself for what they did would make much difference; she went to him willingly enough, for whatever reason. But, like all Chinese citizens, she had lived in the presence of death for so long it no longer held any terrors for her.

Yet Adrian had frightened her, as he had shocked and disgusted her. She had not before come into contact with the true depths of a man's mind. He frightened her because, in

his arms, nothing mattered. Or was it simply true that
nothing mattered compared with the immensity of what she
was taking part in, and which involved lying to, and indeed
betraying, the only brother she truly loved?

Wu Ping bowed before her as she opened the door. If the
Chinese woman felt the slightest pang of jealousy that she
had been replaced she did not reveal it. Victoria supposed
she might actually be relieved.

She went into the back parlour. The doors were open to
the garden and it was an idyllic scene. Adrian reclined on his
settee in an undressing robe, watching the setting sun. He did
not rise when she entered. 'Close the door,' he said.

Victoria obeyed. Her heart was pounding and her hands
inside her gloves were clammy. She had to lick her lips
before she could speak. 'Has the order gone?' she asked.

'Yesterday morning.' He chuckled. 'It was on its way
while that fat toad was actually sitting at Robert's table.'

She stood beside him, looking down at him. 'How long
will it take for the goods to be delivered?'

'About three months.'

'Three months,' she muttered, and felt his hand on her leg,
sliding up the material of her gown to her thigh. Three
months of this? At the end of it she would be utterly
debauched.

'It gives us the time to make other preparations,' he said,
his hand closing on her buttocks in a gentle squeeze. 'Such
as getting you up to Hankow.'

'Will you help me there, too?' She sat beside him.

'Of course. Providing you come to see me, regularly.' He
sat up and unbuttoned her blouse. She wore several layers of
petticoat, but he was not concerned, merely felt his way
through the material to the softness beneath.

'What do you wish to do to me today?' she asked.

'Today . . . today I would have the Jade Girl play upon my
Flute . . . I have dreamed of that, from you, for a long time.'

'You . . . you are unspeakable. I will not do it.'

'Then shall I tell Robert that I have inadvertently ordered

a consignment of modern rifles and ammunition and suggest he sells them to Marshal Yuan? Or the Ch'ing?'

Victoria glared at him, and he grinned, then took her in his arms and kissed her on the mouth. 'Enjoy yourself,' he told her. 'You will, if you would just let yourself. Now strip.'

'You are obscene.' But she obeyed him.

'And you are ungrateful. Do you realise how much I am doing for you?'

'And you do not feel I am doing anything for you back.' She hugged herself, trembling.

'Oh, it is very pleasant to have you being nice to me, Vicky. But man cannot live by sex alone. The time will come when I shall call upon you to repay me for my assistance.'

Victoria frowned. 'What do you mean?'

Adrian lay back, arranging himself comfortably. 'I do not know whether or not your revolution will succeed. I do know that you will foment a great upheaval. It will be a general time for change, in my opinion. I feel that, whether your friends succeed in toppling the Ch'ing or not, it will be a time for change in the House of Barrington. Now, if Dr Sun emerges the victor, there should be no problem. I supported him, Robert did not. If Dr Sun fails, well, there will have to be a little rearranging of facts. The House of Barrington will have shipped arms and ammunition to the rebels. Granted that my signature is on the order. But I always, and only ever, do what I am commanded to by my elder brother, the Master of the House. So there again, it will be time for the traitor to be replaced. Do you understand me?' He put his arm round her naked shoulders, gently stroking the flesh.

'I find you incredible. You mean to replace Robert as Master?'

'Should I not? Have you forgotten I was virtually Master for several years, while Robert was away, and Father was retired?'

'And what do you intend to do with him? He will not relinquish control quietly.'

'I do not see he will have a choice, if he is arrested by

whichever government is in power on a charge of treason.'

Victoria frowned at him. 'You would be risking his execution.'

'Why, yes, I suppose I would,' Adrian agreed.

'You . . . I could never allow that.'

'Why not? Has Robert ever done anything for you? Oh, he and that Chinese whore of his took your son off your hands. But do you suppose Robert has any intention of ever allowing Martin to inherit?'

Victoria bit her lip; he was putting her thoughts into words.

'Exactly,' Adrian said. 'Martin is going to spend his entire life as dogsbody to his cousin, just as you are going to spend your entire life bowing and scraping to your sister-in-law, unless you do something about it.' He grinned. 'Now there is someone I would like to have in here as my slave. God, to get my hands on that ass . . .' Victoria shrugged off his hand and stood up. 'Whereas,' Adrian went on, 'when I am in control of the House, I will make Martin my heir.'

She turned to look at him.

'On my oath. Does that not make you happy?'

'I will not help you murder our brother,' Victoria said, as evenly as she could. 'If necessary, I shall tell him everything.'

'And be executed yourself? You know Chinese law. If you are executed, Martin will die too. And your friend Tang will be hunted down. And the revolution will certainly fail. If you suppose Robert will protect you, well . . .' Adrian smiled. 'You have told me how disgusted he was with you when you confessed your affair with Tang. What do you suppose he will do if he learns of your affair with me? I agree, he is a soft-hearted fellow. He might not have you executed. But he will certainly expel you from the House and from China. With your son. What would you do then, Vicky? I think you need to consider your position very seriously.'

Victoria pulled on her drawers.

'Oh, take those off,' Adrian said. 'I prefer you naked.'

'I am going home,' Victoria said.

'Not yet, my dearest sister. You have not yet played upon the flute.'

*

All Peking was agog that summer, because of the Peking to Paris motor race. The Chinese peasants had never seen automobiles before, and the arrival of the contestants caused a sensation, while the idea that they were actually going to drive across China, and then Russia, and then all of Europe, whether or not there were roads available ... some of the Manchus indeed felt that it was all part of a Russian plot to invade the Empire with these strange, noisy, smelly contraptions, and tried to place all the competitors under arrest. But most people regarded the project as a sign that China had at last moved into the twentieth century, and the Dowager Empress received much praise for her encouragement of the contest.

Tz'u-hsi sat in her straight chair, which had been especially carried into the garden behind her apartments for the occasion. Now she gestured her inquisitive eunuchs and ladies to either side, to form a vast group. 'Where do I look?' she inquired.

The photographer was very nervous. He was an American, and had never expected to be granted this concession, even if he had paid Prince Ch'ing an inordinate bribe. Now he was here, and actually facing the most infamous woman of her time.

He had to lick his lips before he could speak. 'I will hold up my hand, Your Majesty. Look at my hand.'

'Do we all look at your hand?'

'If you would be so kind, Your Majesty.'

The princes of the blood, grouped to one side and out of camera, muttered to each other. This was unheard of. The Emperor certainly disapproved. But then, what the Emperor might approve or disapprove of, was irrelevant.

The photographer held out his hand, and the heads before him turned. There was a puff of smoke and one of the ladies shrieked in terror. 'Take that idiot away and cane her,' Tz'u-hsi snapped. 'Is the portrait spoiled?'

'I should not think so, Your Majesty, but I would like to take another, in any event.'

'Then do so.' The photographer waited while the weeping girl was dragged away by two of the eunuchs. The second time there were no shrieks of terror, and no movement. The photographer bowed, gathered up his equipment, and was hurried from the garden. Tz'u-hsi waved her hand, and her people dispersed, leaving her seated alone.

Prince Ch'ing approached. 'I think that will be very helpful, Your Majesty.'

'Helpful,' Tz'u-hsi growled. 'Helpful to whom?'

She was not in a good mood, and Prince Ch'ing twisted his hands together. 'It creates a good image with the Barbarians, Majesty.'

'The Barbarians,' Tz'u-hsi said contemptuously. 'Fetch that girl back. I wish her caned before me. Stupid girl. Fetch her back.'

'Yes, Your Majesty.' Ch'ing signalled to the eunuchs, and twisted his hands together again. But he had a duty to perform; not to do so would make matters worse. 'I have a report here, Your Majesty . . .'

'Report? All you ever give me are reports.'

'They keep us informed of what is happening in the Empire, Your Majesty. This concerns Marshal Yuan Shih-k'ai.'

Tz'u-hsi's head turned, slightly. She was listening.

'The Marshal has been visiting Shanghai, Majesty. While there, he spent much time with Barrington.'

'They have been friends for many years.'

'The Marshal is an ambitious man, Majesty.'

'I know that. But he is loyal to me. So is Barrington. Barrington,' she said softly. 'I must see him again, before . . .' She glanced at her minister. Ch'ing swallowed. She had nearly put the dread thought into words. 'What is troubling you?' Tz'u-hsi asked.

'It concerns me, Majesty, when two such powerful men meet.'

'Conspiracies,' Tz'u-hsi snapped. 'Always conspiracies.' Her hand slapped the arm of her chair, and Prince Ch'ing shivered. Like all those who had ever served Tz'u-hsi, he had learned to fear her outbursts of temper. 'Those men are my friends!' Tz'u-hsi shouted. 'I will not have calumny spread about my friends.' The veins were standing out in her forehead even beneath the caked white make-up. 'I will not have it, I tell you. I will . . .' Rising from her chair, she gave a little gasp, and fell back with a thump which dislodged her head-dress.

The eunuchs started forward, and then checked, afraid to move. For a moment Prince Ch'ing was also afraid to move, then he realised that his aunt was rigid in her chair, and slowly slipping from it to the ground. 'Help Her Majesty,' he shouted.

Ladies and eunuchs clustered round as Tz'u-hsi was carried into her apartment. There she was laid on her bed, but the eunuchs were afraid to do anything else. Tz'u-hsi was not speaking, but her eyes were open and glaring at them.

Prince Ch'ing sent for doctors, including an Englishman who was with the Legation. No doctor would ever be allowed to examine the Dowager Empress, of course, any more than he would ever be allowed to examine the Emperor. He could not even look at her, had to remain in an antechamber. But Ch'ing was able to describe the symptoms. 'Her Majesty has had a stroke,' Dr Burroughs said. 'That is quite obvious.'

'There is also . . .' Ch'ing gazed at him with a peculiar expression. 'Very unpleasant.'

'Yes,' Burroughs said. 'She will have no control over her bowels, and she will be suffering from a stomach disorder.'

'What is to be done?' Ch'ing asked. 'Will she recover?'

'I believe she may, if she has absolute rest. We must wait. And pray.'

*

Tz'u-hsi recovered, slowly, but, it seemed, completely. She wished to keep the news of her collapse secret, but that was impossible, and word slowly leaked out to the provinces.

Robert expected to hear from Yuan, but did not. And he was distracted, although pleased, by the sudden interest Victoria appeared to be taking in the business. 'Well,' she explained, 'if, as seems likely, I am to be an old maid, I would like to have something to do. With the House. Will you make me a branch manager?'

Robert stroked his chin.

'You are worrying about what sort of treatment I would get from the Barbarians. I don't want to deal with them. Let me deal with the Chinese. Let me go to Hankow, and manage the office there. At least give me a chance, Robert. I would take Martin with me.'

'Vicky, Martin will have his fair share in the House. I want you to understand that.'

'I do understand that,' Victoria said. 'I would like us to learn about the business, together.'

*

It was absurdly easy. Robert was so anxious to be nice to her, to rehabilitate her, she supposed, the more so as Adrian was wholeheartedly behind her idea. Robert was a total innocent in the way he trusted his family, continued to leave the ordering of goods to Adrian, and thus had no idea that guns and ammunition were being shipped into Shanghai under the House flag. Victoria accompanied the first shipment up-river in the spring of 1908. Adrian had arranged for her to rent a house, and she and Martin moved in, thrilled with the journey on the great waterway. But Victoria also waited for

Tang. He arrived a week after her, late at night, with Martin
already in bed.

'The guns are here,' she told him. 'Safely hidden in our
warehouse. And I am in charge. Tell me what you wish me
to do.'

'I wish you to wait. The old devil is dying. It will not be
long now.'

'Then, as we have to wait . . .'

*

Tz'u-hsi had recovered from her stroke, but she never did
shake off her recurrent bouts of dysentery, exacerbated by
her refusal to change her eating habits, which grew more and
more outlandish. Throughout 1908 her health slowly deteriorated, and at last even she realised that her time was fast
approaching. Now she had discovered a new hobby: photo-
graphy. She knew nothing of it herself, but, perhaps in a
desperate search for at least the immortality of celluloid, she
had herself photographed time and again, often inviting
European ladies to take tea with her in the Forbidden City so
that they could form part of the group.

The fact that the woman who had ruined his life was
approaching the end of hers was not lost upon the Emperor,
and Tz'u-hsi's temper was not improved when Prince
Ch'ing brought her a note which was supposed to have been
written by the Kuang-hsu. It said: 'We were the second son
of Prince Ch'un when the Dowager Empress selected us for
the Throne. She has always hated Us. For Our misery of the
past ten years, Yuan Shih-k'ai is responsible, and one other.
When the time comes, I desire that these men be summarily
beheaded.' Tz'u-hsi glared at the Prince. 'What effrontery!
Who is this, one other?'

'No one knows, Majesty. It is supposed that it is Jung-lu.'

'Jung-lu has been dead these five years,' Tz'u-hsi snapped. 'Barrington! I wonder if he means Barrington? It is no
matter. The Emperor has displayed himself in his true

colours. I will appoint a successor. Prince P'u-i.'

Ch'ing goggled at her in dismay. P'u-i was only two years old, but he was the grandson of Prince Ch'un. On the other hand, his father, Prince Ch'un II, had not been the son of Tz'u-hsi's sister, but of a concubine, and thus had none of Tz'u-hsi's blood in his veins. But in any event . . . 'Majesty,' Ch'ing ventured. 'You cannot appoint a new emperor while the Kuang-hsu lives.'

Tz'u-hsi gazed at him. 'Why, Prince Ch'ing,' she said. 'You are absolutely right. But still, it is our responsibility to be ready for every eventuality. Have the pronouncement prepared.' Prince Ch'ing trembled as he performed the kowtow before leaving.

Tz'u-hsi sent for Li Lien-lung. 'How is the Emperor's health?' she asked.

'It is as you wish, Majesty,' Li Lien-lung said.

The Kuang-hsu's eunuchs were all Tz'u-hsi's creatures, and kept him drugged and medicated to her requirements.

'I think the Heavenly Chariot awaits his presence,' Tz'u-hsi said. Li Lien-lung swallowed. To murder an emperor . . . and there was only himself to know who had given the order. 'You must be discreet,' Tz'u-hsi said. Her lip curled as she watched the eunuch tremble. 'Do not fear. It will happen before me. You have but to do as I tell you.'

*

The next day, 14 November 1908, word was brought to Tz'u-hsi that the Emperor was dying. Despite her own ill-health, and her now excessive weight, she waddled along the corridors to the Kuang-hsu's apartments just after five that afternoon, the Hour of the Cock. The Empress Lung-yu and the Lustrous Concubine were with their husband and master, tears rolling down their cheeks as they performed the kowtow at Tz'u-hsi's entry. Tz'u-hsi looked from one to the other, then advanced to stand by her adopted son's bed. The Kuang-hsu opened his mouth as if he would have spoken.

But no sound came, and he fell back upon his cushions, his mouth still open. His face was blackened, and his hands twitched convulsively. Then all movement ceased.

*

It was all so familiar, Tz'u-hsi thought, as at dawn she entered the Great Council Chamber and surveyed the assembled princes and mandarins, to tell them, firstly, of the Emperor's death, and then of her choice as his successor. She watched them all bow in acquiescence, and felt the most utter contempt for them. Thirty-three years before, when they had met for this purpose, there had been some opposition. Ten members of the Council had actually voted for other choices. There had been men in those days. She thought of Kung and Li Hung-chang, of Jung-lu, even of the scholar Wan Li-chung. Now there were none left, she thought, as she looked at Ch'ing, and the younger Ch'un. Not in the Council, at any rate. There were still men in the Empire. Yuan Shih-k'ai, and Barrington.

But were they conspiring against her? Laying plans for after she was dead? She would surprise them yet. As to whether she would order their executions ... it might be a fitting act, she felt. Yuan was a Chinese, and would never truly love the Manchus, or herself. Barrington ... had Barrington ever truly loved her? Or had he just used her body, her needs, as a stepping-stone to greater things? Yes, she thought, as she sat down to her midday meal; they deserved to die.

She surveyed the table before her, the myriad dishes.

'What does Your Majesty desire?' asked Li Lien-lung. He was afraid to leave her side for a moment.

Tz'u-hsi sighed. She did not feel well. She had not felt well for so long. But now that the Kuang-hsu, that hateful boy, was finally gone, she would surely soon feel better. And over there ... 'Is that not my favourite dish?' she asked. 'Crab apples and clotted cream?'

Li Lien-lung signalled to the other eunuchs, and the rich food was piled on a plate and placed before Tz'u-hsi. She ate slowly, relishing the taste of each mouthful, while her eunuchs and ladies waited. She was nearly finished when she gave a gasp and retched. Everyone started forward together as the Dowager Empress fainted, her head falling into the cream. Li Lien-lung gave the orders and Tz'u-hsi was hastily carried to her chamber. There she was washed clean and dressed in the Robes of Longevity. But when she recovered consciousness, Tz'u-hsi knew that the Heavenly Chariot was waiting for her as well.

To Li Lien-lung she dictated a valediction. In it she recalled her girlhood in Wuhu, when she had been wooed by James Barrington, and had first seen Jung-lu; how she had been forced to flee before the T'ai-P'ing; how she had been presented at court and chosen as an imperial concubine; how she had born the Hsien-feng Emperor his only son; how she had fought for her rights as mother of the Emperor when the Hsien-feng had died; how she and Niuhuru had ruled together; how sad she had been when the T'ung-chih had died, and then Niuhuru. She made no mention of milk cakes.

Her voice slowly growing weaker, she recalled how reluctant she had been to take the power from the Kuang-hsu, and how she had done all she could to make China again great. She made no mention of the Boxers. She spoke of Young Barrington, and of Yuan Shih-k'ai, of Li Hung-chang and, with tears in her eyes, of Jung-lu and Chang Tsin. Then, just before three o'clock that afternoon, at the Hour of the Goat, Tz'u-hsi turned her face to the south, straightened her limbs, and died.

She was just short of her seventy-third birthday.

14

THE MARSHAL

'Tz'u-hsi is dead!' The whisper tippled through the Forbidden City, then spread to the Tatar City and the Chinese City beyond that. It travelled down the river to Tientsin, and had the Barbarians scratching their heads. Almost from the time of their first incursions into China, they had been opposed by this one woman – who was now no more. No one paid any attention to the death of the Kuang-hsu Emperor which had so strangely preceded that of his adoptive mother, or to the rumours that he might have been murdered. Only Tz'u-hsi mattered.

The news reached Shanghai two days after the event, thanks to the telegraph. Adrian received the message and took it in to his brother. 'You were her friend,' Adrian said. 'I never even laid eyes on her.'

'Yes,' Robert said. 'I was her friend.' No one, now, would ever know for certain that he had been more than that. But he was the very last of her paladins. Her true paladins. Yuan Shih-k'ai had never been more than a tool. Yuan Shih-k'ai! This was the moment for which the Marshal had been waiting.

'There will be changes,' Adrian said.

'There was a House of Barrington before Tz'u-hsi was born,' Robert reminded him. 'And there is still a House of Barrington now that she is dead. Nothing will change.' Unless Yuan Shih-k'ai wills it, he thought. But it was up to Yuan to come to him.

*

The news took longer to travel up the Yangtse, and it was a month before it reached Hankow. Tang was away in the hills, but Victoria was wildly excited. Yet when he returned, he was curiously muted. 'We must wait for word from Dr Sun,' he said.

They waited, but the only word that came was, wait. Tz'u-hsi had been there for so long no one had really believed she would ever be gone. Dr Sun was not even in China, and if he heard the news soon enough, he had to arrange his return, and even then, he had no real plans laid to take advantage of the situation. Victoria in fact realised that there *were* no plans at all. Dr Sun and his people were theoreticians, dreamers. They had no idea how to react to reality.

But did she? She was perfectly happy, happier, indeed, than ever before in her life. When she had first arrived in Hankow, the local managers and clerks who handled the business of the House had regarded her with a mixture of suspicion and amusement: if China as a whole was undoubtedly ruled by a woman, women had no place in business. But her knowledge of the business, and her understanding of the various factors involved, had won their respect, even as they had understood that Martin Barrington was a future boss and had to be taken seriously. She flattered herself that she had indeed increased business. Certainly Robert seemed pleased from the letters he wrote to her. Just as he was very obviously pleased to have her out of the way; he never suggested she might wish to return to Shanghai.

As to the man who came to see her in the dead of night, no doubt it was well known in the city, but she had no husband to complain and was regarded very much as her own mistress. No one could possibly connect Tang's visits with the store of rifles in one of the godowns, simply because those remained untouched. Only she knew that they waited on Dr Sun's word. Which might never come, she reflected.

So she lived, more freely than ever before, with the certainty of Tang's return to her arms at least once a month. She took precautions to ensure that she did not again become pregnant, and also that Martin never encountered his father; Tang was not interested in the boy, anyway. No doubt Martin also knew of her peccadilloes, but to him she was an aunt, not a mother. And she was a Barrington. He was proud of her notoriety. Once the initial euphoria had settled, she was content to hope nothing would ever happen.

She could even hope she need never see Adrian again.

*

It seemed that everyone was waiting to see what was going to happen. But first of all they had to wait upon the soothsayers, who could not decide upon the most auspicious date for the funerals of the Dowager Empress and the Emperor. Until that was determined, all business in the Empire came to a stop. But from what Robert could learn, Prince Ch'un had taken control of the government in the name of his son, the P'u-i Emperor. This was of course against all the tenets of Confucianism, but then, most of those tenets had been thrown out of the window by Tz'u-hsi during her own lifetime.

And it appeared to work, as the next year drifted by with very little unrest, and the date for the imperial funerals was finally set. 'Will you go to Peking?' Monique asked.

'I think I must,' Robert decided. In any event, he wished to see for himself what was happening.

Monique did not try to dissuade him. She had never probed into his relationship with the Empress, although she had to be aware that he had been a member of her inner circle. But Monique was a very self-contained entity. Now twenty-four years old, she had grown in both stature and beauty, as she had grown into her position as Mistress of the House of Barrington. With her flowing auburn hair and her very pale complexion, over which the freckles were no more than a dusting of colour, and her Paris gowns, she attracted glances wherever she went, and an invitation to her dinner table was highly prized. Robert liked to think that she was a reincarnation of his grandmother, who in her youth had had a similar colouring, he had been told, and a similar presence.

But that was for public show, and he sometimes felt that it was all because she felt it was what he wanted her to be, in public. In the privacy of their own apartment she was a patient and adoring mother. James had a governess, an English lady named Harriet Stringer, a widow imported from Hong Kong. But more often than not Monique attended the schoolroom herself and she often continued the lessons after Mrs Stringer had finished, while she was equally eager to have the younger English factors come in to teach the boy how to play at football and cricket. She wanted him to be a well-rounded person.

Best of all, from Robert's point of view, as a wife she remained the girl he had wooed on the banks of the Han-ho, and thought he had lost, before so magically regaining possession of her. Eight years, and still they loved with a consuming passion.

'You are on a perpetual honeymoon,' Adrian would scoff.

'You should try it for yourself,' Robert would riposte with his customary good humour.

Adrian would look at Monique with lazy eyes. 'Perhaps,' he would say. 'If I could find another Monique.'

*

Robert asked Monique if she would like to go with him to Peking, but she declined. 'It has nothing but bad memories for me,' she said. So he went alone, with only his servants for company, taking a House sampan up the Grand Canal. It was the beginning of November 1908, almost a year since Tz'u-hsi's death. When he arrived at the capital it was crowded with grandees from every part of the Empire.

On the actual day the procession was to leave the city for the Manchu burial grounds the streets were thronged, the people gaping at the myriad soldiers; the cavalry with their pennons fluttering in the breeze; the white-clad princes and princesses of the Dynasty; the equally sombrely dressed mandarins and viceroys; the saffron robes of the Buddhist priests and lamas, including the Dalai Lama himself, all of these garlanded with flowers and walking beneath state umbrellas; the thousands of eunuchs; the animals, camels and llamas; the musicians playing doleful tunes.

The journey took four days as it made its slow way beyond the Great Wall. The route was lined with mourners who burned paper money, paper attendants, paper food and paper clothes to accompany Tz'u-hsi into the next world. The cost was staggering: Robert was told the total sum was two million taels, of which only a quarter was spent on the Emperor, the rest went to the memory of Tz'u-hsi.

But at last, at seven o'clock on the morning of 9 November 1908, the Dowager Empress was sealed in the vault where the Hsien-feng and Tz'u-an already lay.

*

It was time to head for home. And to meet and discuss. On the way from Peking to the Burial Ground it would have been unseemly to do anything but mourn. But once the vault had been sealed, and the imperial party turned back for Peking, Robert was summoned before Prince Ch'un. He had never met this prince before, nor had he ever seen the new Emperor. He performed the kowtow in the imperial tent, gazed at with enormous eyes by the three-year-old ruler of the Empire, and was then escorted into a separate chamber by the Prince.

'Robert Barrington,' Ch'un said. 'The late Empress told me that you could be absolutely trusted at all times and under all eventualities to support the Dynasty.'

'I and my family have always done so, Excellency,' Robert said cautiously.

'These are troubled times. Knowing that there are men I can trust is a great solace to me,' Ch'un went on. 'I will send for you again, Barrington.'

Robert bowed.

It occurred to him that the Regent was a frightened man, seeking support for his regime, uncertain how that support should be used. He was not surprised when on the following day, as he rode with his servants somewhat apart from the rest of the returning procession, which had now dissolved from any semblance of order into a vast, shambling mass, he was joined by Yuan Shih-k'ai. The Marshal wore uniform and had been accompanied on the march by a company of his soldiers, very smart-looking men, also wearing khaki uniforms and armed with rifles and bayonets, in strong contrast to the casually dressed Bannermen.

Robert had of course seen Yuan from a distance on the outward march, but had made no effort to join him. As far as he was concerned, it was up to Yuan to come to him. As he had now done. 'The end of an era,' Yuan remarked. 'For you, more than for most, perhaps. You have not forgotten our conversation of two years ago, Barrington?'

'I have not. And I hope you have not either, Yuan.'

'I accepted your sentiments, then,' Yuan acknowledged. 'Now ... I understand you have had an interview with the Regent. What do you make of him?'

'He is feeling his way. I imagine we will all have to do that, for a while.'

'Some more than others,' Yuan said. 'I too have had an interview with Prince Ch'un.' He gazed at the distant pagoda roofs of Peking, just coming into view. 'I have been dismissed from my posts.'

Robert turned his head in consternation.

'All of my posts,' Yuan went on. 'I am no longer a viceroy, and I am no longer a general in the army. Indeed, I have been commanded to disband my personal troops.'

'But why?' Robert asked.

'It is not my business to know that.'

'What will you do?'

'What can I do, but obey?' Yuan asked. 'Especially in view of our conversation.' Robert shot him a glance, but Yuan's face was blandly composed. 'I think I shall travel.'

'You mean you will leave China?'

'No. I have no wish to leave China. But China is a vast country. I do not know it well enough. Perhaps I do not know it at all. There has never been time before. Now it will be worth exploring, in my retirement. Do you not agree?'

Robert didn't know what to say. The idea of Yuan just retiring was absurd and he knew how deeply angry the Marshal must be, after having spent his entire life in the service of the Dynasty, just to be dismissed with hardly a thank you.

Suddenly he felt very alone. There was no one, such as Chang Tsin or Li Hung-chang, or old Admiral Ting, left with whom he could discuss the situation. When he returned to Shanghai, he mentioned it to Adrian, but Adrian's response was predictable. 'Damned good riddance.'

Robert didn't argue, but he knew that if Yuan Shih-k'ai was prepared to accept his dismissal without question, it could only be because he had some very deep concept at the end of it.

*

'Mistress,' said Lo Yang-li, the butler. 'Marshal Yuan Shih-k'ai is here.'

Victoria looked up from her account book with a frown. 'Here? Or do you mean in Hankow?'

'He is here, Mistress,' Lo said. 'He wishes to speak with you.'

Victoria took a sharp breath. What on earth could the man want? He must know of her dislike for him. And now that he was no longer of any importance in the Government she did not even have to fear him. Indeed, in the nearly three years that had elapsed since Tz'u-hsi's burial and Yuan's dismissal, he had hardly been heard of. It had been supposed that he had indeed retired to private life, as commanded.

They had in fact been three amazingly quiet years, especially up the Yangtse-Kiang. One heard rumours, of course, of mounting governmental debts, of anarchy in several provinces ... Victoria had no doubt that Tang was creating a good deal of that in the south. He came to her less often now, as he was busy travelling the country seeking support wherever there was discontent. And in those three years she had imported three more shipments of arms, to be stored in her warehouses. All that had been necessary was to visit Shanghai, smile at Robert and Monique, give little James a hug ... and brace herself for an afternoon with Adrian. No doubt she was utterly damned. So damned that she even enjoyed the sexual degradation inflicted upon her, even looked forward to it, as such a contrast to Tang's somewhat perfunctory possession of her body. And it was for the Cause.

Supposing the Cause truly existed. There was still no sign of Dr Sun. According to Tang he was laying his plans, which involved waiting for the right moment, which would be when discontent with the ineptitude of the Peking regime reached boiling point. But in Victoria's opinion Peking rule had always been inept, even under Tz'u-hsi. People were conditioned to it. She could not see them boiling over now.

Nor did she wish them to. She had reached contentment. She was thirty-seven years of age. She retained all of her beauty – her slight increase in weight merely accentuated the swell at hip and breast. That those breasts were beginning to sag seemed to make no difference to the two men in her life – she had a husband, at least in her eyes; she had a lover, even if he was her own brother; and she had her son at her side, even if he called her aunt. She was resolved to tell him the truth when he was fully a man; in this autumn of 1911 that time was close – Martin would soon be seventeen. She no longer wanted to see a revolution, or to have her life interrupted in any way. Yuan Shih-k'ai could only be considered an interruption.

Yet it could do no harm to hear what he had to say. 'Then show Mr Yuan in,' she said, and closed her book.

Lo bowed as he opened the door for Yuan. Victoria stood up and thought, how are the mighty fallen. Yuan wore civilian clothes and merely looked a rather old, very fat, white-haired and bearded Chinese of the mandarin class. And this last was indicated only by his silk tunic and good boots. 'Miss Barrington,' he said.

Victoria, who towered over him by some nine inches, allowed him to take her hand. 'Mr Yuan. How good to see you. I did not know you had interests in Hankow?'

'I have interests everywhere, Miss Barrington. Now that I am no longer employed.'

She gestured him to a chair. 'Well, if there is anything the House of Barrington can do to assist you . . .'

'I know this. Your brother remains my fast friend. We have many things in common. Miss Barrington, I have taken a house in Hankow for a week or so, while I conduct my business here. I should be most flattered if you would dine with me.'

'Ah . . .' Victoria tried desperately to think of some excuse, without appearing to be downright rude.

'Tomorrow night,' Yuan went on. 'I was especially asked to remember you, by your brother. I saw him last week in Shanghai.'

Which brother is he talking about? she wondered.

'Robert also asked me to remember his son, who is here with you, is he not?'

'Yes. Martin is learning the business. He is only Robert's adopted son, you know.'

Yuan gave his sleepy smile. 'Of course. I understand this. But a man may be as fond of his adopted son as of his real one. I should be very pleased if you would bring the boy to dinner, tomorrow. Let me see, he is now . . .?'

'Martin is sixteen, Mr Yuan.'

'At sixteen, one's childhood is behind one, and all of one's manhood lies before one. I will look forward to meeting him.'

*

Victoria reflected that the presence of Martin might well be helpful. If only she could determine what Yuan was about. She was in a quandary. She wished she could communicate with Shanghai, but there was no telegraph from Hankow to the coast, and it would take several weeks to reach either of her brothers and get a reply. She had always valued her isolation before.

Equally she wished Tang could be there to advise her. But as usual she had no idea where Tang was, or when he would return. She would just have to use her own judgement.

*

Victoria insisted that they both wear European clothes, just to remind Yuan that he was dealing with the Barringtons, and had the ricksha escorted by several of her servants.

Yuan's house was by the river, and was palatial. He had said he had rented it, but Victoria knew that this house had stood empty for over a year before being suddenly completely redecorated and refurbished – several months before. Therefore Yuan had planned this visit for some time. She wondered if he had actually bought the house.

Bowing servants escorted them through exquisitely furnished halls to an inner room, where the Marshal, wearing a crimson tunic over royal blue pantaloons, but no military insignia, was waiting for them. Victoria looked left and right, but as she had anticipated and feared, they were the only guests.

'How beautiful you are, Victoria,' Yuan said. 'You do not mind if I call you Victoria? I have known your family for such a long time. And this is Martin.' Yuan took the boy's hand. 'I have heard a great deal about you, Young Barrington.' Martin glowed at the form of address. 'Are you going to be a merchant, when you grow up? Or a famous sailor like your father?' Yuan gave his sleepy smile. 'Or even a famous soldier, like me?'

'I would like to be a sailor, or a soldier, Mr Yuan,' Martin said. Victoria had carefully coached him to remember that Yuan was now a civilian, and neither a general nor a minister nor a viceroy – thus he was not entitled to any special address.

'A man can always he what he wishes, with sufficient determination,' Yuan commented. 'I have prepared some entertainment for us.'

They were escorted into another room and seated in comfortable chairs; the Marshal sat between Victoria and Martin. Sake was served. Victoria had never encouraged Martin to drink the seductive liquid, but she did not wish to spoil his evening by playing the heavy aunt, and so she watched him sipping without comment, watched his cheeks redden with the glow of the alcohol, and then even further when the 'entertainment' began. To her dismay she realised it was a decidedly erotic play, in which there was a succession of risqué jokes and situations, and occasional glimpses of naked bodies, both male and female – all the actors and actresses were very young, and very attractive.

Martin watched in fascination, Yuan himself in bland, apparently half-asleep, contentment. 'Did you find that amusing?' he asked, when the actors had withdrawn.

'Oh, yes, sir,' Martin said before Victoria could speak.

Yuan stood up. 'Come. I have some toys which may amuse you more.' The 'toys' turned out to be relics of the Marshal's various campaigns. How they had got to Hankow, and why, was a mystery to Victoria, as this was certainly not Yuan's principal home, and some of the items were quite bulky. But Martin was again clearly fascinated when he was allowed to handle and draw the Marshal's sword, and also examine Yuan's revolver.

'Do not be alarmed, Victoria,' Yuan said reassuringly. 'It is not loaded.'

There was an album of photographs for them to look at, and then a splendid meal, at which a great deal more sake was served.

'I am going to be a soldier,' Martin announced. 'I would like to serve with you, Mr Yuan.'

Yuan smiled. 'Sadly, that is no longer possible. I am retired.'

'But you will fight again should the Empire be threatened.'

'If I were called upon to do so, certainly. Until then . . . I can only attempt to amuse myself. However, would you like to campaign with me, Martin?'

'Is it possible, sir?' Martin's eyes glowed.

'I think the Marshal is speaking of his memories,' Victoria suggested.

Yuan continued to smile. 'A soldier, even a retired soldier, must always keep his body fit and his mind sharp, Victoria. For as Martin so rightly says, were I to be summoned to defend the country, I would have to respond. So, tomorrow I go hunting. Perhaps Martin would like to accompany me.'

'Oh, sir, could I?' Martin cried.

'Hunting?' Victoria asked, alarmed.

'For birds. It is a test of speed and accuracy with a firearm. Do you know firearms, Martin?'

'I shoot at a target every day, sir,' Martin replied proudly.

'Then the next stage in your development should certainly be to shoot at a moving target. Do you not agree?'

'May I, Aunt Vicky?' Martin asked.

Victoria hesitated. To refuse would be churlish. And there could be no danger in hunting birds . . .

'Do not concern yourself, Victoria,' Yuan said. 'I shall take good care of him. I would invite you as well, but I am afraid much of our stalking necessitates finding out way through swamps, sometimes up to our waists. I do not think you would enjoy it.'

'I am sure I would not,' Victoria agreed.

*

They left soon after the meal was finished.

'I have never enjoyed myself more,' Martin said.

Victoria estimated he was quite drunk; the sake had been followed by plum wine. She wished she could summon up the courage to ask him what he had thought, or felt, at the sight of the naked girls. Sex was a subject she had never dared broach; she was not sure how to go about it, and there was the risk that he might ask questions of her in response. But as Yuan had pointed out, Martin was sixteen, and on the threshold of manhood. He was, in fact, by Chinese standards, retarded; he should have lost his virginity by now. She had kept him this way, kept him over-protected. But now there was a crisis rushing at her.

But not to be considered tonight, she decided; she also had drunk a good deal too much. 'Mind you do exactly as Mr Yuan says tomorrow,' she admonished him.

And wondered why she could not sleep, especially after so much alcohol. But she knew that her little boy was about to become a man. From one day's stalking?

*

The hunters were going to be gone all day. Lo Yang-li had the cooks prepare a packed lunch for Martin, and the boy was already mounted when Yuan and his entourage arrived. Yuan waved to Victoria, watching from the front verandah, and then the horsemen moved off down the street towards the city walls.

'Your aunt is a very beautiful woman,' Yuan remarked. 'And a very caring one, about her nephew.'

'I sometimes think she is attempting to take the place of my real mother,' Martin agreed.

'Did you never know your real mother?'

'No, sir. I believe she died when I was born. But my *real* mother was Chang Su.'

'Ah, yes. That was sad. Do you miss her very much?'

'She was my real mother, sir,' Martin repeated with dignity.

'That is a very proper attitude,' Yuan agreed. 'A man should never forget his real mother.'

Martin's whole being swelled. He was being treated as an equal, by this famous man. He needed that. Perhaps it was only since coming to Hankow that he had begun privately to attempt to evaluate his position, his place in the scheme of things.

Before, he had been too young ever to doubt his position. And he had only been six when his 'real' mother had died, and Father had returned to Shanghai with the Belgian woman. Monique had wished him to call her mother as well, and she had always showed him great kindness. But he had always thought of her as an aunt, like Aunt Victoria.

He had also always thought of her as an outsider, a toy for Father, but no one who could in any way impinge upon his position or his rights. As the years had passed, however, he had started to understand certain things. It had begun with the birth of James. Martin had thought of him as little more than a younger brother, until he had heard the servants discussing the situation, and agreeing that here was the true future Master of the House – because he was pure-bred Barbarian.

That was the first time he had realised that it mattered that he was *not* pure-bred. From that moment, whenever he looked in a mirror, he had become increasingly aware of his Chinese characteristics. Just as he had become increasingly resentful of both Aunt Monique and her son.

He had supposed he had concealed his feelings, until he had suddenly been banished to Hankow with Aunt Victoria.

He hadn't known what to do, who to believe. Father had
called him into the study at home and said, 'You are growing
up, Martin. I am going to send you up to Hankow, to learn
the business. Aunt Vicky will be going with you. She is
going to manage the Hankow office.'

Martin's initial reaction had been one of tremendous
pleasure. He had only been thirteen, and here was Father
treating him as an adult. It had only later occurred to him that
he was being banished from the centre of the House of
Barrington's operations to one of its most remote outposts.
Equally, it had only slowly dawned on him that he was not
actually being trained for anything. Aunt Vicky looked after
the House business, and she used her spare time to act as his
governess. He was just a Barrington out-child who was
being shunted aside.

Aunt Vicky was terribly kind to him. Indeed, as he had
told the Marshal, she mothered him in a way not even Chang
Su had ever done. But this he found distasteful. Aunt Vicky,
for all her beauty, and her undoubted peccadilloes – the
servants had told him she had a Chinese lover, and were
shocked by it – was both childless and setting up to be an old
maid. Equally, he supposed, as the last remaining Barrington
woman, she also resented the appearance of the red-haired
Belgian, taking over her prerogatives. Perhaps she was
seeking some counterweight. Or perhaps she was a part of
Father's plot to get his eldest son out of Shanghai and keep
him out, until James had grown up.

These resentments had grown slowly, as Martin himself
had grown. They had slowly become encapsulated in a kind
of hatred for his aunt. He felt she was trying to keep him as
a child, keep him from ever asserting himself as a Barrington. He had even thought of escaping her, and returning
down-river to Shanghai to confront Father. He had not done
so, yet, because he feared Robert Barrington's temper. But
one day, when he was older . . . And in the meanwhile, here
was a man, every bit as famous as his father, prepared to
treat him as a man.

They left the city and went into the swamps that lay at the base of the foothills stretching away to the north, which would eventually become mountains. Yuan had with him a considerable number of servants, and these spread out and entered the swamps first, beating drums and shouting. Martin was even more flattered to discover that he was the only guest, and felt prouder than ever as he followed Yuan into the muddy water, while four servants came behind carrying the fowling pieces and ammunition above their heads. Soon they were up to their waists, and Martin wondered what his aunt would say if she could see him now.

Then Yuan held up his hand. They stopped moving, and immediately the servants handed them their guns, as overhead there rose a flock of geese. Yuan fired, and Martin a moment later. Three birds fell, wings flapping feebly. The rest scattered in every direction. 'Good shooting,' Yuan said, exchanging his empty gun for a loaded weapon.

Martin followed his example. 'I think they were all yours, sir.'

'No, no. One at least was your shot,' the Marshal insisted.

They forced their way further into the swamp, while more birds were put up, and those brought down were retrieved by other servants. The shoot lasted several hours, at the end of which Martin was both soaked through and exhausted, while his shoulder ached. Yuan seemed totally at ease, as they splashed out of the water on to dry land, an island in the midst of the swamp.

Here other servants were already at work, some plucking and cleaning the birds, others lighting fires, and not only for cooking; there were two huge tubs of hot water waiting for them.

'We must not get chilled,' Yuan said.

The Marshal was surrounded by half a dozen very pretty young women, who began removing his clothes with practised speed. But there were equally attractive girls lifting Martin's tunic over his head. He didn't know what to do. His aunt had always insisted that he never undress in front of any

of the servants, or in front of her, for that matter. Yet he had
been thoroughly titillated by the play-acting the previous
night, and the smiling, giggling girls were a treat.

'I have not brought a change of clothing,' he protested.

'That is no matter. It is a warm day, and our clothes will
soon dry,' Yuan pointed out. The Marshal was already
naked, a not very attractive figure because he was both short
and stout, but that did not seem to concern the women, who
were emptying buckets of water over him and vigorously
soaping him.

Martin was totally embarrassed. Being naked before the
women was bad enough, but unlike the Marshal, who
seemed to have himself totally under control, he could not
prevent an erection as the soft fingers soaped him, and
indeed, explored him, caressing his buttocks and penis.
'They will spend you if they can,' Yuan warned. 'Do not let
them.' Then to the girls: 'You may need his services later,
eh?'

The girls giggled some more, but ceased playing with him
in favour of lifting him into the tub, where he sank to his
knees in relief, to be astonished again as two of the girls
stripped off their clothes to get in beside him. Neither was
any older than himself, but fully mature, and their hard little
nipples scraped on his shoulder and back as they resumed
washing him, screaming with laughter. Insensibly he found
his arms going round the lithe yellow-brown bodies, his
hands closing on hips and then buttocks, his fingers sliding
between while their shrieks of joyous laughter grew, and he
hardened ever more.

He looked up with a gasp as the Marshal stood above his
tub, but it was too late; the stroking fingers had caused an
ejaculation. Martin panted with embarrassment, but Yuan
merely smiled, and gestured him to his feet. 'I warned you,'
the Marshal said. 'But you are a boy. Your weapon will be
fully charged again in half an hour. If I let them do that to
me, I would be finished for the day. Let us eat.'

A boat had been following them through the marsh, and

from this more attendants had disembarked, to spread a mat on the ground and lay out a magnificent picnic. Stepping from his bath, Martin was wrapped in a voluminous towel by the eager girls and rapidly dried, but his clothes, which other girls had been washing during the bath, were still hanging on bushes, and he discovered that he was going to lunch naked, as was the Marshal, already sprawled comfortably on cushions, and gesturing him to lie beside him.

The sun was hot, Martin felt clean and, for the moment, sated by his ejaculation, but both hungry and thirsty. And so utterly wanton. For the girls were not dressing either, as they knelt beside their masters, holding cups of warm sake to their lips, and then tasty morsels of food.

As the meal continued, they were joined by boys and young men, also naked, and aroused – as, indeed, was Yuan himself, now. The Marshal smiled. 'Are not the simple pleasures of life the best, Martin? Open air, good food and drink, pleasant company . . . tell me, do you prefer the girls, or the boys?'

Martin hastily swallowed some roast pork. 'The boys, sir?'

'Have you never sampled a boy?' Yuan looked up, and beckoned a boy even younger than himself, Martin estimated. 'Service Young Barrington,' Yuan commanded.

The boy smiled, and knelt beside Martin. Martin had no idea what to do and held his foodsticks almost like weapons between them. But the boy merely took them from his hand and laid them on the mat, then kissed him on the mouth, warmly and intimately. Gently he pushed Martin on to his back, still kissing him, and then lay on him, straddling him with his legs so that their genitals were pressed together. Martin gasped with a mixture of embarrassment and rising passion, but he had nothing to do with his hands and arms, other than close them round the boy.

'Now you can mount him, if you wish,' Yuan said. 'Unless you prefer him to mount you. That is one of the pleasures of a boy, more variety.' The boy released Martin and rose to his knees. Martin looked past him at the other boys, and girls, watching him, some smiling, some serious. 'Or would you rather mount a girl?' Yuan asked. 'As it is the first time, perhaps a girl would be easier. Yan-ling.'

One of the girls who had bathed him came forward. He had caressed her in the tub, without thinking of her as an individual. Now he gazed at very long black hair, a pretty face, full breasts and thighs . . . and she too was kneeling to kiss him, and then lie on him, working her groin on his as the boy had done, rubbing her nipples across his chest, and then spreading her legs to take him inside. He gasped with the ecstasy of it, turned his head from side to side . . . and saw the Marshal mounting the kneeling boy, beside him.

*

'If you knew how much I envy you,' Yuan said as they sipped plum wine. 'To be sixteen again . . . did you enjoy Yan-ling?'

'I have never experienced anything so delightful, sir.'

'Then you must have her again. I give her to you. A man should have a woman,' Yuan explained seriously. 'Whenever he feels desire. At your age, now you have felt it once, you will wish it very often. In fact, I doubt that Yan-ling alone could satisfy you. Which of the others do you like?' He gestured at the boys and girls, who knelt in a group on the edge of the mat, awaiting their next summons. 'Do not worry, Yan-ling will not be jealous. If you are as virile as I am sure you are, she will be glad of the rest, from time to time.'

'Sir, I could not. My aunt would never let me have a woman servant. For enjoyment.'

'Speak plain, boy. For sex. Your aunt does not enjoy sex?'

'I do not know, sir.' He could not betray Victoria's peccadilloes. 'But she would say I am too young.'

'At sixteen?' Yuan appeared to be amazed.

'My aunt is a Barbarian, sir. The Barbarians think sixteen is too young. For anything,' he added despondently.

'That is very sad. One is never too young, for anything, if one has the required physical and mental ability. As you undoubtedly do.' Martin swelled with pride. 'Have you given any thought to your future, Martin?' Yuan asked.

Martin hesitated, unsure how much he could confide in this man, who was, after all, a close friend of his father's.

Yuan smiled. 'You are concerned, with good reason. Your brother will be the next Master of the House.' He glanced at Martin with his sleepy eyes. 'Your father has told me this.' Martin gulped. 'Well, that is natural, I suppose,' Yuan said. 'But he has also told me that he does not know what to do with you. He fears that to keep you in the business may lead to friction. And yet what other career is open to a Barrington?'

'My father himself served the Empress in the navy, sir,' Martin said eagerly.

'So he did. But there is no navy, now. And the army . . . it is a degenerate rabble. However, would you like to serve me, Martin? Oh, I know I have been dismissed from my posts, and officially retired, but this is because those little men who now rule in Peking are both jealous and afraid of me. But I know that they cannot do without me. There are great forces stirring in China, and Prince Ch'un is not the man to deal with them. Sooner or later he will need me, and then he will call for my help. That is why I keep myself fit and ready for action, Martin. But I do more than that. I keep my army in being. It is scattered now, in several camps. But it is in a state of readiness, and the moment the Dynasty calls upon me, I will be ready to respond, and save China. Would you like to help me in that task, Martin?'

'Oh, sir! Is it possible?'

'Of course. I will give you a commission in my personal bodyguard. You will wear a uniform, a sword and a revolver. You will also, of course, be attended by your servants.' Yuan waved his hand. 'The three I have given you, and as many more as you choose. Your salary will be commensurate with your name and rank.'

Martin could not believe his ears. But it all had to be a dream. 'Have you spoken to my father about this, sir?'

'Why, no. I only considered it after meeting you, and discovering your worth.'

'Then . . . I do not think he would agree, sir. He would say I am too young. As for Aunt Vicky . . .'

'Hm,' Yuan commented. 'I understand your point. And if we put the idea to them and you appeared to be enthusiastic . . . you *are* enthusiastic?'

'There is nothing I would rather do, sir, than serve with you.'

'Well said, Young Barrington. And there is nothing I would wish more than to have you with me. But if we are both determined, then we shall achieve our objective.'

Martin shook his head. 'My father is a very stubborn man.'

'Of course. But he is in Shanghai. That is seven hundred miles away.'

Martin looked at the Marshal. 'My aunt is here, and she is just as stubborn. And even more likely to be opposed to our idea.'

Yuan gave his sleepy smile. 'Even your aunt will have to accept a fait accompli. I am leaving Hankow tonight. In fact, I have already left. I am not returning to my house there, but am proceeding to the north, into Shensi, where some of my people are training. It will be a difficult and arduous journey. Can you face it?'

'Willingly, sir. But—'

'Then you will accompany me.'

'But . . .' Martin licked his lips while excitement surged through his brain. 'My clothes! My—'

'You will be going into uniform, immediately, as my aide-de-camp. I understand you have certain possessions which are dear to you, but you would have to leave them behind in any event, even were your father to give you permission to join me. So, boy, have you the courage to do this?'

'But Aunt Vicky will refuse me permission, sir.'

'I have just explained that there is no need for you to ask your aunt, Martin. You will merely accompany me. I think it would be proper for you to write her a letter, explaining what you have done. Otherwise she would worry. There are pens and paper in my bags over there, and I will see to it that your letter is delivered this evening.'

'She will be very angry.'

'Women are always angry about something,' Yuan pointed out, 'except those who are our servants. That is why I have only servants.'

'But Father—'

'Oh, he will be angry as well. But you will be far away, and it will be months before you see him again. By which time . . . let me tell you something about fathers. Especially yours. He wishes the best for you, and yet cannot provide it, or even recommend it. He will, as you say, be angry. He will be angry with me as well, no doubt. But his anger will fade, and when you next visit him, in your uniform and as a grown man, with the experience of having adventured in the mountains, when he realises that you are with me in our determination to save the Dynasty and the Empire, I prophesy that he will throw his arms round you in joy and admiration. So tell me, boy, are you with me?'

'Oh, yes, sir,' Martin cried.

Yuan signalled for the writing utensils to be brought.

15

THE CATASTROPHE

'Victoria?!' Robert Barrington looked up from his desk as his sister swept into the Shanghai office. Robert had never seen Victoria other than neatly groomed, hair freshly brushed, hands manicured, cheeks rouged . . . but this was a wild-eyed creature who did not look as if she had had a bath, much less brushed her hair or painted her nails, for the past week. He got up. 'Whatever is the matter? I had no idea you were coming down-river.'

'It's Martin,' Victoria snapped. 'He's been kidnapped. By your friend Yuan.'

Robert rang his bell, and one of the clerks immediately appeared. 'A glass of brandy for Miss Victoria,' he said. 'Come to think of it, bring the bottle and three glasses, and ask Mr Adrian to step in here, will you?'

Victoria, sinking into a chair before the desk, got up again. 'Adrian?'

'Well, my dear,' Robert said, 'if Martin has been kidnapped . . . not that I can believe it. Yuan? When was Yuan in Hankow?'

Victoria explained, and showed Robert Martin's letter. The brandy arrived, and so did Adrian. Robert showed him the letter in turn while Victoria sipped her drink. 'According to this letter, Martin went of his own free will,' Adrian commented.

'Oh . . . the Marshal turned his head. It was obvious when we went there for dinner. There were guns and swords, just the sort of thing a boy dreams of. Now he's to be Yuan's aide-de-camp. So he can have a gun and a sword of his own. And there's another thing: I wouldn't put it past Yuan to have debauched him. There were naked girls and . . .' she shuddered, '. . . naked boys, at his house. It was disgusting. Robert, you must do something.'

Robert stroked his chin. 'I think you are making a mountain out of a molehill, Sis,' Adrian commented. 'Why on earth should a man like Yuan, a lifelong friend of Robert's, wish to kidnap Martin? All he had to do was ask Robert's permission to employ the boy, and Robert would have given it. Wouldn't you, Robert?'

'But he *didn't* ask Robert's permission,' Victoria said.

They were both looking at Robert now. While his brain was running round itself in circles. Of course Martin had been kidnapped, even if he had been hoodwinked into thinking he was going of his own free will. Yuan sought a hold over the House of Barrington . . . because the House, in the person if its Master, had refused to support his wish to overthrow the Ch'ing. Therefore Yuan's plans must be near fruition.

So what was he going to do? Yuan, in common with most people, believed that Martin was probably Robert's own son, by a Chinese mistress. He therefore entirely over-estimated the value of the boy. Oh, Martin was valuable enough, as Victoria's child. But how valuable? What will I do, Robert wondered, if Yuan approaches me and says that if I do not support a coup d'état he will kill my adopted son? Betray my oath, endanger all my family have built up for generations, and worst of all, endanger Monique and James? He simply had to take the heat out of the situation, and hope to be able to talk sense into the Marshal. 'You say he was in

Hankow a fortnight ago. Where did he go after that?'

'As far as I have been able to find out, into Shensi. Across the mountains.' She dared not tell her brothers her real fear, that Yuan might be seeking Tang. With Martin in tow. Because Tang would never be captured alive.

'I think,' Robert said carefully, 'as Adrian has said, we need to keep a sense of proportion. If Yuan has seduced Martin into working for him, that is reprehensible, I agree, in view of the boy's age. But at the same time, I am positive he means Martin no harm. Now, there is nothing any of us can do about what has happened until Yuan returns to his home. What I shall do is write to him, there, setting up a meeting, at which time we shall determine whether Martin really wants to work for him or not. If not, we shall have him back.'

'Oh . . .' Victoria got to her feet impatiently. 'Of course he'll want to go on working for him. If he's debauched now, he'll be even more debauched then.'

'Then I'm afraid there is nothing any of us can do.'

'You refuse to help.'

'Vicky, try to be reasonable. Martin is almost seventeen. Here in China, he's his own man.' When I was seventeen, he recalled with a touch of nostalgia, I had already been introduced into Tz'u-hsi's bed.

'We could kidnap him back,' Victoria said. 'And send him off to England, or somewhere. I'd go with him.'

'And antagonise the Marshal?' Adrian asked. 'You *are* overreacting, Sis.' He gave one of his sly smiles. 'You will have people thinking Martin is your son, not your nephew.'

Victoria stamped from the room.

*

At Robert's suggestion, Monique went to see her sister-in-law. She found Victoria in a tub, being bathed by her Chinese servants. 'Oh,' she said. 'I'll come back later, shall I?'

'It's quite all right,' Victoria assured her, and got up, to be wrapped in a huge soft undressing robe.

'Robert has told me what happened,' Monique said. 'I am most terribly sorry.'

Victoria waved the girls from the room and sat down, her legs curled up beneath her. 'You know he is really my son?'

'Yes. Robert told me.'

'Then I should think, from your point of view, things have turned out rather well. Martin's departure means there will be no rival to your son for the House.'

'I never supposed there would be,' Monique said, equably. 'I came here to offer you my help.'

'What help can you offer me?' Victoria asked. She got up, and now dry, let the robe fall to the floor.

Monique bit her lip. Victoria remained a beautiful woman; if there was a slight sag to her breasts, a slight widening of her hips, the evidences of approaching age seemed to add rather than detract from her looks. But since the wild adventure of her girlhood during the Boxer Rebellion, Monique had become a distinctly modest woman, and Victoria's casual nudity was embarrassing. 'My sympathy, at least,' she suggested.

'Then I thank you.' Victoria fell across her bed, on her stomach, her chin on the edge; black hair obscured her face.

Monique got up and looked at the naked back. 'It is good to have you home,' she lied. 'We have so much to talk about.'

Victoria tossed hair from her forehead. 'I am not staying.'

Monique, already at the door, checked in surprise. 'Where are you going?'

'Back to Hankow. That is my home now.'

'Yes, but surely . . .'

Victoria rolled over and sat up, cross-legged. 'It is where I wish to live, Monique. It is where Martin will come back to me. If he ever means to come back.'

Monique licked her lips. She had never been one to

criticise others, but there were some things that needed to be said. 'Vicky . . .' She returned to stand beside the bed. 'Do you not suppose that part of the trouble may have been Hankow?'

'I don't know what you mean.'

Monique could feel the heat in her cheeks. 'Well . . . it may be that Martin found out, well . . .'

'Found out what?' Victoria's voice had an edge to it.

Monique drew a deep breath. 'That you have Chinese lovers.'

'I have a Chinese lover, Monique. I am not promiscuous.'

'I didn't mean to offend you.'

'My lover, as you put it, happens to be Martin's father.'

'But . . . you mean this man comes to you in Hankow?'

Victoria realised she had nearly betrayed Tang – and herself. 'What I do with my private life is my business, Monique. You may leave now.'

Monique's head jerked. She was the senior Barrington woman by right of marriage; no one had spoken to her like that since her marriage. 'If Martin found out you had a Chinese lover, and you did not tell him he was his father, then he had every right to leave you,' she snapped, and ran from the room.

She encountered Adrian on the stairs. He smiled at her. 'You look all hot and bothered. Did no one ever tell you how lovely you are when you are hot and bothered?'

'I'm not in the mood for jokes, Adrian,' Monique said. 'You can't go in there. Victoria has nothing on.'

Adrian kissed her hand. 'I'm her brother.' He stepped passed her, went up the stairs, and opened the door, leaving her staring up at him. Then he closed the door behind himself.

Victoria stood by the window, looking down at the garden. She only half turned her head. 'If you lay a finger on me . . .'

'I wouldn't dream of it, in this house,' Adrian grinned. 'I came to find out what really happened.' He stretched out on the bed, hands beneath his head. 'What was Yuan doing in Hankow?'

Victoria put on her robe. 'He said he had business interests there.'

'When is Sun coming back?'

'I have no idea,' Victoria said. 'Look, this has nothing to do with the Cause.'

'Do you honestly expect me to believe that Yuan would risk antagonising the House of Barrington simply to get his hands on a sixteen-year-old boy?'

'Don't be disgusting.'

'So you agree with me. Absolute nonsense. So, Sis, darling, Yuan either knows that the House of Barrington is secretly involved in supplying arms to the Cause, or . . .' He sat up. '*You* wouldn't be engaged in betraying the Cause, would you, Vicky? Like spilling the beans to Yuan, and sealing the deal with Martin? Because if you are doing that, then you are also betraying me.' He got off the bed and stood up. 'I should be annoyed about that.'

Victoria glared at him. 'Get out.'

'I have sometimes wondered,' he said, 'if Tang even knows of that shipment of arms. It seems odd that nothing has ever happened about it.'

'He knows about it. He is waiting on orders from Dr Sun.'

'Then he's a very patient man.' He caught the bodice of the dressing gown and held her against him. 'Or have you confessed all to Bobby?'

'Of course I have not.' She tried to free herself, but Adrian was a very strong man.

'If you have,' he said, 'I'll kill you both. Remember *that*.' He threw her away from him. Victoria stumbled across the room and fell over a chair. When she got up, Adrian had left.

*

Two days later, Monique and Robert saw Victoria off on a House junk, bound up-river for Hankow. They waved her out of sight, then got into their rickshas to be taken back to the Barrington house. 'I wish she had stayed,' Monique remarked.

'So do I. But it's better for her to get on with living her own life.'

Monique said nothing more until they were in the house and she had dismissed the servants. Then she sat beside her husband. 'Did you know Victoria is seeing the man, Tang, in Hankow?'

Robert turned to look at her, frowning. 'How do you know?'

'It just slipped out. She didn't mean to tell me, and she got quite agitated when she realised what she'd said. But I didn't let her see I understood.'

'Holy Christ! What a fool I've been. Why didn't you tell me before?'

'So that you could keep her here, under lock and key? As you said, it's her life, Robert.'

'I don't think you understand, darling. If Tang is in Hankow, then he's there for a reason.'

'You don't think he'd go there just to be with Vicky?'

'No. But I think *she* went there to be near him. As I said, I've been a fool. I actually thought she was trying to live a normal life.'

'What are you going to do? You can't hand your own sister over to the Chinese police. And what about Marshal Yuan? Do you think he's involved?'

'Yuan is playing his own little game. Except it's a very big game. But he's not involved with Sun and Tang. If he was, Vicky would know about it, and she wouldn't have come chasing down here.'

'I'm sorry. Perhaps I should have told you before. Maybe it *would* have been better to keep her here, under lock and key. But Robert, we can still send after her. A horseman will travel faster than a junk.'

Robert shook his head. 'I'd have to send several horsemen, and getting her back here wouldn't solve anything. No. I have to go up to Hankow and try to knock some sense into her, and Tang, if need be. And it's best done up there, far away from any repercussions down here. I'll give her a couple of days start, so as not to be too obvious.'

'Robert!' Monique got up also and held his arm. 'If these people are revolutionaries, it could be dangerous.'

He grinned. 'I've coped with revolutionaries before. And Teng-chin, the Viceroy of Hopei Province, is an old friend of mine. I'll sort them out, never fear.'

*

'Is there any word from Master Martin?' Victoria asked as she entered her house. All the way on the week-long journey up the river she had been praying that he might be there when she got back, that the crisis might be over . . .

Lo Yang-li bowed. 'There is no word, Miss Victoria. But . . .' He rolled his eyes.

Victoria frowned at him, then realised what he meant. She threw her hat on a chair and ran up the stairs to her bedroom. The door was open, and the room beyond was dark. But she could make out Tang, standing by the window. 'Tang!' She was in his arms, and he was holding her tightly, and kissing her mouth. 'Thank God!'

'Where have you been?'

'To Shanghai.'

'Suddenly? Without informing me?'

'I'm sorry. It was an emergency.'

He released her, and she explained about Martin. 'That is not an emergency,' Tang said, when she had finished. 'It may even be useful. But I agree, it presents problems. We need to move the munitions. It would be too dangerous to keep them here if Yuan is poking his nose into our affairs. Do not fret. I will arrange it. You have but to open the warehouse at the appropriate moment.'

'But where will you take them?'

'Not far. We have an agent in the Russian quarter, with an empty godown. I will arrange for them to be moved there. Tomorrow night. Be at the Barrington godown at midnight.'

'Oh.' Waves of relief swept through her; the presence of the munitions in a Barrington warehouse had been constantly on her mind. 'Can you stay?'

He smiled. 'For an hour. It has been a long time.'

*

The excitement of seeing Tang again and the knowledge that the guns and ammunition were no longer to be her responsibility, allowed Victoria to relax for the first time since Yuan had appeared in Hankow. She wished Tang could have been a little more concerned about his son rather than the munitions, but she had long accepted that he was a revolutionary first and a father a very poor second.

The following night she sent her servants to bed early with strict instructions not to move, and then put on Chinese clothes, and made her way from the house to the godown. Tang was already there, with a dozen men, and there were several sampans waiting; the Russian Concession was about half a mile up-river. She wondered at the link with the Russians. From what she had read and been told of the Tzarists, they would only be helping if there was something in it for them. But that was Tang's business, and presumably, if the Russians were prepared to help the Kuomintang, that would greatly add to their strength.

The crates of rifles and ammunition were taken from the Barrington godown to the sampans, the men forming a long procession to and from the dock. Other men stood guard where the road dipped down to the river, to keep off any curious passers-by, but there were few people about. 'You will be glad to see the back of them, eh?' Tang remarked.

'You can believe that,' Victoria said fervently. Soon after two the last crate had been loaded, and the last sampans were ready to leave. 'Do you wish me to come with you?' she asked.

'No,' Tang said. 'It would be better if you did not. Go back to your house and go to bed. I will come to you tomorrow, if I can.'

There were too many of his men watching them, so she merely squeezed his arm and then hurried away. She passed several people and no doubt most of them recognised her even in the darkness, but no one would attempt to interfere with Victoria Barrington. Soon she was home, wet through with sweat. She poured herself a glass of brandy, drank it slowly, then went up to her room. She stripped off her clothing and lay on the bed, and was asleep in seconds.

And awake it seemed only a few seconds later. For a moment she could not decide what had awakened her, then she heard the distant pop-pop of rifle and revolver shots.

She leapt out of bed and ran to the window, looking down the hill at the water. But there was no great activity down there; the shooting was coming from a lot further away. The Russian Concession? Heart pounding, she pulled on a dressing gown and rang her bell. She had to ring it several times before her maid appeared, bleary-eyed and sleepy. 'Send me Lo Yang-li,' she commanded.

Lo by contrast was wide awake. 'What is happening?' Victoria demanded.

'I do not know, Miss Victoria. There was a great bang, and then the sound of shots. You can hear them still.'

'A great bang?' Was that what had woken her up?

'An explosion, Miss Victoria. Like a big bomb.'

'Oh, my God,' she muttered. 'Lo, I wish you to go out and discover what has happened.'

'Now, Mistress?'

'Now,' Victoria insisted.

*

Further sleep was impossible. Victoria summoned her maid

again, had a bath, and got dressed. Then she went on to the
verandah. The sound of shooting had died down, but there
was still a great deal of noise from up-river. Something had
gone dreadfully wrong.

Lo was back just before dawn to confirm her worst fears.
'They are saying that some men, revolutionaries, Miss
Victoria, were stealing arms and ammunition from the
Russian Concession when they were seen by guards and
accosted. Then there was an explosion, and the guards
opened fire. The revolutionaries returned fire, Miss Victoria.
There was a regular battle.'

Victoria's throat was dry. 'Were the revolutionaries
captured?'

'No, Miss Victoria. They shot their way through the
guards and escaped to the north, with the guns.'

Thank God for that, she thought. But ... 'Was anyone
hurt?'

'Oh, yes, Miss Victoria. Five of the guards were killed,
and three of the revolutionaries.'

Victoria's heart gave a painful lurch. 'Do they know who
they were, Lo? Who they worked for?'

'No, Miss Victoria. The men were killed instantly, before
they could be questioned.'

Victoria could not help but be relieved at that . . . save for
the possibility that one of the dead men might be Tang
himself. But she didn't know what to do. She could not ask
Lo any more questions about the dead men without arousing
his curiosity; he had no idea that her Chinese lover was
connected with anything subversive. She realised she would
just have to be patient. Tang would send her a message as
soon as he was able.

*

She went to the office and tried to work, but it was
impossible. She did not suppose anyone in Hankow did any
work that day, as rumours swept the city. She listened to the

tramp of feet and watched Bannermen taking up their positions at strategic points on the walls, apparently expecting some kind of assault. Had Tang received orders from Dr Sun? Or was it something to do with Yuan? Her brain was in a terrible spin. And then, just as she was ready to go home, one of the clerks knocked on her door. 'Pardon me for interrupting you, Miss Victoria,' he said. 'But I have a letter for you.'

Victoria snatched at the envelope. 'Who delivered it?'

'A man, Miss Victoria. He would not wait, but left immediately.'

Victoria nodded, and the clerk closed the door behind himself. She slit the envelope, took out a single sheet of paper. On it was written: 'I am hurt and must see you. Be at your dock at midnight. Tang.'

Relief at having heard from him was immediately overtaken by alarm that he was wounded. But at least he had sent for her. She hurried home, had a bath and pretended to eat a leisurely dinner, dismissed her servants and went to her room. As with the night before, she changed her European frock for Chinese pantaloons and tunic and flat hat. She did not have to worry about her hair, as it was as black as any Chinese woman's, and in the dark it would not be possible for anyone to discern the difference in texture.

She sat at her open window, looking out at the lights of the city, listening to the challenges of the Bannermen, drifting on the still air. But the Bannermen had not been posted around the Barrington godowns.

At a quarter to midnight she stole downstairs through the silent house, and out on to the street. Hankow, like any Chinese city, was still active; dogs barked, music jangled, fire-crackers exploded, people talked in high-pitched voices. As usual, Victoria passed through them without incident and made her way down the beaten-earth road to the dock. Here the noise was even increased by the sounds of the sampancity a little further down-river, but it was also overladen with the whisper of the constantly flowing water. And already waiting was a small rowing-boat, and three men. 'Miss Victoria?' one of them asked.

Victoria held his hand to get into the boat. She sat in the stern, and the man took his place in the bow. The oarsmen bent their backs, and the boat surged away from the dockside.

Within a few minutes they were shrouded in utter darkness as they moved downstream from the city, taking advantage of the current, and swept out into the centre of the stream to avoid the sampan-city. Victoria asked no questions. She was content that they were taking her to Tang. They continued down-river for perhaps a mile below the sampan-city, and then put into the bank. Here there were more men, and several horses.

'How far is it?' Victoria asked as she mounted.

'It is not far,' one of the men answered.

'I must be back by dawn.'

'General Tang will tell you what to do,' the man said.

She was content with that also; Tang could not be very badly hurt if he was still in command. With an escort of six men she rode away from the bank and into the low foothills; the swamp was to her left. They rode for another hour, and she realised that her visit with Tang was going to have to be very brief; it was already past two. But now they were in a defile, and a few minutes later emerged into a little valley, where there was an encampment; fires burned, and there were several tents and huts. Victoria looked up to her left and saw an armed man on the hillside silhouetted against the night sky. That was a relief, but even so . . . 'You are far too close to the city to make a camp like this,' she told the captain of her escort.

He merely smiled. 'We will move on, as soon as you have seen the General.'

The horses were brought to a halt before the largest of the huts, and were immediately surrounded by armed men, and women. Victoria dismounted, and the people came closer to peer at her. She took off her hat to let them see her better, know that she was the General's woman. The captain of her escort gestured at the doorway to the hut, and Victoria pushed it open. She was mentally braced for something unpleasant, blinking in the light which guttered from half a dozen lanterns. Inside the single room there were six men and three women, and, lying on the floor on the far side of the room, Tang's body.

*

Tang's *body*? Victoria's heart gave a great lurch and she stumbled forward, dropping to her knees. But Tang was obviously dead; there were masses of dried blood on the blankets in which he was wrapped, and although he was well bundled up, she thought he might have lost an arm. She was surprised that she had no desire to weep. Their relationship had been too odd, too one-sided perhaps. Equally, perhaps, she had always known it would end like this. Only she had supposed she would be at his side when he fell. 'When did it happen?' she asked.

'After we returned here,' one of the men said. 'But we knew he was dying, when he was hit. He knew it too.'

'And he told you to send for me,' Victoria said. That at least was something, she supposed.

'Great Tang did not send for you, Barrington woman.' Victoria's head turned, slowly. 'He never called your name,' the man said.

'He knew you had betrayed him, betrayed the Cause,' said another.

Victoria rose from her knees and turned to face them. All the faces in the room were hostile. They had summoned her here . . . her stomach felt curiously light. But she could not let them see she was afraid of them. 'That is nonsense,' she said.

'Is it not true that Marshal Yuan Shih-k'ai came to your house in Shanghai, only a month ago?' asked the first man.

'And you went to his,' said the second of her interrogators.

'And then sent your son away with him,' said the third.

Victoria found she was panting, and inhaled slowly to get her breathing under control. 'That is not true. It is true the Marshal came to see me. It was a social call. And I did not give him my son. My son ran away to be with the Marshal.'

'Will you deny that you went down-river but a fortnight ago, to report to your brothers? Men known to be opposed to Dr Sun.'

'No,' Victoria snapped. 'I went to see my brothers to ask for their help in getting my son back from Marshal Yuan.'

'You betrayed Great Tang,' the first man said. 'You betrayed the Cause. How can you explain that only a month after Marshal Yuan's visit the Bannermen knew of Great Tang's decision to move the munitions from your warehouse to one in the Russian Concession? They were waiting for us.'

'I do not know,' Victoria shouted. 'You have no proof that I betrayed you.'

'We will get proof,' the second man said.

'Well, until you do, return me to my home.'

The man smiled. 'You will give us the proof, Barrington woman. You will confess your guilt.'

'I'll see you damned first.'

'Then we will make you.' He waved his hand and four men came forward. Victoria thought of striking at them, perhaps attempting to break out of the hut, then decided against it; there was no way she could escape, and if she tried, they might only hurt her. But they were going to hurt her anyway, she realised; hurt her and humiliate her. Two of the men held her arms while a third lifted her blouse over her head. Another pulled down her pantaloons, and the European-style drawers she wore beneath. 'Be sure my brothers will know of this,' she gasped, still trying to make herself keep still, terribly aware of being stared at by every pair of eyes in the room.

'Your brothers will never know of you again, Barrington woman. You have betrayed the tong, and your oath to the tong. You will confess your betrayal, and you will tell us to whom you betrayed us, and to what extent. Then you will die. Confess now, and you will die with dignity. Refuse to confess, and they will hear your shrieks in Hankow.'

Victoria tried to fight back the panic that was threatening to seize her mind. She was terribly aware that although these men did not know it, she *had* betrayed the tong, to Robert, seventeen years ago in Port Arthur. And then had inadvertently let slip to Monique that Tang had been visiting her in Hankow. Monique would certainly have told Robert, and Robert ... but she had only left Shanghai ten days previously. There was no earthly way that Robert could have alerted the Viceroy in Hankow – there was no telegraph up the river – just as there was no way he could have known about Tang's decision to move the munitions. 'Listen to me,' she said. 'How could I betray Great Tang? Is he not the father of my child? I regard him as my husband. How could I betray my husband?'

'You will suffer the bastinado.'

'No!' Victoria shouted. She had often enough seen men, and women, bastinadoed; it was the standard punishment in China for any offence short of a capital crime, and it was also used for interrogation. But always she had turned away in disgust from watching the caning, the horrible humiliation of being stretched naked on the ground and reduced to a gibbering wreck.

'No!' she shrieked, as the men dragged her forward and forced her to her knees. 'You cannot do this to me! I am a ...' She had been going to say white woman. But that suggestion of some innate superiority would only anger them. 'I am a Barrington,' she cried.

There were men and women all around her now, intent upon enjoying her ordeal with true Chinese pleasure in inflicting pain and degradation. Victoria tried to fight them, but there were far too many people grasping her arms, pulling her legs away from her so that she fell on her face and bit earth. She tried to rise, and her legs were dragged

straight, as were her arms, each ankle and each wrist held by
two pairs of eager hands. She twisted her face in the dust and
tried to shout, but her mouth was filled with dirt. She heard
a swishing sound, and gave a gasp of terror.

Then she felt a tap on her buttocks. Her head jerked, but
it was just a tap. Then there was another, and another. She
knew there would be a man standing to either side of her,
each armed with a bamboo cane, each hitting her with a
steady rhythm. She twisted her head to and fro, as the
succession of taps suddenly started to hurt, while their
monotonous thuds seemed to seize her brain in a giant vice.

Still the blows continued, one after the other. Victoria's
buttocks became a mass of pain, and the agony spread
through her groin, down into her thighs and up into her
chest. She lost control of her muscles and her body ground
into the dust as it writhed, unavailingly. She had no saliva,
could only pant for breath and feel ... the agony continued
even after the caning had stopped. Indeed she was not aware
of the cessation for several moments.

Then she realised that her wrists and ankles had also been
released. She rolled on her side and drew up her knees
against her stomach, hugging herself, and wept and whim-
pered with the pain. The chief interrogator stood over her.
'We will give you the rest of the night to reflect. Tomorrow
you will be caned again.'

They seized her arms to drag her up. She fell over and her
lacerated buttocks touched the earth. She screamed in agony
and leapt to her feet. The men grinned at her and dragged her
outside. They had taken off her boots and her toes smarted
as they encountered stones. She blinked in the darkness, at
the faces all around her, and then again in sheer horror as she
realised she was not going to be given any break in her
ordeal. In front of her was the wooden cage in which
condemned criminals were confined. Its door was pulled
open, and she was thrust inside the wicker struts. She would
have sunk to her knees but several of the men held her
upright while the top of the cage was brought out. This was

fitted over her head, and the inner, steel ring was tightened by means of a screw, so that it gripped her neck, not tightly, but sufficiently to prevent her withdrawing her head. She was thus held upright, unable to move more than her arms and legs.

They did not mean her to die, yet. In ordinary cases the top of the cage was sufficiently far from the floor so that the condemned man had to stand on tiptoe, or strangle. Hers was an inch or two lower, so that she could stand firmly on her feet ... but she would still begin to strangle if she fell asleep or allowed her exhausted, pain-filled legs to give way.

The cage was placed beneath a tree, and a stout rope cable attached to it, behind Victoria's back. This cable was thrown over one of the branches, and the cage was hoisted some two feet from the ground, where it swung in a gentle circle. Victoria immediately lost her sense of balance, and had to stamp her feet to stop herself from falling over and hanging. The men moved away, and she could pray for the swinging to cease. But that was not to happen for some time, as her torment was now taken up by the women in the party, as well as several young boys and girls. These poked at her through the bars, with sticks or their fingers, aiming at her nipples or between her legs, or worst of all, at her buttocks, causing her to whimper with agony and again to have to stamp her feet to stay upright.

The humiliation went on for nearly an hour, but at least it kept her awake. When finally the children got bored and went off to sleep, Victoria's muscles gave way and for a moment she hung from her chin, until she jerked back into wakefulness.

And wondered why? Would it not be better to strangle now, as quickly as possible? She did not know what method of execution Tang's people had in mind for her, but she did not think she could survive another caning: if she did not die she would go mad. Yet survival was an essential part of her personality. She was a Barrington. Barrington women fought to the end. Aunt Joanna had survived the T'ai-P'ing, by refusing to give in. Helen had not survived the Boxers, but at least she had faced them to the end. She could do no less.

As for her grief . . . it still had not come to overwhelm her. Perhaps it never would. Tang must have felt she had betrayed him, at the end, or he would surely at least have spoken her name. Thus perhaps he had never trusted her, however much he had been prepared to use her. Again she slumped, her eyes shut, exhaustion overcoming even the pain in her buttocks. And again she jerked upright as she began to choke. She attempted to lick her lips, but her mouth was too dry. Her thirst suddenly overwhelmed all her other misery. Water! If she could only have some water . . .

Her entire body stiffened at a sound behind the cage. If they were coming back to torment her . . .

'You are in great pain,' a man's voice whispered.

Victoria turned round, slowly, her chin scraping on the iron. It was perhaps an hour before dawn, and very dark; she could only make out a shadow. 'I will set you free,' the man said, and she recognised his voice.

'Ching San!' she gasped.

'Do not make a noise,' Ching said. 'I will set you free. If you will be my woman. I have watched you, with Tang. I remember you, the day we took the oath. I wanted you then, but I knew I must be patient. Now you must be mine, or you must die.'

Victoria did not hesitate. She would have agreed to anything to get out of that cage. 'Yes,' she panted. 'Yes, I will be yours.'

'You must swear this, by the Christian God.'

Victoria drew a sharp breath. But He would have to forgive her. 'I swear it.'

Ching San came up to the cage, and released the bolts. Then he unbolted the collar. Victoria's knees gave way and she collapsed into his arms.

'We must hurry,' he said. 'The camp will stir in an hour.'

'Water,' Victoria begged. 'I must have water.'

Ching San carried her towards the waiting horse, and from

his saddle-bag took a water bottle and held it to her lips. Nothing had ever tasted so marvellous. 'Can you sit?' he asked.

Victoria's buttocks were still a mass of pain. But she could not walk very far either, and the thought of being laid face down across a saddle was repulsive. 'I will sit. Have you any clothes for me?'

'We will find you clothes later.' Victoria was not going to argue at that moment. He had saddled two horses. Cautiously she swung into the saddle, and almost screamed with the agony of it, but she gritted her teeth and followed him as he walked his horse away from the camp. 'If you try to run away, Miss Victoria, I will shoot you dead,' he told her, and showed her both the rifle slung on his back and the revolver hanging from his waist.

'I shall not run away,' she said. 'But what of the guard?'

Ching San grinned. 'I am the guard, at this hour. Am I not clever?'

'Yes,' Victoria said. 'You are very clever.'

*

Victoria had no idea of what Ching San ultimately had in mind. If he meant to return her to Hankow, she thought she could put up with the rape and have her brothers deal with him later. But they hadn't travelled more than half a mile from the encampment before she realised that he was riding north-east, away from the river, as well as from Hankow. If she was going to save herself, she was going to have to do it soon.

'Where are you taking me?' she asked.

'Somewhere safe,' he replied. But they rode only until dawn, and then he drew rein. 'We will camp in that wood.'

They were in fairly heavily wooded country, well away from the river now, Victoria estimated, and in the foothills of the mountains. But they could not be more than ten miles from the Kuomintang encampment. 'You call this safe?' she demanded. 'They will trail us with the greatest of ease.'

Ching San grinned as he led them towards the nearest clump of trees. 'They have no time to chase behind us. Today they attack Hankow.'

'Attack Hankow? Those few men?'

'There are many thousands coming through the mountains to join them. It was already decided, before the fight at the Russian Concession. They cannot be stopped now.'

'But, without Tang, or the extra guns, they will be massacred. The Bannermen are fully alerted.'

Ching San lifted her down. 'That is not our concern now. The more of the Kuomintang who are killed, the better, for us.' She could not avoid his hands, which held her under the armpits, set her on the ground, and then immediately moved over her breasts. 'I have dreamed of possessing these, for many years,' he said.

'I am very hungry. Have you no food?'

'Have you no feelings, woman?' he grumbled. But he turned away from her, to unbuckle his saddle-bags. She gazed at the rifle and the revolver, and also the long-bladed knife which hung at his left hip. But to make a grab for any of those, and fail ... he was as big as she, and he was not exhausted and aching in every bone and every muscle. She would have to be patient.

Ching San threw the saddle-bags on the ground. 'There is food. It is safest for us not to light a fire.'

Victoria knelt beside the bag and found some bread as well as a sack of cold chopped pork. She crammed some into her mouth, then went to the horse and drank from the water bottle. While it was at her mouth, Ching San stood against her to finger her breasts and buttocks, caress her pubes.

'I must relieve myself,' she said.

He stepped away from her and she went into the bushes. But if she hoped to find a weapon, there was nothing. Anyway there was no way she could conceal a weapon on her naked body. She would have to use his. She watched him through the bushes. He took off his rifle, unbuckled his belt, from which drooped both the holster and the sheath, and laid them together on the ground. Then he removed his clothes. Since last she had seen him naked, nearly eighteen years before, he had put on weight. But he was certainly anxious. 'Come out here, woman!' he called.

Victoria stepped from the bushes. She moved slowly towards him, swinging her hips and cupping her breasts, licking her lips and moving her head so that her hair fluttered in the breeze. As she had hoped and estimated, the sight of her apparently actually wanting him was irresistible. He came towards her. She waited until he was almost up to her, his face and penis both the picture of lust, and then she threw herself to one side, falling to the ground and rolling past him, before regaining her feet in a long, panting second. Ching San gave a roar of anger and turned. 'Now I am going to beat you!' he snarled.

But Victoria had reached the discarded clothing and the belts, and now she drew the revolver from its holster. Ching San checked. His tongue came out and circled his lips, for he could read his fate in her eyes, the thin line of her lips. He held up his hands to ward off the first bullet, but it smashed through his fingers and into his chest. Victoria drew the knife and went towards him. He lay on his back, blood gushing from the hole in the breast of his tunic and trickling from his shattered fingers. He was not yet dead, but moaned and coughed blood as Victoria knelt beside him. 'Miss Victoria,' he panted. 'Miss Victoria . . .'

Victoria cut his throat.

16

THE REVOLUTION

Robert used a sampan instead of a junk, in order to make better time. But some hundred miles east of Hankow he was hailed from the bank, and on pulling in, discovered Feng-yu the Viceroy together with a large but discomfited force of Bannermen, in full retreat down the river. 'You cannot go on, Barrington,' Feng-yu told him. 'The whole country is up in arms. The rebels have seized the arsenal at Hankow.'

'And what of my godowns? My sister?'

Feng-yu frowned. 'Your godowns are in the hands of the rebels. As for your sister, I have issued a warrant for her arrest. She is in league with the rebels. This is established by her servants. I am not sure that I should not arrest you as well. Were you aware that your sister was storing arms and ammunition in your Hankow godowns?'

'Of course I was not aware of it! It is not possible.'

'It is true, Barrington. And three nights ago, the night the revolution began, she fled from Hankow to join the rebels.'

Robert bit his lip. He could not deny *that* was possible, if Tang was indeed in the vicinity. But that Vicky should have secretly imported arms for the use of the Kuomintang ... that was *impossible*, without the signature of either himself or Adrian ... By God, he thought. Adrian!

Feng-yu nodded as he watched Robert's changing expressions. 'I think you are beginning to understand.'

'My sister is subject to the laws of extraterritoriality,' Robert said. 'If she is caught, she must be sent to Shanghai to be tried by an English consular court.'

'And be slapped on the wrist?' Feng-yu sneered. '*When* she is caught, she will be decapitated.'

The two men glared at each other, but Robert knew he was too far from his power base to use threats. 'What are your intentions?' he asked.

'Why, to withdraw down the river until I receive reinforcements.'

'In that case,' Robert said, 'you are hardly likely to arrest *any* of the rebels, much less my sister.'

*

He returned to Shanghai and summoned Adrian. 'Tell me of these munitions you have secretly been importing for the use of the Kuomintang,' he said.

Adrian raised his eyebrows. 'What are you talking about?'

Robert told him of Feng-yu's accusation. 'There seems little doubt that he is telling the truth, as he sees it. But it is not possible for Vicky to have done something like that without our knowledge. I certainly did not know of it. So ...?'

'Well, I certainly did not know of it either,' Adrian said. 'But ... my God!'

'What?' Robert frowned.

'It was several years ago now ... just before Vicky said she wanted to manage the Hankow office. Just about then, my seal was stolen.'

'You never mentioned it.'

'I didn't think it was something to bother you with. And in fact, it was found and returned to me, some weeks later. But in that time ...'

'You are saying that Vicky stole your seal and used it to authorise the importation of munitions? She could not possibly have done that all on her own.'

'Couldn't she? I wonder just how much we know about Vicky, Bobby. She has done some very odd things in her life, in the name of that lover of hers and the Kuomintang. Do we really have any idea how many of our people she has suborned with that body of hers?'

Robert stared at him in consternation. 'If she is caught with the rebels, she will be beheaded.'

'If she is caught,' Adrian pointed out. 'From all accounts, we may have a second T'ai-P'ing, a second Boxer movement, on our hands. And this revolution is directed against the Ch'ing, not the foreign devils. But we are associated with the Ch'ing. What happens when Vicky arrives in Shanghai, at the head of a Kuomintang army, a reincarnation of Cheng Yi Sao, perhaps? What happens then, brother?'

*

The soldiers slapped their gloved hands together and peered at the figure stumbling through the trees. Here in Shensi Province winter set in early, and although in late October it had not yet actually started to snow, the wind blowing out of the north was cold.

'It is a Barbarian,' said one of the men.

'And a woman,' said another.

The sergeant stroked his chin. Women by themselves did not approach Marshal Yuan's secret encampment, unless they actively wanted to be raped. As for a Barbarian woman ... but this was definitely not a Chinese. His men were equally confused. 'What shall we do?' asked the senior private.

'Call the Captain,' the sergeant said.

*

'Aunt Vicky?' Martin asked in astonishment. Could this tall, dark-haired, bedraggled creature, armed with rifle, revolver and long-bladed knife, her men's clothes in bloodstained rags, really be his aunt?

Victoria embraced him, and then looked past him at Yuan. 'I have been seeking you this past month.'

'I have heard it said that you belong to the Kuomintang,' Yuan remarked.

'No,' Victoria said. 'I have escaped them. Now I would lead you to them.'

'Can you do this?'

'I know where they are,' Victoria said.

*

Yuan saw that Victoria had a bath, found her a change of clothing, and entertained her to dinner, alone. 'You will have to convince me that I can trust you,' he said. Victoria told him what had happened to her, and what she had done. He listened in silence, stroking his scant beard. When she was finished, he asked, 'Had General Tang lived, you would still be fighting for Sun. Are you that inconstant?'

'I have been constant in love for eighteen years, your excellency. I was never a supporter of Dr Sun – only of Tang.'

'Constant in love for eighteen years,' Yuan said thoughtfully. 'That is a great recommendation. I could value such a woman.' Victoria laid down her foodsticks. 'You are still very beautiful,' Yuan pointed out, 'and my wife has been dead too many years. There have been other women, but . . .' He shrugged. 'You have found your . . . ah, nephew. Do you not wish to stay with him? He is like a son to me, far more so, from what you have told me, than Tang ever was a father to him. And you can never go back to your brothers, because now they will know of your hand in supplying the Kuomintang with weapons. You can only ever return to Shanghai in my care.'

To return to Shanghai, Victoria thought, I need your protection more than even you know. But to do as he asked ... He was fat and unattractive and old enough to be her father, and she knew instinctively that he would demand much more than Tang had ever done. Sex to Tang had never been more than a means to an end; sex to Yuan would be an end in itself.

But to be able to be near Martin, always, and with the promise of avenging herself upon all those who had wronged her, and sought to keep her son from his rightful place as Master of the House, she thought she would yield to the devil himself. Yuan recognised his triumph. 'Take off your blouse,' he said. 'That I may see your beauty.'

Victoria lifted the tunic over her head. Yuan reached across the table with one of his foodsticks. He had just sucked it clean of sauce, and now he used it, slowly and deliberately, to trace round her right nipple, watch it harden. He was taking possession, in his own peculiar fashion. Victoria kept still, and kept her breathing even too. 'You have suffered the bastinado,' Yuan remarked. 'Are there no scars on your buttocks?'

'Yes, there are scars,' Victoria said.

'Show me them also,' Yuan said.

*

'I wish to be avenged on them,' Victoria said. She lay beside the Marshal, beneath the blanket, and found it strange how easily she could adapt. Or did the strangeness lie in the fact that all men, at least of similar race, wanted similar things? She had only had sex with three men in her life. Adrian she discounted, because she was certain that in his depravity he did not represent his own people; he was a monster. Many men considered Yuan Shih-k'ai to be a monster, but in bed he was little different to Tang.

There was not even that much difference in their bodies, and that also surprised her. The Marshal, fully dressed, appeared plump, perhaps even fat. But then the Marshal, sitting quietly as he listened to a report or watched an entertainment, or even supervised his troops drilling, with his straggling beard and his sleepy eyes and his thinning hair, looked like nothing so much as a contented cat on a hearth-rug in front of a roaring fire. Both impressions were utterly false. Yuan Shih-k'ai might indeed be plump, but there was a good deal of hard muscle beneath the apparently soft flesh, and he had the sexual energy of a young man.

Just as she knew that behind the sleepy eyes there was a hard and ruthless brain. To that brain, and this body, she now belonged. She had walked through the mountains, a woman alone. She had fought off men who would have raped her, and men who would have robbed her. She had used her rifle and her revolver, and she had killed, as well as herself robbing, at gunpoint, to survive. She had stalked the mountain trails, in the pouring rain or beneath the scorching sun, like an avenging angel. She had sought her son. And she had found him.

But more than that, she had sought vengeance. And this was the man who could give it to her. So she asked, 'When will we march against the Kuomintang?'

Yuan smiled his sleepy smile and stroked her velvet flesh, as he might indeed have stroked a cat. 'When I am commanded to do so.' Victoria sat up in dismay. Yuan caught her round the waist and pulled her down on top of him. 'Am I not a servant of the Ch'ing?' he asked. 'Would you have me break my oath of allegiance to the Dynasty?' Victoria tried to free herself, and his grip tightened. 'You are impatient, my dearest Vicky. All Barbarians are impatient. There is a time for all things. You will be avenged. When I cut off my pigtail, then will you be avenged.'

Victoria peered past his neck. 'But . . .'

'I have already cut off my pigtail?' Yuan smiled. 'But only you and I, and my immediate aides, know this. Would you have me shout it to the world?'

*

A British warship off the mouth of the Yangtse-Kiang fired a twelve-gun salute. Masses of people lining the waterfront cheered. Armed Chinese – no Bannermen were to be seen – fired rifles into the air, and were accompanied by a thousand fire-crackers. 'Are you going to see the show?' Adrian asked.

He had come over from his house to be with his brother and sister-in-law, and James, who stood on the verandah to watch the excitement. 'He has to come up the river,' Robert pointed out.

'Well, I think I will go and mingle with the hoi polloi,' Adrian decided. 'This fellow may well turn out to be our master, before not too long.'

He has already turned out to be our master, at least here on the Yangtse, Robert thought. With the rapid and complete collapse of Ch'ing authority along the river, an assembly claiming to represent all the Empire – although it had come mainly from the southern provinces – had elected Sun Yat-sen President of the Republic of China . . . before the doctor had even returned from America.

'Can I come with you, Uncle Adrian?' James asked. 'I so want to see the Sun.'

Adrian grinned. 'I think you want to be careful how you refer to him. But you can come, if your ma and pa don't mind.'

Monique looked at Robert, who shrugged. 'Stay close to your uncle. And keep him out of trouble, Adrian.'

Adrian held the boy's hand as they went down the steps and along the road to the Barrington dock.

'What is going to happen, Robert?' Monique asked.

Over the past eleven years she had learned the meaning of the word, security. But here was revolution, all over again.

'I'm damned if I know,' Robert said. 'Although I suspect Adrian is right, and we are going to have to do business with this fellow. His people hold the entire length of the Yangtse.'

'But surely the Ch'ing are going to have to do something about it?'

'It's difficult to see what they can do, save call on Yuan Shih-k'ai, and it appears that their pride is preventing them from doing that. Without Yuan the Banner Army is a joke. And Sun's people are dedicated. It really is rather reminiscent of what Father told me about the T'ai-P'ing. Sun is a Christian, you know. So was Hung Hsiu-ch'uan, who called himself the Heavenly King. He thought he was Christ's younger brother.'

Monique shivered. 'He was mad.'

'Yes, he was. And an utter monster. The point is that the Dynasty couldn't do much about him either, for a long time.'

'Do you think Victoria will come home, now?' They had heard nothing of her since the Hankow revolution, two months ago.

'I wish I could answer that, too,' Robert said.

*

'Mr Barrington!' Sun Yat-sen was a little below medium height, in European terms, but was at once handsome, with his neatly brushed black hair and his pencil moustache, and quietly dressed – in a Western-style suit. If he had been at all impressed by the wildly adulatory welcome he had received in Shanghai he did not show it; nor was there any hostility in either his gaze or his voice as he took in the Barrington house, the splendid crockery, the cloisonné work which filled every brass-topped ornamental table, the parquet flooring ... and the bowing Chinese servants. Which was more than could be said for his aides, who clustered at the top of the steps and muttered amongst themselves.

'Dr Sun,' Robert said in reply. 'May I present my wife and son. My brother you already have met, I believe.'

Sun bent over Monique's hand. 'The Barringtons have always been blessed, so I have heard, Mrs Barrington, in their good fortune.' Monique blushed prettily, and uncertainly, as she glanced at her husband. 'You must meet my wife, Madame Sun, as soon as she arrives,' Dr Sun went on. 'But now, we men must talk business, I am afraid.'

Robert nodded, and Monique escorted James from the room. Adrian would have stayed, but Sun gave him a cool stare, and he bit his lip in anger as he too withdrew to the verandah. Sun seated himself, his hands clasped primly on his lap. 'May I speak frankly?'

'There is no other way, your excellency, if we *are* going to accomplish anything worthwhile.'

'Good,' Sun said. 'Well, Mr Barrington, the situation is a strange one. I am sure you have known of me, and my aspirations, for many years.' He waited for Robert's nod. 'So, you see, I have planned revolution for twenty years and more, at the risk of my life, from time to time, and, sadly, at the cost of the lives of many of my associates.'

Robert realised that Sun would know it was James Barrington who had instigated the arrest of the Shanghai tong back in 1894. But he wondered if Sun also knew that Victoria was one of his most fervent adherents, and had indeed helped him more materially than almost anyone else? He decided against raising her name for the moment.

'I will confess to you,' Sun went on, 'that there have been occasions when I have despaired of bringing my revolution to fruition. And then, suddenly, by mistake, it happens. An over-zealous subordinate, quite unforeseen betrayal, a raid by government forces, and we have an eruption which has convulsed the entire Yangtse-Kiang. It leads one to suppose that the Ch'ing Dynasty and Government is more rotten than one had estimated, if its rule along the Yangtse can collapse so rapidly and so completely.'

'It is not what it was,' Robert conceded.

Sun gave a brief smile. 'Meaning since the death of Tz'u-hsi? However, she is dead, and we now have lesser mortals to deal with. Indeed, I believe there are only two of those giants who stood at the Dowager Empress's shoulder and supported her through thick and thin left alive and in positions of power. I am, of course, speaking of Yuan Shih-k'ai and Robert Barrington.'

'You flatter me, your excellency.'

'Yours is the wealthiest and most powerful trading house in China. You are now, if you will permit me to be crude, in my power, by that peculiar set of circumstances I have outlined. I could close you down. I could have you and all your family shot. Certainly I could put you and all your family on the next ship for England, forbidden ever to return.' Robert licked his lips. 'But what would I have accomplished?' Sun asked. 'I would merely have created an enormous vacuum in the heart of this great country I hope to rule. I think China needs the House of Barrington, Mr Barrington.'

'Now you flatter *us*, Dr Sun.'

Sun gave another of his quick smiles. 'So what I need to know, Mr Barrington, is whether you serve China, or the Ch'ing. Your family has lived in China for well over a hundred years. You were born here and have lived all of your life here. You are a Christian, I imagine. So am I. But I am also sure that we can both appreciate the useful aspects of Confucianism. Would you not say that the Ch'ing have lost the Mandate of Heaven? Now, before you answer, I wish to put your mind at ease on certain matters. I mean the Emperor no harm, nor any of his family, unless they openly oppose me in arms. To this effect I have written to the Regent, offering the P'u-i abdication and honourable retirement, with an income of four hundred thousand pounds a year. That is a great deal of money.'

'May I ask where it is going to come from?'

'From the Government, of course, as soon as we are established in power. Now let me make another point. I say we, because I am an optimist. But this government I speak of will be an elected one. I have been elected President of China, but from a limited franchise. I wish to confirm this with another, more general election. I believe the Kuomintang will

win that election, and that I *will* become President of China.
But if we do not win, if some other party arises under some
other leader, and he is elected, then I give you my most solemn
word that I will retire into private life. However, I will make it
a condition of so doing that any arrangement I may have come
to with the Ch'ing will be honoured by the government taking
office. So now, will you give me your answer?'

Robert had already made up his mind. He knew that Sun
was right, and the collapse of the House of Barrington would
be a disaster for China. Therefore he was in a much stronger
position than might appear to those who saw only the
Kuomintang soldiers thronging the streets and surrounding
his house. But he also knew, as he had known since Tz'u-
hsi's death, that the Dynasty was finished, waiting only for
the push that would overturn it. He flattered himself that he
had prevented Yuan from giving that push by his threat to
oppose it – not for any urgent desire to preserve a moribund
government, but because he knew that Yuan aimed at a
military dictatorship. That Yuan held Martin could not be
allowed to sway his certainty of that.

And now ... here was a man with whom he could do
business. A man who spoke of democracy. Robert remembered that his father had had the most utter contempt for the
prospects of democracy ever working in China. But surely
it had to be tried, before it could be written off as a failure?

More importantly, Sun was a man Robert knew he could
like; he already did so, on this brief acquaintance. And most
important of all, only by dealing with Sun did he have any
hope of discovering what had happened to his only remaining sister ... or of saving her life, if she was still alive. But
did Sun have any idea what he was about? 'I will give you
my support, Dr Sun,' he said. 'Such as it is. Financially I
may be of some assistance. My links with England and
Europe may also be useful. But I do not command an army.
Yuan Shih-k'ai does. What of him?'

'I can only deal with one obstacle at a time,' Sun said. 'I
regarded you as the more important, Mr Barrington. Now

that I am sure of you, why, now I can turn my thoughts to dealing with Marshal Yuan.'

*

Yuan Shih-k'ai unfolded the heavy paper, slowly and with great relish. He reclined in his chair in front of his tent. Around him was all the restless bustle of an awakening army, because here in the mountains there *was* an army, his army, carefully recruited and then trained, thirty thousand uniformed, well-equipped and confident fighting men. He had all but bankrupted himself creating them; they were all he now owned. But he was certain they would restore him all his wealth, and more besides. They but awaited his word to march, and only he knew in which direction he would lead them. But now it was to be made easy for him.

His officers waited as he read the imperial command. Martin Barrington felt a growing excitement. In the months since he had opted to serve this man, he had grown to worship him. It was not merely that Yuan had provided him with everything of which he had ever dreamed; he had also learned to appreciate the Marshal's talent, his determination, and his breadth of vision. Like every soldier in the army, he had no doubt that Yuan Shih-k'ai was the man of the future. That Aunt Victoria had become the Marshal's mistress merely made Martin the more certain that Yuan was *his* future as well; blessed as he was with his own harem of boys and girls – provided by the Marshal – he was not going to criticise anything Victoria did.

Yuan smiled, and folded the paper again. He looked at his officers. 'Gentlemen,' he said. 'I am commanded by the Regent to proceed to Hankow, and put down this rebellion. To do this, I am restored to all my ranks and privileges as a marshal of China.' He looked at one of his officers, recently arrived from the south. 'Tell me again what you saw of the Kuomintang.'

'They are great in number, your excellency. Many

thousands. They control the entire river. They also control
Nanking and Shanghai.' He glanced at the door leading to
the living quarters of the Marshal's house; he knew Victoria
Barrington was in there. 'I have heard it said that they
control the House of Barrington, as well. And now that Dr
Sun has returned, they are claiming he is the true ruler of
China.'

'Which is why the Regent wishes him destroyed,' commented Li Yuan-hung, the Chief of Staff.

'Give me your opinion on the chances of our success in
a campaign against this Kuomintang,' Yuan told the first
officer.

'The Kuomintang are not well disciplined, your excellency. I believe, despite their large numbers, that we should
defeat them. But it will not be a short campaign, or an easy
one.'

Yuan smiled. 'That is a very good report, Colonel.
Gentlemen, we march today.' Once again he smiled at them.
'But we will not go to Hankow, I think. Nor will we go to
Nanking or Shanghai. I think our destiny lies more to the
East.'

*

'Here is a letter from Peking,' Adrian announced.
'Addressed to you, and from Marshal Yuan.' Robert took the
envelope with a frown. 'I did not even know he was in
Peking,' Adrian remarked. 'I thought he was still up in
Shensi, mobilising his army.'

'So did I,' Robert said thoughtfully, slitting the envelope.
'Good God!'

'Well?' Adrian inquired.

Robert read: '"I am sending you this by my fastest
courier, as I wish you to be the first to know. Yesterday, 12
February 1912, I had an audience with the Regent, Prince
Ch'un, at which the P'u-i Emperor was present. I informed
His Majesty and his father that the country could no longer

tolerate the rule of the Ch'ing, and offered them the choice between honourable, and prosperous, retirement, and summary deposition and imprisonment."'

Robert raised his head to look at Adrian; the Ch'ing had not even acknowledged Sun Yat-sen's proposal.

'By God,' Adrian said. 'He's gone and done it.'

Robert resumed reading: '"Prince Ch'un was pleased to accept my offer on behalf of the P'u-i.

'"I understand, Robert, that you have always felt your loyalty to the Dynasty must override all other considerations. The Dynasty is no more. I must now ask you to reconsider the situation, and offer the Empire that loyalty. I understand your suspicions of me. I wish to dispel them. I am assuming the duties of Regent myself, for the time being. But this is only until we can have nationwide elections for the purpose of selecting a suitable governing body, and a suitable executive. In this regard, I wish you to know that I have invited Dr Sun Yat-sen to meet with me to discuss these arrangements, and that I intend to permit him and his followers to partake fully in the coming elections."'

'Have my horse saddled,' Robert snapped, reaching for his hat.

*

He rode into Shanghai, to where Sun had set up his headquarters. Here he was checked and searched by the doctor's bodyguard, under the supervision of their hard-faced young guard commander, Captain Chiang Kai-shek.

But Sun greeted him with a broad smile. 'Well, Barrington, things are moving our way. I have been informed that the Regent, acting for the P'u-i Emperor, has issued a decree that there are to be elections for a General Assembly which will "assist" him in governing the Empire. He has not exactly accepted my terms, but it is a step in the right direction. It is probably best that we hold this first election under the auspices of the Dynasty. Once elected, we can demand his abdication, and that of the Emperor. The whole affair should pass off without violence.' He frowned at Robert's expression. 'This does not please you, Barrington?'

'I'm afraid your news is stale, Dr Sun.' Robert gave him Yuan's letter. 'This arrived not an hour ago.'

Sun's frown deepened as he read, then his brow cleared. 'Marshal Yuan is behaving like a soldier, to be sure. But what can one expect, from a soldier? And to use a Western metaphor, he has certainly cut the Gordian Knot. I must go to Peking immediately.'

'Are you bent on suicide?'

Sun raised his eyebrow. 'You do not trust the Marshal?'

'No, I do not, Dr Sun. You have recently been elected provisional President of China . . .'

'Only by half the country,' Sun pointed out.

'That is something you should not make much of, in my opinion. It is a part of the country which you control. Marshal Yuan has no legal basis for his power, and he understands this. He is seeking one, in the offer to hold elections and in co-operation with you. But until these elections are held, you are President of China. He must come to you, meet you on *your* terms.'

Sun stroked his chin.

'There is much sense in what Barrington says,' commented Captain Chiang Kai-shek.

'And suppose I refuse the invitation, and Marshal Yuan decides to march against us?' Sun asked. 'Will we defeat him, Captain?'

'We will make him rue the day,' Chiang vowed.

'I doubt that. He is a soldier. That is all he has done all his life, soldier. He commands a large and well-disciplined army. These are not effete Bannermen, but professional soldiers like himself. And it will mean many deaths. It will mean civil war. I cannot permit that, if it is at all avoidable. I will go north, to meet the Marshal. But the meeting will take place publicly, before the eyes of the world and the

world's press. There is a body of opinion not even Yuan
Shih-k'ai will wish to offend. Barrington, you will accompany me. Yuan will not want to harm you any more than I
do. Besides, you know the fellow. You will be able to advise
me. But let there be no mistake . . .' He looked over the
anxious faces in the room. 'As Barrington has reminded me,
I have been elected President of China. Until the people
reveal their will otherwise, I am President of China. And I
go north as President of China. You will arrange it, Captain
Chiang, with Barrington here.'

*

'This is madness,' Monique declared. 'You cannot go,
Robert. You know Yuan better than anyone. You know he
means to seize power.'

'He has already seized power. But Sun is right. Yuan's
anxiety to do things legally, to make it appear that he is
acting for the good of the Empire and with the consent of the
people, shows how important it is to him to have world
approval for his actions. I am his link with that approval. No
one is going to shed any tears for the Ch'ing, especially as
their overthrow has been accompanied by a vow to introduce
democracy into China. But the world will be watching to see
what happens next. Yuan is going to have to proceed very
carefully. He cannot afford to display himself to public
opinion as a murderer or a tyrant. I think I at least will be
perfectly safe.'

Monique did not look at all convinced.

Robert smiled at Adrian. 'I leave the House in your hands,
Adrian. Until I return.'

Adrian smiled back. Then he smiled at Monique. 'We will
take care of it for you, Robert. Together.'

*

Robert did not suppose China had ever known an occasion

like this. But obviously the Chinese were already coming to terms with the new regime, the way in which the Tien-an-men had been thrown open – there was talk indeed of tearing it down, and replacing it with a huge square – the way in which the populace could come and go as they pleased into the Forbidden City. Well, not entirely as they pleased. There were soldiers on guard everywhere, very smart-looking men in their peaked caps and khaki uniforms, their bandoliers and their modern weapons. There were even machine-gun emplacements on every street corner. No one could doubt that Marshal Yuan intended to prevent any extension of the revolution into Peking itself.

Blood had already been shed between the adherents of the Kuomintang and the Marshal's troops, in the north. But today, at any rate, there was peace. Excited peace, as the crowds thronged the Grand Avenue and pressed forward to have a closer look at the cavalcade passing before them.

Sun Yat-sen rode immediately in front, his bodyguard and henchman, Chiang Kai-shek, at his shoulder. Robert rode in the second rank, with Sun's other leading captains. They waited for cheers, but despite the interest of the crowds, there were no shouts of 'Sun!' to be heard. This was Yuan's crowd.

But Sun did not seem to be dismayed, or even concerned, as he approached the Tien-an-men, where Yuan awaited him, wearing a crimson tunic, decorated with medals, and white breeches. His white cocked hat sprouted a cluster of ostrich feathers. He had a gold-plated scabbard on his thigh and a white holstered revolver on his belt. His face, as ever, was relaxed and almost sleepy. He looked contented. Well, Robert thought, he had every reason to be.

He looked past the Marshal at the aides-de-camp, no less brilliantly clad, and found it easy to pick out Martin, who was taller and more heavily built than the others. The boy – he was still not yet eighteen – gazed straight in front of himself, his left hand lightly holding his horse's reins. But he too looked utterly confident, and utterly contented.

Behind and to either side of the Marshal were his élite troops, standing strictly to attention. Behind them again were the open carriages of those dignitaries invited to the ceremony, with their wives, and presumably Yuan's concubines as well, Robert thought, as he picked out a group of carriages containing only women, some distance apart from the others.

Then his heartbeat quickened and his eyes narrowed. One of the women ... she could have been Chinese, because of her lustrous dark hair. But she was too tall, and her skin was too fair. Her face was indistinct at this distance, but he knew ... Was it a sense of great relief, or one of great concern? From Tang to Yuan? Ardent revolutionary to military despot? From a man she had claimed to love to one she had always claimed to hate? But at least now he knew she was alive ... and perhaps she no longer needed rescuing.

*

Monique Barrington stepped down from her ricksha, aware of a strange sense of mixed apprehension and exhilaration. No member of the family, to her knowledge, had ever been invited to dine at Adrian's house before.

She had considered for some time before accepting. It was not possible to be unaware of Adrian's searching eyes, the way his gaze would mentally strip a woman naked, moving from her shoulders, slowly and thoughtfully, down past her bodice to her waist and then her hips. It was the sort of look that might frighten or disgust some women, but leave others merely sorry for a man who, presumably because of some character defect, had never been able to make himself do more than look, who had always been forced to content himself with serving girls. She knew all the stories, of course, that he treated his servants as slaves, flogged them as he chose. This had always distressed Robert. But Robert, with his innate reluctance to interfere in the private lives of others, as long as those private lives did not become in any way public, had always reflected that Adrian's servants, even the women – or was it especially the women? – all seemed devoted to him.

Robert had never been invited to dine.

So then, her brother-in-law would wish to look at her with those longing eyes ... and what else? She wondered if Robert would approve, or disapprove, of her decision to accept? But he had to approve, in the long run, of anything she did to bring this doomed family closer together, especially since the disappearance and almost certain death of Victoria. Did she approve herself? In fact she knew that secretly she disapproved. But she had come. She was too curious.

*

The butler greeted her gravely. 'I am Chiang Lu, madame.' A solemn, sober man of hardly less than fifty, wearing a silk tunic and pantaloons. No signs of depravity here.

Monique entered the drawing room, and was greeted by a tall, thin Chinese woman, who also bowed to her. 'Welcome, Madame Barrington. I am Wu Ping. The master invites you to take an apéritif.' Monique was more intrigued than ever. Wu Ping wore a pale blue cheong-sam, which enclosed her slender body like a glove; Monique could see no sign of any underclothes. But she too was over fifty, and there was no suggestion of beauty in either her face or her body.

She followed the woman into an inner reception room, where Adrian waited for her. He wore European dinner dress, white tie and black tail-coat, and took her hands as if they had been strangers. 'Monique, how beautiful you are.'

For Monique was in a green evening gown with a deep décolletage, her auburn hair upswept in a pompadour, her pale, lightly freckled skin almost translucent. 'Thank you, Adrian. I am not the only guest, I hope?' She had known all along that she would be, but she felt it necessary to make the comment.

'Why should we be bored by company?' he asked, leading her to a settee. Chiang Lu hovered with a tray of glasses of champagne, and Adrian handed her one before taking another for himself and sitting beside her. Then, much to her reassurance, the butler withdrew, but only as far as the wall, while the woman Wu Ping also entered the room and took up her position on the other side of the door. Perhaps, Monique thought, he is as apprehensive of being entirely alone with me as I am with him. 'I think your house is charming,' she said.

'You did not expect to find it so,' he suggested.

'Well, a bachelor, living alone ...' She glanced at Wu Ping. 'But I imagine you are well looked after.'

'I am very well looked after. I will show you the rest of the house, after dinner.' They dined on Western food, and drank French wine. Adrian was an attentive but quite charming host. Monique found herself wondering if she, and everyone else – including his own brother – might not have misjudged him over the years. It was not until the meal was ended and they were drinking brandy that he asked, 'Have you heard from Robert?'

'No, I have not. I expect he is very busy.'

'I wonder if we shall ever hear of him again.' Monique's head and hand jerked, and brandy slopped from her goblet. Instantly Wu Ping hurried forward with a napkin to dab her gown dry. 'I'm sorry,' Adrian said. 'But the future has always fascinated me. I wonder what will happen if he were to be executed by Yuan, together with Sun, of course.'

Monique drank the remainder of her brandy. 'You can say something like that, about your own brother?'

'And your husband,' Adrian smiled, signalling Chiang Lu to refill her goblet. 'But it is certainly a possibility. Do you never consider possibilities, even if they may be unpleasant?'

She gazed at him, and drank some more without thinking.

'And of course,' Adrian went on, 'there is really no necessity for that possibility to *be* unpleasant. It isn't as if you were newly-weds. Why, I would suppose you are thoroughly bored with that dry old stick by now, and desperate for some new attraction.' He continued to smile at her, while she stared at him as if he were a snake.

'It is odd the way things turn out,' Adrian went on. 'Can turn out. We Barringtons were quite a clan once. Brothers, sisters, cousins all over the place. Now, well, Vicky gone off with her bandit lover, probably dead as we haven't heard from her for so long. Her son is soon to be dead, I imagine. Yuan won't be interested in keeping him alive. Robert, probably dead. Everyone dead, save for you, your son, and me. I think that is all rather cosy. Don't you?'

Monique picked up her glass, realised it had been refilled, and put it down again. She stood up, somewhat uncertainly. 'I think I will return home now, Adrian, if you do not mind. It has been a splendid dinner, and I do not wish to spoil it by dwelling on unpleasant matters.'

Adrian stood up as well. 'But I do mind, dear sister-in-law,' he said. 'It is far too early to end the evening. I promised to show you the rest of the house.'

Monique glanced at him, then at the two servants, waiting on either side of the doorway. She had had too much to drink, and this was confusing her judgement. She genuinely did not want to quarrel with her brother-in-law, and she could not make up her mind whether or not to be afraid of him. Equally she could not believe he meant her any harm; for all his dinner conversation, he surely could not doubt that Robert was coming home. 'Very well, Adrian,' she said. 'I should greatly enjoy seeing the rest of your house. But I did tell my servants that I was returning early. I shall just go and inform them I will be a little delayed.'

'That is not necessary,' Adrian said. 'It has already been done.' He went to the door and waited for her, and after a moment's hesitation she joined him. He let her climb the stairs ahead of him, and as seemed usual, he was in turn followed by his two servants. Earlier she had found this reassuring; now she wasn't sure.

Adrian reached past her to open the first door on the landing. 'I am sure it is not as grand as yours at the Barrington house,' he said. 'But I have done the best I could.'

The electric light was already on in the room – Robert had installed a generator to serve both the houses as well as the office – and to Monique's surprise there was another Chinese woman waiting. 'This is Shu Lai-ti,' Adrian explained.

Monique gave the woman a brief nod, more than ever mystified. Shu Lai-ti was a handsome woman, and must once have been quite pretty. She was more voluptuous than the average Chinese. But she also was not a day under forty, Monique estimated. 'What do you think of it?' Adrian asked.

Monique gazed at a large, panelled room, dominated by the huge four-poster in the very centre. The floors were deep-piled carpet, and there were Chinese paintings on the walls.

'It even has its own bathroom,' Adrian said.

'It is very civilised,' Monique agreed.

'It awaits my bride,' Adrian said.

Monique was too surprised to think before she replied. 'Your bride? You, Adrian? I thought you were the most confirmed of bachelors.'

'My misfortune,' Adrian said, 'is that the women I would take to wife have always been bespoke, or unattainable. As wives, I mean. All women are attainable. For instance, were Vicky not my sister, I would have married her. I do wish to have beauty around me, and, how shall I put it? An intimacy beyond that of being merely husband and wife.' Monique frowned at him, trying to reconcile his separate statements with belief. 'Now, I fear she is gone forever,' Adrian went on. 'But before she went, I had already replaced her in my dreams with another.'

Monique listened to a soft sound, and realised the door to the landing had closed. She turned sharply. The three servants again waited, one woman on either side of the door, Chiang Lu standing immediately in front of it.

'Chiang Lu and Wu Ping and Shu Lai-ti are my alter egos,' Adrian explained. 'There is no need to be afraid of them.' He stepped behind her, put his arms round her waist, and kissed her neck. As he kissed her, his hands came up her bodice to hold her breasts. She gasped, and tried to step away, and his grip tightened. 'I mean to marry *you*, now that Robert is dead,' he said.

Monique pulled herself free; but his fingers remained lodged in her décolletage and she listened to the material ripping as she staggered across the room. She regained her balance, clasping the ruined gown against herself. 'You are drunk!' she snapped.

'I do not think I am, save with desire for you.' He moved towards her.

Monique turned to the door, and the servants. 'If you attempt to stop me leaving,' she said as evenly as she could, 'I will have you flogged.'

'Oh, you are welcome to punish them,' Adrian said. 'Providing you flog them yourself, while I watch.'

The servants had not moved, the door remained shut. Monique turned back to face her brother-in-law. Now she could not stop herself panting. 'You're mad!' she shouted. 'When Robert hears of this . . .'

Adrian grinned. 'Robert is not going to hear of this, dearest sister-in-law. Robert is dead. Or he soon will be. He will not be coming back. There are only you and me left, now.'

He reached for her bodice again, and she struck at him. He swayed his face back out of reach of her nails, and before she could decide what to do next, her arms were grasped from behind by Chiang Lu and pulled backwards. She tried to kick, but was hampered by her gown. Adrian merely stepped round her feet and pulled the bodice free, leaving it trailing from her waist to expose her breasts. These he now fondled. 'They are quite magnificent,' he said.

She strained on the arms holding her, without success, while Adrian slid his hands round her thighs to lift her from the floor; Chiang Lu still held her arms, and between them they laid her on the bed. She jerked both arms and legs, but they were too strong for her. She thought of screaming, but knew it wouldn't do her any good. In fact she was aware more of anger than fear. To have survived the Boxers to be raped by her own brother-in-law . . . Adrian was now tearing the remainder of her gown from her body. 'Don't fret, dearest Monique,' he said. 'I will replace the gown.'

When she was naked, he knelt beside her and looked down at her. Chiang Lu now held her wrists, extending them above her head, but also looking at her, as were the women, who had come to stand on the other side of the bed. Monique wanted to kick at them, but she felt it was more important to keep still, before they hurt her.

Although this was difficult when Adrian sat beside her and began to stroke her thighs, before sliding his hand across to caress her pubes. She could not stop herself from straining on the hands holding her wrists, and drawing up her knees.

'I will see you *hang*,' she spat at him.

'To possess you is going to be the supreme moment of my life,' Adrian said.

*

Robert had visited the Forbidden City on many previous occasions, but never had he been entertained there at a state dinner; the Ch'ing had not indulged in such Barbarian antics. But Yuan was determined to show the world that he was a civilised Western gentleman. What else he was determined to show the world remained to be seen.

For the past twenty-four hours there had been lavish entertainments as well as serious conferences between Yuan and Sun. Robert had been called upon from time to time as financial matters were discussed, but the two men appeared to be getting on amicably, feeling their way towards a

solution to the problem of a democratic China. Thus mostly
Robert had been left on his own. He had indicated to Yuan
that he would like to speak with his adopted son, and even
more with his sister, and Yuan had nodded gravely and said
it would be arranged. But it had not yet been arranged, and
now . . . As he entered the hall where the reception was being
held, and found himself in the middle of all the uniforms,
and all the black-coated officials as well – there was no one
present, not even Dr Sun, wearing Chinese dress – he
realised that he was also in the presence of a good number
of women. This was a surprise in that it was so totally
untraditional.

And the ladies also wore Western-style ball-gowns, some
with considerable embarrassment: a Chinese lady never
revealed any part of her body below her neck to any male
save her husband or her lover. But here were exposed
shoulders and plunging décolletages.

Even more surprising, and a little alarming, there were no
foreign diplomats present. There was Yuan and his entourage, male and female, and there was Sun and his entourage,
entirely male, amongst whom Robert supposed he must
count himself.

But at least there was Martin, resplendently uniformed
almost like a British guards' officer, in red tunic and blue
trousers, sword at his side, saluting. 'Father! I saw you at the
Tien-an-men. It is so good that you are here, to help us
rebuild the greatness of China.'

Robert clasped the boy's hand. 'It is so good to be here.'
He looked past him. 'And to see Aunt Victoria looking so
well. We had feared for her life.'

'She wishes to speak with you,' Martin said. 'Will you
come with me?'

Robert followed him across the floor. Victoria was obviously and by some distance the outstanding woman in the
room, by reason at once of her height and voluptuous build.
But in addition, here was a Victoria who exuded health and
confidence, which merely added to her outstanding beauty.

'Robert!' she smiled. 'How good to see you.'

He held her hands. 'We thought you were dead. You never wrote . . .'

'I was not in a position to do so, in the beginning,' she said. 'And these last couple of months, life has been so busy . . .' Her gaze drifted over his left shoulder, and he knew she was looking at Yuan.

'Will you forgive me if I say I find what you have done difficult to understand?' he said in a low voice. Martin had moved away to leave his supposed father and his supposed aunt in private.

'I think you probably will, when you know the truth of it,' Victoria said. 'I would like to have a private conversation with you. Tomorrow.'

'Are such things permitted, to a concubine of the warlord?'

He immediately regretted putting it that bluntly, but Victoria did not take offence. She merely smiled. 'Certainly, where one's brother is concerned. If you think I live in a harem surrounded by eunuchs . . . Shih-k'ai has abolished eunuchs.' Robert wondered what the shades of Chang Tsin must be thinking. But now Victoria was openly looking past him. 'The Marshal.'

Yuan clapped Robert on the shoulder. Tonight his uniform was white, with a liberal use of gold braid; his left breast was covered with medals. His expression was as genial as ever. 'You must be very pleased to be reunited with your sister, Robert. You will take her in to dinner. We are about to go in. Robert . . .' He gazed into Robert's eyes. 'You once refused to support me in overthrowing the Ch'ing. I have never pressed you. Now it is done. But now, as I prophesied, there is a great deal to do. Will you support me now?'

'I will support the de jure ruler of China, your excellency.'

Yuan smiled. 'De jure, de facto, you are about to indulge in Latin semantics. No matter.' He glanced at Victoria. 'Is she not the most beautiful woman in all China? Save perhaps for your own wife, Barrington. And look . . .' They followed his gaze to where Martin was deep in conversation with a Chinese woman, or rather, girl, Robert supposed, would be more accurate. 'Have you not the two most handsome sons in all China? Do you think that girl is pretty, Barrington?'

With her long black hair, her pert features – accentuated by the use of Western rouge on both cheeks and lips – and her crimson ball-gown which left the smooth yellow-brown shoulders exposed, the girl was in fact strikingly lovely. 'Yes,' he agreed. 'She is.'

'I have her in mind as a wife for Martin.'

Robert heard the sharp intake of breath which indicated that Victoria had also been unaware of her lover's plan.

'So,' Yuan said. 'As life is going to be so very pleasant for all the Barringtons, in the coming years, barring of course some entirely unforeseen misfortune to which we are all subject, I am confident that you will support whoever is forced to take on this great burden of ruling the Empire. Shall we go in?'

*

The dining room was dazzling, with its gold service, its eager, brilliantly dressed waiters, its walls draped with imperial yellow and red dragons, its orchestra, playing somewhat discordantly, but fortunately quietly, at the far end. Robert held Victoria's chair for her, and she smiled at him as she seated herself.

They were some distance away from Yuan, who had Sun on his right hand, but that was a relief, as they were enabled to talk, in English, and in almost complete privacy, despite the chatter all around them. 'So what happened to Tang?' Robert asked.

'Tang is dead.'

'And with that you changed sides?'

'It was not quite as simple as that.' She turned her head to look at him, very directly. 'I have been tortured by the

Kuomintang. I suffered the bastinado, Robert. Me. Victoria Barrington, stretched naked in the dust before a hundred people. Then they put me, naked, in a cage, to be tormented some more.' She gave a little shudder.

He bit his lip, trying desperately not to use his imagination. 'But you escaped.'

'Yes. I was rescued by Ching San. Do you remember him?'

'Good Lord, of course I do. Do you mean he was one of them too?'

'Ching San and I were initiated into the tong on the same day, standing shoulder to shoulder. It seems he always wanted me,' Victoria said. 'So he rescued me. To take possession. I killed him.'

Robert coughed into his napkin, as he realised how little he knew of his sister.

'After that,' Victoria said, 'I sought only revenge. I still do. On everything to do with the Kuomintang.'

'Seeing Yuan and Sun sitting together, I would say you might have to wait a while,' Robert suggested.

Victoria smiled. 'About an hour, I suppose.'

*

Robert looked around him at the smiling faces, the eager servants, and frowned as he saw, as the meal went on, that the servants were slowly being joined by armed men. These entered the room very discreetly, standing half concealed by the drapes, noticeable only to someone who cared to look. The Marshal was still engaged in flowing conversation. Robert found Martin looking at him and smiling, but at the same time giving a quick shake of the head. He was being warned against doing anything rash. And now the dessert course was being served, and removed.

'Why, Bobbie,' Victoria murmured. 'You've hardly eaten a thing.'

Before he could reply there was a fanfare from the

orchestra, and their leader announced, 'His Excellency, the President-Elect of China, Marshal Yuan Shih-k'ai.'

Yuan stood up, smiled at the assembly. 'My friends,' he said. 'This is an unique occasion. We are gathered here tonight, not merely to celebrate the downfall of the Ch'ing, the end of the Manchu tyranny which has sat across the Middle Kingdom for nearly three hundred years. That is indeed a cause for celebration. But we are looking to the future. We are gathered here to inaugurate a new era, an era of China ruled by Chinese, and by Chinese who have been democratically elected to office.'

He waited while the applause rang out. 'To accomplish this,' he went on, 'I have invited Dr Sun Yat-sen to Peking, that we may discern this great future of our country the more clearly.' He smiled at them. 'You all know that I have been elected President of the Republic of China by the people north of the Yangtse. No election with my name on it was ever held south of the river.'

Another pause, and now there came the first ripple of unease amongst the Kuomintang representatives. Chiang Kai-shek in particular glared left and right with angry insecurity.

'However, there has been an election, of sorts, south of the river,' Yuan continued. 'This was held by the Kuomintang, then in military control of the river and the adjacent provinces, and in the absence of their leader, Dr Sun, and consisted not in a vote of the people, but in a vote of an assembly of Kuomintang representatives. In these, shall I say, prejudiced circumstances, Dr Sun was elected *provisional* President of China.'

Now the rustle of whispered comment grew louder. But Yuan continued, his face blandly relaxed. 'Now, obviously, China cannot have two presidents. Equally obviously, my friends, the election held by an assembly of the Kuomintang must be considered invalid.'

There were shouts of anger and dismay, but these died as Yuan looked from face to face in turn. 'It is invalid because it was not democratic. Only Kuomintang representatives were present, and only one name was put forward, that of Dr Sun. On the contrary, here in the north, every adult male who could prove he has paid taxes during the past year was allowed to vote, and he was allowed to vote for whom he chose. And I was elected.'

There was a stunned silence, broken by the quiet voice of Dr Sun. 'Did these voters know their fate if they chose otherwise, Marshal Yuan?'

His supporters cheered, Yuan's scowled. But Yuan continued to smile. 'An unworthy remark, Dr Sun. My point is unarguable. When my name is put before the *voters* of the south, as opposed to the members of the Kuomintang, there can be no doubt of the result. This will be done as soon as is practical. But in the meantime, China must be governed. And it can only be governed by someone capable of exercising total authority, in the name of the people by whom he has been democratically elected. Now, as we all know, the Kuomintang is not a political party: it is a revolutionary organisation dedicated to overthrowing the Ch'ing.'

'That makes it a political party,' Sun said.

Yuan looked down at him for a few seconds, then continued. 'Thus the objectives of the Kuomintang have been achieved. The Ch'ing have been overthrown. Not, I may say, by the efforts of the Kuomintang, but by the loyalty and devotion of my soldiers, many of whom are in this room tonight.'

There was a storm of cheering which drowned the hisses of the Kuomintang, who seemed to notice for the first time that the room was indeed full of soldiers.

'Therefore I say without fear of denial,' Yuan said, looking from face to face to make sure everyone understood him, 'that it is time for the Kuomintang to disband, and to yield whatever political ambitions it may have accumulated during the past few weeks to those who are both equipped and prepared to govern. I lay claim to no party. I lay claim to an army, which will support me in anything I choose to do. I lay claim to the support and devotion of the Chinese people. And as one who has throughout his life been close to the centres of power, a member of the Grand Council for the past thirty years, I lay claim to the experience needed to govern this country. I do not accept that anyone who has spent most of those thirty years in exile from China, who has no army to carry out his decrees, and who has no standing with the ordinary people of this Empire but only with a small band of revolutionaries, can possibly hope to oppose me. I therefore, in the interests of us all, but above all, of China, call upon Dr Sun Yat-sen to resign his pretensions to the presidency.'

The great hall was absolutely silent. Robert glanced at Victoria and saw her eyes gleaming with vengeful delight.

'And if Dr Sun prefers not to resign?' asked a voice. It could have been Captain Chiang, but Robert rather felt the question had actually been put by one of Yuan's own officers, coached by Yuan himself.

Yuan gave an elaborate sigh. 'Then I will be forced to take whatever measures may be necessary to preserve the peace of the Empire.' He paused to let that sink in, and the room was deafened by the click of a hundred rifle bolts. The members of the Kuomintang exchanged glances, but they were mostly frightened glances.

'Let me say,' Yuan went on, 'here and now and unequivocally, that I mean no harm to Dr Sun or any of his followers. Dr Sun has merely to sign the document I have had prepared, resigning the provisional presidency he has so rashly claimed, and he is free to do what he wishes for the rest of his life, as are his people. Remembering always that I will have no subversion against the State, against the people, of China.'

For a last time he looked around the assembly, then he sat down.

All eyes were on Dr Sun. The doctor's face remained calm, but it was possible to see the various emotions drifting

across it. Anger, certainly, at the way in which he had been
trapped; outrage, perhaps, at so shabby an ending to his
dream. Robert could see no visible evidence of fear, but
perhaps he detected some despair. There were several
moments of silence, then Sun rose and left the table. Some
of his aides also rose, but these were immediately restrained
by Yuan's men. Other soldiers followed the doctor from the
room.

*

Yuan received Robert in his office late that night, and
gestured him to a chair. 'He signed,' he said. 'Under protest,
but he knew he had no choice.'

'You do not consider that you have behaved in a most
treacherous and underhand way? You gave Sun a safe-
conduct.'

Yuan raised his eyebrows. 'And has a hair on his head
been harmed?'

'Suppose he *had* refused to resign?'

Yuan smiled. 'To succeed in any struggle, Barrington, one
must study one's opponent. Sun is a dreamer, not a man of
action. He has, to my knowledge, never fired a shot in anger.
I do not say he is a coward, merely that he lacks the
resolution to initiate a course of action that may cost lives,
or bring misery to people. Oh, he has subordinates who are
very different men – that fellow Chiang Kai-shek is a thug
– but they have elected to tie themselves to Dr Sun's
fortunes. They think he is a great man. Perhaps he is, but he
will never be great in the field of politics. As for the manner
in which I removed him from office, I too wish to avoid
bloodshed if possible. And this I have done. I am surprised
that you feel sorry for Sun, Barrington, or for anyone
connected with the Kuomintang. Do you not know what they
did to your sister?'

'She has told me,' Robert said.

'And you can forgive them that? I am amazed that you

have not come here demanding the execution of them all.'

'Victoria dug her own pit and then climbed down into it,' Robert said. 'And in any event, none of the men here tonight are in any way responsible for what happened up the Yangtse.'

'It was their people,' Yuan said. 'But I wish to speak of more practical matters. The future. Are you with me?'

'Do you seriously intend to hold elections?'

'The very moment the country is in a suitable state.'

'And when will that be?'

'It must be my business to create conditions where democracy can flourish, just as rapidly as possible.'

'Would I be right in assuming that means getting rid of every Kuomintang member you can lay hands on?'

'You persist in seeking tyranny, Barrington. I have just overthrown a tyranny. Why should I seek to replace it? No, no, I merely wish the country to be at peace, and prosperous. This is where I need your help. I am afraid China's finances are in very bad shape. Do not worry, I do not intend to increase taxes. That would be bad politically. What we need is an injection of foreign capital. I wish you to arrange this for me.'

'Why on earth is any foreign government going to lend money to China? They know the state of your finances.'

'That was my principal reason for not allowing the Kuomintang to contest the government. We need to prove to the Europeans that stability has returned, and good government. The very fact that we no longer have to support the enormous expense of the Ch'ing Dynasty should be proof of that. The fact that you, an international businessman of proven integrity, are prepared to back the new government should be additional proof. You may offer the salt tax as security. That should satisfy anybody. Get me the money, and help me bring China into the twentieth century.'

Robert studied him. 'You have been kind enough to describe me as a businessman of proven integrity. To have proven integrity means that I must preserve that integrity at all times.'

'I will not let you down, Barrington. If you will help me. The alternative is chaos.'

'And presumably the execution of Victoria and Martin, and any other member of my family you can lay hands on.'

'I am not a Manchu monster, Robert. You have my word as to the safety of your sister and the boy, whatever you may do, and so long as they remain under my protection. But I cannot guarantee that safety, or yours, if we find ourselves in the midst of another civil war. And it will happen if I cannot persuade the people of China to back me.'

Robert got up. 'You don't leave me with a lot of choice.'

Yuan smiled.

17

THE LAST BANNERMAN

Robert visited Victoria to say goodbye. 'Are you satisfied?' he asked.

'Not really.' She reclined on a chaise longue in her private apartment. Her gown was expensive, the skirt slit to the thigh to reveal her legs, and she wore several rings of incalculable value. She looked in fact the picture of contentment ... and utter beauty. 'I would have liked to see that little toad bastinadoed, and then castrated.'

'Yuan is more interested in getting what he wants than in bearing grudges,' Robert suggested. 'And he does always get what he wants, doesn't he?'

'He is an admirable man,' she agreed.

He wondered if she believed that herself, just as he wondered how she could yield that exquisite body to Yuan's fingers. 'But Sun aside, you are content?'

'Should I not be?'

'Well, I shall see you again the next time I am in Peking. Yuan even has me working for him now.'

*

Robert also said farewell to Martin.

'I am to be married in a month, Father. Will you not attend my wedding?'

'Of course I shall. I will bring Mother Monique with me,' Robert promised him.

*

Chou Li-ting was waiting for him, with the sampan flying the phoenix flag of the House of Barrington. Captain Shung had been replaced by another longstanding employee of the House: Captain Wong. 'Home, Chou,' Robert said, and retired beneath the tent. He felt exhausted, physically and mentally, and there was so much to be thought about, because so much had happened since he had left Shanghai. It would all have to be analysed ... but the analysis would be meaningless. He was, as much as ever in the past, committed to the cause of the governing élite, simply because, in his successful business and his family, he had offered too many hostages to fortune.

Therefore his sole problem at the moment was to arrange Yuan's loan ... and hope that the Marshal would prove to be as disinterested a ruler as he claimed. But how he yearned for Monique's arms, the cool reassurance of that tawny beauty ... He slept on the journey down the upper canal to the river, waking only as the sampan tied up. He was served his evening meal while his people cooked their own food on the bank.

Chou Li-ting himself served his master, as he had always done, assisted by a young Chinese Robert did not remember seeing before. 'His name is Tao Wan,' Chou explained. 'I have employed him in place of Too Ching.'

Robert raised his eyebrows. 'What happened to Too Ching?'

'He was taken ill, Master.' Chou grinned. 'In a Peking brothel. This boy also comes from Shanghai. I will train him to be better than Too Ching.'

'You're the man for it,' Robert agreed. He drank some plum wine, looked at the evening, which was indicative of all the beauties of spring, and heard a choking gasp. He turned in his seat and saw Chou fall to his knees, while blood flowed from his mouth. Robert started to his own knees, gazing past his dying servant to the boy Tao Wan, and the bloody, long-bladed knife he held. Tao Wan hissed, and leapt forward. Robert hurled himself to one side; he did not wear arms when eating in the midst of his own servants. 'To me!' he shouted.

The other servants looked up in alarm, but he realised he would have to settle this on his own; they had all removed themselves a polite distance from their master, and Tao, lips drawn back in a snarl, was coming forward again.

Robert reached his feet, whipping off his belt as he did so. As Tao lunged, he swung the heavy leather; it struck Tao's hand and half turned him as he fought to retain his grasp on the knife. Before he could regain his balance, Robert had kicked him in the thigh with all his force. Tao yelped and fell to his knees, and Robert kicked him again. Before the boy could recover, Robert had landed a third kick, this time on his knife arm. The knife spun away over the side and splashed into the water. Tao Wan panted, but by now the other servants had come up, and his arms were seized.

Robert knelt beside Chou; no man had ever had a more faithful servant. But Chou was dead. 'What are we to do with this carrion, Master?' asked Captain Wong.

Robert stood above Tao Wan; the boy shook violently with fear – he could see the anger in Robert's face. 'Who sent you to do this?' Robert asked. His brain was already ranging over the possibilities. Yuan? But Yuan needed him, at least until the loan was arranged. One of Sun's men? Chiang Kai-shek, perhaps, in a spirit of vengeance because he had changed sides?

The boy continued to shiver, but his mouth was closed. Robert knelt beside him. 'Listen to me, boy. You are about to die. It can be a clean cut. Or I can give you to my men.

What will you do to him, Wong?'

Wong smiled. 'I will burn off his genitals,' he said. 'That way he will suffer great agony, and he will never enter Heaven.'

Tao Wan rolled his eyes, but did not speak.

'Very well, Wong,' Robert said, and stood up.

Wong grinned. 'Bring him ashore,' he told his men. 'And take down his pants.' He went to the nearest fire and withdrew a flaming brand. 'This will take much time,' he promised Tao Wan as the boy was dragged before him and spreadeagled on his back on the ground, eager hands holding his wrists and ankles, while his body twisted with antici- pated pain. 'Perhaps all night.'

Robert had remained on the boat, but he watched Wong stoop over the boy, the brand in his hand, to send the flame stroking along the inside of his thigh. 'Master Adrian!' Tao Wan screamed.

Wong stopped in consternation, and looked at the sampan. Robert leapt over the rail and ran to them. 'What did you say?'

Tao Wan panted and slobbered. 'Master Adrian sent me. He said that you would be killed by Marshal Yuan. But if by any chance the Marshal did not kill you, then I was to join your people and slay you.'

'Then it was you had Too Ching poisoned in the brothel,' Wong growled. 'Go back to the sampan, Master. Leave him with me. He killed Chou.' The two men had been friends.

'Adrian,' Robert muttered. He had always refused to recognise either Adrian's jealousy or his revolting personal habits. But Adrian was at the moment in charge of Shanghai ... and Monique and James were there too. 'Cut his throat,' he commanded. 'And then let us make haste.'

*

Adrian Barrington left his office and went up the street towards the Barrington Mansion. He walked with a swagger,

swinging his cane; four male servants followed him, armed
with sticks. People on the street stopped to stare. Shanghai
was rife with rumour about what was happening both at the
Barrington Mansion and at the offices of the House. But no
one short of the Viceroy would dare interfere with Barrington affairs; they were not subject to European law, and it was
well known that Adrian Barrington was a dangerous man to
cross.

As well as an important man to know; several people
raised their hats to him, and were acknowledged with a brief,
contemptuous nod of the head. He stamped up the steps to
the verandah, past the bowing servants. They were as
confused as everyone else, but none of them was going to
oppose Mr Adrian, until Mr Robert returned ... and the
rumours being spread by Mr Adrian's servants indicated that
Mr Robert was not coming back.

Eleven-year-old James was waiting in the drawing room.
James was as confused as anyone, but principally because of
the summary dismissal of his governess, who had been put
on a boat to Hong Kong. Regarding his mother's sudden
illness, he believed what his uncle had told him; Adrian had
always been at great pains to be friends with the boy and was
constantly giving him presents. 'When will Mother be well
enough to see me?' he asked.

Adrian ruffled his hair. 'Soon, boy. In a couple of days.'
He was in fact surprised, and a little concerned, that he had
not heard before now.

He went through the house and up the stairs to the private
apartment shared by Robert and Monique, and into which he
had moved when he had had Monique taken home from his
dinner party. Outside the door Chiang Lu waited, as usual.
No one except Master Adrian and his intimate servants were
allowed in and out of the apartment, since Mistress Monique
had been 'taken ill'.

Chiang Lu opened the door and Adrian stepped inside. Wu
Ping was in the sitting room and bowed before her master.
No doubt, Adrian supposed, she was pleased with the

situation, in that since he had taken possession of his sister-in-law she had been enjoying a rest. But it was difficult to be sure with Wu Ping; her eyes were pools of the darkest midnight. He knew she hated him, of course; presumably they all did. But they were all terrified of him as well, and he intended that they should stay that way. They would be even more terrified once he was truly Master of the House.

He opened the inner door, and Shu Lai-ti leapt to her feet; she had been seated in a chair at the foot of the bed. Monique, sprawled naked on the bed – Adrian would not allow her to dress – merely opened her eyes, and then closed them again. She seldom left her bed. When she had first been brought here, she had fought him and tried to escape. He had had the women hold her down while he caned her, and then had thought of a more efficient way of obtaining her co-operation. 'If you do not stop fighting me,' he had told her, 'I will take this cane to James.'

That had gained the day. She had had to content herself with saying, 'When Robert gets home . . .'

To which he always smiled and replied, 'But Robert isn't coming home, my dearest Monique.'

He knew she refused to believe that, but also that she understood she could do nothing until and unless Robert did appear; she had given up fighting him. And he had been content that it should be so. He did not trust her, of course, not to attempt either escape or suicide. Thus one of his women stayed with her every minute of the day and night, even when he was with her himself; he had no secrets from them, anyway.

Now he stood above the bed and poked between her buttocks with the end of his cane; it was an utter delight to be able to treat so much beauty with so much contempt. Monique winced and her whole body quivered, but she would not turn her head. Adrian grinned. 'I would have the blue phoenixes dance in pair,' he said.

Shu Lai-ti stripped off her robe without hesitation, and then undressed her master. Monique remained lying on her

side, looking away from him, shivering. When Adrian was
naked, he went round to her side of the bed and rolled her
on her back. 'Stimulate her, Lai-ti,' he said.

Lai-ti grinned and crawled on to the bed; she also enjoyed
tormenting the former mistress of the House. But as she did
so, the bedroom door opened. Adrian turned with a snarl of
rage, and glared at Chiang Lu. 'What the devil do you think
you're doing?'

Chiang Lu fell to his knees. 'Master, a messenger has
come. From up the river, Master. He has galloped all night
and all today. He says there is a sampan coming down-river,
with Master Robert on board.'

Monique sat up, throwing auburn hair from her eyes. Shu
Lai-ti checked, still kneeling on the bed. Wu Ping stood in
the doorway behind Chiang Lu.

'You expect me to believe that?' Adrian demanded.

'The man swears he saw the master, Master.'

'Well, *brother*?' Monique asked in a low voice.

Adrian faced her, mouth twisted. 'She must die,' he said.

Monique gasped. She had not anticipated that.

'Chiang Lu,' Adrian commanded. 'Strangle the mistress.'
Chiang Lu got to his feet.

'You would not dare,' Monique whispered. 'You would
not *dare*.' Chiang Lu stood beside the bed, and she shrank
back against the headboard.

'And then what, Master?' Wu Ping asked, softly. Adrian
turned his head, frowning at her. 'Will you fight the master,
Master?' Wu Ping asked, still speaking very softly. 'Because
if you mean to fight your brother for possession of the
House, there is no need to murder the mistress. Rather is she
a weapon for you to hold. But you do not mean to fight your
brother, Master. You are afraid of your brother.' Her voice
was heavy with contempt.

'I am going to *flog* you,' Adrian snarled.

Wu Ping never moved. 'I will tell you what he means to
do, Chiang Lu,' she said. 'He means to have you murder the
mistress, then hand you, hand us all, over to his brother as

the assassins. We will all die, Chiang Lu.'

Chiang Lu hesitated, looking from one to the other uncertainly, while Monique held her breath.

'Do as I have commanded,' Adrian said. 'Then come here and deal with this bitch as well.'

'You will remember, Mistress,' Wu Ping said, 'that I have saved your life.' It was Monique's turn to look from one to the other, seeking some sign, and gasping as from behind her back Wu Ping brought a long, sharp-bladed knife.

'You bitch!' Adrian stepped towards her, and without hesitation she moved against him and drove the knife into his stomach. He gave a ghastly shriek and fell to his knees, holding his belly, from which blood spurted as the knife was withdrawn.

'Chiang Lu,' Wu Ping commanded. Chiang Lu licked his lips, then went to her. Adrian, still on his knees, had fallen forward so that his forehead rested on the floor, while blood spread around him. Chiang Lu took the knife from Wu Ping's hand and drove it into Adrian's side. Once again blood spurted, and Adrian's head jerked as he fell over, his scream now nothing more than a gurgle.

'Shu Lai-ti,' Wu Ping said remorselessly. Lai-ti scrambled off the bed. She was shaking so much even her hair was trembling, but she had no pity in her face. Even through her horror at what she was watching, Monique wondered at how much, and for how long, must these people have hated their master.

Shu Lai-ti grasped the knife. Then she seized Adrian's hair to pull his head back, and cut his throat.

Wu Ping took the knife from her hand, and advanced to the bed. Every muscle in Monique's body was tensed as she gazed at the woman, and the bloodstained blade. 'You will remember that we acted in your defence,' Wu Ping said again.

*

'I gave them my word,' Monique said.

'Under duress,' Robert pointed out. 'Didn't they torment you as well?'

'Yes. Under duress. You can have no idea what those three have suffered, Robert, for more than twenty years.'

'I have some idea,' Robert said. 'And the fault is largely mine, for being so blind to what a creature he was. Anyway, had they not killed him, I would have.' He looked at the three kneeling, trembling figures before him. 'I will tell the Viceroy that you murdered my brother and escaped. Here are thirty taels of silver. There will be no pursuit for twenty-four hours. But do not ever return to Shanghai.'

Chiang Lu took the money, glanced at the two women, got to his feet, and backed from the room. Shu Lai-ti and Wu Ping followed. Outside the door was a crowd of curious servants, but Robert closed and locked it.

Monique drew a long breath; she was fully dressed, but she had still not been able to bring herself to leave the apartment. Adrian's body had been removed, but she still had not seen her son. Now she asked, 'What will you do with me?' She raised her head to gaze at him. 'You saved me from the Boxers.'

'But I could not save you from my own brother. As I have said, the fault is mine. But do you think I care what has been done to you, as long as you have survived, and are safe and unharmed?' He took her in his arms, held her close.

'What will we tell James?' she whispered through her tears.

'Why, that you were ill, and are now well again. Now is no time for looking over our shoulders, Monique. As it has turned out, there are only you, and me, and James left of our family. We have a lot to do.'

*

It was Robert's nature to attack life, where he could see his way. He set the negotiations for the loan going immediately, but he knew that he would have to visit both Europe and

America to secure the backing of the international bankers.
He would be the first Barrington since his immortal
namesake to set foot in England. Monique and James
accompanied him, the House being left in the care of Min-
chung, a Manchu who was his chief clerk. But Robert feared
no interference in his absence; he was far too valuable to
Yuan.

They travelled first of all to Peking to attend Martin's
wedding. Even Monique, conditioned by her experiences to
be suspicious of all things Chinese, was impressed by the
evidence of Yuan's benevolent power, the confident beauty
of Victoria, and the elaborate celebration of the wedding
itself, when the handsome boy was married to the lovely
Chinese girl.

'Are they going to be happy?' she asked Robert, as they
took the train to Tientsin, from whence they would join their
ship – a Barrington ship – for Yokohama and thence San
Francisco.

'As long as Yuan is in power, certainly,' Robert said. 'But
then, that goes for all of us.'

*

Robert's journey took longer than he had expected, not only
because the negotiations took longer than he had anticipated,
but because Monique and James naturally wanted to do
some sightseeing as well. Most important of all, he and
Monique needed to get to know each other again, as bit by
bit what Adrian had done to her slipped out, and had to be
absorbed into his love for her. But the love remained
constant; he felt indeed that her experience had brought
them closer together – certainly she more than ever looked
on him as the man who would always protect her and guard
her. It was a heavy responsibility – but also a heady one.

The United States bankers were not inclined to lend Yuan
money, so they went on to Europe, crossing the Atlantic in
a liner on which the talk was all about the tragedy of the

Titanic, which had gone down only the previous month. It was a sobering thought that while the 'civilised' world of the North Atlantic communities regarded China as one of the most dangerous places on earth to live, they had managed to lose, in one night, more lives than were lost in the entire Chinese revolution.

In Europe, Robert succeeded in raising twenty-five million pounds, from a consortium of British, French, Russian and Japanese bankers, secured, as Yuan had instructed, by a tax on salt. The deal was completed in June, and Robert, wiring the good news to Peking, informed the President-Elect that he would be taking a brief holiday before returning; the letters he had been receiving from Min-chung assured him that the House was prospering as always. Meanwhile, he actually intended to implement a plan he had had in mind for some time. He had already completed the correspondence and entry forms, and all James had to do was sit, and pass, an entrance examination before he was admitted to Eton. 'It's time the Barringtons ceased to be pirates and became gentlemen,' Robert told him. 'Don't worry, the House is waiting for you when you leave school.'

James was not due at Eton until the commencement of the autumn term in September, so the three of them went off touring the continent. It was not until they reached Rome, at the end of July, that Robert, to his concern, read newspaper reports that there had been a 'Second Revolution' in the southern provinces, centering on Nanking. He booked his return passage immediately. Monique was disappointed, and it was agreed that she should remain with James for the rest of the holiday, returning to China at the end of September.

*

Robert had wired both Min-chung and Martin, seeking information. Both replied reassuringly, if in different contexts. Min-chung said that the Yangtse was temporarily closed, but the loss of business would be minimal, because

Marshal Yuan was moving forces against the rebels. Martin was ebulliently confident as he actually held a junior command in the army marching on Nanking. Neither stated whether the rebellion was Kuomintang inspired, and once Robert was at sea, communications were difficult. The voyage took six weeks, through the Suez Canal and thence the Indian Ocean, which meant, Robert noted with pleasure, that he was the first Barrington to circumnavigate the globe. It was mid-September before he reached Shanghai, to be greeted with the news that Nanking had fallen only a few days before, to Yuan's army.

'It was a massacre,' Min-chung told him. 'Now they are carrying out wholesale executions.' Which wasn't going to go down very well with Yuan's European backers, Robert thought. He remained in Shanghai only long enough to check the books, then put to sea again, in another of his own steamships, for Tientsin, where he caught the railway to Peking. The journey which had once taken several weeks now needed less than a fortnight.

*

Robert had wired ahead, and was escorted immediately into the Forbidden City, and Yuan's presence. Where he received a shock. The Marshal did not look well; his complexion seemed to have darkened and occasionally he seemed to be in pain, while from time to time during their conversation it appeared that he had difficulty in staying awake. But he appeared as delighted as ever to see Robert. 'Robert!' he said as they embraced. 'I am very pleased with you. Very pleased. I did not expect you back so soon.'

'I came as soon as I heard of the rebellion,' Robert said.

Yuan waved his hand. 'It has been put down.'

'So I gather. Isn't now the time to show some mercy?'

'To those scum?'

'It is what will be expected of you in Europe.'

'Europe,' Yuan sneered. 'This is China.'

'As long as you are dependent on them for money—'

'The money has been paid into our bank accounts,' Yuan said. 'It cannot now be recalled.'

Robert was aghast. 'You do not mean to repay it?'

'Certainly I mean to repay it. Or enough of it to obtain some more when I need it. But I am pointing out that there is no way it can now be recalled, however much your Barbarian governments and bankers may disapprove of my methods. That being so, their only concern will be that my regime should be bolstered in order that they do obtain repayment, of at least their interest. Am I not right?'

'You have obviously studied the West very carefully,' Robert said.

'It is the duty of a statesman to study both his opponents and his allies very carefully,' Yuan said. 'I seek stability for China, Robert. That means I must have total acquiescence in my rule, whatever means I must employ to obtain that.'

'With respect,' Robert said, 'where there is total acquiescence in the rule of one man, or even one group of men, especially where that acquiescence has been imposed by force, you no longer have a democracy.'

Yuan smiled. 'You are speaking of a European-style democracy, Robert. I am speaking of China. China understands only the rule of force. That is all she needs to understand.'

*

Robert visited Victoria, who was as he had left her, sensually content with her surroundings. 'Yuan must be a marvellous lover,' he suggested.

'He is. Oh, I am not pretending that he is a young man. He can no longer perform with great regularity. Sometimes he cannot perform at all. He falls asleep at the oddest times. But his fingers . . .' She gave a languorous sigh.

Robert had not really come to discuss Yuan's amatory ability; he found it both distasteful and embarrassing, with

his own sister. But he did seek information. 'And his general
health?'

'I could wish it were better.'

'What, for instance?'

She gave a little shrug. 'Obviously sexually. But it is that
whole area. Sometimes there is difficulty in passing water.
And then . . . well . . .'

'His breath is bad, and his sweat.'

She frowned. 'How do you know?'

'I have observed him at close range.'

'It is a bladder complaint. Nothing more. Will you stay
until Martin gets back?'

'No. I am needed in Shanghai.'

'He has covered himself in glory. There is to be a medal.'

'Why, that is splendid.' He gave her a hug. 'And you are
happy?'

'I am more happy than at any previous time in my life,'
she told him.

*

Robert had to believe her. And he found a visit to Lu-shang
rewarding; already a mother, she remained exquisitely
beautiful, and anxious to entertain her father-in-law, while to
hold even a step-grandson in his arms filled him with pride.
But he returned to Shanghai with a lot on his mind. He
summoned Dr Simkins, an English doctor who practised in
the International Concession and attended the Barringtons as
necessary, and told him what he had been able to garner. 'I
would say he is suffering from uraemia,' Simkins concluded. 'A disease of the kidneys.'

That made sense. 'How serious is it?'

'It comes in two forms, acute and chronic. Chronic is what
it says, and is merely a continuous source of pain and
discomfort. The acute variety is a very serious matter.'

'What causes it?'

'I'm afraid we aren't quite sure. It is a malfunction of the organ, and its effect is that poisonous matters which are normally excreted by the kidneys through the bladder are instead allowed to enter the bloodstream, but I'm afraid medical opinion has not yet determined whether the illness is caused by a failure of the kidneys to excrete all such matter, or by an excess of such matter proving more than the kidneys can handle.'

'What about symptoms?'

'Oh, physically, as you describe. In a white man the most obvious symptom is a yellowing of the complexion, as in jaundice. This obviously would be less noticeable in a Chinese, but the presence of the poisons in the blood can be detected on the breath and in the sweat, and there is a general decline in the ability of the penis to perform its function, either as an excretory or a sexual organ. There are other effects which may not be immediately noticeable, such as weight loss, and a general dryness of the skin. A general debility . . .'

'What about the mind?'

'Ah, well, you must remember that the blood is what keeps the brain working. When the blood is poisoned, the brain suffers. In the early stages, the symptoms are likely to be as you described, an ever-present drowsiness. But as the disease takes hold, there can be no doubt that the brain is affected. Loss of perspective, even dementia, are not unknown.'

'You are not being very reassuring, doctor,' Robert growled. 'So, what's the cure?'

'The cure is to get rid of the poison before it takes too firm a hold. This can only be done by purging, or even bleeding.' He paused.

'Neither of which Yuan is likely to accept. Thank you, Doctor. What we have said here today is very strictly confidential. It wouldn't do Chinese politics any good for it to become known that their President-Elect is a sick man.'

*

But Robert remained very worried, on two counts: equally that Yuan might prove physically incapable of continuing his rule, or that his illness might lead to irrationality, as Simkins had suggested. To a man like Yuan, the slightest loss of political or military perception might well involve the gravest consequences. His concern increased as the year went on. Yuan duly held his election, and was duly chosen as President, with Li Yuan-hung as his Vice-President. This was in October, but when it became apparent that the Parliament wished to have a mind of its own, sparked by the return of a surprisingly large number of Kuomintang members, Yuan did a Cromwell. He descended upon the assembly at the head of a body of troops, arrested and expelled all members with any affiliations to the Kuomintang, and early in the new year, dissolved Parliament altogether. Everyone assumed that there would now be new elections, but to general consternation on 1 May 1914 Yuan announced that there had been a 'constitutional compact' between himself and his people, which gave him a ten-year term of office . . . without any formal vote.

*

Monique quickly discerned that Robert was far from happy with the situation. 'The Empire is at peace,' she pointed out. 'Trade is prospering. Does it really matter that he's not being strictly democratic about running the country? Didn't you tell me once that your father always said that China just wasn't made to be a democracy?'

Robert sighed. 'And he was probably right. What would you say if I told you I am thinking of getting out? Abandoning China.'

'But why?'

'Because I think there is a disaster ahead. Yuan means to

establish a dictatorship. Which will collapse when he dies, and he is already a sick man, even if he doesn't understand it himself. What happens then? Dr Sun has proved a broken reed. There is going to be a situation where other army commanders are going to snatch at power. There is going to be civil war on a scale which will make the T'ai-P'ing, or the Boxers, look like an old ladies' tea party. The country is essentially bankrupt. All of its revenues are committed, either to indemnities or to the repayment of loans. And what is the loan money I negotiated being used for? Increasing the Army, not improving the Government, or the lot of the people. I told those bankers Yuan wanted to build schools and universities; what do you think they are saying to themselves now? I can tell you that at the first sign of real trouble any possibility of future overseas financing will be finished. Then you will have a bankrupt government trying to rule a bankrupt and angry nation.'

'The Ch'ing were always on the verge of bankruptcy,' she ventured quietly.

'As you say, they were used to it. Besides, they were the Dynasty. As long as there was any leadership, there was no chance of any revolution succeeding.'

'If you had your way, you'd bring Tz'u-hsi back to life,' Monique said.

'Yes. It would take someone like T'zu-hsi to restore the situation now.'

'Did you love Tz'u-hsi, Robert?'

For on their trip, and as a counter-weight to Adrian, he had confessed his relations with the Dowager Empress to her.

'I never loved her, Monique. Any more than she loved me. But I understood her strength. It came from her belief in her past, and the past of her ancestors, her belief in both the Manchus and the Ch'ing. Yuan is an adventurer. He has no foundations driven deep into the soil of China. So, I must either pack up and flee China . . .'

'You'll not do that, Robert. What of the House? Oh, you may have salted away sufficient to keep us in comfort for the rest of our lives, but the House ... well, it is synonymous with the name of Barrington, is it not?'

'Yes, I suppose it is. The alternative is to go to Peking.'

She was aghast. 'Not to conspire against Yuan?'

'To talk to him, convince him that what he is doing runs against the tide of history.'

She held his hands, not reassured. 'For God's sake be careful.'

*

In fact, Monique would have liked to accompany him, if only to see her step-grandson. But Robert decided against it. He was not at all sure how his journey was going to turn out.

On the surface, China seemed more at peace than for several years. People worked, and waved at the train as it chugged its way from Tientsin to Feng-tai, the Peking railway station. The country looked prosperous; the streets of the capital were as busy and excited as ever in the great days of the Ch'ing.

But there were soldiers everywhere, groups of them on every railway station, just as there were armed sampans patrolling the Canal and the rivers. And there were more convicts to be seen, manacled men, and women, labouring on public works, clearly political prisoners. Yuan had only one remedy for dissent: arrest and hard labour.

Thus Robert had no idea whether to be relieved or sorry to find that the Marshal appeared to have overcome his illness, and indeed looked almost as healthy as in the early days of their acquaintance. But if the sleepy look was back, it was too often shot through with the quick, suspicious glances of a caged tiger.

Yet he greeted his old friend jovially enough. 'What do you think of the news from Europe?' It was the end of July, and word of the assassination at Sarajevo had just been received.

'I'd say that is a most unhappy house,' Robert said. 'The Empress assassinated, one heir committing suicide, and now the next also assassinated . . .' He could not help adding, 'It makes one wonder if trying to rule an empire composed of so many disparate peoples is really worth it.'

'It depends upon who is doing the ruling. I am advised that there is certain to be a war, that Russia and France will fight Germany and Austria. Do you agree with that assessment?'

'I would say war is a strong possibility.'

'What will Britain do?'

'I have no idea. There is a rumour that she is tied to Russia and France by a secret agreement, but I find that hard to believe. You should ask the British Minister.'

'I have. He also is totally non-committal. But in any event, Robert, if there is a general European war, even if Britain does not take part, she will be fully occupied with it. That opens wide vistas,' Yuan said. 'A period of non-intervention by the Barbarians, no matter what happens here.'

'Will you explain what you mean?' They were alone together in Yuan's office, and Robert could be blunt.

Yuan gave one of his sleepy smiles. 'To you, certainly. As I *can* be frank, to you, Robert. I am not happy with the way things have gone since the fall of the Ch'ing. More important, China is not happy. As I said when last we met, this country needs to be ruled, and it needs to be ruled by someone all the people can accept. The Chinese people will never accept as their ruler a man who can be expelled from office after a four- or five-year period, simply by the casting of a few votes.'

'You have secured office for ten years,' Robert pointed out.

'Even ten years is not very long. And what of my successor? My people want permanency. They seek a restoration of the Mandate of Heaven. That is something they can understand. On all sides, I hear people saying that there has been no sacrifice to heaven for more than a year. This disturbs them.'

'You are thinking of restoring the Dynasty?' Robert asked, astonished.

'The Ch'ing? Never. It is unacceptable for China to be ruled by foreigners. But I am saying that it is necessary to *have* a dynasty. A Chinese dynasty.'

Robert stared at him; this was even more extreme that he had feared. 'Have you one in mind?'

'Of course. My own.'

'You have no sons.'

'I will adopt sons. I will adopt Martin, Robert. He can never be emperor, because of his foreign blood. But he will be a prop to the throne, firstly to me, and then to my successor. You will be very proud of that, I know.'

'You intend to make yourself emperor,' Robert said, determined that there should be no question as to the fact.

'Yes. That is my intention, Robert. With your support, it will be a simple matter.'

'It will be opposed.'

'Who by? The Barbarians? I have just pointed out that they will be too occupied with their own quarrels for the foreseeable future. Some of our own people? I will know how to deal with them. Dr Sun? Well, that is obvious. But he is far away, and I do not intend to allow him back.'

'What of your marshals?'

'They are soldiers. They obey their commander-in-chief, or they face a firing squad.'

'And if I oppose you, will I too face a firing squad?'

'You?' Yuan seemed genuinely surprised.

'I told you, I would never support the overthrow of the Ch'ing.'

'Yet you did.'

Robert gave a wry smile. 'Yes. You took me by surprise. And I felt too vulnerable, in my family and my business.'

Yuan regarded him, sleepily. 'Now you no longer feel vulnerable, is that it? What has changed?'

'Shall I say that during the past year I have taken certain precautions. I have transferred all my surplus funds from China to Hong Kong, where you cannot touch them. I have, while arranging your loan, increased my standing in the international community, and I have taken out British nationality. If you arrest me, I come under the laws of extraterritoriality, and must be handed over to the nearest British consul. The same applies to my wife. No matter what is happening in Europe, if you break those laws you will find a British squadron blockading the Pei-ho, and the Huang-ho, and the Yangtse. My son is already in England. As for my sister and her son, well, she has made her own bed and seems prepared to lie on it, indefinitely. However, should you harm either of them, be sure I will bring you down. And I can, Yuan. There will be no more money after that I have secured for you. And that is already spent, as you have told me.'

Yuan studied him. 'How vehement you are, Robert. And how carefully have you thought out all of your plans. Then you do mean to oppose me?'

'I cannot support you in founding a dynasty.'

'And this is obviously something you have determined some time ago, or you would not have taken so many precautions. Will you tell me why? Is it because I am a common man of the people? Many of China's greatest dynasties have been founded by a man of the people. Will you deny that I am a great soldier? All great leaders need also to be great soldiers. Is it because I am prepared to be harsh to those who would rebel against my authority? Again, this is a sign of greatness in a leader. I am appointed by fate to rule this country. I am the man, and this is the moment. There is no one can stand against me. Not even you, Robert.'

'I am not opposing you, Yuan. I have said I will not support you. If you intend to persist in your plan, then, as I have said, I will leave China.'

'You have still not told me why.'

Robert gazed at him. 'I do not believe you have the

character of an emperor, Yuan. You have the character of a conqueror. The two are not synonymous. I believe you will bring untold suffering upon the people of China, and that you will inaugurate a generation of war and suffering. I want no part of that.'

Yuan smiled. 'I understand your reservations, Robert. I respect them. There is no need for us to quarrel, however much we may differ. China needs the House of Barrington. You may be sure always of my friendship and protection, at the least. Now go with your god.'

*

He was a difficult man to oppose, in his refusal ever to lose his temper, or even to appear to do so. In that, he was in the strongest possible contrast to Tz'u-hsi. But was he any more to be trusted? Robert doubted it.

Seeing Victoria was a waste of time. Robert called instead on Martin, where he was entertained by Lu-shang, whose son was now a year old. 'Are you not proud of your grandson, Mr Barrington?' she asked.

Martin was equally proud, but he frowned when Robert suggested he should resign his commission and come back to work in the House. 'Under James, you mean?' he asked.

'I was thinking of an equal partnership,' Robert said.

'Are you then going to retire? You are only forty-seven.'

'These are things to be discussed,' Robert said. 'But not here in Peking.' His trouble was that he did not know how much the boy was in Yuan's confidence – how much anything he said might be relayed straight back to the Marshal. 'It's just that I feel troubled times may be ahead, and that it might be a sound idea for all us Barringtons, and . . .' he glanced at the open doorway, beyond which he could hear Lu-shang playing with her baby, '. . . our loved ones, to get together and stick together.'

'You are mistaken, Father.' Martin's face shone with ardour. 'China is being better governed now than for many years. It is an honour and a privilege to serve the Marshal. I could not conceive of doing anything else. It is my most fervent wish that little Robert may grow up to serve in his turn.'

Robert gave up and went home. It was time to think of Monique and himself, and thank God he had got James out. He reached Shanghai ten days after leaving Peking, and was greeted by a very nervous Lin Pang, his butler. Inside the drawing room there was an equally nervous Monique.

'What in the name of God has happened?' he demanded.

Monique turned her head to look at the door to the back parlour, and the man standing there. Dr Sun!

*

'He came three days ago,' Monique whispered. 'Dressed as a peasant. He has re-entered the country secretly, and was supposed to have transport arranged into the interior, where he has friends. But the transport has not materialised, and he is afraid of betrayal. So—'

'He has been here, in this house, for three days?' Robert demanded in consternation.

'What was I to do? He appealed to me in the name of your friendship, of the fact that you had once promised to support him . . .' She bit her lip. 'He has been a perfect gentleman.'

Robert went into the parlour. 'Just what have you come back for, Sun?'

'To save my people from the tyranny of Yuan,' Sun said. 'My people are ready, in the mountains. They are going to launch an offensive which will drive Yuan from Peking, and re-establish the Kuomintang.'

'I see. They are going to do all of this, but they cannot even carry out their arrangement to meet you here in Shanghai.'

Sun looked utterly woebegone. 'I do not understand it.'

'I understand it very well. You have been betrayed, not for the first time.'

Sun's shoulders drooped. 'Will you hand me over to the Viceroy?'

'Of course I will not do that, Sun. But I must see about getting you out of here, as quickly as possible.'

'Out of China? I will not go. Two years ago my nerve failed me. I admit it. But then, did not yours? We sought a modern, democratic China, and we allowed ourselves to be pushed aside by a tyrant. It has lain heavy on my conscience. Has it not lain heavy on yours?'

Robert had no reply to make to that, because it had. As had, more especially, his failure to support Sun at the crucial moment. 'So what has happened?' Sun asked. 'China groans under this tyranny. My people cry out for help. And who can help them, save me? I am back now, Barrington, and I am not going to run away again. If you will not help me, then I will leave the shelter of your house and take my chances on the street. But I am never going to leave this country again.'

Robert looked at Monique, standing in the doorway. 'Could we not arrange passage for Dr Sun, up-river?' she asked. 'In a House sampan?'

Robert nodded. 'Yes, we can do that. If you are prepared to risk all. For if we are found out ... This is not your land, Monique, or your quarrel. You have had only unhappiness from the Chinese.'

'On the contrary,' she said. 'For is not my husband Chinese?'

*

Even when it came to his own people, Robert was not sure whom he could trust. The domestics he felt were faithful to whichever way the Barringtons might incline, but the House clerks and officials, even Min-chung, were necessarily supporters of whichever government was in power in Peking, as opposed to revolutionaries who would disrupt trade and profits.

He therefore merely announced that he was going up the river on a tour of inspection, and that his wife would be accompanying him. There was nothing unusual about that, and the only way he could feel sure of getting Sun out of Shanghai was by going with him – besides, he wanted to see for himself this army which was going to depose Yuan Shih-k'ai. Sun was kept in the house out of sight of prying eyes until the boat was ready. Here the domestics *had* to be trusted, but none of them seemed unduly disturbed by the situation. Robert even began to feel that everything was going to work out, as Monique packed her bags and prepared for her journey. 'I am looking forward to it,' she told him. 'We shall have a second honeymoon.'

They were having dinner on the last night before their departure, and, as usual, Sun had joined them. 'Believe me,' he said, 'this time we shall triumph. As soon as I have joined forces with my generals ... Chiang Kai-shek is there. You remember Chiang, Barrington?'

'I remember Chiang,' Robert said.

'He has the making of a fine soldier,' Sun said. 'Perhaps a great one. All he needs are the sinews of war ...' He paused.

'I cannot help you there, Sun,' Robert said. 'Even if I wanted to. With Europe on the point of eruption, there will be no munitions for sale to any disinterested parties.'

'There are always munitions for sale,' Sun argued. 'Providing one is prepared to pay for them. We have the funds, Barrington, all we need—' He checked and half turned his head as there was an eruption of noise at the front of the house.

Robert put down his napkin and stood up, facing the door, which opened to admit Lin Pang, looking very alarmed. 'The Viceroy, Master,' he stammered. 'With soldiers.'

'Quick,' Robert said. 'Get upstairs, Sun.'

Sun hesitated, then made for the other doorway, but he was too late. The doors were thrown open again, and Lin Pang was shouldered aside. The new Viceroy, one of Yuan's generals named Yun Li-chow, stood there, and at his shoulder were six soldiers of the viceregal guard and a captain. 'You will see I came myself, Barrington,' Yun Li-chow said. 'Do not move, Dr Sun. My orders are to capture you, dead or alive.'

Sun waited. Monique had also risen, and held her napkin to her throat. Yun came further into the room, while his men moved to either side; the Captain remained standing in the doorway, beside Lin Pang. 'I was informed that Dr Sun was in Shanghai several days ago,' Yun said. 'But as I was also informed that he had been given shelter in this house, Barrington, I felt it necessary to seek a higher authority before acting. I therefore wired the President, asking for instructions. Do you know what his reply is? It is to the effect that I should place you, and your wife, and Dr Sun, under the most strict arrest, and send the three of you to Peking under guard, that you may be tried for treason.'

Robert heard Monique's sharp intake of breath. Sun made no comment, but he was gazing at Robert. As was Monique. They were relying entirely upon him, upon his known courage and determination . . . and his ruthlessness as a man of action. Monique in particular would be remembering how he had killed the Boxers. But then he had Chou Li-ting at his side.

'However,' Yun continued, 'as you are one of China's most famous citizens, Barrington, the last of a long and glorious house, I do not propose to drag you and . . .' he glanced at Monique, standing like a statue against the table, '. . . your wife out into the street in chains to be humiliated by the mob. That is, if you will agree to accompany me without delay.'

'Are we not allowed to collect some changes of clothing?' Robert asked.

'My people will bring your clothes,' Yun said, and gave a grim smile, 'not that you will need much finery where you are going. We leave now.' He had been moving all the time as he spoke, and Robert knew it had to be now or never; if once he allowed himself to be taken out of this house and on to a government ship, he was finished; he could not imagine Yuan even considering a public trial. He, and Sun, and Monique, would all conveniently die on the voyage to Tientsin – no doubt somewhat unpleasantly.

He never hesitated. Yun was just within reach, and the meal had consisted of a joint of pork, carved at the table. With a single tremendous movement, Robert seized Yun's arm and spun him round and against him, at the same time whipping the razor-sharp carving knife from the platter and holding it against the Viceroy's throat.

Yun gurgled in a mixture of fear and outrage. His guards levelled their rifles, but could not shoot for fear of hitting their master. Monique brushed past Dr Sun as she ran from the room into the antechamber beyond, where she knew there were weapons. Dr Sun allowed himself to be pushed aside and remained standing still against the inner doorway.

Yun got his voice back. 'Are you mad?' he snarled.

'Quite,' Robert said. 'Tell your people to put down their guns, slowly and carefully.'

'Never!'

'Then you will die.'

'You will suffer the death of a thousand cuts,' Yun snarled. 'You and your wife, face to face, hanging from the same scaffold.'

'But you won't be there to see it,' Robert told him. Behind him he heard movement, and knew that Monique had returned. He pressed the knife blade against Yun's pulsing flesh. 'Well, if that is how you want it . . .'

Yun gasped as a trickle of blood dribbled over Robert's knuckles. 'Put down your guns,' he panted.

The guards obeyed, as did the Captain. 'Pick them up, Sun,' Robert said. Sun collected the rifles and the Captain's revolver. Monique came further into the room; she carried two revolvers. Robert was reminded of his escape from Chang Tsin's house fourteen years before, and wondered if Monique remembered it too. But it was not going to be so easy this time, and not only because they were fourteen years older.

'Monique,' he said. 'Go outside and make sure none of the servants leaves the house. Assemble them all in the pantry and keep them there. Shoot anyone who attempts to disobey you.'

Monique swallowed, but nodded and left the room, pushing Lin Pang before her.

'I will cover these people, Sun,' Robert said. 'You tie their wrists together. Use their belts.'

'It would be safer to kill them all,' Sun pointed out.

'I know. But we are not in the business of murder, are we?'

Sun tied the soldiers' hands behind their backs, and then did the same for Yun, who continued to glare at them most malevolently. 'They will be free in half an hour,' Sun said.

'Sooner than that, I would say.' Robert went outside, to where Monique was confronting the scandalised servants, who had never seen their mistress in quite this mood. 'You will all go into the cellar,' he commanded. 'You'll bring Yun and his people down, Sun,' he called. 'Now listen to me, Yun,' he told the Viceroy, when they were all assembled. 'I am going to lock you in. Do not worry, there will be people along shortly.'

'Do you really think you can escape me?' Yun demanded. 'I know all about the sampan you have waiting. You will be stopped on the river.'

'Then you've nothing to worry about, have you?' Robert closed the door and shot the bolts. Sun and Monique watched him, their faces indicating their feelings that they were lost.

'Monique,' Robert said. 'Go upstairs and change that dress for travelling clothes. Pack a small valise.'

'Have we time?' she asked.

He grinned. 'We are going to have all the time in the world. Off you go.' He watched her leave the room. 'Now, Sun, help me.'

He led the doctor to the storeroom where there were several

large drums of kerosene, which was used in the lamps.

Sun looked horrified. 'You intend to destroy your own house? This beautiful house?'

'Houses can be rebuilt. People can't.'

'I do not understand. You would not let me kill those soldiers or the Viceroy, yet you are going to burn them to death?'

'They're not going to die. That cellar was especially constructed by my grandfather during the T'ai-P'ing revolt, to withstand fire. I'm not saying it won't get a little hot.'

'Then you will also, how do you say in England? Have burned your bridges forever. The House of Barrington will be finished.'

'Not if you succeed in your revolution, doctor. If you do not, well, my bridges are burned anyway. Come on.'

Between them they pushed several of the upholstered chairs and settees from the drawing room to the top of the cellar stairs, and soaked them in kerosene. Then they spread a trail of kerosene throughout the house, and thoroughly impregnated all the carpets and the foot of each drape.

By this time Monique had returned, wearing a riding habit and carrying two valises. 'I packed something for you as well . . .' She stared at the mess. 'What on earth . . . and what is that smell?'

'Kerosene,' he told her.

'But . . . my God!'

'You can design our next house,' he promised her.

By now there was a banging on the cellar door, so he went back down to it. 'Any more noise,' he called, 'and I'll put a couple of bullets through this.'

There was no way, of course, that a bullet could get through the fireproof door, but the people inside didn't know the door was fireproof. Robert and Sun went to the stables and saddled three horses, then Monique joined them. As soon as they were ready, Robert returned to the house, and went to the piled furniture. He stood for a second, looking at it, and then around himself at the house. This house had been built by his grandfather, as a seaside holiday home when the family had been based in Nanking. It had become the family home when Nanking fell to the T'ai-P'ing in 1853, and over the years had been added to in all directions, outwards as well as upwards, to make the Barrington Mansion. He had been born here, and he had fully expected to die here. Well, he thought, he very nearly had.

There was no time for regret or hesitation. He struck a match and threw it into the pile, waited for it to catch well alight, then left, locking the front door behind himself. From the paddock there was at the moment no sign that anything was amiss; the huge building merely glowed with light, as usual.

Monique and Sun waited with the horses. 'Why cannot we use the sampan?' Monique asked. 'Is it not ready?'

'Indeed it is, and Yun knows all about it. We need to go across country, and find Chiang Kai-shek.'

He led them out of the paddock and on to the road. They walked their horses away from the other houses in the Concession; some people passed them but no one greeted them – they had not been recognised in the dark.

Then they heard a shout from behind them, and looked over their shoulders. Flames were flaring from the windows of the Mansion, licking upwards. Now the shouts of alarm grew, and in the distance they could hear the bell of a fire appliance.

'Time to ride,' Robert said, and swung into the saddle.

*

Yuan Shih-k'ai raised his head from studying the report on his desk. He moved slowly, as if exhausted. 'Barrington,' he said. 'I could not believe he would dare do anything overt, while I held his sister and his adopted son.'

'Shall we have them executed?' asked one of his aides.

'No,' Yuan said. 'Not at this time. They may still be useful. This report says Barrington and Sun made their escape by horse towards the south-west. Viceroy Yun is a fool not to have been able to catch them.'

'I gather that being locked in a cellar while the building burned around him has had a bad effect on his personality,' Chief of Staff Li Yuan-hung said. 'He thought he was going to die.'

'He is very likely to die,' Yuan growled. 'Have him dismissed, at any rate. Send a competent commander to Nanking, and give him *carte blanche* to smoke out these rebels as quickly as possible.'

Li got up. 'And Sun? And Barrington?'

'Sun should be executed at the moment of capture,' Yuan said. 'He is a dangerous man, and he has too many secret followers. With him dead, they will lose their purpose.'

'And Barrington and his wife?'

'I want them alive,' Yuan said. 'Barrington is too useful to me.'

'Can you ever trust him again?'

'No. But I will make sure he can never betray me again. The important thing is to maintain the House of Barrington, both because of its earnings of foreign exchange, and because through it I can obtain financing. It is a matter of bringing James Barrington back from England; when I have Barrington and his so beautiful wife in my power, I will soon persuade them to bring their son home. Then we will have a Master of the House I can manage. Failing that, there is always Martin. But they are both very young. For the time being, we need Robert Barrington.'

'You shall have him,' Li promised. He went to the door, paused, and looked back at the desk. 'I am worried about your health, Shih-k'ai.'

The Marshal's head had drooped again. Now it raised; his breath rasped in his nostrils. 'I am tired,' he said. 'Would you not be, with so much to manage? I shall be all right.'

He went to the women's quarters, to Victoria's apartment.

'So Europe is at war,' she remarked. 'Will that make any difference to us?' With her usual arrogance she had not even risen, as any Chinese woman would have done, at his entry, but remained lounging on her divan. She wore silk pantaloons and a silk blouse, both pale blue and both sheer, no shoes. Her hair was loose. She was the most beautiful creature he had ever seen, and she was all his.

Yet suddenly she was loathsome to him. Not that he wished her to know that ... yet. He sat beside her, stroked her hair; its texture, so un-Chinese, had always fascinated him. 'It can only be good for us,' he said. 'Have you heard the news from Shanghai? A report has just arrived. Your brother has thrown in his lot with the Kuomintang.' Victoria sat up, the newspaper slipping from her lap to the floor. 'He escaped that idiot Yun Li-chow and has fled to the interior, with his wife. He burned his house before leaving. I have to admit that Robert does things in the grand manner.'

'What will happen to him?' she whispered.

'I had no idea you were that fond of him, Vicky.'

'He is my brother! I do not approve of what he has done, of course, but I would not like him to ...' She hesitated.

'Be decapitated? I assure you that if I did mean to execute him, I should think mere beheading far too simple. Or for his wife. But I mean him no harm. He is a poor, misguided fool. Oh, I intend to fetch him back, and teach him the error of his ways. But execution ... that would not be right.'

'What of Sun?'

'Ah, Dr Sun. I have no reason to keep *him* alive. But I am sorry, Vicky, I doubt you will actually be able to watch his execution. I have no intention of bringing him back to Peking.'

Victoria drove her hands into her hair. 'What can have possessed Robert to do such a thing?'

Yuan smiled, and fondled her breasts. 'When he is captured, we will have to ask him.' She gasped as his hands suddenly closed on her flesh, driving rivers of pain through her chest.

*

Robert Barrington stood on the hillock and watched the men streaming by beneath him. They were the remnants of an army.

But that was paying them a compliment. They had never been an army. Now, shattered by the artillery and machine-guns of Yuan's well-trained levies, they were retreating into the mountains south of Hankow, shoulders bowed, many of them walking wounded ... and yet, every man still carried his rifle and his bandolier. He heard movement behind him, and turned, to see Chiang Kai-shek dismounting from his horse. 'Not a pleasant sight,' the young colonel remarked.

'I do not think I bring fortune to warring armies,' Robert remarked. 'Or navies.'

The grim face relaxed into a half-smile. 'We will outlast that old bastard yet, Mr Barrington.'

They regained the encampment, having made sure that the Government forces were not in close pursuit. Here Sun held his usual court, issuing decrees, listening to petitions, as if it were he and not Yuan who ruled China, as if his domain was even a few square miles rather than the few square feet presently occupied by his army.

But here too was Monique, working with the Chinese women at ladling soup into bowls for the hungry men. She wore Chinese clothes, her blue tunic and pantaloons wet with rain, her boots soaked with mud. Only the auburn hair escaping from beneath the flat straw-hat indicated that she was any different to her companions. That and the way her eyes lit up as she saw her husband. 'I was afraid ... but you're here, now.'

'We break camp in an hour,' he told her. 'Yuan's people are too close.'

Her shoulders slumped for a moment. 'Further into the mountains? At this rate we will wind up back in Canton.'

'You will go there anyway. Sun is sending his wounded there,' Robert told her. 'You will go with them, and take a ship for Hong Kong. I have money on deposit there, and you can wait in safety until I can come to you.'

'When will that be?'

'God knows. When Sun gets tired of fighting.' They had already been in the field for more than eighteen months, chased from place to place by the Government troops, always avoiding a final, catastrophic defeat, just. But they were not winning, and this was no place for a woman like Monique. There were times, indeed, when he all but despaired. Had circumstances been different, he would have gone to the coast himself, and to Hong Kong, and even to Europe, in an endeavour to raise help. But Europe, the entire world, was locked in war. And throughout 1915 the Allies had equally given no sign that they were on their way to victory. They had been defeated in the Dardanelles and their massive campaigns on the Western Front had ended in mud and blood; there was little hope that this year of 1916 would be any better.

'If you are remaining with the army,' Monique said, 'then I will stay too.'

'This isn't your fight, Monique.'

'Is it yours?'

'Yes, it is mine. I let Sun down once before. I cannot let him down again.'

'But can you help him, fighting as a common soldier? Even an officer? Wouldn't you do more, if you yourself were in Hong Kong, raising money?'

'It is a matter of morale, my darling. My presence makes his people feel they are not forgotten by the Barbarians.'

'And you and I know that they are. Robert—'

'I must stay, Monique, and there is an end of it.'

She shrugged. 'Then I must stay too. Until the end of it.'

*

Yuan Shih-k'ai gazed at the sheet of paper on his desk. 'What is this?' he demanded. 'What is this?' he shouted.

Everyone in the room trembled, even Li Yuan-hung. 'It was handed me by the Japanese Minister this morning, your excellency.'

'They have the effrontery to send me this?' Yuan bellowed. 'Twenty-one demands? Demands? They wish the right to occupy the Shantung Peninsular? To control Manchuria? To have us trade with them and no one else? What do they take me for, their puppet? Are they mad, to think they can force this upon us?'

Another tremor ran round the room. 'They are taking advantage of the situation, certainly,' Li ventured. 'The fact that there is no end to the war in Europe; that the French and British campaigns last summer have been failures; that the British failed to force the Dardanelles; and now that the Germans are launching such a massive onslaught at Verdun ... they know not only that the Barbarians have neither the will nor the power to intervene at this time, but also that the French and British and Russians need Japanese support.'

'We shall see about that,' Yuan growled.

'They also,' Li continued, 'I am afraid to say, regard you as an impostor, who will soon be swept away by events. They are of course aware of the rebellion in the south.' Yuan glared at him, but Li had been his comrade-in-arms for too long to be browbeaten. 'It is necessary to know these things, your excellency, so that your enemies may be combated.'

Yuan got up and began to stride the room. 'An impostor, am I? We will show them. I will declare myself Emperor. I have long had this in mind. Now is the time. I will found a new dynasty. Let the Japanese scoff at that.'

There was an uneasy shuffling of feet, and Yuan looked from face to face before coming back to Li. 'They will not accept it, your excellency,' Li said.

'Who will not accept it? The Barbarians? What can they do? You have just told me that the Japanese are grasping at our sovereignty because they know that the Barbarians are too preoccupied with fighting each other to remonstrate. Well, what is food for the goose is also food for the gander, eh?'

'I was not speaking of the Barbarians, your excellency. I do not think the people will accept it.'

'The people?' Yuan roared.

'And the literati, the magnates. They will not accept you, your excellency. As for Sun's people . . .'

'Sun's people!' Yuan bellowed. 'Sun's people are defeated. Word has just arrived that they have been defeated again.'

'They have retreated into the mountains, your excellency. They have been defeated, but they have not been destroyed.'

'Destroyed,' Yuan snarled. To the consternation of his officers his legs gave way and he half fell on to a settee, his breath rasping. But he was still talking. 'Yes, they will be destroyed. Send word to my commanders. I want every man, woman and child, every cow and every sheep, every dog and every chicken in those mountains destroyed. I want the rivers and lakes to be poisoned so there will be no fish. I want every tree cut down and every field of grain trampled underfoot. I want every house in every village or town burned to the ground. Is that understood? I want those people *destroyed*!' His officers gulped, and exchanged glances. 'All except Dr Sun, and Barrington, and Barrington's wife,' Yuan said in a low voice. 'I want them brought here, in a cage, so that I can see them. Do you know what I am going to do to them? You, Martin Barrington, come here.'

Martin licked his lips as he stepped from the ranks of the aides-de-camp and stood to attention before his master.

'I will tell you what I am going to do to them,' Yuan whispered. 'I am going to castrate the men and I am going to cut the breasts from that woman, and then I am going to sew them up and expose them in cages, from one end of China to the next. I am going to feed them their own flesh to eat. I am . . .' His voice grew hoarse with his own raving, and he collapsed.

'He is demented,' Li Yuan-hung told the little group of men. 'Fortunately, he is also dying. There can be little doubt of that. We can but wait, and until then, keep ourselves ready.'

'What do you intend, your excellency?' one of the men asked.

'To restore the republic,' Li said.

'With yourself as president?'

'That may be necessary, to begin with. But I shall also restore relations with Dr Sun.'

'And the Japanese, your excellency?'

Li shrugged. 'We will have to deal with the Japanese, gentlemen. At some stage.' He looked over their faces, his gaze coming to rest on that of Martin Barrington. 'I beg of you all, do nothing rash.'

*

Martin sat with Victoria, whispering in her ear. Her face was set in hard lines. 'Marshal Li is a traitor,' she said. 'He waits only for Yuan to die.'

'We are all doing that,' Martin said.

'And what do you suppose will happen then?'

'Marshal Li intends to open negotiations with Dr Sun.'

'Never!' Victoria declared.

'Aunt Vicky, this is inevitable. Yuan has turned out to be a disaster. All he does is hold reviews of his army. All he dreams of is becoming Emperor, even though he knows that is impossible, because the Empire will not accept him. Of course we can defeat Sun's people in the field. We have done so, time and again, but if we cannot force them to abandon the struggle, then we are going to lose, eventually. And with the Japanese breathing down our necks, we must stop the internal struggle, as quickly as possible.'

'You mean to depose the Marshal,' Victoria said. 'To allow that slimy toad to take power.'

Martin sighed. 'I mean to save China from an unthinkable civil war, in the course of which we are going to lose God knows how much more territory.'

'You are a—' Victoria checked what she was going to say as the door opened. Hastily she got off her settee and bowed. Martin stood to attention.

Yuan gazed at them for some seconds, while the room

filled with an unpleasant odour. Then he said, 'Conspiring against me?'

'Of course not, your excellency,' Victoria said. 'We were discussing affairs.'

'Affairs,' Yuan snarled. 'I know you, whore!' Victoria stiffened, but made no reply. She remained standing still, even as Yuan crossed the room and thrust his fingers into her hair. 'Whore!' he bellowed again. 'You are a whore, and a treacherous whore! You go where you think you will be welcomed. You fled your brothers to be with the rat Tang, and you fled Tang to be with me.'

'Your excellency...' Victoria was trembling, but it was with anger more than fear.

'Now you are planning to flee me,' Yuan said. 'You and that bastard brat of yours.'

Victoria's eyes rolled towards Martin, who had been a silent spectator of the scene. 'Leave us,' she said.

But Martin stepped forward, seeing her face twisting in pain as Yuan's fingers tightened their grip on her hair. 'Your excellency...'

'Attacked!' Yuan screamed. 'I am attacked!'

The doors burst open and guards hurried in. Martin was unarmed, but even if he had been armed he would have had no chance against the sudden crowd of men, who seized his arms and forced him to his knees. 'Your excellency,' he protested.

'You are going to die,' Yuan snarled.

'Die?' Martin shouted. 'What have I done? Have I not served you faithfully throughout my life?'

'You are a Barrington,' Yuan said. 'I am going to exterminate everyone who bears that name. Everyone. Take him away.'

'Yuan!' Victoria screamed. 'You cannot kill my son!' Yuan glared at her, while Martin looked at her in consternation. 'Yes,' Victoria panted. 'You are my son, by Tang Li-chun. I gave you to Robert to adopt, because they would not let me bring you up as my own. But you are my son! Yuan—'

'A fitting son, for such a mother. You shall die the death of a thousand cuts. All of you. And that bride of yours, and that son. They are Barringtons. All of them. Take them out. I will witness their executions. Take them out!' He fell across the settee, panting.

*

Li Yuan-hung stood beside the doctor as he washed his hands. On the bed the warlord lay and panted; the rank odour of his sweat pervaded the room.

'I can do nothing,' the doctor muttered. 'The poison from his kidneys is throughout his system. I can do nothing.'

Li waved the man away and went to stand by the bedside. Whatever this man had become, they had once been friends, had served together and fought together for more years than he cared to remember. More important, they had believed in China together. It was only at the end that their views on what was best for China had diverged. 'What does he say?' Yuan asked.

'He says that there is no hope,' Li replied.

Yuan was silent for a few seconds. Then he muttered, 'There is so much to be done.' He grasped his friend's hand. 'Will you carry out my dream, Li?'

'I will do what must be done,' Li said, carefully.

Yuan's eyes opened, and he stared at him for several seconds. 'You will do nothing,' he said at last. 'You are not a Bannerman. You have never been a Bannerman.'

'Neither have you,' Li pointed out. 'Only Manchus were Bannermen, and you destroyed the Manchus.'

'I was made a Bannerman, by the Empress,' Yuan said. 'By Tz'u-hsi herself. I was her last Bannerman. She said so.' He gave a great sigh. 'The last Bannerman,' he muttered. The room was quiet, until Yuan opened his eyes again. 'Kill the Barringtons,' he said. 'They are a canker in our side. I thought Robert would support me. But he has not. They must all die. I wish to see them die. Do it now. The death of a thousand cuts. Have it done beneath my window, that I may watch.'

Li Yuan-hung looked from the mottled face in front of him to the other men in the room. He was in a quandary. He had no love for the Barringtons, and especially for Victoria and her son. But he knew he would have to deal with Sun Yat-sen ... and that meant dealing with Robert Barrington as well.

On the other hand, were he to disobey, or even to temporise, Yuan might very well order his execution as well.

But the death of a thousand cuts ... It was the oldest and most terrible of punishments; the naked body of the condemned was encased in a chain-metal jacket, the links of which were wide enough to allow his flesh to bulge through when the jacket was drawn tight. The bulging flesh was then sliced away, and the jacket was drawn tighter yet, before the operation was repeated. By staunching the blood as necessary, a skilful executioner could keep his victim alive for hours, even days, before a vital part was reached, and the torment to be endured was unthinkable. 'Are they ready?' Yuan muttered.

'I am arranging it now,' Li said. He beckoned one of the waiting officers to the far side of the room, and gave whispered instructions. The officer then saluted and left the room.

*

Martin Barrington raised his head at the sound of footsteps in the corridor leading to his cell. For the past several days he had lain here, not knowing what had happened to his mother and his wife, or his son. His mother! How obvious it all seemed now. How many oddities about his life had suddenly dropped into place. If only he could have known sooner.

Now he had no idea what the future was going to bring. He had snatched at freedom from the cloying uncertainty of

being a Barrington out-child, and tied his fortunes to a
madman. Now he was going to suffer, he had no doubt. But
Lu-shang and the boy! And Mother! It was very likely that
Victoria had only followed him, and given herself to Yuan,
because she wanted to be near her son. Thus his own wilful
pride and ambition was going to cause her death.

There was only one man outside his door, a captain. The
door swung in, and Martin stood to attention. The Captain
wasted no time. 'You are condemned to death, and the
sentence is about to be carried out.' Martin inhaled, slowly.
The Captain drew his revolver. 'I have been sent by Li Yuan-
hung to give you this.' He held out the gun, butt first.

Martin gazed at it, but did not take it.

'Your mother, your wife, and your child are in a cell
further along this corridor,' the Captain said. From his belt
he took a set of keys, selected one. 'This will open their
door. After that it is up to you.'

Still Martin did not take the revolver. 'There is a
guardroom up the steps,' he said.

The Captain nodded. 'It is full of armed men. They are
waiting for you. For all of you.'

Martin frowned in bewilderment. 'And you expect me to
take my family to be murdered?'

'It will be very quick,' the Captain promised. 'You have
my word and the word of Li Yuan-hung. The men are
waiting to take you and your mother, your wife and your
child to the courtyard beneath Marshal Yuan's window.
There you will all suffer the death of a thousand cuts,
beginning with your son, then your wife, then your mother,
and finally you. It is your choice whether you allow that to
happen, or whether you will attempt to escape and be shot
down. I repeat, you have my word that my men will shoot
to kill, and that there will be no mutilation of your bodies.
If you can act well enough, your loved ones will not even
know they are to die, until the last moment.'

Martin gazed at him, then at the revolver. His brain
seemed to have frozen; he had never expected to have to

make such a terrible decision. His entire family ... one half of him was screaming for him to let things happen, because as long as there was life there was hope. But the other half was telling him there was no hope, and if he did not act, he would have to watch his mother and his wife, and his son, slowly cut to pieces before his eyes. Their screams would accompany his own on the way to hell. 'You must choose, now,' the Captain said.

Martin drew a long breath, and took the revolver.

*

Fire-crackers exploded, guns were fired, people screamed and cheered. Sun and Robert, Monique and Chiang Kai-shek watched the approach of the white flag, held by the herald in the uniform of one of Yuan's officers. The herald dismounted and saluted, then held out the piece of paper. Rumour had preceded him, hence the celebrations, but this was official confirmation. Sun read, and then raised his head. 'It is true. Yuan Shih-k'ai is dead. It is over.'

'Because Yuan is dead?' Chiang was sceptical.

'Li Yuan-hung invites me to meet him,' Sun said. 'He wishes an end to fighting.'

'That *is* promising,' Robert said, and waited.

Sun handed him one of the sheets of paper. 'There is a message for you, Barrington.'

Robert read. It was from Li Yuan-hung. 'I regret to inform you that your nephew, Martin, having secured a weapon, attempted to escape from prison with his mother, his wife, and his child. All four were shot by the guards. They had been placed in prison by order of Marshal Yuan, who I am afraid lost his senses towards the end of his life. He had condemned them to death, but I had some hopes of keeping them alive until after the Marshal's death. These hopes cannot now be realised. I hope you will accept my sincere condolences, and my prayer that now that the monster is dead, we may again work together. Li.'

Robert handed the paper to Monique. 'Do you believe him?' she asked.

'No. But I believe him when he says they are dead. I suppose you could say that Vicky played dice with the devil just once too often.'

'I am so very sorry,' Sun said. 'But there is a great deal to be done. First, we must gain the coast.'

'You are going to trust Li?'

'According to this letter, he has made the news of his desire to meet me and discuss the future of China public to the world. I must believe him. Besides, he is a different man to Yuan.'

'That is true enough,' Robert conceded. 'He does not have the strength of character, or the ruthlessness. That may be good for you, but there is a negative side. He will be less able to dominate his army commanders, his viceroys, his mandarins.'

Sun nodded. 'I never supposed unifying China as a democracy would be a simple task. But as I have devoted my life to that task, I am not going to give up now. Will you help me, Barrington?'

Robert hesitated, glanced at Monique. Her face was expressionless, but he could imagine some of the thoughts which must be racing through her brain. 'No,' he said.

Sun's head jerked.

'Do not misunderstand me, Sun,' Robert said. 'I have the greatest respect for you, and for your cause. But I cannot serve it. My great-great grandfather, Robert Barrington, came to China to serve the Ch'ing. For three generations and more than a hundred years, we have done that. Now the Ch'ing are no more, and my family is no more, save for myself, my wife, and my son. I do not think the Barringtons have any longer anything to offer China. I see too much misfortune ahead.'

Monique gave a sigh of relief.

'And the House?' Sun asked.

Robert grinned. 'I bequeath it to the Kuomintang.'

Sun considered for some moments, then he nodded. 'Perhaps you are right. I accept, on behalf of the Kuomintang.' He smiled in turn. 'You served the Ch'ing, as you say, long and faithfully and well. You know, Yuan Shih-k'ai was fond of calling himself the Last Bannerman. But you were more faithful to the Dynasty than he ever was. I believe that you are the very last of the Bannermen, Robert Barrington. Go with God, and prosper.'

Epilogue

Robert Barrington was proved right in his fears for the future. Li Yuan-hung proved to be both honest and weak. Out of the chaos which descended upon China, Sun Yat-sen carved a viable state, but his hold was only south of the Yangtse-Kiang. The north of the great country was divided up amongst warlords of varying strength. Sun flirted with the Russian Communists as he sought aid, but his death in 1924 left the nation adrift. Chiang Kai-shek ruled in his stead, but the anarchy grew as China developed a Communist Party of its own.

Internal squabblings were submerged in the great war against Japan, which lasted from 1937 to 1945, and when it ended, the Communists were ready to seize power, and at last to unify the country in a way not known since the death of Tz'u-hsi.

But by then the House of Barrington had been long forgotten.

THE EIGHT BANNERS

Alan Savage

As Lord Macartney's embassy to the Manchu court sailed into the Gulf of Chih-li, Robert Barrington knew the British attempt to establish links with the vast Chinese empire was doomed to failure. But for Barrington it was the opportunity to found his own dynasty amongst the fabulous wealth of the Middle Kingdom.

Abandoned by his compatriots, Barrington begins to build his fortune during one of the most glittering, violent and decisive episodes of Chinese history: the bloody exploits of the pirate Chen Yi and his beautiful consort; the disaster of the Opium war; the startling career of a sultry young Manchu girl who is destined to become the infamous Dowager Empress.

The saga of the Barrington family, set against the vast tapestry of China, is a brilliant and action-packed story which recreates the splendour and brutal squalor of the eight Manchu tribes who carried their banners against the decaying Ming dynasty.

'An epic tale by a masterly storyteller.'
Eastern Daily Press

OTTOMAN

Alan Savage

In 1448 an English master-gunner, John Hawkwood, arrives in the fabled city of Constantinople. He intends to enter the service of the Byzantine emperor, whose capital is this astonishing meeting-place of East and West – now in dire threat from the Ottoman Turks.

But even gun-powder cannot prevail and, in 1453, Constantinople falls to the foe. By fate the Hawkwoods have already changed allegiance, and now serve the conquerors in their victorious surge across eastern Europe and the Mediterranean shores.

Though showered with wealth and privilege, they need every ounce of political cunning to survive the swirling intrigues and bloody massacres which dominate the Ottoman realm. For four generations the Hawkwood men are military leaders and envoys, while their women are beautiful captives or dutiful concubines trained in the arts of sensual pleasure.

But always the grim spectres of betrayal and sudden death, of ravishment and torture lurk behind the gilded pillars of their palaces and harems . . .

☐ Ottoman	Alan Savage	£4.99
☐ Moghul	Alan Savage	£4.99
☐ The Eight Banners	Alan Savage	£5.99
☐ Queen of Night	Alan Savage	£4.99
☐ Queen of Lions	Alan Savage	£4.99

Warner Books now offers an exciting range of quality titles by both established and new authors. All of the books in this series are available from:

Little, Brown and Company (UK) Limited,
P.O. Box 11,
Falmouth,
Cornwall TR10 9EN.

Alternatively you may fax your order to the above address. Fax No. 0326 376423.

Payments can be made as follows: cheque, postal order (payable to Little, Brown and Company) or by credit cards, Visa/Access. Do not send cash or currency. UK customers and B.F.P.O. please allow £1.00 for postage and packing for the first book, plus 50p for the second book, plus 30p for each additional book up to a maximum charge of £3.00 (7 books plus).

Overseas customers including Ireland, please allow £2.00 for the first book plus £1.00 for the second book, plus 50p for each additional book.

NAME (Block Letters) ....

....

ADDRESS ....

....

....

☐ I enclose my remittance for _____

☐ I wish to pay by Access/Visa Card

Number ☐☐☐☐☐☐☐☐☐☐☐☐☐☐☐☐

Card Expiry Date ☐☐☐☐